FROZEN HEAT

Heat Wave

Naked Heat

Heat Rises

FROZEN HEAT

RICHARD CASTLE

TITAN BOOKS

NIKKI HEAT: FROZEN HEAT
Print edition ISBN: 9781781166338
E-book edition ISBN: 9781781166345

Published by Titan Books
A division of Titan Publishing Group Ltd.
144 Southwark Street, London SE1 0UP

First edition November 2012

1 3 5 7 9 10 8 6 4 2

This edition published by arrangement with Hyperion.

Book design by Shubhani Sarkar.

A CIP catalogue record for this title is available from the British Library.

Printed and bound by CPI Group (UK) Ltd, Croydon, CR0 4YY

Did you enjoy this book? We love to hear from our readers.
Please email us at readerfeedback@titanemail.com or write to us at
Reader Feedback at the above address.

To receive advance information, news, competitions, and exclusive offers online,
please sign up for the Titan newsletter on our website:
WWW.TITANBOOKS.COM

To all the remarkable,
maddening, challenging,
frustrating people who inspire us
to do great things

ONE

"Oh, yeah, that's it, Rook," said Nikki Heat. "That's what I want. Just like that." A trickle of sweat rolled down his neck to his heaving chest. He groaned and bit down on his tongue. "Don't stop yet. Keep it going. Yes." She hovered over him, lowering her face just inches from his so she could whisper. "Yes. Work it just like that. Nice, easy rhythm. That's it. How does it feel?" Jameson Rook stared at her intently just before he pinched his eyes into a squint and moaned. Then his muscles went slack and he dropped his head backward. Nikki frowned and brought herself upright. "You can't do that to me. I cannot believe you're stopping."

He let the dumbbells hit the black rubber floor beside the exercise bench and said, "Not stopping." He pulled in a chestful of air and coughed. "Just done."

"You're not done."

"Ten reps, I did ten reps."

"Not by my count."

"That's because your mind wanders. Besides, this rehab is for my own good. Why would I skip reps?"

"Because I turned away once and you thought I wasn't looking."

He scoffed, then asked, ". . . Were you?"

"Yes, and you only did eight. Do you want me to help you do your physical therapy, or be your enabler?"

"I swear I did at least nine."

A member of Rook's exclusive gym slid in behind her for some free weights, and Nikki turned to gauge how much of her and Rook's childish exchange he'd picked up. From the tinny music spilling from his earbuds, the only thing the other man heard was the Black Eyed Peas telling him it's gonna be a good night while he stared in the mirror. Heat couldn't tell what the guy admired more, the row of plugs from his new hair transplants or the snap of his pecs under his designer wife beater.

Rook stood up beside her. "Nice chesticles, huh?"

"Shh, he'll hear you."

"Doubt that. Besides, who do you think taught me the word?"

Chesticle man caught her eye in the mirror and favored her with a wink. Apparently surprised that her knees didn't turn to jelly, he racked his weights and moved on to the tanning beds. Moments like that were precisely why Heat preferred her own gym, a throwback joint downtown with painted cinder-block walls, clanging steam pipes, and a clientele there to work instead of preen. When Rook's visiting physical therapist—whom he'd dubbed Gitmo Joe—called in sick for his morning session and Nikki volunteered to spot him in his rehab routine, she had considered using her club instead. But there were negatives there, too. Well, one. Namely Don, her ex–Navy SEAL combat training partner with whom she had a history of grappling in bed, not just on the wrestling mat. Don's trainer-with-benefits days had come and gone, but Rook didn't know about him and she couldn't see the point in forcing an awkward encounter.

"Whew. I don't know about you," said Rook, toweling his face, "but I'm ready for a shower and some breakfast."

"Sounds great." She held out the dumbbells to him. "Right after your next set."

"I have another set?" He maintained the innocent pose as long as he could pull it off, and then snatched the weights from her. "You know, Gitmo Joe may be the spawn of an unholy union between the Marquis de Sade and Darth Vader, but at least he cuts me some slack. And I didn't even take a bullet to save his life."

"One," was all she said.

He paused and then did his first rep, grunting, "One."

They kidded about it, but that night two months before at the sanitation pier on the Hudson, she thought she had lost him. The ER doc assured her afterward that she indeed almost had. In the blink of an instant after she beat down and disarmed one bad cop in the garbage transfer warehouse, his crooked partner took an ambush shot at her. Heat never saw it coming, but Rook—damn Rook—who wasn't supposed to be there, leaped out and tackled her, taking the slug himself. Over her NYPD career as a uniform and a homicide detective, Nikki Heat had seen many bodies and watched many men die before her, and as the color left him that winter night and she felt his warm blood flow out of his chest across her arms, the vision resonated with all the fragile breaks and hopeless endings she had witnessed. Jameson Rook had saved her life, and now his own survival was nothing less than a miracle.

"Two," she said. "Rook, you're pathetic."

Out on the sidewalk, he took in a long, exaggerated breath. "I love the smell of Tribeca in the morning," he said. "It smells like . . . diesel."

The sun had risen just enough for Nikki to peel off her sweatshirt and enjoy the April air on her bare arms. She caught him looking and said, "Careful, you're one hair plug from becoming chesticle man."

She walked on and he fell in stride with her. "I can't help it. You know, any moment can become romantic. I saw that on a TV commercial."

"Let me know if you need me to slow down."

"No, I'm good." Heat gave him a side glance. Sure enough, he was keeping up. "Remember my first shuffles around that hospital corridor? Felt like Tim Conway on the old *Carol Burnett Show*. Now look at me. I'm back to my superhero stride." He demonstrated and powered ahead to the corner.

"Nice. If I ever need help, and Batman or Lone Vengeance are booked, I know who I'll call." As she drew up to him, she asked, "Seriously, you doing OK? I didn't tax you too much with that workout?"

"Naw, I'm fine." He placed the tip of her forefinger on his ribs. "I just feel a little tugging sometimes when I stretch." They waited for the light to change, and he added, "Speaking of tugging."

Nikki gave him her best blank expression. "Tugging? I'm sorry, I don't follow." They held each other's gaze until he arched one brow and cracked her up.

Rook laced his arm through hers as they crossed the street. "Detective, I do believe if we skipped breakfast, you could still get to work on time."

"Are you sure you're ready for this? Seriously, I can wait. I'm the queen of delayed gratification."

"Trust me, we've waited long enough."

"Maybe you should double-check with your doctor to see if you're healthy enough for sexual activity."

"Oh," said Rook. "So you've seen the commercials, too."

Instead of stopping for a bite at Kitchenette, they made a sharp turn at the corner and headed toward his loft, arm in arm, picking up the pace as they went.

They kissed deeply in his elevator on the way up, pressing against each other, his back to the wall, and then, suddenly, hers. Then they broke away, resisting or maybe teasing, or maybe a bit of both. Their eyes locked in on each other's, only flicking away to monitor the floor count.

Inside his front door, he reached to kiss her again, but she ducked him and raced through the kitchen, bolted up the hall at a sprint, and leaped at the bed, flying airborne like a club wrestler and landing with a bounce, laughing out a "hurry up" while she kicked off her cross trainers.

He appeared in the doorway, completely naked. At the foot of the bed, he struck a regal pose. "If I am to die, let it be this way."

And then she grabbed him and pulled him on top of her.

The heat took them beyond caution, even beyond play. Lost time, raw emotions, and aching need all cycloned into a swirl of passion with no mind, only frenzy. In minutes the room itself was in motion, not just the bed. Lampshades swayed, books toppled on shelves, even the pencil cup on Rook's nightstand tipped, and a dozen Blackwing 602s rolled onto the floor.

Then it was over and they flopped back, panting, smiling. "Oh you're definitely healthy enough for sex," said Nikki.

All Rook could manage was a dry-throated "That was . . . Whoa." And then he added, "The earth moved."

Nikki laughed. "Feel good about you."

"No, I think it literally moved." He got up on one elbow to look at the room. "I think we just had an earthquake."

By the time she came out from drying her hair, Rook had tidied up the fallen items in his loft and planted himself in front of the TV. "Channel 7 says it was a 5.8 on something called the Ramapo Fault Line, epicenter in Sloatsburg, New York."

Nikki put her empty mug on the counter and checked her cell phone.

"I've got service back. No messages or TAC alerts, at least not for me. What's the impact?"

"They're still assessing. No fatalities, some injuries from fallen bricks and whatnot, nothing major, so far. Airports and some subway lines closed as a precaution. Oh, and I won't have to shake the orange juice. Want some?"

She said no and put on her gun. "Who'd have thought? An earthquake in New York City?"

He put his arms around her. "Can't complain about the timing."

"Hard to top."

"Guess we'll just have to try," he said, and they kissed. Her phone rang, and Heat pulled away to answer. Without being asked, he handed her a pen and notepad and she jotted an address. "On my way."

"You know what I think we should do today?"

Nikki slipped her phone into her blazer pocket. "Yes, I do. And as much as I'd love to—believe me, I'd love to—I've got to get to work."

"Go to Hawaii."

"Very funny."

"I'm not joking. Let's just go. Maui. Mmm, Maui."

"You know I can't do that."

"Give me one reason."

"I've got a murder to handle."

"Nikki. If there's one thing I've learned in our time together, it's never let a murder get in the way of a good time."

"So I've noticed. And what about your work? Don't you have some magazine article you should be writing? Some exposé of corruption in the dark corridors of the World Bank? A chronicle of your ride-along with a bin Laden hunter? Your weekend in the Seychelles with Johnny Depp or Sting?"

Rook pondered that and said, "If we left this afternoon, we could be in Lahaina for breakfast. And if you feel guilty, don't. You deserve it after taking care of me for two months." She ignored him and clipped her detective shield onto her waistband. "Come on, Nikki, how many homicides are there in this city in a year, five hundred?"

"More like five thirty."

"All right, that's fewer than two a day. Look, we peace-out to Maui today and come back in a week, you'd miss, maybe, ten murders. And not all of them would be in your precinct anyway."

"You're making a very clear point here, Rook."

He looked at her, mildly taken aback. "I am?"

"Yes. And the point is, I don't care how many Pulitzer Prizes you've won. You still have the brain of a sixteen-year-old."

"So is that a yes?"

"Make that a fifteen-year-old." Nikki kissed him again and cupped him between the legs. "By the way? So worth the wait." And then she went to work.

The crime scene was on her way to the precinct, so instead of going up to the Twentieth first to sign out a car and double back, Heat got off the B train a stop early at 72nd Street to hoof it. The bomb squad had ordered a precautionary traffic shutdown at Columbus Avenue, and Nikki came up the subway steps near the Dakota to witness nightmare gridlock backed up all the way to Central Park. The sooner she finished her investigation, the sooner relief would come to the stuck drivers, so she quickened her stride. But she didn't short her contemplation.

As always, on approach to a body, Detective Heat steeped herself in thoughts of the victim. She didn't need Rook to remind her how many homicides there were in the city every year. But her vow was never to let volume dehumanize a single lost life. Or inure her to the impact on friends and loved ones. For her, this wasn't lip service or some PR tagline. Nikki had come by it honestly years ago when her mother was murdered. Heat's loss not only spurred her to switch college majors to Criminal Justice, it forged the kind of cop she vowed to be. Over ten years later, her mother's case remained unsolved, but the detective remained unbending in her advocacy for each victim, one at a time.

At 72nd and Columbus she picked her way through the knot of spectators who had gathered there, many with their cell phones aloft, documenting their proximity to danger for whatever street cred that gave them on their Facebook pages. She reached down to draw back her blazer and flash her shield to the uniform at the barrier, but he knew the move and gave her the fraternal nod before she even showed it. Emergency lights strobed two blocks ahead of her as she headed south. Nikki could have taken the empty street but kept to the sidewalk; even as a veteran cop, it unsettled her to see a major downtown avenue completely shut in morning rush hour. The sidewalks were vacant, too, except for uni patrols keeping them clear. Sawhorses blocked 71st, also, and a few doors west of them, an ambulance idled in front of a town house that had shed its brick façade in the earthquake. She passed one of the green ash trees growing from the sidewalk planters and looked up through its budding limbs at dozens of rubberneckers leaning out of windows and over fire escapes. Same on the other side of Columbus. As she drew closer to the scene, dispatch calls from the roundup of emergency vehicles echoed off the stone apartment buildings in enveloping unison.

The bomb squad had turned out with its armored mobile containment unit parked in the center lane of the avenue, just in case anything needed detonating. But from twenty yards off, Heat could tell from body language that Emergency Services had pretty much stood down. Elevated above the roofs of vans and blue-and-whites, she caught a glimpse of her friend Lauren Parry walking around inside the open rear cargo door of a delivery truck in her medical examiner coveralls. Then she ducked down and Nikki lost sight of her.

Raley and Ochoa from her squad stepped away from a middle-aged black man in a watch cap and green parka, who they were interviewing beside the Engine 40 fire truck, and met up with her as she arrived. "Detective Heat."

"Detective Roach," she said, using the partners' house nickname that amicably squashed Raley and Ochoa into one handy syllable.

"No trouble getting here," said Raley, not asking, not expecting that she, of all people, would ever have any.

"No, my line's running. I hear the N and the R are down for inspection where they go under the river."

"Same with the Q train coming out of Brooklyn," added Ochoa. "I made it across before it hit. But I'll tell you, Times Square station was unreal. Like a Godzilla movie down there, the way people were screaming and running."

"Did you feel it?" asked Raley.

She replayed the circumstances and said, "Oh, yeah," trying to sound offhanded.

"Where were you when it hit?"

"Exercising." Not a total lie. Heat side nodded to the armored blast container. "What are we working here that warrants the parade of heavy metal?"

"Suspicious package lit things up." Ochoa flipped to the first page of his notepad. "Frozen food delivery driver—that's him over there—"

"—in the green jacket—" chimed in his partner in their usual duet.

"—opens the back of his truck to unload some chicken tenders and burger patties at the deli here." He paused to allow Nikki a beat to eyeball the All In Bun storefront, where a trio of cooks in checked pants and aprons slouched at the window counter waiting out the closure. "He slides a carton aside and finds a suitcase sitting there between the boxes."

"I guess 'See Something, Say Something' is working," Raley said, picking up. "He books it out of there and calls 911."

"Emergency Services Unit deploys and sends Robocop in to check it out." Detective Ochoa beckoned her to walk with him while he led her past the bomb squad's remote control robot. "The 'bot does a sniff and an X-ray. Negative on explosive elements. Their bomb tech was suited up anyway, so—abundance of caution—he pops the lock and finds the body inside the suitcase."

A few feet behind her, she heard Detective Feller. "That's why I go strictly carry-on. Those checked bags'll kill ya." She snapped her head around and saw the surprise on his face, while his audience of two uniforms laughed. He'd been speaking in a low voice, but not low enough. Feller's cheeks reddened as Heat left Raley and Ochoa to cross to him. The unis melted away, leaving him alone with her. "Hey, sorry." Then he tried to charm it away with a preemptive grin and the self-effacing cackle that always reminded her of John Candy. "Don't think you were supposed to hear that."

"Nobody was." She spoke so quietly, so evenly, and so without expression that the casual observer would think they were simply two detectives comparing notes. "Look around, Randy. This is serious as it gets. A murder scene. My murder scene. Not open mic night at Dangerfield's."

He nodded. "Yeah, I know I stepped in it."

"Once again," she noted. Randall Feller, perennial class clown, had a nasty habit of cutting up at crime scenes. It was the one bad habit of one great street detective. The same detective who, along with Rook, had gotten shot saving her life on that sanitation pier. Feller's gallows humor might have fit right in during the years he spent in the Special Operations Division, riding around all night in undercover yellow cabs in the macho, kick-ass, Dodge City world of the NYPD Taxi Unit, but not in her squad. At least not inside the yellow tape. This wasn't their first conversation about it since he'd transferred to her Homicide Unit after his medical leave.

"I know, I know, it just sort of comes out." She could tell he meant it, and there was no point belaboring it. "Inside voice next time, I promise." Heat gave him a short nod and moved off to the delivery truck.

From street level at the rear hatch, Nikki had to tilt her head back to look up at Lauren Parry, who squatted on the floor inside the cargo hold. The stacks of cardboard cartons deeper inside wept with condensation; some even glistened from ice crystals encrusting their sides. Even with the freezer motor off, refrigerated air rolled out cool across Heat's face. At Lauren's knee, a blue-gray hard-side suitcase rested open and flat with the lid clamshelled up, blocking Nikki's view of its contents. She said, "Morning, Dr. Parry."

Her friend pivoted to her and smiled. When she said, "Hey, Detective Heat," Nikki could see puffs of Lauren's breath. "Got a complicated one here."

"When isn't it?"

The ME rocked her head side to side, weighing that and agreeing. "Want the basics?"

"Good a place as any to start." Nikki took out her own notebook, a slender, reporter's cut spiral that fit perfectly in her blazer pocket.

"Female Jane Doe. No ID, no purse, no wallet, no jewelry. Estimating age as early sixties."

"Cause of death?" asked Heat.

Lauren Parry's eyes left her clipboard and settled on her friend's. "Now, how did I guess that would be your question?" She glanced inside the suitcase and continued, "I can't say, except preliminarily."

Nikki echoed back, "Now, how did I guess that would be your answer?"

The ME smiled again, and small trails of vapor floated from her nostrils. "Why don't you come on up here, and I can show you what I'm dealing with."

Detective Heat gloved up as she ascended the corrugated metal ramp sloping from the pavement to the back ledge of the truck. As she stepped aboard, her gaze momentarily stuck on the suitcase, and when it did, her teeth clacked with an icy shiver. Attributing it to crossing climates—leaving behind the mild April morning for a January chill inside the cargo hold—she shook it off.

Lauren stood so Nikki could squeeze by to get a view of the corpse. "I see what you mean," Heat said.

The woman's body was frozen. Ice crystals like the ones shimmering on nearby boxes of ground beef, chicken, and fish sticks glistened on her face. Clothed in a pale gray suit, she had been folded into the fetal position and fit into the suitcase, where she now lay on her side. Lauren gestured with the cap of her pen to the frosty bloodstain covering the back of the suit. "Obviously, this here is our best guess for cause of death. It's a significant puncture delivered laterally to the posterior of the rib cage. Judging from the amount of blood, the knife entered sideways between the ribs and found the heart." Heat experienced that uneasy déjà vu she felt every time she saw one of those wounds. She made no comment though, just nodded and folded her arms to warm the gooseflesh the refrigeration had no doubt raised on them, even through the blazer. "With her frozen like this, I can't do my usual field prelim for you. I can't even unfold her limbs to check for other wounds, trauma, defense marks, lividity, and so forth. I can do all that, of course, just not yet."

Nikki kept her gaze fixed on the stab wound and said, "Even time of death is going to be a challenge, I suppose."

"Oh, for sure, but not to worry. We can still come close when I get a chance to work on her down at Thirtieth Street," said the medical examiner. And then she added, "Assuming I don't get back there to a major situation following the quake."

"From what I hear, it's mostly a small number of treat-and-release injuries."

"That's good." Lauren studied her. "You all right?"

"Fine. Just didn't know I'd need a sweater today."

"Guess I'm more used to the cold, right?" She uncapped her pen.

"Why don't I stand aside and make some notes while you do your be-ginn-y thing?" Parry and Heat had worked enough cases together that they knew each other's moves and needs. For instance, Lauren knew that Nikki had an initial task she performed at each crime scene, which was to survey everything from every possible angle with what Heat called beginner's eyes. The problem with veteran detectives, Heat be-lieved, was that after years and years of cases, even the best investiga-tors became numbed by habit; counterintuitively, experience worked against them by blunting observation skills. Ask a refinery worker how he deals with the stink, and he'll say, "What stink?" But Detective Heat remembered how it felt on her first homicides. How she saw everything and then looked for more. Every bit of input held potential significance. Nothing could be overlooked. Just as the experience of her mother's killing ritualized her empathic approach to the crime scene, her belief in keeping it fresh prevented her survey of it from lapsing into ritual. As she often reminded her squad, it's all about being present in the moment and noticing what you notice.

Detective Heat's eyes told her this truck was not likely the murder scene. Walking the tight area of the cargo section, flashing the beam of her Stinger on the floor between boxes and on the walls, she saw no signs of any blood spatter. Later, after the body removal, the Evidence Collection Unit would offload all the cartons for a thorough inspec-tion, but Nikki was satisfied in her mind that the suitcase had been brought aboard with the victim in it and, possibly, dead already. Time of death and a timeline of the truck's loading and unloading would help button that down. She turned her attention to the victim.

ME Parry's pick of early sixties seemed right. Her hair was flatter-ingly cut to a shorter business length correct for a woman of that age and, from the roots that were starting to show some gray and dark brown in the part, her honey blond do, subtly streaked with caramel, indicated two things. First, she was a woman with some money who cared enough about her hair to have an expensive cut and a skilled col-orist. Second, in spite of that, she was long overdue for a visit. "What kept her away?" wrote Nikki in her notebook. The clothes were simi-larly tasteful. Petite size. Off the rack, but clearly the rack lived on one of the upscale floors of the department store. The blouse was from the current season and the gray suit was a lightweight wool with some function to it. The feeling Heat got wasn't so much expensive as good quality. Not the uniform of the lady who lunches, but the woman who power lunches. Nikki crouched to look at the one hand that was visible. It was partially closed and tucked up under her chin, so she couldn't see all of it, but what she could see told a story. These were busy hands, toned without being muscular or abused by hard labor. The slender fingers had the kind of strength you see on tennis players and fitness enthusiasts. She noted a small scar on the side of the wrist, which looked years, maybe decades, old. Nikki stood again and looked straight down at her. The body fit the profile of a runner or cyclist. She made another note to have the vic's picture shown at fitness clubs, the New York Road Runners, and cycle shops. Heat squatted again to examine a grimy, dark brown dirt scuff on the knee of the woman's pants, which could say something about her last moments. She made a note of it and scooted around to look more closely at the knife wound. Furthering Heat's notion that the victim had been killed before being put in the truck, the frozen bloodstain formed a wide pond, as if she had bled out facedown. The width of the stain indicated great volume, yet there was not much blood in the satin of the suitcase interior other than from abrasion smears on the lid. Nikki shined her flashlight where the victim's back met the inside hinge of the suitcase and saw only similar bloodstain rub-off, with no evidence of pooling. Again, when they removed her later, better measurements could be taken, but Heat was getting a picture of a murder not only outside the truck, but outside the luggage.

One more indicator would be to look at the exterior of the suitcase for any major blood collection along the hinges or seams. Taking care not to disturb it, she knelt on both knees, palmed one hand on the cargo deck for balance, and dropped her head, leaning over far enough for her eyebrow to nearly touch the floor. Slowly, methodically, she ran the beam of her flashlight from right to left along the bottom edge of the case.

When her light reached the left corner of the suitcase, Nikki gasped. Her vision fluttered and a vertigo sensation swept over her. The light slipped from her hand and she toppled over onto her side.

Lauren said, "Nikki, you all right?"

She couldn't really see anything in that moment. Hands came on her. Lauren Parry cradled her head off the floor. A pair of EMTs started for the ramp, but by then Nikki had recovered enough to sit herself up and wave them off. "No, no, I'm fine. It's OK." Lauren crouched beside her at eye level to check her out. "Really, I'm OK," said Nikki.

But to her friend, her face said anything but. "You scared me there, Nik. I thought you went over in an aftershock or something."

Heat swung her legs over the back of the truck and let them dangle. Raley and Ochoa approached, followed by Feller. Ochoa said, "What's up, Detective? You look like you saw a ghost."

Nikki shivered. This time, not from the refrigeration. She twisted to look behind her at the suitcase and then slowly turned back to the others.

"Nikki," said Lauren, "what is it?"

"The suitcase." She swallowed hard. "My initials are on it."

The detectives and the ME all looked at one another, puzzled. Finally, Raley said, "I don't get it. Why would your initials be on that suitcase?"

"Because I carved them there when I was a kid." She could see them processing that, but it was taking them too long, so she said, "That suitcase belonged to my mother." And then she added, "Her killer stole it the night she was murdered."

TWO

Nikki Heat marched toward the homicide bull pen of the Twentieth Precinct at a determined clip that left little doubt in the minds
of the detectives trying to keep up with her that she had recovered from the shock of her discovery, and then some. "Briefing in
ten," she called out to her squad as she strode through the door. On her
way to her desk, she said, "Detective Ochoa, fire off the Jane Doe head
shot to Missing Persons. Include Westchester, Long Island, New Jersey,
and Fairfield County cops while you're at it. Detective Raley, erase that
whiteboard and roll the second one over beside it so we can work both
Murder Boards at once." Heat broomed aside the morning's pile of message slips and dusted away grains of acoustical ceiling tile that the 5.8
shaker had snowflaked onto her desktop. Then she hit her keyboard,
e-mailing Lauren Parry at the Office of the Chief Medical Examiner
the same message she had given her verbally fifteen minutes before at
the crime scene: to interrupt her the moment she had any information,
no matter how minor.

She hit send and a cardboard coffee cup materialized on her blotter.
Nikki swiveled in her chair to find Detective Feller lurking there. "In
lieu of flowers, consider this the apology coffee for my big mouth this
morning. Tall, three pump, hazelnut mocha, if I remember. Right?"

Actually, her drink of choice was a grande skim latte with two pumps
of sugar-free vanilla, but "Close enough" was all she said. He was trying
to make amends, but she was focused places other than coffee flavorings
at the moment. "Thanks. And let's put it behind us, OK?"

"Won't happen again."

As soon as Feller stepped away, she set the tepid cup at the back of
the desk, beside her unread messages, and started a to-do list on a letter
pad. One third down the page, she bulleted "additional manpower" and

stopped. That would require clearance from the precinct commander, a hurdle the detective didn't relish. Heat scanned across the bull pen into the PC's glass office that looked out onto her squad. The glass also let the squad look in and had the effect of a creating a life-sized diorama out of that movie *Night at the Museum.* Captain Irons was inside the exhibit, hanging his jacket on a wooden hanger. Heat knew he was next going to go through his ritual of tugging the fabric of his white uniform shirt, and he did—all in his constant quest to eliminate button pucker on the gut that lipped over his low-slung belt.

"Excuse me, Captain," said Heat at his door. "A word?" True to form, Wallace "Wally" Irons paused before he invited her in, as if he were searching for a reason not to but had come up empty. He didn't ask her to sit, which was fine with Nikki. Every time she sat across the desk from him, all she could do was envision the wonderful man who had occupied that chair until he got killed and Irons, a career administrator, got tapped to replace him. Captain Irons was no Captain Montrose, and Heat bet both cops in that room knew it.

Adding further awkwardness to the dynamic, the top brass at One Police Plaza had offered her Wally Irons's job after she passed her exams for lieutenant with record scores. But Heat got soured by the ugly departmental politics surrounding the whole process. It made her realize how much she would miss the street, so Nikki not only declined taking Irons's command from him but passed on the gold bar, too. Yet the fact that she had come a hairsbreadth from being the one on the other side of that desk made the unspoken friction between the detective and her commander loud and clear. From her perspective, he was an organizational survivor concerned more with career than justice, someone she constantly had to out-think or out-maneuver to get the job done right. For Irons, Nikki Heat was his Faustian bargain. She was a detective of incredible value whose case clearances made his CompStat numbers look hot 'n' juicy downtown, but that same damned competency also diminished him. In short, Nikki Heat represented a daily reminder of everything he was not. Ochoa had told her he recently overheard Irons whisper to Detective Hinesburg in the kitchen, "Know what it's like having Heat around? It's like a football team with two head coaches." Nikki shrugged it off and reminded Ochoa she wasn't one for the gossip mill. Besides, she'd kind of known that without him telling her. To smell the paranoia you didn't have to be much of a detective. Kind of like Irons.

"Word is you made quite a discovery this morning," he said, not sounding so much interested in the actual discovery as praising his networking. Nikki kept her briefing to the broad strokes, building it as a multiple homicide worthy of high status and, most importantly, of added manpower from the beginning. The captain held out two palms to her. "Whoa, whoa, let's not run away with the bit in our mouth here. Now, I understand your personal enthusiasm to hit code red with this, but, somehow, these resources have to be accounted for."

"Captain, you see my numbers. You know I always exercise great restraint in overtime and—"

"Jeez, overtime?" He shook his head. "So it's not just pulling uniforms and detectives from other squads, it's OT for your crew, as well? Oh, man . . ."

"Money well spent."

"Easy for you to say. You don't know what it's like to have this job and . . ." He realized the road he'd put himself on and slapped it in reverse. "Easy for you to say, is all."

"Captain, this is big. For the first time in ten years, I have a fresh lead to my mother's murder." She had learned never to take his obtuseness for granted, so she spelled it out for him. "The stolen luggage is a direct link between the two cases, and I am confident that if I can find the killer of this Jane Doe, I can find my mother's killer, as well."

He softened his face into a doughy grimace attempting compassion. "Look, I know this is charged by a highly personal element for you."

"I can't deny that, sir, but I assure you that I would pursue this just as vigorously regardless of my—"

"Knock, knock?" Detective Sharon Hinesburg leaned in the door. "Bad time?"

Captain Irons beamed at Hinesburg and then reeled his unmoored attention back to Nikki, offering her a sober look. "Detective Heat, let's put a pin in this discussion until later."

"But a simple yes would wrap it up."

He chuckled. "A for effort, I've got to respect that. But I need more convincing, and right now, I've got Detective Hinesburg on my calendar." He made a gesture to his desk agenda as if that settled that.

Apparently, thought Heat, Hinesburg was now booking formal appointments for her brownnosing. She slipped by her detective, the low performer in her unit, on her way out of the office. "Squad meeting in three minutes, Sharon." The glass door closed softly behind her and she heard muffled laughter.

Detective Heat put her irritation in her back pocket. Nikki was too professional to get sucked into that quicksand and too driven by the gravity of the new lead to let petty office politics draw focus from her mission. Raley had finished positioning the two large blank whiteboards in an open V-angle against the painted brick wall of the bull pen, and she went right to work, prepping the Jane Doe Murder Board first. At the top corner of the left-hand board, Heat posted eight-by-ten color prints of the victim from various angles: a facial close-up; a side view of her head; an overhead shot of her body in the fetal position inside the suitcase; and a detail view of the stab wound. Beside these, she put up photos of the delivery truck from five angles: front, rear, the two sides, and an overhead she had asked the photographer from the Evidence Collection Unit to grab from a fire escape. In New York City people did a whole lot of looking down at the street from their apartments and offices. The top view of the cargo box, including its telltale graffiti, might jar an eyewitness's memory and help that wit track the vehicle's journey. Any information like that, however small, could nail down how and when the suitcase got inside the truck. Or who put it there.

A burst of applause made her turn from the boards. Jameson Rook had entered the bull pen for the first time since he took the slug to save her life, and the full squad rose to its feet, cheering him. The intensity of the clapping grew as patrol uniforms, civilian aides, and detectives from other squads in the station gathered at the doorway behind Rook and joined in the standing o. He seemed taken aback and caught Heat's eye, clearly moved by the spontaneous group welcome. As if the morning hadn't been emotionally raw enough for her, Nikki found herself choking up at his reception and all that a gesture like that meant from the fraternity of cops, who weren't known for overt demonstrations of sentiment.

When it died down, he swiped at one of his eyes, swallowed hard, smiled at the gathering, and said, "Garsh, do you do this for everybody who delivers coffee?" During their laughter, he crossed to Nikki and handed her a paper cup. "Here ya go. Grande skim latte with two pumps of sugar-free vanilla."

"Perfect," she said, and as soon as she had, Randall Feller's face peered around from behind Detective Ochoa, wearing a slighted expression.

Rook noticed the group had remained in place, staring at him. "I guess I should say a few words."

"Do you have to?" said Detective Raley, eliciting more chuckles.

"Just for that, I will. But I'll be quick." He indicated the Murder Boards behind Heat. "I heard there's some new casework to be done, and I don't want to slow it down."

"Too late," said Nikki, but she was smiling and they both laughed.

"I guess 'thank you' is my beginning and end. Thanks for the support, the cards, the flowers . . . Although a naughty nurse would not have been unwelcome."

"As long as he didn't have too much back hair," said Ochoa.

Rook continued, "And I'll say it for the last time. Thanks to Detectives Raley and Ochoa. Roach, thank you for rolling up your sleeves for my transfusion that night. I guess that now makes us officially . . ."

". . . Creepy," called out Detective Rhymer, who had come down from Burglary.

"No, man, it's all good," said Ochoa. "Know what you have now, Rook? You have the power of Roach Blood."

Raley added, "Use it wisely."

Nikki cleared her throat. "About done?"

"Done," answered Rook.

Heat went official. "My squad, pull up chairs for the briefing."

As the visitors departed and her people began to form up around the Murder Boards, Rook got close and studied her, speaking in a gentle voice. "Hey. You doing any better since our call?"

She shrugged ambivalently. "I'll be fine. Putting the shock behind me. I'm sort of in all-out task mode now. Except I got Iron-gated." Rook followed her glance to Irons, who was still in his office with Hinesburg. "He's balking at giving me OT and resources."

"Drone."

"I don't know what I can do to convince him." She shook it off. "Hey, thanks for the latte. Any chance you can swing by my apartment to see how it did in the quake?"

"Already did. Minimal breakage. I re-straightened the pictures, re-fruited the fruit bowl, re-tchotchked your tchotchkes, and sniffed the range for gas. All is well. Oh. Except your elevator is out. Three flights was no picnic, but I'm a trouper."

Nikki thanked him, but instead of saying you're welcome, he rolled up a chair. "What are you doing?"

"Getting ringside for my briefing." He read her objection and said, "Come on, you really didn't think I came all the way up here to bring you coffee, did you?"

Heat began with details. The major headline, she didn't need to put into words. Not with this group. It rang loud and clear to everyone in that room who knew the lead detective and her history. If that didn't say it, the parallel boards and her ultra-focused demeanor did. This was The Big Case. The case of Nikki Heat's lifetime.

Attention was sharp. Nobody interrupted, nobody joked. Nobody wanted to blow this for her. They all shared one thought: Bring this one home for Detective Heat.

Quickly recapping the discovery of the suitcase by the bomb squad, she used the Jane Doe photos as reference for her grand tour of the victim, explaining her frozen state, lack of ID or personal effects, and apparent—but unconfirmed—death by single stab wound to the back, expertly delivered. Next she indicated the array of truck pictures. "The driver is cooperating fully, and, along with his employer, we are establishing the timeline of deliveries to see when the suitcase got put in there. We can assume the luggage was deposited along his delivery route, but I want no assumptions. None. That brings us to my first assignment. Detective Hinesburg."

Nikki caught Hinesburg off guard as she joined the meeting late from the captain's office. "What's up?" she asked from a half-sit.

"I want you to run a check for priors on the truck driver and anyone at the loading dock who had access to that vehicle before it rolled out this morning. That means anyone who cleaned it, loaded it, inspected it, or who could have slipped the suitcase in there before it left the facility." Hinesburg found a seat and nodded. "Sharon, do you want to write any of this down?"

"No, I got it." And then, as she processed, Hinesburg added, "If the driver called in the 911, we probably don't like him as the perp, do we? Isn't this kind of busywork?"

If thought bubbles were visible in life, the one over Heat's head would have said, You bet. Nikki had learned the hard way that the best way to contain the damage Sharon Hinesburg caused on a case was to give her assignments where her laziness and sloppy detail work would do the least harm. "Guess we'll only know after you get busy, Detective." She scanned the room. "Detective Feller."

"Yo." He had been leaning forward, intent, with his elbows on the thighs of his jeans. Hearing his name, he sat tall and poised his pen.

"You'll work the delivery route. That means not only checking out the workers at the delis and bodegas he hit, but did he stop for gas? Did he leave the truck to use a restroom? Does he have an affair going on the side that made him park for a quickie? Is he skimming food off the books and dropping calamari at his uncle's with the loading door unlocked? You get the idea."

"On it."

"Interface with Raley. As our King of All Surveillance Media he's going to find all the security cams working the delivery route. And Rales?" The detective raised his chin to her, signaling complete attention. "Of course we're hoping to score footage of the suitcase and the person or persons who put it on the truck, but also scrub the video for eyewits. Pedestrians, news vendors—you know what I want."

"Anybody who saw the truck and anything that was happening around it, everywhere it went," answered Detective Raley, making it sound daunting and doable at the same time.

"Detective Ochoa, you run the fingerprints as soon as we get a set.

Also, contact the Real Time Crime Center. See what their database spits out as far as disturbance calls, women screaming, even if they're classed as domestic disputes."

"Time frame?" asked Ochoa.

"We can't fix our time of death until OCME can do some extra lab work after she thaws, so let's tentatively set the kill zone in the past forty-eight and widen later, if we have to."

As she noted that on the board, Feller asked, "You think this could be a serial killer? I wouldn't mind running the MO through the database. Also see how the two kills match up with prison release times, stuff like that."

"Good idea, Randy, do that."

"What if it's just a coincidence?" asked Sharon Hinesburg. The other detectives shifted in their chairs. Ochoa even dropped his face into both hands.

"I believe you know what I think about coincidences, Sharon," Nikki said.

"But they do exist, right?"

"Come on," said Feller, unable to contain his contempt. "You mean a different killer with the same MO just happens to defy all odds and put the body in the suitcase owned by the prior vic? If that's so, I'm buying a lottery ticket."

As the derisive laughter quieted, Heat said, "Tell you what. Just to cover the base, let's check out eBay and area thrift shops to see if we get any tracking on the suitcase." And then, to show how much faith Nikki put in that road, she said, "Sharon, why don't you work that, too."

Heat then lowered her gaze to a photo on the table, and when she saw it, the crackling energy she had been running on since her discovery on Columbus Avenue took a slight dip. Then she straightened up, willing herself back to full speed, and held the eight-by-ten for them to see. "This . . ." she said, then had to come to a full stop, fearing her voice would crack. Something moved in her periphery. It was Rook clasping his hands together and squeezing them before him in a gesture of strength. That small, secret move bolstered her, and Nikki felt a rush of gratitude that she hadn't kicked his ass out of there, after all. Composed again, she resumed, "This is a detail shot of the bottom of the suitcase." She posted it on the upper right corner of the Jane Doe board. The silent room creaked with the sound of Sam Browne belts as they all leaned forward for a good look. The ECU camera flash had brightened the suitcase from blue-gray to a sky at high noon. In the center of the shot, two initials were crudely scratched into the case: N H.

While the squad silently absorbed the haunting significance—that the little girl whose hand had marked the suitcase now stood before them—the adult hand of the little girl slapped a duplicate photo of the initials on Murder Board 2. "Here is our connection," said Detective Heat, accessing a reserve of coolness and control in denial of her emotional turmoil. "Our hot lead runs to the unsolved ten-year-old homicide of Cynthia Trope Heat." She traced an invisible arc back and forth in the air between the photos of her initials on both boards. "This case is going to help us solve the cold case."

"And vice versa," said Roach, in unison.

"Damn right," said Nikki Heat.

As the group broke up to work its assignments, Detective Feller made his way to Heat through the dispersing crowd. "We'll crack this one," he said. "In my mind, this is my only case."

"Thanks, Randy. Means a lot." He waited, standing there looking like he wanted to say something else. Once more, Nikki read the unspoken crush on his face. She had seen it there from the first day they had crossed paths the autumn before, when his undercover taxi had been first to respond to her officer-in-distress call. Ever since, this rough-and-tumble street cop melted into the shy kid at the junior high sock hop whenever he was alone with her.

"Listen, I was wondering. If you hadn't partnered up with anyone yet . . ." He had let it hang there, leaving her to figure out how to deal with it, when Rook swooped in.

"Actually, I was thinking Detective Heat and I would pair up on this case."

Feller looked Rook up and down like he had just jumped out of a clown car. "Really." And then he turned back to Nikki. "I was thinking a veteran detective might work out better than . . . a ride-along writer. Maybe that's just me."

"You mean, the ride-along writer who got shot saving her life?"

Nikki said, "Um, OK, listen."

"I mean, the veteran detective who got shot saving her life," said Feller, pulling back his big shoulders and taking a half step to Rook.

"I know how to settle this," Rook said. "Rochambeau."

"You're on."

Nikki said, "Seriously? No, you two are not doing rock, paper, scissors."

Rook leaned close to her and whispered, "Don't worry. I know the type. Macho guys like this always go for the rock." And before she could protest again, he counted, "One, two, three, shoot." And put out his flat hand for paper—to Feller's scissors.

The detective cackled. "Hah-ha. Nice playing with you, Rook."

"Sorry to throw cold water on this dance of the peacocks," said Heat, "but Randy, I have plans for you that would put your talents to better use than duplicating effort with me. And Rook? Don't take this personally, but this isn't a case I want to be tripping over you every time I turn around."

"Gee, how could I take that personally?"

Then Captain Irons stepped up from behind them. "Mr. Jameson Rook. Welcome back to the Two-oh." A chamber-of-commerce grin pulled back the skipper's fleshy face. He bumped aside Detective Feller reaching to grip Rook's hand in a damp shake while he clapped his shoulder. "To what do we owe the honor? You writing a new story, perhaps?"

The precinct commander's shameless attempts at self-promotion were always embarrassing, but clearly not to him. Wally Irons, who once accidentally knocked over a toddler after her AMBER Alert rescue while rushing to get his face in front of a TV camera, lacked the mortification gene when it came to massaging the press. But Jameson Rook had spent a career dealing with his type and didn't miss a beat. In fact he grabbed the opportunity, for a cause.

"Hm," he said. "Depends. Think there might be a story here, Captain?"

"Uh, Rook," cautioned Heat.

"Ducks in a barrel," Irons said, grinning. "To me, this new development cries out for a follow-up to your earlier article on my Detective

Heat." Nikki tried to get Rook's attention, drilling him with her eyes and shaking her head no. Rook knew how much she hated the attention his cover story in *First Press* had brought, but Rook pretended not to notice her.

"A follow-up?" he said, as if taken by the notion.

Irons said, "To me, it's a no-brainer."

"Well, you'd be the expert there," Rook said, and the captain's quick "thank you" certified that the insult had gone over his head. "Could have some merit. I'm not the editor, though, so don't hold me to this. But I like it." Rook stroked his chin and said, "I suppose it would hinge on action, not just rehash, Captain."

"I hear you."

"For instance, I know Detective Heat's fully engaged and so is her squad. But the story really gets easier for me to sell to a publisher if it goes bigger. I assume, in your leadership role, you've already marshaled all the forces you can." He resisted winking to Nikki as he continued, "For instance clearing overtime and . . . I dunno . . . tapping extra manpower from other squads and precincts?"

A cloud crossed over Irons's brow. "It has come up."

"See, that's something new I could run with. A precinct captain fighting the bureaucracy to rally the resources for his detectives. A leader who can crack a cold case and a frozen one in the same stroke." He chuckled. "What do you know: Headline!"

The captain nodded like a bobble head and turned to Nikki. "Heat, let's move forward with the resources we talked about earlier."

"Thank you, sir." She half-smiled at Rook.

"And I was also thinking, Captain Irons."

"Yes?"

"Now that I'm back to a hundred percent, it might not be a bad idea for me to return to the arrangement I had with the first article and partner with Detective Heat. It's a great way to follow up, plus it would help me document the fruits of your command from street level so—if there does turn out to be an article in this—I'd already be boots on the ground."

"Done," said Irons. Feller shook his head and walked away. "Heat, looks like the dynamic duo rides again," said the captain on his way back to his office.

"Anything else I can help you with, Detective?" asked Rook.

"I just want to note for the record that, after that manipulative display of yours, I now know you are devious and can not be trusted. Ever."

Rook just smiled at Heat and said, "You're welcome."

THREE

R ook disappeared to the battered desk in the corner where he used
to perch during his old ride-along days, dragging along the same
orphaned chair with the loco wheel he always ended up with.
Heat immediately got on her computer to make her manpower
grabs before Captain Irons realized he had just gotten his pocket picked.
Detective Rhymer made a good fit from Burglary, so she put in her bid
for him. As partners, Malcolm and Reynolds—also from the Burglary
Unit—were nearly as formidable as Roach. She had heard the duo was
already out on loan working undercover for Surveillance and Apprehension, but she sent an e-mail to their skipper anyway, asking for their
use and nesting her personal IOU between the lines.

Randall Feller returned to Heat's desk showing no hint of bother
over basically getting hip checked by Rook minutes before. The detective, like everyone else in that room, had his head solidly on task. He gave
her the photocopy he had scored of the truck driver's route sheet for her
to examine. "I'm going to hit the bricks with this and get interviewing at
his stops before shifts change and people's memories go south. So you
know, I'm tearing Raley away from his work wife so he can come with
me and eyeball security cams."

"Ochoa will understand for one day. Their bond goes deeper than
that," she said with a dry smile before he left.

One of the administrative aides called across the chatter of the bull
pen that Lauren Parry was on hold from the coroner's office. Heat
snatched up her phone before she finished her sentence. "Your e-mail
said not to worry about being a pest," said the medical examiner.

"You, Lauren? Never. Especially if it's good news."

"It is."

"You have an ID on my Jane Doe?"

26

"Not yet."

"Then it's not good news to me, girlfriend." Nikki gave her jab a light touch, but the truth lived inside the soft wrapper.

"What if I told you I'm already starting to get some pliability in the joints?"

Heat picked up a pen and sat at her desk. "We're upgrading to pretty good news, Laur. Keep going."

"First off, this tells us our Doe is not frozen solid." The detective pictured a Thanksgiving turkey coming rock-hard from the freezer and nudged the thought aside. "The significance of this is helpful in multiples, Nikki. I put her in front of oscillating fans to bring her gradually to ambient temp so I wouldn't destroy tissue, and the joint movement means we should be able to test sooner than later."

"How soon?"

"This afternoon." And then the ME added, "But beyond that, her semifrozen state tells us she did not get put aboard that truck at midnight at the food packer. That many hours inside an insulated container at sub-zero would have solidified her pretty good, so you can hypothesize—at least for now—that she was loaded somewhere along the route after the truck left early this morning." Heat considered pulling Detective Hinesburg off her assignment at the loading dock and then rejected it. Better Sharon do a little wheel-spinning there than a lot of damage elsewhere. "This also means there's a shot I can give you a more accurate time of death since there may not be any rupturing of cell walls by ice crystals. If we're lucky there, I can get a decent measurement of melatonin from the pineal gland and urine for an accurate TOD window."

Detective Heat had worked enough autopsies to grab hold of all the indicators and form the right questions. "Are you seeing any hypothermia?"

"Negative."

"So we also can assume she was already dead when she became exposed to the frigid temps?"

"I'd definitely make that bet," said Dr. Parry. "One more thing. I should have enough digital flexibility to get some fingerprints for you soon. I know you need these yesterday, but I'm being patient so I don't tear tissue by being hasty."

"How soon?"

"Hasty girl."

"How soon?"

"Within the hour, for sure."

"Hey, Lauren?"

"Yeah?"

"This *is* good news," said Nikki. "Thanks for being a pest."

After she hung up, Rook came over to join her and said, "You do know that if we weren't in your workplace, I'd give you a shoulder rub or a hug or both."

"Thank you for not."

"You're my hero, seriously. I don't even know how you are coping."

"Don't," she said. "Please, not here, not now."

" 'Nuff said." He raised both hands in a surrender gesture. Rook knew her well enough to know that, in spite of all the passion that boiled inside, Nikki came factory-equipped with a firewall that kept it locked up. Her feelings ran deep and hot, which made it a life's work for her to compartmentalize. Jameson Rook unexpectedly held some keys to those locks and wisely let the subject drop. He switched gears with a survey of the room, which buzzed with a level of activity he'd never seen before. "Looks like you've got the taskmaster thing down, Detective Heat. Or is it taskmistress? So hard to know these days."

"It's a start" was all she allowed.

"And what are you planning to do?"

"Me? Keep riding herd. Beg, borrow, and steal a bunch of uniforms to get out and canvass with the Jane Doe photo, as soon as I have a clue where to show it. Maybe I'll take a drive down to Thirtieth Street to surf the autopsy when she thaws."

"I think you and I have more important work to do."

Nikki gave him the wary squint he'd seen so often. "Why am I not liking this already?"

"Cute," he said. "Always your first reaction. Until what? Sweet vindication." He left for the Murder Boards, and, after hesitating, she surrendered and followed. When Nikki got there, he faced the two boards, balancing his hands like scales. "Is it I, or does there seem to be a bit of an imbalance?"

"First off, plus ten for grammar."

"All part of the writer's toolbox," said Rook.

"And, secondly, yes, I focused my briefing on the new murder. The details of my mother's case are too vast to post on one board." She tapped her temple. "But trust me, it's all in here."

"Which is why," he said, matching her move by tapping the nearly blank board, "we need to concentrate our efforts here."

"Rook, I have been there. I have lived it for over a decade."

"Not with me, you haven't."

"But I cannot lose traction on the new case."

"Come on, you yourself said solve one, solve the other." He swept his arm to the bustling squad room. "You've already got one plate spinning beautifully. What's to lose by sorting through the cold case with your experience and my fresh eyes?"

"But that means going backward. More than ten years."

He smiled and nodded. "With apologies to Prince, we're going to partner like it's 1999."

"Prince may forgive you but rule me out." Rook held his ground, affirming the logic of his idea by letting brash silence and flickering eyebrows do the work. At last, she said, "We don't have time to go through the whole case."

"Well, how about we start by talking to the lead detective on it?"

"He retired," she said, the quickness of her reply designed to tell him she not only kept up on the details but that this would be no small undertaking. "Who knows where he is now?"

"I don't know about right this minute, but at noon today Carter Damon, NYPD, retired, will be at P.J. Clarke's on West Sixty-third having lunch with us."

"Rook, you are incorrigible."

"I know. I tried being corrigible once. Lasted a summer right before puberty. Corrigible was kinda dull. Incorrigible was not only more fun, it got me laid a lot. Which is also fun." He checked his watch. "Ooh, quarter to twelve. Subway, or are you driving us to our appointment?"

Rook didn't say much on the short walk to the 79th Street station. He kept the walk brisk to thwart Nikki from changing her mind and staying at the precinct to probe the new lead rather than traveling back in time with him. Standing in the aisle of the subway car for the two-stop ride south, she did say, "You actually knew the name of the lead investigator and where to find him?"

"Let's just say I needed a hobby during my recuperation. A guy can only watch so many *telenovelas*." The doors parted and she followed him out onto the platform.

The subway station at West 66th Street was always busy around lunchtime; however, damage from the earthquake made the pack of humanity extra dense that day. The rails and underground structure had been OK'd by MTA engineers, but superficial damage still needed a cleanup and the platforms there were halved by caution tape to keep riders away from all the tile that had broken off the walls. Many subway stops in the city had public art installations themed for their neighborhood, and their stop; the one for Lincoln Center for the Performing Arts had an impressive wall mosaic stretching the length of the station. Whole chunks of the masterpiece had fractured in the morning shake, sending glass bits of costumed warriors, opera singers, and back-flipping gymnasts to the floor. The elevator up to the sidewalk had also been tagged out of service, and Heat and Rook found themselves blockaded by an elderly woman struggling her walker up the steps. They introduced themselves to her by first names and each offered Sylvia an arm to grip for the remaining five steps. A stranger behind them, a hard-looking gangsta from Uptown with a neck and arms full of scary ink poked Heat's shoulder. Then he volunteered to carry the old woman's walker. Welcome to New York City in an emergency.

Up top, Sylvia left them for the Barnes & Noble, singsonging her thank-yous to Heat, Rook, and the gangsta, who had quietly gone his way in the opposite direction, toward Juilliard. Nikki noticed he had a clarinet case over his shoulder.

Walking through Dante Park where Broadway crosses Columbus, they saw a small band of demonstrators rallying under the Philip Johnson Timesculpture shouting warnings of doom to them about the omen of the quake. One shook a homemade sign at Nikki as she passed. It read, "The End Is Near!" Crossing the street to the restaurant, she paused to look back at the words on the sign and hoped so. Then Jameson Rook took her elbow and escorted her back to the beginning.

The P.J. Clarke's at Lincoln Square had only opened for business two years before but already vibed old New York saloon, the sort of joint where you could get a great burger and a brew or order something icy fresh from the raw bar without a health care card. The original P.J.'s, which opened on the East Side more than a century before, was where Don Draper and his fellow mad men hung out, as did real-life throwbacks like Sinatra, Jackie-O, and Buddy Holly, who proposed to his wife there on their first date. When Nikki Heat followed Rook across the distressed wood plank floor to their table, she only spotted one familiar face. He wasn't a celebrity but he made her knees go weak.

Carter Damon might have retired from the NYPD, but a cop's habits run deep, and he sat with his back to the wall so he could monitor the room over his Bloody Mary. He stood to shake both their hands but kept his gaze on Nikki, even as he gripped Rook's. Something broken lurked in that look; something that, for her, read sadness or awkwardness or, maybe, vodka. Perhaps all of the above.

"You grew up," Damon said as they all sat. "I just got older." Sure, he had more salt in with the pepper of his brush cut and cop-stache, and some pouches had begun to swell his eyes, but Damon, at fifty, still had the lean body of a guy who kept himself in shape. He fit perfectly into the image frozen in her head from the first time she saw him on the worst night of her life.

"I'm sorry for your loss" had been his first words. Nikki, nineteen years old then, looked up at the floating head from where she sat in the living room chair beside the piano. She hadn't even noticed him approach. Lost in a fog, she had been transfixed by her mother's blood, still damp but cooled on the thighs of her jeans from when Nikki had cradled her body on the kitchen floor until the paramedics and the policewoman finally coaxed her away. As Detective Damon had introduced himself, camera flashes from the kitchen strobed behind him, each one making her flinch. When he had told her he would be the detective investigating this crime, the defining word—"crime"—came punctuated, like chain lightning, by a double strobe that jolted her, ripping away her haze, and hurtled her into an alertness, a hyper-clarity, that had made every minute detail store itself like digital video. She had noticed his gold shield clipped to the breast pocket of his sport coat, but instead of a dress shirt underneath, he had worn an old, stained Jets tee with a threadbare collar, as if he had rushed there from home, his Thanksgiving eve turned upsidedown by a phone call from Dispatch at the Thirteenth Precinct. Nineone-one from a Gramercy Park apartment. Units responding. Report probable homicide. Suspect or suspects fled before discovery.

Nikki had been two blocks away, in the spice aisle of the Morton Williams supermarket, when it happened. In hindsight, it always seemed so trivial, so banal, to be running her fingertip along the alphabetical row of jars, her biggest problem in the world trying to find cinnamon sticks—sticks, not ground—while her mother was drawing her last breaths. Elated to find them, she had cell-phoned to do a victory dance and to ask if she needed anything else. After six rings the answering machine grabbed the call. "Hello, this is Cynthia Heat. I'm unable to come to—" and then a squeal of feedback as her mother picked up. She'd been kneading crust for the pies they were baking and had to wipe the butter off her hands before she could get to the phone. And, as usual, she didn't know how to turn off the answering machine without disconnecting, so she let it roll, recording everything while Nikki listened.

"I may need evaporated milk. I have an open can in the fridge, let me see how much is left." Then a crash of glass followed by her mother's scream. Nikki had called out to her loud enough to turn heads in the market. Her mother hadn't answered her, only screamed again, and the phone dropped, smacking onto the floor. By then Nikki had bolted from the market, forcing open the in door with all her strength, dodging cars across Park Avenue South, calling to her mother, begging her to speak to her. In the background, she had heard the muffled voice of a man and a brief scuffle. Then her mother had whimpered, and her body dropped hard beside the phone, followed by the clang of a knife also hitting the floor. Then Nikki heard suction, as the refrigerator door opened. The wine bottles, chilling on the door for their Thanksgiving feast, had tinkled. Then she heard the snap and hiss of a soda can popping open. A pause, then footsteps walking away, followed by silence. She still had a block to go when she heard her mother's weak moan, and her last word. "Nikki . . ."

"Thank you for coming on short notice," said Rook.

"You kidding? Whatever I can do." He glanced at Nikki again. "I will admit, though, this is tough for me." He drank down another swallow of his cocktail, observing her over the rim. Nikki wondered if Carter Damon was tasting failure.

"Me, too," she said.

Damon set down his glass. "Sure, I bet it's ten times worse for you. But as a cop yourself now, you've got to know how it gnaws at you. The ones you never solved. They keep you awake."

Nikki gave him the best smile she could muster and said, "They do," letting her neutral reply politely acknowledge a fellow detective's pain over justice left unserved, without letting him off too easy for not getting the job done.

Her response had an effect. His face ashed and his attention went to Rook. "Is this meeting about an article? You going to write a story about this case? Because I think you pretty much covered it in the one you did a couple months ago." There it was again. How Nikki hated that article. Favorably as it portrayed her, as one of the city's top homicide investigators, CRIME WAVE MEETS HEAT WAVE, Jameson Rook's cover profile for a major national magazine, gave Heat fifteen minutes she wanted back. Damon must have clocked the disdain in Nikki's expression, and he lobbied her, saying, "It's not like there's anything new to bring to the party."

"Actually, there is," said Rook.

The ex-cop's shoulders drew back, and he raised his head a little taller as he took the writer's measure, too experienced, too wary to buy some journalist at face value. But when he saw Detective Heat's nod of affirmation, he said, "Well, hot damn. Seriously?" He smiled to himself. "You know, they say don't cash out, never give up hope . . ."

Carter Damon's words rang hollow to Nikki because he had done exactly both. But she hadn't come there to cast blame. Rook's strategy to revisit history with fresh eyes held enough merit for her to play it out. So she briefed the ex-lead on the developments of the morning: the Jane Doe knife vic in her mom's suitcase. He perked up with every detail, nodding with his full body. When she finished, he said, "You know, I remember logging that stolen luggage." He paused while the waiter took drink orders. Nikki asked for a Pellegrino and Rook a Diet Coke. Damon pushed his unfinished Bloody Mary across the red-and-white checked tablecloth and said, "Coffee, black," and the instant the waiter cleared earshot, he inclined his head back to stare at the ceiling and recite from memory. "Large American Tourister, late seventies vintage. Blue-gray hardside with a chrome T-bar pull handle and two wheels." He tilted back to Rook, since he knew Nikki knew the rest. "We figured it for carrying the haul from the burglary."

Rook asked, "Is that where you left it, as a homicide to cover an apartment burglary?"

Damon shrugged. "Only thing that made sense." But then, when Rook peeled the elastic band from around his black Moleskine to take notes, the ex-detective bristled and said, "This isn't for an article." When they both shook no, he cleared his throat, no doubt relieved he wouldn't appear in print as the cop who couldn't bring it home. "There had been a burglary along with it."

"When?" asked Rook. "Nikki got back to the apartment within minutes of the murder."

"Whoever did the burglary did it before. The theft came from the back of the apartment, the master bedroom and the second bedroom–slash–home office. Could have even been done while the two ladies were in the kitchen. They had the mixer going, the TV on, busy talking and whatnot. But my money is it came down during the substantial time gap after she left for the market."

Rook turned to Nikki, having heard this for the first time. "I took a walk." The muscles tightened in her neck. "That's all. It was a nice night. The weather was mild for then, and so I just walked for about a half hour." She crossed her arms and turned profile to him, clearly shutting down that subject.

"What got stolen?"

"It's all in the report," said Damon. "She has a copy."

"Broad strokes," said Rook.

"Some jewelry and small decorative pieces, you know, antique silver and gold. Cash. And the desk and files got a good cleaning out."

Rook asked, "How common is that? Jewelry, gold, and papers from a desk?"

"It's different. But not unheard of. Could have been an identity thief going for socials, passports, and like that. Or just an amateur doing a quick grab to sort later." He picked up on the skeptical glance Rook gave Nikki and said, "Hey, we'd ruled out everything else."

"Take me through it," said Rook.

Carter Damon said to Nikki, "You have all this."

The ex-detective had a point. But the value of this began and ended with Rook hearing the first-person take from the official investigator, not his girlfriend and victim. "He's new," she said. "Humor him."

The drinks came and they waved off ordering. Damon blew across his coffee, took a sip, and started counting on fingers. "One, we ruled out Nikki. Obviously not on premises, we have her alibi on the phone machine married to the time code on the supermarket security cam, end of that story. Two, no sexual assault."

"But that doesn't mean it couldn't have been a motive, even if it never happened, right?" asked Rook.

The ex-cop made a face and bobbed his head side to side. "I don't like it. That's not to say you don't get both a burglary and an assault, because you do see that. But in a tight time frame like this one—and I'm assuming it came down in the half hour she took her walk—experience tells me it's going to be one or the other. I think Mrs. Heat spotted the burglar and that was that."

"Three," said Rook, waiting.

"Three. We cleared her dad. Touchy subject, but always the top of the list is husbands and, especially, ex-husbands. The Heats' divorce had been recent but, by all accounts, amicable. And just to dot the i's, Jeffrey Heat alibied clean. He was away on a golf vacation in Bermuda, where we had local authorities notify him of the murder." Rook side-glanced to Nikki, who remained stoic, giving him her profile, as before. At least until Damon asked her, "So how's your dad doing now?" and some unseen string pulled her face taut. "You in touch with him lately?"

"Can we move this along?" Heat checked her watch. "I need to be getting back to the squad."

"Sorry. Sore subject?" She didn't respond so he'd ticked off another finger for Rook. "Four. Her mother hadn't reentered the dating pool yet, so there were no suitors to shake down." Nikki made an impatient sigh and took a long pull of her mineral water. "Workplace conflicts," he marked with his pinky finger, "none. Cynthia Heat tutored piano and everyone was very happy with her. Except, maybe, for a couple of eleven-year-olds who hated doing scales." He went back to counting on his forefinger. "Enemies? Check the box that says 'none apparent': no neighbor disputes in the apartment building; no legal disputes pending."

Nikki jumped in, questioning him for the first time. "Did you ever get any trace on that speeding blue Cherokee that had the fender bender at the end of our block that night?"

"Hm. No, I put the word out, but you know how they are. They never got back to me. It's a crapshoot, no plates and all in a city this size."

Then she said, "Mind if I ask when the last time was you checked Property to see if any of the stolen jewelry or antique pieces got fenced or pawned?"

"Hello. I retired three years ago." A family at the next table turned to stare. He softened his voice and leaned forward to her. "Look, we all did our best with this. I gave it my shot. So did your old skipper."

"Montrose?" The family looked again, and it was Nikki's turn to tone it down. "You talking about Captain Montrose?"

"You didn't know? Your skip reached out to me right after you joined his squad. He asked me to take him through my investigation, and he didn't find anything, either. But he must have thought a hell of a lot of you to do that."

"Captain Montrose was a special man," she said simply as she absorbed this news.

"Guess you gave back." He took a sip of his coffee. "I know all about what you did to clear his name."

"It's what you do."

Damon made a side nod referring to Nikki as he spoke to Rook. "And I saw on the news how you took a nine in the chest saving this one."

"It's what you do," said Rook.

"I took a bullet my rookie year in uniform." He tapped the tips of two fingers to his right shoulder. "Getting shot was a picnic compared to the rehab, am I right?"

"Torture," said Rook.

"Hell on a daily schedule." Damon laughed.

"With brief moments of purgatory. I have a visiting sadist named Gitmo Joe."

"Your therapist calls himself Gitmo Joe?"

"No, I do. Actually it's Joe Gittman."

"Love that," said Damon. "Gitmo Joe. Any waterboarding?"

"Might as well be. He comes over every day and makes me wish I had some sleeper cell to throw in just to make him stop." That made Damon laugh again, until he caught Nikki staring at him and it withered.

"Two thousand three," she said. "The last time you checked Property for those fenced items was 2003. Seven years ago."

"How do you know that?"

"Four years before you retired."

"If you say so."

"February 13, 2003, was your last Property check."

When the waiter returned and read the tension, the silence that hung there sent him away without a word.

At last, Carter Damon leaned forward with something resembling a plea deep inside the red rims of his eyes. "Nikki . . . Detective . . . Sometimes the trail runs cold, you know that. It's nobody's fault. You move on." When she didn't reply, he continued, lowering into a hoarse rasp. "I worked your case. I. Worked. It."

"Until you stopped working it."

"Do I need to tell you how many people get murdered in this city?"

"And just how many of my mothers have been murdered?"

He shook his head and retrenched. His moment of vulnerability hardened into defensiveness. "Nuh-uh, no you don't. That's too easy. See, to you it's one case. To me, it ended up being one case on my list. I couldn't help that. The job swamps you."

"Mr. Damon," she said, shunning the respect of using his former rank. "You're talking as if you actually did the job. Seems to me you stopped working about four years before you retired."

"That's not fair."

"Funny," she said, "I've been thinking the same thing."

"Hey, bitch, if you think you can solve this, then do better."

Heat rose. "Watch me."

Rook tossed some cash on the table and left with her.

They splurged on a cab for the twenty-block ride uptown to the precinct so Heat could work her cell phone on the way instead of losing signal underground. After Rook gave the driver the address, he said to her, "You know the doctor said I had to get some weight back on me, and may I point out you are not helping me meet my goal?"

She scrolled through her messages and said, "What are you babbling about, Rook?"

"This morning we skipped breakfast, but I suppose that's OK because it was to have wild sex." Rook caught a flash of eyebrows in the rearview mirror and leaned forward, framing his head in the plexi window for the cabbie. "It's all right, she's my cousin, but my second cousin." Nikki slouched down in the seat, trying not to laugh, because that's what Rook did—especially when the grim darkness reached for her—make her laugh and keep on. He turned back to her and continued, "And now what happens? We have lunch with Mr.—not Detective—Carter Damon . . . and don't think I didn't catch the nuance of the omission . . . and my total nutritional intake from that repast came from a diet soft drink."

"Who says repast?" she said, finishing a voice mail and pressing call back.

"A wordsmith delirious from low blood *sucre*."

Nikki held up her palm. "I'm calling Lauren Parry."

"Perfect, the coroner. If I don't eat, I'll be seeing her soon enough."

Rook dropped her at the precinct and held on to the cab to take him back to his loft in Tribeca so he could do some independent research and read the case file Nikki had promised to e-mail him. After she sent it off, Heat assembled her squad for a midday update around the Murder Boards beginning with the news from Lauren. "I just got word from the ME that our Jane Doe now has a preliminary time of death, which would have been the night before last, in a window of ten P.M. to two A.M." She paused to let them keep up with their notes, then continued, "They were also able to lift some clean prints that Detective Ochoa has already circulated on the database. So far, no hits, but let's hope. Forensics news. They found residue on her skin of a cleaning solvent generally used in labs." Nikki used a capped marker to point to the grime smudge on the knee of the victim's pants. "Also, early results of this dirt, as well as similar material on her shoes, contained elements linked to train environments."

She took a moment to survey her group. "Nice to see Detective Rhymer in the big kids part of the building again."

Detective Ochoa led the traditional chorus of "Welcome to Homicide, Opie," using the Southern transplant's house nickname.

"Rhymes, you'll be partnering with Feller when he gets back from screening security video with Raley. Why don't you get a head start running a check for missing pharmacists, lab techs, medical professionals, and so forth? Any other profession you can think of that would need to use industrial strength lab solvent, hit them, too."

"Like, maybe, Ochoa's dry cleaner," said Detective Reynolds, kicking off a string of catcalls aimed at Oach.

"Ah, yes," said Heat, "the irrepressible Detectives Malcolm and Reynolds, in the house. Going to put you two right to work checking out the rails and subways to see if she worked for any of them. So, flash her picture around the MTA offices, the Long Island Rail Road, PATH, and MetroNorth. As you can see," said Nikki, gesturing to the overhead shot of the victim in the suitcase, "she is dressed like a manager or an executive, so start there with HR, but don't rule out conductors or yard workers."

"Got it," said Detective Malcolm.

"And ask railroad security to screen their cams for you. Jane Doe may not be an employee but a commuter who tried to escape her killer on the tracks."

In the back of the bull pen, Raley and Feller burst in and then stopped short, seeing the briefing still in progress. She read their excitement and said, "Meeting adjourned."

As Heat closed the door to the glorified closet up the hall where Raley tirelessly screened security video, Feller said, "You were right to have us check cams near the delivery drops." He picked up the truck driver's route sheet and showed Nikki where he had made ticks in order down the page leading up to a deli address with a Sharpie circle around it. "This footage comes three doors from the driver's last stop, at a gyro place in Queens, before he left for Manhattan."

"Northern Boulevard near Francis Lewis and Forty-fourth Ave.," added Raley while he keyed some commands on his computer. "We lucked out. I pulled this from a jewelry store that's had so many smash and grabs, they recently upgraded their video to HD. You won't be unhappy." He made sure she was ready and hit play.

The video showed blue velvet in the store's empty window display, which had been cleared out at closing for overnight security. The time stamp read just before five-thirty that morning and registered only light traffic with just the occasional taillight rolling by in the darkness. The sidewalk remained empty until a figure appeared from the parking lot behind the P.C. Richard electronics store across the street. He had his head down, and a drape of hair fell across his face, obscuring it. But Heat's attention focused on the blue-gray American Tourister he rolled behind him by the T-bar through the crosswalk toward the jewelry store. The man turned his back to the camera as he used both hands to tug the heavy luggage up the access incline from the gutter to the sidewalk. The case lost balance on its way up. It would have toppled over, but he flung an arm out to trap it before it could fall, and the shadows defined some major arm muscles pressing the sleeves of his T-shirt. With the suitcase steady now on its two wheels, he continued on, passing directly by the store window, where the bright light inside must have caught his attention because he turned to look in the window. Raley froze the frame and grabbed a crisp, high-def, full-face shot of their man. His deep-set eyes almost looked right into the lens. The frozen glance left Nikki momentarily speechless as she realized she could be looking into the face of her mother's killer.

"You OK?" asked Feller.

She only said, "What do we gather from this shot?"

Raley looked at notes he had already made. "I make him about forty-five, give or take. I'll go with five-eleven to six feet, and two hundred, maybe two-ten considering those guns. Some kind of tattoo peeking out the neck of the shirt. Nose broken years ago, and all around a pretty hard look to him."

"I'm betting he's done time," Feller said. "I know a yard face when I see one."

"Wonder if that's where he's been for ten years," added Detective Raley.

"Let's not get ahead of ourselves," Heat cautioned, saying it as much for herself to hear as the other two. "Write up your physical description to accompany the APB. Make a close-up of the tatt, and get it to the ink and scar database at RTCC. Even though it's a partial, they've worked wonders finding matches with less. And, yes, let's do make sure we get this still frame checked against prison records when we circulate it. Which should be immediately, or sooner."

"Already created the JPEG," said Raley. "Anything else?"

"Yes. You truly are King of All Security Media."

An herbal scent greeted Heat when she opened the door to Rook's apartment. The entry and kitchen were dark, and she caught the ambient dance of candlelight against the walls and the brushed metal appliances. The flickers came from the great room on the other side of the counter, along with dreamy New Age music. Nikki quietly slipped her keys onto the hook, hoping he wouldn't be disappointed when she asked for a rain check on the romantic evening. After the wrenching day she'd just experienced, pizza, CNN, bath, and bed held all the allure she needed. Hell, she might even skip the food and TV.

"I'm in here," came his voice, sounding a little throaty and disconnected, as if he'd gotten a head start on the Sancerre. Nikki stepped into the kitchen and peered across the counter to discover Rook in the dusky light, prone on a massage table. He had a towel across his ass, and a strikingly gorgeous woman in nurse's scrubs kneaded one of his hamstrings, her long fingers just a little too close to that perfectly rounded cheek. Rook made introductions without lifting his head from the foam donut. "Nikki, this is Salena. Salena, Nikki."

Salena looked up briefly at her, only long enough to show perfect teeth through her smile. She whispered a hello then resumed her interest in the spot where the upper thigh met the hem of his towel. "Mmm," said Rook.

Salena said, "This is very tight."

"Mm-hm," he answered.

"Excuse me," said Nikki. She left them and found her way up the dark hallway of his loft to the bedroom and closed the door.

When he came to her afterward in his robe, he found Nikki crosslegged on the bed, working her laptop. "You didn't have to hide in here."

"Well, I wasn't going to stand out there while you were having your 'me time' with your masseuse."

"Actually, licensed physical therapist. The agency sent Salena over to replace Gitmo Joe. How cool is that?"

She closed the lid of her MacBook. "He still sick?"

"No, he quit. So it's Nurse Salena for the rest of my rehab. It's only a few more sessions, but I can live with that." He did a few twists and bends. "I'm feeling better already."

"He just quit?"

"I think he knew I never liked him. Sadist. Dude probably didn't like it that I talked back and offered too much resistance."

"That wasn't a problem with Salena. Not from what I saw."

"Are you jealous? Seriously? That was a therapeutic session from a licensed professional."

She laughed. "Complete with tea tree oil and Enya. Jeez, Rook, I felt like I walked into a porn video."

"There is no Enya in porn video."

The door buzzer sounded. "I'll get that," she said. "I ordered us a pizza."

He followed her out of the room. "Ooh, pizza delivery. Now we are talking porn video."

They ate camp-style, right out of the box, while she filled him in on the surveillance HD Raley pulled from the jewelry store cam and the forensic news about the lab solvent and train residue on Jane Doe. When they were finished eating, he said he'd do the dishes and did so by dropping the pizza carton into the recycling. "Good call on the pie," he said. "Although I can't decide whose I like best. Original Ray's, Famous Original Ray's, or Swear to God, Folks, This Really, Really Is Ray's."

They adjourned from the counter to the dining table, where that afternoon he had spread the printouts he'd made of the PDF case file she sent him alongside his typed-up notes from their meeting with Carter Damon. "In case you're wondering, Detective Heat, that was a very useful exercise for me to be able to sit down with that guy."

"I'm glad somebody got something out of it. All I got was pissed."

"I hadn't noticed."

She scanned his notes and said, "But I can't see anything new that you got. Damon was right, it's all information already in the case file."

"What I got is a sense of his laxness. Maybe he wasn't when he started the case, but this is a detective who dropped the ball when it got hard and the investigation called for some old-fashioned doggedness. To me, Carter Damon is Sharon Hinesburg without the nail extensions and push-up bra. The headline for me is that we have to go back ourselves and dig deeper."

"I disagree. Much as I don't like Damon's slacker mentality—"

"—more cop-out than cop—"

"—these are dead ends. Captain Montrose always drilled us to follow the hot lead. And that means we focus on the fresh trail off that suitcase."

"We can do both."

Nikki ignored him, plowing onward. "And when we ID our Jane Doe, we'll be even closer."

"Why are you resisting this?"

"Beer?" she said, and left him for the fridge. Nikki had just finished pouring them each a perfectly cloudy Widmer Hefeweizen when her cell phone rang. After she listened briefly, Heat said, "Got it. Meet you downstairs from Rook's in five," and hung up. "That was Roach. If you want to come, you'd better wear more than a robe."

"Where are we going?"

"Queens. They found our guy with the suitcase."

FOUR

The tattoo busted him. As Heat had hoped, the Real Time Crime Center had a match in its computer that connected to a suspect. A week before, the owner of a convenience store in the Bayside neighborhood of Queens had called in a complaint on a shoplifter. The surveillance cam picked him up, and even though the petty crime didn't have the weight to make the news or light up an All Points, the RTCC logged the tatt into its database, and the hit came within minutes of Detective Raley posting his JPEG on the server. Uniform patrols flashed the picture around Bayside, and a night watchman at a used car lot recognized him as a guy he had seen hanging around lately. The break came when the security guard spotted him again a few hours after the uni visit and tailed him to a nearby house while he put in a cell call to NYPD.

Heat, Rook, Raley, and Ochoa rode in tense silence under the flashing gumball, shoulders swaying and knees bumping against the doors of the Roach Coach while Detective Raley threaded the needle through evening cross-town traffic to the Midtown Tunnel and onto the Long Island Expressway. The only gap in Raley's concentration came on the straightaway passing the steel Unisphere at Flushing Meadows, when he side-glanced Ochoa in the shotgun seat and rabbit wrinkled his nose. His partner suppressed a smile about Rook, whose fragrant herbal massage oil had also hitched a ride in back. Heat picked up on it, but all she said was, "ETA?" Her succinct way of urging focus and speed.

Their Crown Vic rolled up to the tactical staging area at Marie Curie Park in Bayside six minutes later, and Raley angled it nose-out with the other police cars. Emergency Services Squad 9, including a unit of SWATs, stood by in black helmets and body armor. The ESS field commander greeted her as she climbed out. "You made good time, Detective Heat."

"Thanks for waiting."

"Listen. Going to let this be your show," he said.

The underlying message of respect embedded in that gesture nearly choked her up, but she let it go with a crisp, "Thanks, appreciate that, Commander."

"Got it all buttoned up for you," he said. "Suspect is inside a single-family two-story on Oceania, next street over. Con-Ed records list the owner as a J. S. Palmer, although the bill hasn't been paid for six months and the juice is off at the resident's request." He used the red filter on his flashlight, so he wouldn't night blind her, and spread a map full of neatly drawn deployment markings on the roof of the car. "It's the corner house here. I've got a tight perimeter covering all possible exits, including canines here and here. Blue-and-whites have Northern Boulevard choked off, and we blockaded Forty-seventh Avenue after you came through, so we own the streets. I also have a team inside the neighboring house, and we've moved that family out the side door."

"Sounds like you've covered everything."

"Not done yet." He keyed his walkie-talkie mic. "ESU Nine to Chopper Four-one-four."

"Go, ESU Nine," replied a calm voice with a high-pitched purr behind it.

"Ready in five."

"Confirm five minutes, on your signal. We'll bring the daylight."

Raley popped the trunk. Heat moved around to join him, Ochoa and Rook at the rear bumper. While the three detectives vested up, she said, "Rook, you wait here."

"Come on, I promise I won't get shot. I can wear one of those vests."

Ochoa indicated the bold white lettering across his chest and back. "Check it out, bro. It says 'POLICE.'"

Rook peered into the trunk. "Do you have one in there that says 'WRITER,' preferably in a large tall? You're gonna like the way I look. I guarantee it."

"Give it up," said Nikki.

"Then why did you even bring me?"

Nikki almost let slip the truth and said, For the moral support. But she replied, "Because if I left you behind, I'd never hear the end of the whining."

"That's why?" said Ochoa, as the three detectives fell in with the SWAT unit. "I thought it was 'cause Rook's like the human Air Wick. Won't need that cardboard pine tree in the Roach Coach with him around."

ESU swarmed the house with a tactical precision that belied the laid-back demeanor of the commander and his team. Heat and Roach double-timed with the SWAT unit on foot, using the armored Bearcat vehicle for cover as it roared up the driveway. When the black truck came to a stop, the Bell helicopter thundered up the street and the pilot hit his Nightsun, beaming a dose of hot light to blind anyone looking out windows as the team deployed. They approached in efficient, textbook sequence, taking cover behind the porch rail, trash cans, and shrubs as they moved in. When Heat and the crew carrying the battering ram gained the front door, she knuckled it and called over the din of the chopper, "NYPD, open up." After a pause too short to measure, Heat gave the go sign for the ram.

The thud of the door into the wall matched the pounding under Nikki's vest as she entered the unlit house, leading the SWAT team in a surreal ballet of flashlight beams and rapid incursion. She called out, "NYPD, identify yourself!" but only heard the slap echo of her own voice in the near-vacant house. The assault force fanned out, a third rolling to the right side of the downstairs with Heat, a third going left, circling toward the dining room and kitchen, with Roach and the remainder heading upstairs to the second story and attic. The spotlight from the circling copter pierced the windows and crept along the walls, making the house feel like it was spinning. Each terse update whispered in Heat's earpiece confused and disheartened her. "Dining room: clear." "Kitchen: clear." "Master bed: clear." "Hall closet: clear." "Attic: clear." "Basement: clear." The downstairs pincer groups met up in the kitchen, which smelled from enough stacked garbage to qualify for a cable TV hoarders show.

But no suspect.

"Garage status?" she said into her mic.

"Clear."

The ESS commander came downstairs with Roach and met her in the living room. "Doesn't make sense," he said. "And there's no place to hide. Closets are empty. Only a ratty mattress on the floor of the master."

"On the vacant side down here, too," said Detective Ochoa. He traced his Stinger LED across the nail hooks, illuminating the spots where pictures once hung above an unbleached rectangle in the hardwood the size and shape of a sofa. Now only a pair of mismatched patio chairs sat off to the side of a grimy, secondhand rug.

"Any false walls?" asked Rook, coming in the front door. "I know for a fact some of these old houses have fake doors behind bookcases."

Heat sounded a familiar refrain. "Rook, I told you to wait outside."

"But I saw the pretty light from the helicopter and it pulled me in against my will. It's like *Close Encounters* for me. Or the rose ceremony on *Bachelorette*."

"Outside. Now."

"Fine." He backed up to leave and stumbled to the floor, landing on his butt.

Ochoa shook his head. Raley helped him up and said, "See? This is why we can't take you anywhere."

"It's not my fault. I tripped on something under that rug."

"Well, lift your feet," said Nikki. "On your way out."

"Detective?" said Ochoa. He was down on one knee, running his palm across a lump in the stained green shag. He rose and whispered to her, "Hatch handle."

They peeled back the rug and exposed a three-by-three square of plywood with a pull ring handle and hinges embedded into the floor. "I'm going in," said Heat.

The commander cautioned her. "Let's drop some gas down there first."

"He'll get away. What if there's a tunnel?"

"Then we'll send a dog."

But adrenaline called her shots. Nikki slid her forefinger into the pull ring and threw the hatch back. She shined her light into the emptiness and shouted, "NYPD, show yourself." A startled moan came from below.

"See anything?" asked Raley.

Heat shook no and swung a leg into the opening. "There's a ladder."

"Detective . . ." said the ESS commander. But too late. Overwhelmed by the drive to capture her suspect, Heat broke from procedure and descended. Ignoring the rungs, she slid down the outer rails, using the ladder like a firehouse pole. Nikki landed in a crouch, Sig Sauer ready in her right hand. She plucked the flashlight from her teeth and shined it across the cellar.

He stood completely naked in the center of the partitioned-off section of basement, staring at her with detached eyes that appeared to see and not to see. "NYPD, freeze." Her suspect didn't respond. Besides, he had already frozen, standing there motionless yet unthreatening as SWAT backup rained down to join her, training assault weapons with tactical-mount lights on him. "Hold fire," said Heat.

She wanted him so dead, but she needed him alive.

All the flashlights revealed a sea of shoes surrounding him. Hundreds and hundreds of shoes: men's and women's, old and new, pairs and orphans—all in neat rows of concentric circles around the center, toes pointing at him. "So," he said. "You came for my shoes."

"What do you answer to, William or Bill?" Nikki waited again for him to speak and would wait as long as she had to. The suspect had remained silent since they sat down to face each other in Interrogation One ten minutes before. Mostly, he just studied himself in the observation mirror. Occasionally, he looked away, then back, as if to surprise himself. He rolled his muscular shoulders so that they flexed against the orange fabric of his jumpsuit.

At last he asked, "Is this mine to keep?" and seemed to mean it.

"William," she said. "I'm going to call you what it says here on your rap sheet." He broke eye contact and looked back in the mirror. Detective Heat studied the file again, although by then she had committed the salient facts to memory. William Wade Scott, male cauc, age forty-four. Basically a low-end drifter whose arrest record traced his movements through the Northeast following his dishonorable discharge on drug charges after Desert Storm in 1991. His beefs ran on the petty side, a ton of shoplifts and disorderly conducts, plus a few arrests that raised the bar, most notably a 1998 electronics store smash-and-grab in Providence that earned him three years as a state guest. Nikki tasked Ochoa to run a double-check with Rhode Island Corrections for the release date because that incarceration alibied him for her mother's murder.

Behind the mirror in Observation Room 1, Detective Ochoa texted her, confirming William Wade Scott's prison release in 2001—a year and a half after her mom's killing. She read it passively, but Rook watched her fists ball under the table after she slipped her cell phone back into her pocket.

In the wake of so many setbacks on her mom's case over the years, Nikki had hardened herself against despair, but this one stung. However, as ever, Heat's response to disappointment was greater resolve. And a reality check. Did she honestly believe the killer would fall into her lap on the same day as the new lead? Hell, no. That's what tomorrow was all about.

Rook turned to Raley and Ochoa in the Ob Room. "That still leaves him as a possible for the Jane Doe killing, doesn't it?"

"Possible?" said Raley. "Yeah, possible . . ." The "not likely" was silent. After the raid in Bayside, neighbor interviews said the naked man in the basement was not the owner of the residence on Oceania Street but a homeless squatter, one of a number who had moved into nice, suburban neighborhoods throughout Long Island after residents simply walked away from upside-down mortgages. The block had filed several complaints about the man, but they grumbled that nothing had come of them. But Raley's follow-up check on the absent homeowner suggested this vacancy hadn't come from a mortgage walk-off. He pulled up an old 1995 New Jersey arrest against the owner for operating a hydroponic pot farm in the basement, which not only accounted for the floor hatch in his next residence—the Bayside house—but also his abandonment of the property to keep a step ahead of drug enforcement.

"OK," said Rook, grasping for any good news, "there's still the suitcase. He possessed the suitcase that connects to Heat's mom. If he's not the killer, maybe he knows him."

Ochoa said, "She'll get there. You watch. This is her art."

"Why were you hiding from us in that basement?" Heat asked. No reply. "We identified ourselves as police. Why did you need to hide?"

He released his gaze from the mirror and smiled. "I don't need to hide. I could get out of here now, if I wanted to." Scott yanked up both wrists beside him, pulling his manacles taut and then releasing them. "These mean nothing to me."

Nikki played along on the tightrope walk of trying to pull straight answers from a delusional, likely schizophrenic, man. But right then William Wade Scott was her best hope. If he wasn't a good suspect, he might be a great witness. Acting unfazed, she moved a mental chess piece, a pawn. "Was it about the cigarettes you stole the other night?"

"This is all bullshit once I am taken up. You must know that."

"Maybe I'm not as informed as you. 'Taken up'?"

"To my vessel," he said. "I received the special communication."

"Of course. Congratulations, William." Her affirmation surprised him and made him rivet her with a penetrating squint, listening intently. "Is that why you needed the suitcase? For your trip?"

"No, for the shoes! I found it and thought there'd be more shoes inside." He leaned forward and winked. "They'll be so pleased when I bring them shoes."

She leaned forward, also. "But weren't there shoes inside the suitcase? Didn't you see shoes?"

"I . . . did." He began to fidget but stayed with her. "But they were . . . They were still on her."

"On whom?"

"Her!" he said, then stooped over to grind his eye sockets with the heels of his palms. "I couldn't take them off her." He grew more agitated. "I couldn't keep her."

"Did you kill her?"

"No. I found her."

"Where?"

"In the suitcase, pay attention."

"Where did you find the suitcase?"

"Behind the nursing home around the corner." He calmed and confided his big secret with a stage wink. "They throw out lots of shoes there."

Heat made a hand gesture to the mirror, but inside the Ob Room, Raley and Ochoa were already on their way out the door for a return drive to Bayside and the nursing home.

"So when you saw her in the suitcase, why didn't you take her back to where you found her?"

"The nursing home? Why? She was dead," he said as if the logic of that should be obvious. "But I didn't know what to do with her. A body is, well, it's a complication to The Plan." Nikki opted not to press and gave him plenty of line. He fidgeted some more and said, "I dragged her around all night. Then I saw it. A preservation vessel. It was perfect. Plenty cold inside. Even had a ramp."

"You sure you don't want to just crash?" asked Rook when he and Nikki got back to his loft. "It's coming up on two A.M. No harm, no foul if you want a rain check."

"I'm too wired to sleep. And besides, you promised me one of your Killer Caipirinhas, and I'm holding you to it, writer boy."

"You're on. Worth every bit of being held at gunpoint by an international arms dealer just to score his bartender's recipe." He opened the fridge to hunt fresh limes. She settled on the bar stool at the counter to watch the magic.

Long as the day had been, Heat's fatigue couldn't match her frustration. When Roach called in from the security office of the nursing home in Bayside, they had mixed news. Due to the late hour, they were fortunate to interview the same watchman who had been on duty the night before, when William Wade Scott said he found the suitcase there. Unfortunately, however, the facility had no surveillance cams at the disposal Dumpsters, which meant no pictures of the homeless man finding the suitcase and, worse, no shots of whoever left it there. The security guard did recognize the freeze of Scott rolling the luggage and verified seeing both him and the baggage leaving the property about two hours before Raley's surveillance picture had been taken. He also said he saw Scott arrive empty-handed, validating his story that the case had been scavenged. Adding more cold water to the embers, he didn't recognize the Jane Doe. Roach had called in the Evidence Collection Unit to survey the Dumpster area—a long shot that had to be covered—and then clocked out, telling Heat they'd return at sunup to interview staff and residents about the suitcase, Jane Doe, and whatever some nonagenarian insomniac might have seen staring out a window in the long night of the soul.

"What's going to happen to Willie Shoetaker?" asked Rook as they clinked glasses.

"Real sensitive, Rook." She sipped her cocktail. "But I forgive you because this Caipirinha is awesome. To answer your question, I Article Nined William Scott for an involuntary psych evaluation. It lets me hold him a few days, plus he's better off in Bellevue. Not that I expect to get any more from him. I'm afraid he seems to be a gap in the chain, not a link."

"Hey, you never know."

"Don't patronize me. I do know."

Recognizing the rise of her firewall, Rook busied himself with his drink to fill the strained silence with something other than strain. After a decent interval, he said, "Well, here's what *I* know. This may be a dead end, but only on one front."

"Here we go. Are you back to 1999 again?"

"No. Before that. I want to look into your mom's life."

"Forget it, Rook."

"Carter Damon said your mom was a piano teacher, right?"

"Tutor. Piano tutor."

"What qualified her for that?"

Nikki scoffed. "Qualified? Pal, do you have any idea how qualified?" But then she was surprised by the answer he gave without taking a beat.

"You mean like an advanced degree from the New England Conservatory of Music while training to become a top concert soloist? That kind of qualified?" As she sat there just gawking at him, he clinked her glass and said, "Hey, you don't get a pair of Pulitzers by being a slouch in the research department."

"All right, so you have your special gifts, smarty. Where's this going?"

"Riddle me this: What is Detective Heat's First Rule of Investigation?" Before she could reply, he answered it himself. " 'Look for the odd sock.' The odd sock being the one thing that doesn't go with, or seems out of place in, all the evidence."

"And?"

"And what is the odd sock of your mother's life? Simple. Why have all that passion, talent, and classical training only to give it up to teach rich brats 'Heart and Soul'?" He waited, same as he'd seen her wait out the homeless man through the glass.

"I . . . uh . . ." She lowered her gaze to the counter, having no answer to share.

"Then let's find out. How? Let's follow the odd sock."

"Now?"

"Of course not. Tomorrow. Tomorrow's Saturday. We're going to Boston to visit your mom's music school."

"Do I have a say in this?"

"Sure. As long as it's yes."

They certainly seemed to know Jameson Rook at the front desk of the Lenox Hotel. After a short walk from the Back Bay Amtrak station, the two of them had planned to drop their overnight bags at the bell desk and move on with their day, but a beaming old gent whose nameplate read "Cory" welcomed the famous writer back and offered them a suite upgrade to something called "Heaven on Eleven" and early check-in. Looking out their top-floor room at the view of the Back Bay, Rook said to Nikki, "I used to come to this hotel a lot because it's next door to the PL." He made a nod to the Boston Public Library below. "Logged a lot of hours in there working on a romance."

"Which book was that?"

"Not a book. Sandra, in the microfiche section."

"You're dating yourself."

"I was then, too. Sandra proved immune to my charms."

His phone buzzed. It was Cynthia Heat's music professor from the New England Conservatory returning his call with apologies that she wouldn't be available until the next morning. Rook set a time to meet, thanked her, and then hung up. "I hereby declare this day to be an RTWOTC."

"What's RTW . . . whatever?"

"Romantic Trip While On The Case. And you call yourself a cop?"

They had set out to stroll Newbury Street to select one of the thousands of sidewalk cafés for lunch, but on Boylston, when they got a whiff of a gourmet food truck selling pulled pork Vietnamese noodles and rice bowls, a quiche on Newbury didn't stand a chance. They unpacked the white paper bag on a park bench in Copley Square and began their impromptu picnic. "Nice view," said Rook, pointing to the bronze statue in front of them. "The ass of John Singleton Copley and a twenty-four-hour CVS." He put his hand on her knee and added, "Wouldn't have it any other way." When she didn't reply, he repeated, "Wouldn't have it any other way."

"I should never have left New York."

Rook put his container of noodles down to give her his full attention. "Look, I know it's not your nature to take what feels like a step back in the middle of a case. Especially this one. Trust me, I know you are all about pure effort. But you have to try to see this as work. Even if it doesn't feel like it every second, you are still investigating something my gut tells me is important. And remember, that squad of minions you browbeat are hard at it back home. This is good strategy. It's divide and conquer, in action."

"Doesn't feel like it to me." Heat set aside her rice bowl and made phone rounds of the investigation while he ate. When she had finished, she couldn't mask her disappointment. "They came up empty at the nursing home."

"Too bad. I halfway wondered if that lab cleaning residue might have come from there. They must have some medical solvents in a place like that."

She shook her head. "Roach checked that already."

"You know, we ought to have a name like that. A compressed nickname like Raley and Ochoa. Roach." And then he added, "Only ours would be romantic. I mean there was Bennifer, right? And there's Brangelina. We could be . . ."

"Done with this relationship?" She laughed. But he kept on.

"Rooki? . . . Naw."

"Would you stop?"

"Or how about . . . Nooki? Hm, I like Nooki."

"Is this how you lost Miss Microfiche? Talk like this?"

He hung his head. "Yes."

A rain shower rolled into Boston, so they took things indoors, to the

Museum of Fine Arts. They dashed through a downpour from their taxi, past a group of guerilla artists on the sidewalk with political works on display. One was a lovely, if unimaginative, acrylic painting of a greedy pig in a top hat and tails, smoking a cigar. It caught Rook's eye, though, and as he ran by, he almost tripped over a sculpture of a three-foot-tall gold leaf fist clenched around a wad of cash. "What a way to go," he said to Nikki once they got in the lobby. "KO'd by the 'Fist of Capitalism.'"

Just by entering the museum, he sensed Nikki had become temporarily released from her cares. She grew animated, telling him the MFA had been a weekly pilgrimage when she went to college at Northeastern. She hooked his arm and took him to see all of her favorites in the collection, including the Gilbert Stuart oils of Washington and Adams and *The Dory* by Winslow Homer. Transfixed, Rook said with reverence, "You know, his water is the wettest you'll ever see in a painting." The John Singer Sargents triggered warm memories of the print of *Carnation, Lily, Lily, Rose* Rook had given her when they first started seeing each other. Heat and Rook kissed under *The Daughters of Edward Darley Boit*, a masterpiece from the period when the artist made a living painting American expatriates in Paris. The four daughters didn't seem to mind the PDA.

Another Sargent, on loan from a private collector, hung to the side by itself. Also painted in Paris, it was the artist's portrait of a Madame Ramón Subercaseaux.

"I've never seen this one," said Rook. "Isn't it amazing?" But a shadow fell over her demeanor again. All Nikki did was grunt a cursory "uh-huh" as she moved on to the next gallery. He lagged behind to take in the portrait. It captured an elegant young woman with dark hair seated at an upright piano. Mme. Subercaseaux was posed turning away from the instrument. Her melancholy eyes stared out, meeting the viewer's, and one hand rested behind her on the keyboard. The painting evoked the feeling of a pianist, interrupted.

Rook followed after Nikki, understanding her discomfort with it.

The showers had cleared out, and Heat asked him how much he would hate getting dragged along on a nostalgia tour of her alma mater, just across the street. "On an RTWOTC Saturday?" he asked. "First, I'd love to."

"And second?"

"If I said no, I'd be kissing off any chance of hotel sex."

"Damn straight."

"Then what are we waiting for?" he said.

Frankly, the notion of a tour didn't excite him, but he didn't regret a bit of it, simply because he could see how the visit energized her. Rook watched Nikki's cares shed at each point of interest and every old hang she showed him. She snuck him in the backstage entrance to Blackman Auditorium to see where, as a freshman, she played Ophelia in *Hamlet* and Cathleen, the summer maid, in *Long Day's Journey into Night*. At Churchill Hall, where Heat studied Criminal Justice, they found the doors locked but she pointed to the fifth floor so he could see the window of her Criminology lecture hall. Looking up at it, he said, "Fascinating, the actual window," then turned to her, adding, "That hotel sex better be mighty raucous." He paid for that crack by having to endure small talk with her freshman Medieval Lit professor, whom she stumbled upon in the campus Starbucks grading *Beowulf* term papers. Crossing the quad took them to the bronze statue of Cy Young. Relishing her role as tour guide, Nikki proudly informed him it stood on the exact location of the mound where Young had pitched the first-ever perfect game when the site had been the old Huntington ballpark.

"Photo op," he said, handing her his iPhone.

Nikki laughed. "You're such a boy."

"I wish. This is so I can pretend I know something about baseball. When you grow up without a dad, raised by a Broadway star, there are gaps. Swear to God, until this moment I thought Cy Young was the composer who wrote 'Big Spender.'"

She snapped one of him aping the legendary pitcher, reading signs from the catcher. "Let me get a close-up." She zoomed in on his face and, in the viewfinder, saw him looking past her, frowning.

Nikki turned to see what Rook was reacting to and said, "Oh, my God . . . Petar?"

The skinny man in the Sherpa cap and designer-torn denim who was walking past, stopped. "Nikki?" He pulled off his sunglasses and beamed. "Oh, my God. This is crazy."

Rook stood by, leaning an elbow on Cy Young's pitching arm, as he watched Nikki and her old college boyfriend hug. And just a little too exuberantly to suit him. Now he did regret the campus tour. This guy Petar went up his ass from the day he had met him last fall. Rook convinced himself it was not some possessive, irrational jealousy of an old flame. Although Nikki said that's precisely what it was. Petar Matic, her Croatian ex, screamed Eurotrash, and Rook couldn't believe Nikki didn't see it. To Rook, this journeyman segment producer for *Later On!*, a post-midnight talk show he looked down on as Fallon-lite, posed as if he held the pulse of late night comedy in his pale-fingered grip. Rook knew there was only one thing Petar Matic held the pulse of every night, and he tried not to imagine it.

"Oh, and James is here, too," Petar said, parting at last from Nikki.

"It's Jameson," said Rook, but Petar was too busy delivering a man hug shoulder bump for it to register.

Nikki touched his cheek and said, "Look at you, you grew your beard back."

"Just stubble," Petar said. "Stubble's like the new deal."

"All the rage in Macedonia," said Rook. Petar seemed oblivious to the jab and asked what they were doing there. "Just a getaway." Rook draped his arm around her shoulder and said, "Nikki and I are grabbing a little alone time."

"Thought I'd show him our old stomping grounds," she said. "What about you?"

"I'm having alone time, too. But alone." He chuckled at his own joke and continued, "I came up from New York for the day to guest lecture a Communications seminar about the future of late night talk shows."

"Professor Mulkerin?" asked Nikki.

"Yep. Funny, I barely got a C in that class, and now I'm the star alum."

"Well, it was great to see you," Rook said, the verbal equivalent of checking his watch.

"You, too, Jim. I wish I had known. We could have planned dinner together."

Nikki said, "Let's!" The smile she gave Rook held the hotel sex card clenched in its teeth.

Rook forced a grin. "Great."

On the cab ride back to the Lenox, since Nikki didn't have a knife, she cut the silence with her tongue. "Know what you've got, Rook? Petar envy."

"Don't make me laugh."

"You have a thing against him, and it shows."

"I apologize. I just didn't see dinner with your old boyfriend as part of the RTWOTC plan. Is this payback because I got a massage from a practitioner who happened to be somewhat attractive?"

"Rook, she was a Victoria's Secret model without the angel wings."

"You thought so, too, huh?"

"Your jealousy is transparent and over-the-top. Forget old boyfriend. Yes, Petar did try to rekindle when we ran into him last fall, but I ended that."

"He hit on you? You never told me that."

"Now he's just an old friend." She paused to peer up at the top of the Pru then said, "And yes, this still is an RT-whatever. But just to remind you, since you may have been too traumatized—or in denial after your gunshot—Petar was a huge help breaking that case. This is my chance to say thank you."

"By having me buy his dinner?"

She looked out the window and smiled. "Win-win for me."

He booked a table at Grill 23 for the simple reason that, if it was good enough for Spenser, it was good enough for him. After starting off with topneck clams and an extraordinary Cakebread Chardonnay, dinner wasn't pure hell for Rook. Perhaps just purgatory. Mostly he smiled and listened as Petar gassed on about himself and his exciting behind-the-scenes role booking guests for *Later On!* "I'm this close to the big get," he said, and lowered his voice. "Brad and Angelina."

"Wow," said Nikki, "Brangelina."

"I hate those cute nicknames," said Rook.

Petar shrugged. "Nikki, remember what they called us? Petnik?"

"Petnik!" She laughed. "Oh my God, Petnik." Rook reached for the ice bucket and filled his own glass, wondering what the hell it was about scruffy waifs with sad, soulful eyes that attracted women. What was this magical allure of underachievement and unruly hair?

After a main course of memory lane conversation and Nikki's fifth cell check of messages from the precinct, Petar came out of his self-absorption to observe that she seemed preoccupied. Nikki set down her fork, leaving a perfectly good duck fat tater tot still speared on it, and napkinned her mouth. The clouds that had parted for her rolled in on a new cold front. She told Petar about the new development in her mother's case, pausing only for the plates to be cleared before she resumed.

To his credit—for once—Petar listened intently and without interruption. His face sobered and his eyes grew hooded by an old sadness. When she finished, he shook his head and said, "There's no such thing as closure for you, is there?"

"Maybe I can close the case someday. But closure?" She dismissed the entire concept with the wave of a hand.

"I don't know how you got through it, Nikki." He rested his hand on her wrist. "You were very strong then." Rook signaled for the check.

"Maybe strong is what broke us up."

He smiled a little and said, "And not me cheating?"

"Oh, right." She grinned. "That, too."

On their way out, Nikki excused herself to the ladies' room and Petar thanked Rook for the nice meal. "You're a very lucky guy, Jameson Rook," trilling the R, a remnant of the accent. "Take this the right way, OK? I honestly hope you're luckier than I was. I could never get through that protective wall of hers. Maybe you won't give up."

In spite of himself, Rook had to admit maybe he and the old boyfriend had something in common, after all.

The April air had chilled overnight, and as they waited Sunday morning on the empty sidewalk outside of NEC's Main Conservatory Building to meet her mom's former professor, Nikki could see vapor trails from Rook's nose. It reminded her of Lauren Parry's breath inside that freezer truck, and she turned away to watch a bus roll by on Huntington Avenue. Then they both heard bouncy synthesized music followed by a man's amplified voice singing the *Flashdance* song "Maniac." The two of them turned all around, searching for the source.

"He's up there," said the gray-haired woman approaching from the bus stop. She pointed to an eighth-floor open window in an apartment building behind the NEC residence hall, where a black man in a red long-sleeved shirt and matching black leather vest and fedora sang into the mic of his karaoke machine. "That's Luther." She waved up to the window, and Luther waved back, still swaying and singing, his booming voice echoing off the face of the building. "Every morning, when he sees me, he auditions like this for the Conservatory. I told him once we don't do pop, but he seems undaunted." Professor Yuki Shimizu extended her hand and introduced herself.

The three of them ascended the foot-worn marble steps and entered through hallowed wooden doors into the vestibule. "I guess you know NEC is a national landmark," said the professor. "The oldest private music institution in America. And no, I wasn't here when it opened. It just feels like it."

As they signed in at Security, Professor Shimizu said, "Pardon me for staring, but I can't help it. You look just like your mother." The old woman's smile filled her entire face and warmed Nikki. "Take that as a supreme compliment, my dear."

"So taken, Professor. Thank you."

"And since it's my day off, how about calling me Yuki?"

"And I'm Nikki."

"Most people call me Rook," he said. "But Jameson's fine, too."

"I've read your magazine articles."

"Thank you," he said.

A twinkle played in the woman's eyes. "I didn't say I liked them." She threw a wink Nikki's way and led them down a corridor to the right. In spite of the gray hair earned over seventy-six years, she strode with vitality and purpose, not a bit like she even knew what a day off felt like.

As they passed a rehearsal hall, a scattering of students awaiting their turns sat cross-legged on the brown and tan carpet, beside their backpacks and instrument cases, listening to iPods. From inside the hall, *Boléro* pounded against the closed door, all lush and percussive. Rook leaned over and whispered to Nikki, full of suggestiveness, "Mm, *Boléro*."

Professor Shimizu, strides ahead of them, stopped and turned. "You like Ravel, Mr. Rook?" she asked, clearly having nothing wrong with her hearing. "Almost as sexy as *Flashdance*, eh?"

She took them downstairs to the Firestone Audio Library, where she had arranged a booth for them to meet in, for quiet and privacy. Once they all sat, she regarded Heat again and said, "Nikki, you became a police officer, right? So much for the apple falling from the tree theory."

"Actually, I had planned on becoming a performer myself," she said. "I went to college next door at Northeastern and was on track get my degree in Theater Arts when my mother was killed."

Professor Shimizu surprised her. The old woman rose to her feet and crossed to Nikki's chair, clasping both her hands in both of hers. "I have no words. And we both know none can fill that void."

Rook could see Nikki blink away some mist as the woman returned to her seat, so he began for her. "Professor, may I go back for a moment to our metaphorical apple tree?"

She turned aside to Nikki. "Writers."

"You feel her mom was quite promising as a performer?"

"Let's talk about the whole student, Jameson. The goal of this institution is not simply to grind out performers like sausage. This is a school, but it is also a community. We stress collaboration and growth. That means artistically, that means technically, and, most importantly, as a person. They are all connected if one is to achieve mastery." The old teacher turned to address Nikki. "Simply put, your mother embodied those values like few I have seen in my almost sixty years here, both as a student and as faculty." She paused for effect and said, "And do I look like I'd blow smoke up your skirt?" Heat and Rook laughed, but the professor remained serious. "Your mother also confounded me, Nikki. She studied, she practiced, she inquired, she experimented, and then she studied and practiced some more—all so she could realize her passion, her dream of becoming a concert pianist of the first order. I knew she would get there. The faculty had a pool going about when she would get her first recording contract from Deutsche Grammophon."

"What happened?" asked Rook.

"Wrong question. You mean, 'What the hell happened?'" She looked at Nikki and said, "You don't know either, do you?"

"That's why we came to see you."

"I've seen this sort of thing before, of course. But usually, it's alcohol or drugs, or a man or woman derailing them, or burnout, stage fright, or mental illness. But your mother, she simply went to Europe on holiday after graduation and . . ." The professor lifted both hands off her lap and let them drop. "No reason. Just a waste."

Rook broke the brief silence. "Was she really that talented?"

The old professor smiled. "You tell me." She swiveled her chair to the console behind her and switched on the TV monitor. "Lights, please," she said. Rook got up to kill the overheads and rolled his chair beside Nikki's in front of the screen. The image that appeared there, 16mm film dubbed to VHS years before, fluttered and resolved. They heard applause and young Professor Yuki Shimizu, with jet-black hair and a polyester pantsuit, stepped to a podium. The subtitle lettering read, "Keller Recital Hall, February 22, 1971." Beside them, Yuki whispered, "Anyone can pound out Beethoven and hide in the spectacle. I chose this because of its simplicity, so you could see all her colors."

"Good evening," said the professor on-screen. "Tonight, a rare treat. French composer Gabriel Fauré's *Pavane*, Opus Fifty, performed by two of our outstanding students, Leonard Frick, playing cello, and, at the piano, Cynthia Trope." Upon hearing her mother's maiden name, Nikki leaned closer as the camera panned to an impossibly skinny student with muttonchops and an explosion of kinky hair behind a cello. Then the TV screen included Cynthia in a sleeveless black formal with dark brown hair brushing her shoulders. Heat cleared her throat at the sight. Rook felt like he was seeing double.

The piece began on the Steinway grand, slowly, softly, plaintively; Cynthia's elegant arms and slender fingers rode the keyboard like gentle waves and then became joined by the cello in harmony and counterpoint. "One bit of color, and I'll shut up," Yuki said to them. "This is a choral work, but in this arrangement, the piano carries that part. It's amazing what she does with it."

For six minutes they sat, mesmerized, watching and listening to Nikki's mother—only twenty—weave under, inside, and through her partner's plaintive cello line in graceful motion, playing fluid and sure, her swaying body connected to the music and the piano, a picture of natural poise on the bench. Then the velvety opening turned sharply dramatic, signaling distress, tragedy, and discord. Cynthia's unruffled flow broke and she threw thundering, athletic stabs at the ivory. Her neck and arm muscles were sculpted into sharp definition with each of the concussions she delivered, etching the recital hall with crisp shocks of upheaval before returning seamlessly to the melodic, stately dance, with the whole effect of her contribution elevating the performance above melodrama to fully realize the composer's intent, which was its sophisticated cousin, melancholy. At the end, her fingers gently shaped the notes into softness, not just heard but felt. Ending solo, her tender creation conjured a vision of puffy snowflakes gently lighting on frozen branches.

During the applause, her mother and the cellist stood for humble bows. Rook turned to Nikki, expecting to see tears glistening on her cheeks in the reflection of the video. But no, that would be melodrama. Her response was in tune with her mother's in the piece—melancholy. And longing.

"Want to see one more?" asked the professor.

"Please," said Nikki.

The video continued to roll as the duo quickly set up to became a trio and a classmate joined them on stage with her violin. Heat and Rook both reacted at the same time. Rook said, "Stop the tape."

Nikki shouted, "No, don't stop it, freeze it. Can you freeze it?"

Professor Shimizu punched the pause button and the image of the violinist froze as she brought her instrument and bow up, revealing a small scar on her outer wrist.

"It's her," said Rook, voicing what Heat already knew. "That violinist is our Jane Doe from the suitcase."

FIVE

A s the Acela Express sped toward New York's Penn Station, Rook stared out his window at a snowy egret fishing the bank of a salt marsh on the Connecticut shoreline. "God, I wish you'd say something," said Heat.

"What do you mean, 'say something'?" His eyes rose to the archipelago dotting the horizon, where several hulking mansions jutted up, each stately home rooted fast to one of the tiny rock islands scattered offshore. Over a century ago, millionaires from New York and Philadelphia looking for isolation and privacy built what they whimsically called their summer cottages on those mounds of granite, appropriating Long Island Sound as a castle moat. Their perfect seclusion made Rook reflect on Petar's comment the night before about Nikki's defensive wall. He turned to face her across the table from him. "I think I've been a total chatterbox since Providence. Do you really want to hear more about my theory on why Ravel's *Boléro* is such a surefire, panties on the floor, bedroom seducer?"

"Rook."

"Hands down, the most hauntingly erotic piece of music ever. Except maybe 'Don't Mess with My Toot Toot.'"

"You're driving me crazy, so just say it. If you hadn't pushed me to go to Boston, we never would have popped this lead." Nikki's cell phone vibrated and she took a call from Detective Ochoa. "That's great," she said and made a few notes. She hung up and said, "Case in point. In the time since we ID'd Nicole Bernardin as our Jane Doe this morning, Roach has located her apartment. It's on Payson Avenue near Inwood Park. They're rolling there now."

"No such thing as Sunday off for Roach."

"Or Malcolm and Reynolds. They volunteered to pick us up at Penn so we can Code Two up there." She checked her watch for the tenth time in as many minutes. "We'll still get there sooner than if we had waited for a flight."

Rook smiled. "I can't quite put my finger on it, but there's something I like about Malcolm and Reynolds."

Heat went back to looking over the photocopies Professor Shimizu had made for her of the student file and 1971 yearbook photos of Nicole Aimée Bernardin. As Nikki studied the French violin student's young face in one picture, snapped in a candid moment laughing with Nikki's mother and Seiji Ozawa at Tanglewood, she felt Rook's stare.

"Know what I can't wrap my brain around?" he said. "That your mom never mentioned her to you. Let's look past the obvious stunner that the lady in your mom's suitcase was a classmate of your mom's. They weren't just classmates. The professor said your mom and Nicole were inseparable back then. Friends, roommates—hell, they even formed their own chamber ensemble. Why do you think she never told you about her?"

She turned the page to another yearbook shot of her mother and Nicole. This time they were at the 1970 French Cultural Festival at the Hatch Shell on the Charles River Esplanade. The picture captured them eyeing each other peripherally as they played. The caption read, "Trope and Bernardin, Keeping Time," but to Nikki the look carried more. If it were present day, the caption would simply say, "BFFs."

Rook asked, "Do you think they had some big falling out?"

"How would I know if I didn't even know about her?"

"Hey, here's a theory."

"I was waiting. Are you sure you don't want to put on your foil cap?"

"Nicole Bernardin killed your mother."

She just stared at him. "And?"

"Hang on, I'm formulating thoughts. . . . And that is how Nicole had your mom's suitcase."

"And then, ten years later, someone else killed her, same MO, and just happened to stuff her in it?"

"Oh," he said, wiggling in his seat. "What if . . . What if Nicole's husband was your mom's killer? That's how she ended up in his suitcase."

"You know, at least that has possibilities."

"Really?"

"Yes. So quit while you're ahead." She closed the file and stared at the passing marshes and woodlands, seeing none of it, really. Less than a minute passed, and Rook was back, as if he'd hit reset. "There must be some reason your own mother never mentioned such a good friend."

"Rook?" she said. "Don't make me shoot you."

"Shut up?"

"Thank you."

He concentrated on the view again, glimpsing the last of the solitary islands of rock just before the train entered an underpass and the concrete wall blocked it from sight.

Even though they had to detour around a frozen zone set up on Dyckman due to a gas leak caused by the earthquake, they still made record time getting to Nicole Bernardin's apartment in the northernmost section of Manhattan. Her building, a slender two-story town house facing Inwood Hill Park across the avenue, would be Realtor-listed as a charming Tudor. The neighborhood felt safe and looked well maintained, the sort of quiet street where people used canvas car covers and the half walls surrounding porches gleamed with fresh coats of paint. Heat and Rook entered the town house to find a different picture entirely.

From the downstairs foyer, in every direction they looked, the disarray was alarming. Cabinets and closets stood ajar. Paintings and pictures ripped from hooks sat askew, with busted frames tipping against wainscoting and doorjambs. An antique china cabinet in the dining room lay split open on its side with shattered crystal glassware surrounding it like ice chips. Strewn decorative objects covered all the floors as if the whole place had been shaken. "Tell me this wasn't from the earthquake," said Rook.

Detective Heat put on a pair of blue gloves. Raley handed him a pair and said, "Not unless the earthquake walked around crushing everything under size eleven work boots."

Touring the ransacked town house shrouded Nikki in yet another suffocating cloud of déjà vu. Her own apartment—once the scene of her mother's murder—had also been tossed back then, although not so thoroughly violated. Detective Damon had called that an interrupted search.

This one clearly went on nonstop until the perp either found what he was looking for or was satisfied he never would.

Ochoa met her in the doorway as she entered the upstairs master bedroom. As they stepped around the fingerprint technician who was dusting the cut glass knob, she asked her detective, "Any sign of blood anywhere?"

He shook no and said, "No obvious sign of struggle, either. Although I don't know how you'd ever be able to sort that out a hundred percent in all this mess."

"I can give you about ninety-nine-point-nine percent, if that's helpful," said the lead for the Evidence Collection Unit, Benigno DeJesus, as he rose up from kneeling on the rug behind a tossed mattress. Nikki's shoulders immediately relaxed when she saw him. The crime scene was in excellent hands.

"Detective DeJesus," she said. "To what do we owe this honor on a Sunday?"

He pulled down his surgical mask and smiled. "I don't know. I had an uneventful day planned when Detective Ochoa called to tell me about this case of . . . ," he paused and then, in his typically understated fashion, continued, "some interest. So here I am." She gave Ochoa a quick study, wondering what favor Miguel had traded for pulling in the best evidence man in the department on a day off, but Oach's stoic face gave nothing away.

DeJesus gave her and Rook an overview tour of the town house, with his preliminary assessment being that the disarray constituted a property search without an assault associated with it. He pointed to the second bedroom, which Nicole Bernardin had set up as a home office. That had received the brunt of the rummaging. He used a penlight to indicate four tiny circular marks where the rubber feet of her laptop had lived before it got taken. The charger cord as well as the USB cable to her missing external hard drive all remained where they had once connected to the computer. Desk drawers and files all sat open and empty, except for stationery odds and ends. "The level of meticulousness here tells me whoever searched the residence focused most of his attention and care in here," he said.

Back in the bedroom, the ECU detective said the owner of this place wasn't sharing it with a spouse. All the toiletries, clothing, foods in the kitchen, and other tells suggested a mature woman living alone, although she had kept a supply of condoms in the nightstand and a new toothbrush, shaving cream, and a package of disposable razors in a bathroom cabinet. Hearing that, Nikki and Rook side-glanced each other, each tentatively ticking one unspoken thought off a mental list about Cynthia Trope Heat and Nicole Aimée Bernardin. The prescriptions in the medicine cabinet all matched Nicole's name, and the few pictures in broken frames on the floor showed the victim in Europe at various ages with people resembling parents and siblings. Nikki crouched over, curious to see if her mother appeared in any of them, but she did not. She stood up and observed Rook doing the same thing in the next room.

Roach had already briefed Detective DeJesus about the traces of lab solvent and the railroad grime found on her body, and he promised to be on the lookout, as well as to coordinate with Lauren Parry at OCME on Nicole Bernardin's toxicology to match prescription use and any other findings she learned in her postmortem. Heat was content to leave it in the capable hands of ECU, but she indulged herself in a solitary, sense-of-the-house tour before she drove back to the Twentieth Precinct. One thing she wanted to see satisfied a big piece of curiosity for her when she found it. In the downstairs closet she discovered a complete set of luggage, including the exact size of her mother's stolen piece. All were empty, and there was no space left in the closet for the suitcase the victim's body had been found in. That was not definitive information, but it did lessen the likelihood that Nicole Bernardin had been in possession of that American Tourister, and therefore it moved her one step down the roster of her mother's potential killers. A bittersweet thought for Heat since, ten years later, that roster was still empty.

The silence that fell over the bull pen while Detective Heat updated the pair of Murder Boards was so complete the only sound was the squeak of her marker on the white surface as she printed in red block letters: "1. WHY KILL NICOLE BERNARDIN? 2. WHY KILL NICOLE BERNARDIN NOW?" As she wrote, she said, "As the connections between the old murder and this new one deepen, we need to be thinking about not just the why but the timing, the ten-year lag between the two."

She turned to the room, where Rook and her squad formed a semi-circle around her. Even though she had called them in on a Sunday afternoon, the detectives had turned out without complaint. In fact, beyond just showing commitment, they seemed energized by the mission sense of working this one all-out for her. Some had even brought the group snacks that they had stopped for on the way in from their homes or from the town house up in Inwood. The take-out containers of bagels, cookies, and salads sat behind them on the desktop of the lone no-show, Sharon Hinesburg, who had her phone turned off, a violation of policy. Heat tapped the board with the marker cap. "Keep coming back to these, OK? When this falls together for us, it will be because, above all else, we found the answers to these two questions."

Their attention was on her, but their eyes were riveted on the new photos Nikki had posted, and the profound—literally graphic—story they told. On the left whiteboard, the familiar death pose of Jane Doe, now Nicole Bernardin. Inches away on the right-hand board, Nikki's mom's suitcase, bearing Nikki's girlish initials, and the new addition, the blowup of Nicole and Cynthia in performance forty years ago at the Esplanade. Not only did the connection between the two victims drawn by the photo impact on the group, but the striking resemblance of young Cynthia Trope Heat to their squad leader dramatically underscored the stakes they already felt.

"By now, you all know about the lead we picked up in Boston," she began. "And that her apartment has been tossed and, most likely, scrubbed of evidence. That includes, paperwork, laptop, even her mail. Now, these two apartment searches—my mother's and now Nicole Bernardin's—tell us that this one," she said pointing to her mom's Murder Board, "was not likely a simple burglary gone bad. Someone was searching hard for something in both places."

Feller's hand went up. "Do we assume it's the same person?"

"We don't assume. And we sure don't know. Yet. We also don't know if the hunt was for the same object. All we have is the common MO. Just like the killings."

Rook said, "Here's a notion. Nicole was French. What about international jewel thieves looking for two halves of a treasure map?"

Malcolm kept his face deadpan and said, "Oh. Like *The Pink Panther.*"

Rook was about to say yes, but he felt their stares. "Well. One possibility."

Nikki continued, "Of note, all Nicole's suitcases are apparently accounted for, as are all knives, which are in the wooden holder. I've assigned a group of uniforms to canvass neighbors and Parks PD for unusual activity or strange vehicles. We have some of our own work to do."

On the Nicole Murder Board, she began a list of new assignments, placing the initials of detectives beside each. "Detective Ochoa, I'd like you to look into her personal life. Hit all the usuals: boyfriends past and present; stalker complaints; restraining orders; family feuds. If you have trouble finding anything official, check with her hairdresser. You'd be amazed what you can learn."

"Like maybe doing something about that bald spot," said Reynolds. "You're blinding me, homes."

"Detective Reynolds, you'll contact the local sports and running clubs again now that we have a name to go with the face. And also check out Internet dating services. See if she was registered and if she had any hookups that might have gone bad. Do the upscale matchmakers, too. A professional woman might have gone to them."

"And what do we know about the profession?" asked Detective Malcolm.

"Letterhead and business cards that turned up at the town house indicate the victim worked as the owner of her own business as a corporate headhunter." Heat read from one of the cards. " 'The NAB Group. Discreet and confidential executive searches for industry and institutions, worldwide.' NAB being her initials."

Rhymer asked, "Address?"

"Mail drop. No offices evident. Phone is an eight-eight-eight. I've put in for a check on that number and any other phone accounts she had. Landline, if she even had one, got taken. And, as you recall, she had no cell phone on her."

Rook said, "No cell phone? That's like one step away from cave paintings and medicinal leeches."

Heat posted the business card. "She had a Web site, but it's one page stating all of the above plus an added line, 'References and testimonials on request.'"

Raley said, "Sounds like a front or a home business."

"Rales, you work that thread. Put on your media crown and surf for any hits on executive placements, business testimonials, you know what I'm after." He nodded as he jotted his note. "Detective Feller, you do a search for her state and federal tax ID. That will also tell us if she used an accountant."

"And if so, I follow the proverbial money," Feller said.

"Like the bloodhound you are. That includes all bank accounts, safe deposit boxes, credit cards, credit check—the works. Detective Malcolm, do you own a suit?"

"Birthday," his partner, Reynolds, heckled him.

"Whatevs," said Heat. "Nicole Bernardin was a French national. Take a jaunt across Central Park and visit their consulate when they open. See if she's known to them. Also put in a call to the French consulate in Boston." She indicated the Esplanade photo. "This was for a cultural program they sponsored. Maybe she kept in contact. Find out."

Rook had his hand up. "A thought?"

"Let's hear it," said Nikki.

"Her laptop is missing, right?"

"And her external drive and memory keys."

"Right," he continued, "but in my own travel experience with a notebook computer, I always do compulsive backing up, either by e-mail attachments I send to myself or, the new fail-safe, syncing everything to a remote internet storage cloud service like Dropbox."

Heat said, "That's actually a good idea."

"Second one today," said Rook.

Ochoa said, "I tell ya, the man's got the power. The power of Roach Blood."

"Detective Rhymer," she said. "Soon as we adjourn, bust down some geek doors at the Computer and Information Technology Unit to see if they have any Big Bangers who can work a trace on whether she used a Web cloud for data backup."

The soft-spoken detective formerly from the South lived up to his nickname of Opie by politely asking, "And it's cool if I kick some butt, even if it's a Sunday?"

"Even better," said Detective Heat. "That way, they'll know how important this is."

After dinner they arrived at Heat's apartment building to find the elevator still had the out of order seal on its doors. On the second landing of the stairs, Rook paused momentarily to swap grips on his Boston overnight bag. "Now I know why these are called carry-ons and not carry-ups."

"Want me to take yours?"

"Ah-ah," he said, shooing her hand away. "I'll just consider this my rehab for the day."

"Let me see if I can write the story, Pulitzer boy. Rehab today, naughty nurse massage tomorrow?"

"Now, there's a story with a happy ending," he said as he resumed his ascent.

Rook found an '07 Hautes-Côtes de Nuits in the back of the fridge that he accused her of hiding from him, and then he settled beside Nikki on the couch to look through the photo albums with her. "This is all I have left," she said, indicating the banker's box of family keepsakes on the floor beside her. "I don't even know what's missing. Whoever searched this apartment the night of the murder got the rest and must have left before he got to these."

"Nikki, if this is hard for you . . ."

"Of course it's hard for me. How could it not be?" Then she rested her palm on his thigh. "That's why I'm glad to have you here with me to do this."

They kissed, each tasting Burgundy on the other's tongue. Then he surveyed the room and gave her a thoughtful look. "I've always wanted to ask, and I never quite knew how."

"You mean, ask how I could live here after her murder?" When he reacted, she said, "Come on, Rook, the way you just scoped out this place was the most ridiculous tell I've seen. Well, since the last time I beat you at poker." He didn't respond, but just watched her.

She swiveled her knees to the coffee table and traced her fingers around the edges of a photo album. "It's hard to say why. People encouraged me to move, back then. But leaving here felt like I would be leaving her. Maybe I will want to move out sometime. But it's always seemed right to be here. This was always home; this is our connection." She sat up straight and clapped her hands twice to bring a mood change. "Ready to look at some boring pictures?"

They began slowly at first, turning pages that led off with her parents' individual grammar and high school portraits along with serious and goofy poses with family, mostly elderly. Her dad's college photos from George Washington University included a few action shots of him playing basketball for the Colonials and cradling his business school diploma at commencement on the DC Capitol Mall. There were numerous pictures of her mother at the New England Conservatory, mostly at a Steinway or standing in front of one. There was even a picture of Professor Shimizu handing her a bouquet and a trophy, but no chamber duo shots, except for one with Leonard Frick. No glimpses of BFF Nicole Bernardin. When Nikki closed the back cover on the first album, Rook said, "It's like a mash-up Syfy Channel meets Lifetime movie where a rip in the space-time continuum removes all traces of the best friend."

She stared at him and said flatly, "That's right. That's exactly what it's like."

But that did coax a smile out of her, and he said, "Know what we should do? No-brainer. Ask your father."

"No."

"But of all people, wouldn't your dad—"

"Not going to happen, OK? So drop it."

Her sharpness left him nothing to say but "Moving on?"

The second album of the pair chronicled the courtship of Jeff and Cynthia Heat, a young trophy couple about Europe, including Paris, but still without Nicole. When Rook asked if she might be in the wedding party, Nikki told him there hadn't been one. Products of the seventies, her mom and dad had succumbed to a bout of post-hippie rebellion and eloped. The ensuing series of photographs were taken of baby Nikki in New York, including a hilarious snapshot of her when she was barely walking, holding on to the wrought iron bars of Gramercy Park, peering through them angrily at the lens. "I've seen that expression from most of the prisoners you put in the holding cell." She laughed at that but then closed the album. "That's it? Come on, it's just getting to the good stuff."

"We're done. The rest is mostly me at my gawky worst and we're not doing this for your entertainment or my humiliation. I got enough of that in seventh grade. I know for a fact there's no sign of Nicole in these."

"I have another crazy thought."

"You, Rook? Imagine that," she said, refilling their glasses.

"Actually, it's not so out there. Has it occurred to you since we found out her name this morning that you might actually be Nicole's namesake?" He watched the impact of that play across her brow. "Ah, not so crazy now, is it?"

She tossed it around and said, "Except my legal name isn't Nicole."

"So? Nikki, Nicole. Not so far off. Makes sense, especially if they were such close friends. . . . Although, from this," he said, indicating the photo albums, "Nicole's looking more like she turned into an imaginary friend."

Nikki went to her desk in the second bedroom to make her cell phone and e-mail rounds on the case progress, and when she returned, she found Rook cross-legged in the middle of the living room floor. "What do you think you are doing?"

"Being incorrigible, what else? It's my job." He pressed the play button on the old VHS player and the TV screen resolved into a video recording of Nikki, seated beside her mother at the piano. The date stamp read: "16 July 1985."

"OK, Rook, that's fine, you can turn it off."

"How old were you then?"

"Five. We've seen enough. We're good."

A man's deep voice came from off camera. "What are you going to play, Nikki?"

"Your dad?" asked Rook. She shrugged as if she didn't know who and just stood in place, watching.

On the twenty-five-year-old video, young Nikki Heat, decked out in a yellow jumper, swung her feet to and fro under the bench and smiled. She talk-shouted to the camera, "I am going to play Wolfgang Amadeus Mozart." Rook expected to start hearing "Twinkle, Twinkle, Little Star."

Instead, the girl looked to whoever held the camera and confidently announced, "I would like to play his Sonata Number Fifteen." Cynthia gave her a nod to begin, and Nikki poised her hands over the keyboard, counted silently to herself, and began the piece, which was immediately familiar to Rook. He moved closer to the TV, impressed to say the least. The piece was challenging but doable for small hands, and she struck all the notes without a miscue, although her cadence felt rote, but hell, the kid was only five. As the little girl continued to play, her mother leaned close to her and said, "Beautiful, Nikki. But don't rush. Like Mozart said, 'The space between the notes is music, too.'"

Heat indulged Rook his voyeurism but hit the stop button as soon as the song ended. Rook applauded, and meant it. He turned to the piano across the room: The same one, situated exactly as it had been in the video. "Do you still know the song?"

"Forget it."

"Come on, command performance."

"No, show's over."

"Please?"

Nikki sat on the couch and positioned herself turned away from the piano. Her pose gave off the vibe he got from the Sargent painting she had avoided in Boston. "You need to understand. I haven't even opened the lid since her murder." Her features tightened and her complexion took on a slight pallor. "I can't bring myself to play it. I just can't."

A pair of sirens screamed by, wailing beneath her window in the middle of the night, and Nikki stirred. Somebody heading to emergency or jail, as that old Eagles song about New York had gotten so right. The alarm on the nightstand read 3:26 A.M. She flopped an arm to Rook's side of the bed and found nothing but cool sheets.

"Please tell me you're not surfing porn," she said, tying a bow on the front of her robe. He sat in his undershorts at her dining table in the darkened room, his face cast in creepy lunar light from his laptop screen.

"In my own way, I am. Writer's porn." He looked up at her. The spiky bed head didn't make him look any less crazy. "What is it that is so darn satisfying about a Google search? It is kinda like forbidden sex.

You wonder, should I/shouldn't I? But you can't get it out of your head, so you say the hell with it, and, next thing you know, you're sweaty and panting with excitement as you get exactly what you need."

"Look, if you'd rather be alone . . ."

He spun his MacBook toward her so she could see the search results. "Leonard Frick. Remember the cello guy in your mom's video?"

"Otherwise known as the cellist."

"Who also played the clarinet in her chamber trio with Nicole. Multitalented." Rook hitched a thumb to the screen. "Leonard Frick, graduate of the New England Conservatory, is currently employed as principal clarinetist for the Queens Symphony Orchestra."

"Otherwise known as the principal clarinet."

"This is why I gave up the bassoon. Too many rules." He stood. "This guy had to know both your mom and Nicole as well as anyone. We need to go see him."

"Now?"

"Of course not. I need to get dressed first."

She pressed herself against him and caressed his ass with each hand, then jerked him to her by his cheeks. "Now?"

He untied her robe and felt her skin spread warmth across his chest. "I suppose we could go back to bed. You know, for a bit. There'd still be time to see him on our way to the precinct."

At seven-thirty that morning, Heat and Rook waited at the cross-walk outside her neighborhood Starbucks, holding three coffees: one for each of them and the other for Rook's car service driver, who waited leaning against the fender of the black Lincoln across East 23rd. Traffic stopped and they got the walk signal, but halfway across their driver called, "Heads up!" They heard the roar of an engine and turned to face the grill of a maroon van mere feet from mowing them both down. They jumped back just in time, and it charged through the intersection and raced on. Shaken, they hurried across while they still had the right of way.

"Holy fuck, scared the hell out of me. You guys OK?"

Nikki saw that she had a case of latte leg, nothing unusual for her, and blotted it with a napkin. "What was that guy doing," she asked, "texting?"

"No, must have been drunk or high," said their driver. "He was looking right at you." Nikki stopped cleaning the stain and took a step to the curb to see if she could get a plate on the van. It was long gone.

"Am I a suspect?" asked Leonard Frick. The once-skinny kid in the tux with the cloud of steel wool hair had filled out over the decades. Now, sitting across from him in the rehearsal hall at the Aaron Copland School of Music at Queens College, Heat put him at two-seventy, and the only hair on his head was a silver goatee framed by the dimples that appeared like parentheses when he smiled.

"No, sir," said Nikki, "this is purely for background."

Rook asked, "You didn't kill them, did you?"

"Of course not." Then he said to Nikki, "He's not a cop, is he?"

"What gave him away?" That brought out the dimples as Mr. Frick laughed. He seemed happy for the company and told them how his career in music had ebbed and flowed since the seventies. First came fill-in work as a substitute for some of the smaller symphony orchestras in the Northeast. Then a bit of commitment-testing unemployment until he landed steady work in a few Broadway orchestra pits, including *Phantom*, *Cats*, and *Thoroughly Modern Millie* before he settled into the QSO.

"OK, it's not the New York Phil, but it's a great bunch, union benefits, plus, once a year I get to play that solo clarinet opening in Gershwin's *Rhapsody in Blue*. Worth the whole trip just to lay out that great ascending note and see every face in the orchestra break into a grin. Even the bassoon players, and they're all nuts." Rook smiled and nodded in agreement. Leonard offered Nikki his condolences. "I loved your mom. I loved them both, but trust me, your mother outshined all of us. And I'm not saying that because I had a crush on her. All the guys did. She was pretty like you. And had this special gift, this . . . force that made her competitive and driven to excel, but also very kind to her fellow students. Nurturing, even. And music conservatories are notoriously cutthroat at that level."

"Let me ask you about that," said Rook. "Were there any ugly rivalries that might have lasted over the years?"

"None that I know of. Plus, Cindy was too into her music to make enemies or get involved in the petty stuff. That girl worked. She studied every great piano recording—Horowitz, Gould, the lot. She was the first one in the rehearsal studio in the morning and the last one out at night." He chuckled. "I spotted her at Cappy's Pizza one Sunday and was going to go to her table and kid her, asking her how she could live with herself, not rehearsing, and with a Chopin recital the next day. Then I look over and see she's moving her fingers along her placemat like it's a freakin' keyboard!"

"Mr. Frick," said Nikki, "do you know anyone from back then who would have a reason to kill them? My mother or Nicole, or both?" His answer was the same no. "Has anyone contacted you looking for either of them?" Again, it was a no.

It fell to Rook to steer the interview back to the Odd Sock. "You're just one of many to talk about Cynthia's drive and determination."

"And talent," said Leonard.

"What happened?"

"Beats me. It turned like that." He snapped his fingers. "The change came when Nicole invited Cindy to come stay with her folks in Paris for a couple of weeks after graduation." He turned to Nikki, explaining, "The Bernardin family, they were wealthy. Nicole's parents offered to pay for the whole trip, and the plan was for your mom to come back in time to do her tryouts for all of the symphony orchestras that had been talent scouting her. She was supposed to be away for two or three weeks. That would have been June 1971. She didn't come back until 1979."

"Maybe she had opportunities with orchestras over there in Europe," Nikki suggested.

He shook no. "Nah. Cindy never auditioned for an orchestra here or there. Never got a recording contract. She just kissed it all off."

"What do you suppose changed her?" Rook asked. "Was it Nicole?"

"Maybe. But not like a relationship thing. They were too into men." He paused. "Except one, and you're looking at him." He smiled, then the dimples faded. "Something happened over there that summer. Cindy went away a ball of fire and let it all go cold." His fellow orchestra members began to file in for rehearsal. Leonard stood and picked up his Members Only jacket off the back of his chair. "What I'd still give to have one ounce of your mom's talent."

Rook dialed the car service driver he had hired for the morning to let him know they were finished, and the black town car pulled up to Gate Three of the campus just as he and Nikki finished their short hike from the Copland School. "Tell you one thing I've learned," he said when they had merged onto the LIE for the ride to the precinct. "The way he described your mom . . . driven, competitive, but nurturing? Professor Shimizu was wrong. The apple didn't fall far from the tree."

"Rook, would you mind if we not?" Nikki lowered her window and closed her eyes, putting her face to the wind while she thought.

After a mile of silence, the driver said, "Mr. Rook? Since you were kind enough to get me a coffee, I picked up a paper, if you'd like to read it."

"Sure, why not?

The driver backhanded the *Ledger* to him. Rook had hoped for the *New York Times*, but a little sensationalism never hurt anybody. At least that's what he thought until he saw the headline on the front page of the tabloid. "Holy . . ."

Heat half turned from the window. "What?" Then she saw the headline herself and grabbed the newspaper out of his hands and read it, speechless with anger.

SIX

FROZEN LADY THAWS C-C-OLD C-C-ASE
LEDGER Insider Exclusive

By Tam Svejda, Senior METRO Reporter

As if last week's grim discovery of a woman's frozen body inside a reefer truck on the Upper West Side wasn't enough to get New Yorkers' teeth chattering, now the gruesome case has taken an even more chilling turn. Exclusive *Ledger* sources with knowledge of the investigation confirm that the unidentified stabbing victim has not only been identified as Nicole Aimée Bernardin, a French national with an Inwood address, but that the suitcase police found her in once belonged to a similar stabbing victim from a 1999 case that remains unsolved. The two killings struck an even more bizarre note yesterday when investigators learned Mademoiselle Bernardin knew the prior victim, Cynthia Trope Heat, who was stabbed in her Gramercy Park apartment on Thanksgiving eve ten years ago. Ms. Heat's daughter, NYPD Homicide Detective Nikki Heat, the modelicious cover cop in a recent magazine article on our Finest, has been assigned the lead role on the case by Precinct Commander Wallace "Wally" Irons, whose savvy choice of Heat has already brought fast results. Are these double DOAs an odds-breaking coincidence or cold serial? Capt. Irons was not available for comment, but this reporter can suggest one: When it comes to cold cases, warm globally, thaw locally.

Heat folded the tabloid in half and slapped the seat with it. Rook didn't often hear Nikki swear, but this might be an occasion. "Well this just sucks," she said. Her jaw muscles knotted and her lips whitened from flexing them together.

He should have known better, but Rook said, "Well, it is factual, at least."

"Don't even," she said. Then a thought came to her and she gave him an appraising look. And he knew why. They'd been down that road before with this reporter.

"No, I did not source that story to Tam Svejda." Her gaze stuck, and it made him uncomfortable the same way he'd seen her make hardened suspects come unglued in the interrogation box. "First of all, when would I?"

"During your Google session in the wee hours this morning?"

"Ha!" He took the *Ledger* from her and examined the top of the front page. "Past deadline for this edition." He handed it back to her. "Plus, why would I?"

That slowed her down but didn't end it. "Well, you and this Tam Svejda, your bouncing Czech . . ."

". . . Have a history, I know. Just because I slept with her a couple of times doesn't indenture me to source all her stories."

"You told me it was once."

"True." He smiled. "Meaning once upon a time. In a galaxy far, far away." When she seemed partially mollified, he said, "Want me to call her?"

"No." And then, after reflection, "Yes." But her look said not really.

The earthquake was still managing to keep the city scrambling. The latest infrastructure fail forced their car to detour onto the Queensborough Bridge to get across the East River, because the Midtown Tunnel had been shut down by the Bridge and Tunnel Authority. The driver turned on 10-10 WINS, which reported that the closure was due to slight water ponding mid-tunnel from a mystery leak. "Leaks. Seems to be the theme of the morning," said Rook. Nikki didn't appear amused.

After dropping Rook curbside in front of the Midtown offices of the *New York Ledger,* Heat continued on to the Two-oh, where she entered to the buzz of her squad working its assignments. She spotted Sharon Hinesburg hastily closing an Uggs shopping window on her computer, boss-buttoning the screen to the fingerprint database homepage. "Missed you yesterday, Detective Hinesburg."

"So I hear. It's what I get for not plugging in my phone Saturday night."

"No, it's what I get, which is one of my detectives out of reach, and that cannot be. Are we clear?" Hinesburg answered with an overblown military salute, which, like most of what she did, irritated the piss out of Nikki, but she let it slide, point having been made. She assigned her to follow up on Nicole Bernardin's phone records for any leads and moved on to her own desk.

To her disappointment, the pitch of activity in the bull pen was just the sound of wheels spinning. Every update she got—on fingerprints at the Inwood town house, on tracking her headhunter business to get a tax ID, on sports clubs, on credit card statements—all came up either empty, delayed, or devoid of useful leads. On any other case, she would have called on her wisdom and experience gathered over the years to remind herself that it's impossible to see the trail until it reveals itself. She would remember that crimes got solved by hard work and patience. But this was not any other case. Even though she had succeeded in not only ID-ing the victim but finding a huge connection to her mom's cold case, Nikki wanted to capitalize on the momentum, and immediately would be nice. A decade was a long time to be patient.

Rook came in with a grin to go with her latte. "You find out who leaked to Tam?" she asked in hushed tones after she drew him into the kitchenette.

"I did. And I didn't even have to sleep with her to find out. I just tricked her by pretending I already knew. I don't know if you've noticed, but Tam Svejda's not the smartest one in the room, even when she's the only one in it."

"Very witty, Rook. Save it for your next article. All I want to know is who." She scoped the area for privacy. "It's Irons, right? So obvious."

"Well now, there you go, running off on one of your cockamamie conspiracy theories."

"OK, let it out; have your fun."

He stroked his chin theatrically, relishing the opportunity to feed the great detective some of her own words. "I prefer to deal in hard facts rather than indulge myself with a mere crumb of a hunch."

"Do you want to wear this coffee?"

"It was Sharon Hinesburg."

Heat was still weighing how to deal with that information when Captain Irons called her into his glass office for an update. Even knowing he had a short attention span and simplifying her briefing to the broad strokes didn't stop him from wandering off-topic, and early on. "Since I called you from Boston yesterday to tell you about what Rook and I learned about our Jane Doe and her connection to my mother, we've been focusing on anything we can learn about Nicole Bernardin."

"Did you get any seafood up there?"

"Excuse me, Captain?"

Irons leaned back in his leather chair and his weight caused the springs to groan. "Man, I loves me my Boston chowdah. Legal Seafood's a must on every trip."

"Yes, they're quite well known," she said, but only to keep him engaged while she continued with the business of a double homicide investigation. "So, now that we have the Bernardin ID, we are tasked with following a series of new avenues. We have limited forensics leads from her town house, but we can track other aspects of her life through her banking, business and personal. These haven't borne fruit just yet, but—"

"Was Rook doing any writing on your getaway?"

"Sir?"

"Any new magazine pieces in the mix?" Irons sat up in his chair to the twang of sprung metal protesting. "It's just he mentioned the other day he might be doing something to follow up the other article, and I was wondering if he'd been on that, or not." Maybe Irons didn't have a short attention span. Maybe his attention was just stuck on other things. "You see my mention in the fish wrapper this morning?"

"Yes I did. In fact, sir—"

"You ought to show it to Rook. Let him see other reporters are nibbling at this, too."

It wasn't lost on her that Irons's take-away from the piece was his own mention. "Rook is not only aware of the article, but he knows it was sourced by a leak, sir. Inside our squad."

"Someone here slipped that to the *Ledger*?" Irons tilted his head and peeked over her shoulder through the big window that looked out onto the bull pen. "Know who?"

For anyone else, Heat would have claimed ignorance. "Detective Hinesburg," she said.

"Sharon? You sure?"

"Yes, sir."

"Huh. Well, they had to get it from somewhere." He took a pull from his coffee mug, seeming unfazed by the leak, and then confirming it after he swallowed with a loud gulp. "Probably a good thing it's out there."

"I disagree, Captain." Heat didn't like the look of self-amusement she saw after she said that, she but pressed on. "This case is at a stage where we don't want it played out in public and have to deal with the circus that comes with that. Not before we have a chance to run down all our investigative threads."

"Yeah? And how's that going, Detective?" His smile made the wisecrack worse, in her view. It wasn't just dismissive, it illustrated a closed mind-set.

"As I was just telling you—so far, it's slow going. But to be realistic . . ." she said, then paused to give it emphasis, recognizing that her commander's background was administration. His police experience came from quiet offices on floors numbered by double digits instead of street-level investigation. So she offered a version of the speech she'd given herself minutes before. ". . . to do this properly, we need to be patient, work it tenaciously, and understand that it's still very early in this case."

"Ha. This case has been ten years of stall." He flicked his copy of the *Ledger* so it slid across his empty desk toward her. "The paper has it right. This thing ain't cold, it's frozen." He stood, signaling the meeting was over. "Let's air it out and see what a little publicity brings." Sure, thought Nikki. Like his fifteen minutes of fame.

Sharon Hinesburg's phone rang as Heat passed her. She heard the detective say that she'd be right in and saw her hurry into the captain's glass cube, closing the door. Nikki sat to read a file at her desk, but couldn't resist swiveling her chair so she could look over the top of it into Irons's office. Roach came over to her.

"Just to let you know," said Ochoa, "I came up zip on stalker complaints by Nicole Bernardin. Same with orders of protection. Nothing. Her hairdresser has Monday off, but he's happy to meet, so I'm heading to his place in the West Village now to see what dish he has that might be useful."

"Good, keep me up," she said. But then the partners lingered, so she waited.

Raley cleared his throat. "I know you don't go for gossip."

"You're right."

"But this, you need to know," said Ochoa. "Tell her, pard."

"They're sleeping together," Raley said in his lowest whisper. He didn't turn, but he let his eyes flick toward Irons and Hinesburg. Heat let her eyes drift to the pair in the office and saw Irons wagging a finger at Detective Hinesburg, but they both seemed to think something was funny. "On the way in this morning, I saw Wally drop her at the far corner down on Amsterdam so they wouldn't walk in together."

Heat remembered how she and Rook used to put on charades like that before they were a public item, but she said, "That doesn't mean anything."

"They kissed each other before she got out. And it was full-tonsil exploratory."

Sharon Hinesburg falling off the grid Sunday and the media leak that had made Irons the hero now made sense in a way that got Heat angry. Angry at being saddled with Hinesburg in the first place. Angry that Irons had crossed the line with a squad romance. Angry that, as a result, a toxic dynamic had been created in her unit that jeopardized her case. And angry, most of all, at herself for not having seen it coming. But she took a beat and said, "You two know how I feel about gossip. So this goes no further." And then she added, "But keep me posted."

As Roach moved off, Rook came to her desk. "Did you tell him it was Hinesburg?" She nodded and he said, "Think he's going to give her a tongue-lashing?"

"Oh, count on it."

"Listen, Nikki, one more thing about this leak." And then he spoke the worry that had been nagging her from the moment she read the article in the car. "I imagine your dad reads the papers and watches the news, huh?"

She nodded solemnly, got her cell phone from her pocket, and then surveyed the openness off the bull pen. "I'll be outside," Nikki said. "I need to make a personal call."

. . .

Heat came back into the bull pen ten minutes later smelling like fresh air and asked Rook if he wanted to take a ride to Scarsdale. He didn't say any more than "Sure," lest she change her mind about bringing him to meet her father. But by the time their gold unmarked crossed Broadway heading toward the West Side Highway, he felt his seat was adequately secured and said, "Can I tell you I'm surprised you asked me along?"

"Don't feel too flattered. I'm using you." Nikki's comment came without eye contact because she was making a show of putting her attention on the road instead of him. "You're my rodeo clown to distract him so things don't get too mired."

"A high honor, indeed. Thanks. Mired, how?"

"With any luck, you won't have to know."

"That bad between you two?" Her shrug didn't satisfy him, so he asked, "How long since you last saw him?"

"Christmas. We see each other birthdays and major holidays." Rook let silence work for once. Sure enough, nervous spaces need filling. "We're sort of living the cards and calls relationship. You know, e-gifts instead of gifts. Seems to work for both of us." She ran a dry tongue across her lips and focused on the road again. "Or seemed to."

"Didn't you want that on-ramp?" he asked. Heat blew an exhale through her teeth and circled the 79th Street rotary back to the entrance she had passed in her distraction. Rook waited until she settled into her lane. Out her window, to the west, he watched thunderheads building into giant cauliflowers across the Hudson. "Were you two always arm's length?"

"Not so much. Didn't help that my parents got divorced while I was away on my semester abroad in college. They didn't tell me until I got back and he'd already moved out by then."

"That was the summer before the . . . ?" He left it unsaid.

"Yeah. He got one of those corporate extended-stay apartments. The Oak, on Park Avenue. Then, after Mom got killed, Dad couldn't deal. Quit his job, left for the burbs, and started his own small real estate business there."

"I'm looking forward to finally meeting him. This is kind of a big deal for me."

"How so?"

"I dunno. . . . Let's call it future relations."

Now she did look over at him. "You slow it down, there, bucko. This visit is strictly to tell him firsthand about the new developments in the case. It's not . . . I don't know what."

"*Father of the Bride?*"

"Stop right there."

"Part Four. Diane Keaton puts Steve Martin on a colon cleanse right before the wedding. Anything can happen, and does."

"I could let you out right here and you could walk back."

"Hey," he said, "you wanted a rodeo clown, you got a rodeo clown."

Twenty minutes later, they pulled into the driveway of a gated condo complex about a half mile from the Hutchinson Parkway. Nikki punched some numbers into the security keypad and waited, running the fingers of both hands through her hair. A sharp buzz vibrated the tiny speaker on the kiosk, and as the gate rolled aside, thunder growled in the distance. Rook said, "Rumble thy bellyful! Spit, fire! Spout, rain!"

"Seriously, Rook? You're meeting my dad and quoting *King Lear?*"

"You know," he said, "there's no bigger pain in the ass than a literate cop."

To Rook, the Jeffrey Heat who waited for them standing in his open front door held only a faint resemblance to the photos he had seen in the family album. Sure, many years had passed since those pictures captured a more robust version of the man, whose life had been under his own command and whose future loomed brightly, but at sixty-one, time hadn't aged Jeff Heat, life had. The thousand blows of grief had tempered his kindly, jovial face into a guarded replica, one that had come untethered from trust itself and permanently inclined downward, braced for the next jolt. When he reached to shake Rook's hand, his smile qualified as a best effort; not fake, just unable to access anything inside that passed for simple pleasure. Like the hug he gave his daughter, it was all about getting it as right as he was able.

His condo had a beige feel. Not just clean, but orderly and male. All the furnishings had the same vintage, circa Y2K, including the beached walrus of a big screen TV, the predictable indulgence of the new bachelor. He asked if they would like anything to drink, and it struck Rook that Nikki seemed almost as much a guest there as he was. They declined, and her father took the leather easy chair, establishing himself in his command center flanked by side tables bearing his phone, TV remotes, a flashlight, a portable scanner, newspapers, and a short paperback stack of Thomas L. Friedmans and Wayne Dyers.

"You home for lunch, Dad?"

"Haven't gone in yet. Everything you've heard about this real estate market? It's worse. Had to let one of my agents go yesterday." He reached down to hike up his socks. One of them was black, the other navy.

If her father felt any slight at first reading of the latest on his ex-wife's murder case in the tabloid at his elbow, he didn't let on. Instead, he listened quietly as Nikki filled him in on the particulars of the case, the only spike in his emotions coming when she recapped their lunch with the former lead detective, Carter Damon. "Ass," he said. "And useless. That clown couldn't find sand at the beach."

"Tell me something, Dad. Everyone says Mom and this Nicole Bernardin were such good friends. But I never heard of her." His expression remained neutral, so she said, "Kind of strange, don't you think?"

"Not really. I never liked her, and your mother knew it. Bad influence, let's leave it there. After we moved back here to the States about a year before you were born, Nicole Bernardin was out of our lives. Good riddance."

Nikki filled him in on the visit to the New England Conservatory and described the video of her mother's recital. "I knew Mom could play, but jeez, Dad, I never saw her like that."

"Wasted gift. That's why I nagged her the whole time we were in Europe that she was squandering her talent."

"So you two knew each other a long time over there?" Rook asked. "When did you and Cynthia meet?"

"1974. At the Cannes Film Festival."

"Were you in the film industry? Nikki never mentioned that."

"I wasn't. After business school I got hired by a big investment group to be their man in Europe. My job was to find small hotels to buy and remodel as elite boutiques, basically copying Relais et Châteaux. I'll tell you, it was a plum job. In my twenties, full of my own bullshit, bopping around Italy, France, Switzerland, West Germany—that's what they called it then—all on an expense account. You sure you don't want a soda? Beer, maybe?" he asked hopefully.

"No, thanks," said Rook. He noticed the wet ring on the coaster beside Jeff's chair and it saddened him to see how badly he longed to put a fresh glass on it.

"Anyway, one of our investors also put money in films, and he took me to this incredible cocktail party the famous director Fellini threw. There I was with big movie stars like Robert Redford and Sophia Loren. I think Faye Dunaway was there, too, but all I cared about was the hot American girl near the bar, playing Gershwin while everybody ignored her and drank free champagne. We fell for each other, but Cindy and I were both traveling a lot. We got more serious, though, and I started to work my itineraries around wherever she was doing her thing."

"Playing at cocktail parties?" Rook asked.

"Some. Mostly she'd be spending a week here or a month there as live-in music tutor for rich families at their ritzy vacation homes. Like I said, a waste of a gift. It all would have been so different . . ." A somber quiet fell, punctuated by a rattle of thunder and rain plinking on the windowsill.

Nikki said, "We should probably head back." She started to rise, but Rook had other ideas.

"Was she scared of the spotlight, maybe?"

"No way. I blame Nicole. The party girl. Every time I felt like I'd finally convinced her to get serious again, Nicole showed up like the devil on her shoulder, and, next thing I know, Cindy's off to St. Tropez, or Monaco, or Chamonix, paying her way by selling her talent cheap." He turned to his daughter. "Things got better when you came along. We had the place in Gramercy Park, your mom settled down into raising you, and loved that. She loved you so much." When he said that, some of the old Jeffrey Heat found his face and Rook could see in it the same jawline he saw in Nikki's whenever she smiled.

"It was a very happy time," she said. "For all of us." Then she reached for her keys.

"Those things don't last, though, do they? When you turned five she went back to the old habits. Tutoring kids of rich New Yorkers, sometimes gone weekends with their families or keeping strange hours, nights even. And never talked to me about it. Said she needed her independence and just did her thing. Shut me out." He paused as if making a decision, then said, "I never told you this, but I even got paranoid your mother was having an affair."

Nikki shifted the keys to her right hand. "OK, well, maybe this isn't the time and place to get into this."

Rook asked, "Did you ever tell the police you suspected that?" and caught a slight elbow from Nikki. He ignored it. "Seems they'd want to know."

"I didn't mention it."

"Because you had already divorced?" This time the elbow came a little sharper.

"Because I already knew she wasn't." He closed his mouth and sucked in his cheeks. Then he continued, with his lower lip trembling. "This is awkward for me, especially after what happened." Nikki slid forward on the couch and reached a hand to rest on his knee. "I'm ashamed now—but I hired a private detective to, um, follow her." And then, regaining himself a bit, he added, "Came up with nothing, thank God."

Lightning struck with a simultaneous cannon crash in the woods behind the condo complex, hurrying their jog back to the car. When they got in, Heat checked her cell phone and found a text invitation from Don, her combat trainer. "Whip yr ass 2nite? Y/N."

Rook asked, "Something new on the case?"

She shook her head, texted, "N," and fired up the ignition. He must have read her mood, because, for a change, Rook respected her silence the whole ride back to Manhattan.

The squad worked the case diligently, but their results still didn't move the needle on the case. The French consulates in both New York and Boston had no recent dealings with Nicole Bernardin, she had no record of a landline, and her cellular calls were mundane take-out orders and mani-pedi appointments. Ochoa came back with confirmation of two, uncharacteristically last-minute color-and-cut cancellations made from the cell. Her stylist, who grieved the loss of one of his best clients, said she was a very nice, albeit private lady who seemed scattered lately.

Neither of much use in furthering the hunt for her killer. Rook took a cab back to his place, leaving Heat to update the murder boards. Unfortunately, that amounted to writing check marks beside each bullet instead of entering new information.

The elevator doors opened for Nikki in the lobby of Rook's building that evening and a massage table rolled out on two wheels followed by Salena, the rehab babe. "Hiyee!" she said, finger waving with her free hand, making her triceps ripple. "He's all yours."

"Gee, thanks. Appreciate that." The last thing Heat saw was that row of perfect white teeth as the door shut, making her ruminate the whole ride up about Cheshire cats and how she'd seen grins without airheads but never an airhead without a grin.

By the time Rook came out from his shower, she had plattered the antipasto ingredients she had picked up at Citarella and poured them some wine at the counter. "Thought we'd stay in and do some grazing tonight," she said.

"Fine with me." He looked at the wine label and said, "Ooh, Pinot Grigio."

"Yeah, perfect accompaniment to tea tree oil and pheromones." They clinked. "I passed your naughty nurse on the way up. How was your 'rehab'? And yes, those were air quotes."

"Sadly, my last one. But I needed it after those rib shots I took from your elbow this afternoon."

"Really?" She forked a slice of prosciutto and rolled it around a ball of *bufala* mozz. "It didn't seem like you were even aware of them. Remember, you were supposed to be the rodeo clown, keeping my dad from getting mired?"

"Yes, it was quite a role reversal, wasn't it?"

She set her food down and dabbed her fingers with her napkin. "What's that supposed to mean?"

"Well, I was prepared to run interference for you, but you weren't asking any questions. So I did."

"Rook, we didn't go there to ask questions. I went as a courtesy to my father to fill him in on the case because it ended up in your old girl-friend's tabloid."

"Let's ignore that second jealous comment you've made in under a minute and focus on the visit with your dad." He nibbled the meat off an olive and placed the pit on the side of his plate. "Yes, we went there for one purpose, but he kept sharing things that made me want to know more. His suspicion about the affair was too big to just let pass. When you didn't say anything, I assumed you were too busy absorbing it emotionally and I picked up the slack. He never mentioned it to you?"

"You heard him. He said no."

"And you had no clue?"

She took another sip of wine and watched the ripples on the surface as she swirled the stem. "Can I share something with you?"

"Anything, you know that."

She paused to ponder, mirroring her father's tortured expression, hours before. "Yes. I suspected my mom might be having an affair, too." She took another drink from her glass. "Not until I was older, in my teens, but I started noticing the same things my dad brought up today. Gone a lot. Sometimes a weekend or nights, out late. You know, when you're in high school, it's all about you, and you feel angry and lonesome. And then I started to wonder if there was more to it. Also the tension between my parents was a big elephant in that apartment. I even started trying to get to our mail before she did so I could look for any letters from men or anything. It's crazy, but it's what it became."

"Was she seeing someone?"

"I never knew."

"And you never talked to her about it directly?"

"Like I'd do that."

"And she never confided in you? Not even a hint?" Nikki gave him a derisive sniff. "Hey, just asking. I got the impression you and your mom were close."

"In our own way, yes. But my mother had this very private side to her. It was a bone of contention between us. Even the night she was killed. Know the reason I was gone from the apartment for such a long time before I went to the market? I needed to take a walk because things were tense between us about her . . . what should I call it . . . ? Separateness. Don't get me wrong, my mom was warm and loving to me, so I'm not invalidating that. But . . . there was a part of her that she kept totally to herself. As close as we were, she had this wall that divided us."

Understanding now why Nikki had balked at digging into her mother's past, Rook said, "There's no shame here. We all have our private areas, right? Some people erect a little more protection around theirs than others. What did my man, Sting, call it, 'A Fortress Around Your Heart'?" He ate a marinated artichoke with his fingers and added, "You, of all people, should know that."

Nikki frowned and studied him. "Meaning?"

He swallowed wrong, coughing on some vinegar as he realized his mistake. Trying to contain the damage, he said, "Nothing. Forget it." But it was out there.

"Too late. What exactly should I know that you have now somehow become an expert on from listening to Classic Rock?"

"Well . . . OK, look, we all have aspects we inherit from our folks. I have my mother's brash theatricality and adorable impulsiveness. As for my dad, I have no clue. Don't even know who he is." He hoped that sidetrack would end that thread of discussion, but he was wrong.

"Spit it out, Rook. Are you saying I'm inaccessible?"

"Not at all." He felt himself trapped in a sparring match he didn't want to be in and that everything he said was the wrong thing. Such as stupidly adding, "Not all the time."

"And at what times am I inaccessible?"

He tried to dodge. "Not most of the time."

"When, Rook?"

Seeing no way out, he chose the Robert Frost path and went through. "OK, sometimes, when I want to broach certain subjects with you lately, you do ice me."

"You think I'm cold?"

"No. But you do know how to freeze me out."

"I freeze you out, is that your point? Because that's ridiculous. You're the first person I've ever heard say that about me."

"Actually . . ."

She had started to take another sip of wine, but the color left her face and she clanked the glass down on the cold stone countertop. "You'd better finish that." Already feeling up to his neck, Rook's brain clawed for a way out, but all the passages were marked "No Exit." "I mean it, Rook. You can't lay something out there like that and retreat.

Finish it." She fixed him with that unblinking X-ray stare he'd seen her melt bull-necked sociopaths with during interrogation.

"All right. The other night in Boston, Petar and I were talking and—"

"Petar? You were talking to Petar about me behind my back?"

"Briefly. You went to the loo, and I was just minding my own business—I mean, what do I have to say to Petar? Anyway, he brought up the notion—Petar did—that—his words, now—that you had a protective wall."

"First of all, I think it's cheap of you to throw Petar under the bus like this."

"He brought it up!"

She ignored him, swept up in her anger and the release it was giving her. "And second, I would rather have a slightly cautious, slightly controlled side that values privacy and discretion than be a reckless, immature, self-centered jackass like you."

"Look, this came out all wrong."

"No," she said, "I think it just finally came out." She grabbed her blazer off the back of her bar stool.

"Where are you going?"

"I'm not sure. I suddenly feel the need to have a wall between us." And then she left.

Don took the brunt of it. Seeking an outlet to subdue the riot coursing through her veins, Heat had texted back her combat training partner, and thirty minutes later the ex–Navy SEAL landed facedown on the gym mat with the air knocked out of him. He drew himself up on all fours, gasping, but Nikki smelled the fake. He sprung at her shoulder-first, his long arms octopussed out to wrap up her legs for a takedown. Before he got there, she dropped to a crouch and hooked the inside of her elbow into his armpit, then kicked herself upward off the mat, lifting and flipping him midair. Don crash-landed on his back with her on top of him for the pin. Nikki hopped to her feet, panting, blowing sweat droplets off the tip of her nose, as she danced side to side, ready for more. No, craving more.

At the close of the hour, both drenched in sweat, they bowed and shook hands, center mat. "What got into you?" he asked. "Fierce tonight. Did I piss you off somehow?"

"No, it's not you. Got a lot on my mind. Sorry if I made you my punching bag."

"Hey, anytime. Keeps me sharp." He dabbed the perspiration off his face with the belly of his shirt and said, "Got enough energy left for a beer or something?"

Nikki hesitated. The "or something" meant bed, and they both knew it. He made it sound casual because it was. Or had been once. Before she met Rook, Nikki and Don had no-strings sex on a semiregular basis for two years. They both got the same thing out of it, which amounted to a full-contact, no-commitment, physical relationship without the emotional hangover or jealous inquiries when one or the other passed. When they both wanted to, it was fine. When not, same deal. It never interfered with their jujitsu sessions, and Don hadn't pressed or sulked once in the months since she'd chosen to remain exclusive to Rook, who knew nothing about her arrangement with her combat TWB. "Beer would be nice," she said on impulse, feeling a flutter in her rib cage that might be guilt. But hell, it's just a beer, she decided.

"Wouldn't mind a shower first," he said, plucking the wet shirt from his skin. "No hot water here. They shut it off after the earthquake, and I guess the city's backed up on inspections."

The flutter rose again, but she ignored it and said, "You can get a shower at my place."

Heat stayed in her gym clothes but changed into a dry tee shirt while Don hit the shower. She checked her cell phone again for case updates from the squad and got nothing but three more voice mails from Rook she didn't listen to. In the refrigerator she found a six-pack and tried to decide whether to drink there in such proximity to the bedroom or go out to the Magic Bottle after Don made himself presentable.

She washed her face in the kitchen sink to rinse the sweat salt from her eyes. As she dried herself with a paper towel, Nikki tried to figure out what she was doing with Don back in her apartment. Was she seeking escape? The mere company of a friend? Or was she testing the old waters of independence again to see what that would feel like? She told herself, if any more did come of the evening, that it would not be to spite Rook.

Then why did she take that extra step to invite Don over? Was it because their relationship was shallow enough that he wouldn't be asking her too many questions or try to go deep when she didn't want to? Was she looking for mind-numbing sex as an escape?

What bugged her about Rook wasn't so much that he had pushed a hot button with the accusation about her wall—and then hidden behind her old boyfriend. It was that he insisted on poking around in places he had no business. Dragging her back over family secrets she wanted to be done with. Quizzing her father like he was in the interrogation box up at the precinct . . . And then, tonight, pushing her to talk about her relationship with her mother. How could Nikki explain something like that— and all it encompassed—to him or to anyone? And why should she have to? Did she have an obligation to share with Jameson Rook the way her mom made her feel when she bandaged her skinned knees? Or how she dropped everything and took her right out to a Broadway show when her junior prom date stood her up? Or how she taught Nikki the joys of Jane Austen and Victor Hugo? And that practice, whether it was for the piano or anything else in life, should be a journey of discovery. Not just about the music but about herself.

She couldn't tell him all that. Or wouldn't. These, and the hundreds of thousands of other random memory slideshows, were journeys to the places Nikki seldom ventured herself. Like the lid of the piano across the room, those were doors too painful to open. Maybe Rook was right. Maybe her defenses did constitute a fortress wall.

Was it one just like her mother's?

And if so, was that really a character deficit, or simply one more valuable life lesson Cynthia Heat taught her daughter by example? Like demonstrating how to let the spaces between notes breathe, because they are music, too.

The shower water shut off, forcing Nikki to ask herself what this moment was all about, because she could not deny she had put herself at a crossroads. Why? But, as the bathroom door opened, Heat knew that wasn't the most pressing question. The immediate issue was what she would do on this night full of risky impulses.

He came up the hall with his skin glistening and nothing but a towel around his waist. "I believe you mentioned something about a beer," he said. Before she could agonize over it too much, she grabbed the pull handle on the fridge, popped open a pair of bottles from the six, and set them on the counter between them. They side-clinked necks and each took a sip. "Gonna be hurtin' for certain tomorrow," he said.

There was a soft knock at the door. "Expecting anybody?" he asked as he stepped toward the entryway.

Rook had a key, but maybe he was learning to be discreet for a change, so she whispered, "Don't say anything, just look." She came around the counter trying to figure out how to handle the introductions as Don's towel slipped and it landed on the floor before he could snag it. He turned to her with a wink and impish grin and then leaned forward to look though the peephole.

The shotgun blast punched a hole clean through the door and threw Don backward with such impact that he landed headfirst at Nikki's feet. A seemingly endless flow of blood rivered out of him where his face had been, and pieces of his brain stuck to the front of Heat's legs and shirt.

SEVEN

I f she let the fear in, it would paralyze her. If she contemplated the horror facing her, she'd be done. So before the tsunami of feelings that bore down on Nikki could immobilize her, she threw the cop switch. She made her emotional disconnect. She became all about balls and action. She went to work.

Throwing herself low, Heat rolled backward on the rug, to where the corner of the entry hall met the end of the counter, and snapped off the lights. A table lamp still burned in the living room, but any dimness helped give cover. Protected by the wall, Nikki stood on shaky legs and grabbed for her Sig Sauer and cell phone off the granite countertop. Her arm bumped one of the beers and it sailed into the kitchen, slamming against the oven door. The bottle was still spinning when she knelt at Don's side, hitting 911 send while she pressed two fingers to his carotid.

"911, what is your emergency?"

"This is Detective Heat, One-Lincoln-Forty, reporting a ten-thirteen, officer needs help, shots fired." With eyes on the door, Nikki spoke as low and calmly as she could, giving her address and cross street. "One man down, deceased." She took her fingers off Don's neck, wiped his blood on her gym shorts, and gripped her Sig. "Shooter has a shotgun. Shooter still at large."

"Help is on the way, Detective. Can you describe the shooter?"

"No, I never saw—"

The chilling sound of a pump-action racking a round *snick-snicked* on the other side of the door. Nikki let the phone drop to the rug. Light that had been streaking in the gaping hole from the outside hallway got blocked out, eclipsed by movement. From her mobile on the floor, the small voice that kept asking, "Detective Heat? Detective, are you there?" grew smaller as Heat duckwalked back, taking cover once more around the corner and under the kitchen counter. Keeping in a low crouch, she peeked around the edge just as the fat muzzle of the single barrel poked through the ragged hole it had put in the wood. She knelt again, this time with both hands in an isosceles brace against the wall. "NYPD, drop it!" she called.

The barrel adjusted its aim an inch toward her. Nikki spun back around the corner for cover. A deafening blast filled the room and tore fragments from the wall beside her. Before he could rack another round, Heat rolled out, braced, and, with ten quick reports, emptied the magazine of her Sig in a diamond cluster under the shotgun. She heard a man moan, and the black barrel chafed as it tipped upward and retreated from the hole in the door. But amid the muffled neighbors' voices of alarm coming through walls and windows, she heard another round getting pumped into the shotgun. Heat dove in the darkness, across the entryway to the living room, ejected her clip, and snatched a fresh magazine of 9mms from the gym bag she had left on a chair.

As she tiptoed through the entryway with her back hugging the wall, Nikki's cross trainers crunched on bits of glass from lamps and a mirror shattered by the lead spray. She pressed herself against the cold plaster beside her front door to listen. After half a minute, she heard soft retreating footfalls on the carpet. Then a pause before a squeak of hinges and the hollow slam of a metal door. Heat pictured it as the service stairwell up the hall to the left. The elevator was still out and the shooter was avoiding the main stairs. Or wanted her to think so.

Heat heard a knob turn and a door hitting its security chain. A woman's voice she recognized as her neighbor Mrs. Dunne's said, "I don't see anything, Phil. Smells bad, though. Come here, is this gunpowder I smell?" Nikki took it as a sign the shooter had left the hall, but she entered it cautiously, gun at the ready.

She walked to the right first to make sure he wasn't faking her out and hiding in the open main staircase. After she'd cleared that, Nikki moved back with her Sig up in both hands, toward the service door with the creaky hinges. Nikki stepped over two spent shotgun shells and then saw Mrs. Dunne's face pinched in the open sliver of her door. Heat put a finger to her lips to signal a shush, but the woman spoke in a whisper as loud as her normal voice. "Are you all right, Nikki?" When she didn't reply, the old lady said, "Want me to call 911?" Nikki nodded, just to get her out of there, and Mrs. Dunne said, "OK," and finally went.

The prospect of using that squeaky door didn't thrill Heat, but she didn't have much alternative if she wanted to pursue. Questions pinged in her head in milliseconds. What if he was waiting there to cut her in half when the door opened? What if he wasn't alone? Should she take the main stairs instead and hope to cut him off on the sidewalk? Her questions all led to bad options and caution signs. She pressed her ear to the metal. Listening told her nothing about what lay on the other side, and time ticked onward. The caution signals flashed again. Nikki ignored them.

She took a step back, hit the push bar with her hip to fling the door open, and rolled onto the landing, coming up in a squat with her weapon raised and her lower back to the cinder-block wall.

It was dark in there. Except for ambient light from the first floor, all the overhead bulbs were dead. Unscrewed, she figured. Whoever had done this had a plan.

Nikki listened for anything. Breathing, movement, footsteps on the metal stairs, a stomach gurgle . . . but heard nothing. Nothing but the *plink* of water hitting the landing beside her. Water? Even if the roof leaked, it hadn't rained in days, and there were no exposed pipes in that stairwell. Heat felt the corrugated metal landing until the tip of her finger found the drip. She rubbed her fingertips together. They were sticky. Not water, she thought. Blood. Dripping from above.

She could wait him out or take him out.

Since he was lurking, expecting her to go down the steps, Heat decided to try to draw his fire and hit him before he could re-rack. A good strategy as long as she was quick, had a clear shot, and he didn't have another gun. To fake him out, she would turn the darkness he had created to her advantage. She felt along the threshold beside her and located the heavy wooden wedge the super used for a doorstop. Rising up, but stooping to keep underneath the protection of the metal staircase, she walked toward the turn in the landing as if to go downstairs. Instead, she lobbed the wedge down.

He fired immediately at the decoy. Heat swung around the railing and fired two shots upward but must have missed because she heard him scampering up the stairwell toward the roof, two floors above. As she followed, Nikki heard the metal door above her open and slam.

At the top she confronted another damned door with more vulnerability on the other side of it. By then he could have set up a hide behind a vent or a chimney and be waiting to saw her off. But when she listened, she could hear him beating feet away from her across the flat of the rooftop. She ripped the door open and raced out, praying he didn't have a partner.

Detective Heat got her first look at the shooter as he reached the far side of the rooftop and turned to descend the front fire escape. Male about five-ten, strong build—possibly Caucasian—but no features to ID. He wore a gray hoodie topped with a black Yankees cap, and a dark mask or scarf over his nose and mouth. Nikki also got a look at the shotgun, a short barrel with a pistol grip that he held in gloved hands. He rested the stock on the lip of the roof and took aim from the ladder. She dove behind a chimney. He fired and peppered the brick with the spray of lead.

At risk of losing him, Heat dashed for the other fire escape, the one on the back of her building. Lucky was one thing, but the exposure from descending open stairs above a man with a shotgun would be pressing her luck, and that would be stupid. And deadly.

She rode the bottom ladder down on its springs and made a short dismount four feet to the service alley and flattened against the side of the building. Heat made a fast recon around the corner and pulled back. He wasn't waiting for her; the narrow driveway between apartment buildings was empty. Then she heard running. Nikki peeked again and caught a flash of him sprinting by on the sidewalk. She charged up the service drive after him.

When Heat passed through the gate at the top of the incline and looked up the sidewalk, it was empty. He couldn't have rounded the corner at Irving Place already. She sprinted down to it, passing into the construction zone for the building being renovated there. Slowing at the end of the sidewalk, she knelt at the corner wall formed by the temporary plywood work barrier and carefully looked down that stretch of sidewalk but saw no one. Where could he have gone? She remembered the outhouse back near the construction trailer. Heat backtracked to it, approaching it cautiously. But it had a padlock on it. So did the trailer door.

She went back to the corner and turned south toward East 19th Street, moving vigilantly under the corridor of scaffolding that wrapped around the building. Sirens approached, but Nikki couldn't chance losing her man by breaking off the chase to go back and meet them. When she reached the corner at 19th, she stopped again, and once again saw no shooter. A man walking a Chihuahua and a golden retriever approached from the west, but he told her he hadn't seen anyone matching the description. She asked him to go to her building and tell the police where she was, and he did. After the dog walker moved on, she waited. Nikki was just about to give it up and go back herself when she heard it.

Above her, one of the scaffolding planks creaked and a sprinkle of dust cascaded down onto the ground beside her. Unless New York was experiencing another aftershock, her killer was hiding above her, using the scaffolding as an elevated escape route.

Heat ducked between the lattice of support tubes and backed out into the street to see if she could spot him. No, her view was blocked by a waist-high plywood debris shield. The protective barrier ran continuously along the second floor of the scaffold, halfway to Park Avenue South, providing perfect cover for him all along the block. Making soft steps, she reversed course on Irving Place. Halfway back up the street, Nikki Heat started climbing pipe.

On the second-floor level Heat pushed through the nylon catchnetting, quietly rolled herself over the plywood barrier, and squatted behind a tool storage cabinet that sat chained to a stanchion. She braced her gun and peered around the metal Jobox. There on the scaffolding, at the far corner of the building, knelt the dark figure with the shotgun, waiting. She had gotten as far as "Drop i—" when he fired and lead shot hit the toolbox like a hail of bullets. When Heat looked again, he was gone.

Through the ringing in her ears, Nikki could hear the pounding of his feet as he ran away on the wooden slats. She followed. Pausing before she rounded the corner, Heat reconned and glimpsed him at the end of the plankway just as he jumped down the debris chute to the sidewalk below. Heat got to the opening, and just as she measured the risk of leaping down it right into his line of fire, his shotgun blasted, tearing a hole through the floorboards a yard from where she stood. She heard the metallic *snick* of the pump racking a new round. Nikki jumped to the other side of the chute. The next blast chewed through the exact spot she'd just moved from. He pumped in another round. Not sure where to stand, whether to just run away or to take her chances with a chute slide with her gun blazing, she heard a helicopter drawing near. He must have heard it, too, because someone from a window across the street yelled, "There he is. See? He's getting away."

Heat crossed her arms in front of her and jumped feet-first into the chute. She popped up, gun ready, over the rim of the debris bin and caught sight of him halfway to Park Avenue South, cradling his shotgun.

She vaulted the container and gave chase. He was wounded, so Nikki made good time on him. As he reached the intersection, she called, "NYPD, freeze!" Nikki had a perfect bead on him, a high-probability shot, too, but a laughing group of college students rolled out of the Magic Bottle and she held back. Resuming her chase, she sprinted to the corner and spotted him heading north, running against the downtown flow of cars. The traffic light was with Nikki. She crossed the street easily and followed him, cop and killer both hugging the curb of the center divider. At 20th Street she saw the front of her building jammed with emergency vehicles and flashing lights. A blue-and-white was making a turn to join the party, and she called out, "Police, here!" They didn't notice her and drove on.

But the shooter heard her. He twisted for a look over his shoulder, saw Heat gaining, and made himself a moving target, weaving between the planters spaced along the median, then switching to the uptown lane, then hopping back over to the downtown side. Crossing the intersection at East 21st, Nikki got cut off by one of those stretch Humvee party limos when the driver realized too late he didn't have the steering radius to make his turn. He flipped her the bird as she palmed her way around the hood of his vehicle, and by the time she had, her shooter had bought almost a block on her.

But he began to slow. On one of his over-the-shoulder glances, Heat could see a growing red stain on the chest of his gray hoodie. At 22nd, he gave up the run but not his flight. He aimed his shotgun at a taxi driver waiting at the stoplight, who bailed out instantly, hands up. Her suspect got behind the wheel and floored it through the red, clipping the tail of another cab crossing by, but recovering after a fishtail and bearing down on Nikki.

Heat took a side step up on the center divider, but he came for her anyway, roaring right at her spot on the curb. She braced for a shot, and when he saw that, he jerked his wheel hard right to spoil her aim, then slung the barrel of the shotgun out the side window, ready to deliver a blast as he went by. Instead of diving for cover, Nikki brazenly held her ground, made sure she had a clear field behind him, and squeezed off three rounds as he sped past. Two in the windshield missed him as he lurched the steering wheel evasively again, but the third shot, right through the open side window as he passed her, landed home. She saw the fabric rip where the neck of his hood met his shoulder, and his head wrenched suddenly to the side. He wove crazily in his lane but righted himself and continued speeding downtown. Nikki memorized the cab number and started walking back to her place.

For the shooting report, she also made note of where she was standing. Right across from the Morton Williams supermarket, exactly where her nightmare began ten years ago.

When Heat had finished her statement to the detective from the Thirteenth Precinct, Lauren Parry took a break from her work over Don's body and handed her a glass of orange juice. "Found this in your fridge. Drink it. It'll get your blood sugar back up." Nikki took a small sip and put the glass down on the end table. "You didn't drink any of that. What's wrong, you feeling nauseous? Any chest pains? Dizziness?" The medical examiner checked her pulse. Satisfied Nikki wasn't in shock, she handed her friend a box of sanitary wipes. "I've got to get back to my prelim. You clean up." She gestured to the dried blood and tissue caked onto Heat's legs and arms, adding as she stepped away, "Don't forget your face, too."

Nikki did none of that; only set the box of wipes down beside the orange juice and stared, eyes glazed, at the corpse of her friend. Voices pulled her attention to the doorway that stood open to the hall. Detective Ochoa came in first, grim-faced but sharing a low, discreet wave to his girlfriend, Lauren. His partner followed, Raley also glumly taking in the scene. Heat got up to meet them, and on her way over, Raley turned to look behind him. He said quietly to someone in the hall, "You sure you want to do this right now?" Rook appeared in the door and nodded to him.

As Nikki approached, he took her in his arms and pulled her to him. She wrapped herself around him and squeezed hard. They clung tight to each other a good while. When they finally separated, he still held her, resting a palm on each arm. "Thank God, you're OK." And then his gaze drifted over her shoulder to the body on the floor, naked except for the paper modesty towel Lauren had just finished draping over the groin. "Who's this?" Rook asked.

Nikki sucked air deeply in through her nostrils, wondering where to begin. Before she could, the lead investigator stepped over. "Wondering the same about you. I'm Detective Caparella, Homicide."

"Oh, Detective," said Nikki. "This is my friend, Jameson Rook."

Caparella noticed they were still holding hands and looked from him to her to the body. "Think I'd like to get a statement from you, if that's all right, Mr. Rook."

"Me? About what?"

Nikki said, "He really has nothing to do with this."

"You know we need to cover the bases, Detective," said the other cop. "Two boyfriends, one alive, one dead . . . ?" He held his arm like a gate between Rook and Nikki, signaling this would be without her input. "Now would be good, sir."

Heat used the time they were in the second bedroom for Rook's interview to pluck some wipes from the box and clean herself off. As she dabbed her forehead, it occurred to her that Lauren probably had heard from her boyfriend Miguel that he and Sean had picked up Rook in the Roach Coach on the way there, and leaving the towelettes was her attempt to let her neaten up before he arrived. Scrubbing something crusty off her chin, Nikki turned to the back hallway, figuring it would be a short conversation since Rook didn't even know Don had existed. That would certainly back up the answer she gave when Caparella had asked Heat if she was in any other relationships besides the one with the victim. He'd made a note when she mentioned Rook's name, but she said, "He didn't know him. Far as I know, he didn't even know *about* him."

If she had been in the other detective's shoes, she would be asking the same questions—as he put it, covering the bases—but Heat wholeheartedly believed she was the target, not Don, who had fulfilled the wrong-place-and-time maxim in the most tragic fashion. The awkward part of the interview for her had been filling her colleague in on what she knew about Don, which amounted to so little, it might have come off like a dodge of the question: ex–Navy SEAL; single, so he said; they'd met at her gym two years ago when she signed up for hand-to-hand combat training; he was her instructor; the two began meeting outside formal classes for one-on-one workouts and then a beer after. And then a casual . . . physical . . . relationship. The other detective paused, frowning at his notepad, either processing, judging, or fantasizing, she couldn't tell. Nikki knew it wasn't the sort of thing easily explained to a disinterested third party, and his reaction made her worry anew how Rook—a decidedly interested third party—would react.

Nikki had moved things off Don and filled Detective Caparella in on the twin murder cases she was working and her belief the killing was meant to shut her down. "Any idea who would do that?" he asked.

"Detective, I've spent ten years trying to answer that question. Trust me. My life is about nothing else but finding that out and bringing him down." Appearing satisfied, he made a few more notes, asked her to e-mail him a copy of the case files that were relevant, and that was that.

Lauren Parry wrapped her exam in record time and managed to get Don's body removed before Rook could emerge from the back bedroom and be confronted again by the nude mystery man on the floor. "How did it go?" Nikki asked when he finally appeared.

He gave her a cool, appraising stare. "Only tough as hell." He bit off the words. Rook's initial relief had been joined by an anger that floated a mere inch beneath the surface. "You know how hard it is to find fifty different ways to say, 'I don't know'? And I'm a fucking writer."

A ballistics technician passed by to flag a hole where lead shot had bored into the oak bookcase beside them. Heat drew Rook over near the piano to find as much privacy as she could in a room full of detectives and evidence collectors. Even though he went along, Rook's arm felt stiff to her, and she said, "I know this is a big piece to swallow."

"Big? For once, Nikki, I am speechless."

"I get that, but . . ."

"But what?" His hurt, confusion, apprehension, and—yes, anger— came all rolled up in two small words.

"This isn't what it looks like."

"That's usually my line." But he wasn't amused. "What is it, then?"

"Complicated," she said.

"I can do complicated." He waited, but she didn't speak. Nikki was flat-out at a loss as to where to begin and anxious about where it would likely go once she started. Instead, she looked over at the red stain on the entry rug where Don's head had landed and he'd bled out—and she said nothing. Rook's patience gave. "OK, look. You've got your keys to my place, right? Best thing to do now is to let Raley and Ochoa take you over there for a shower and some sleep."

"You're not coming?"

He didn't have a cop switch, so he hid in logistics. "I'll hang out here to make sure the place gets locked up when all this is finished."

She repeated, "You're not coming?"

"I'll call your super. Jerzy should be able to cover that hole in the door."

"Thanks," she said but laced it with edge and sarcasm. "Comforting."

"What do you want, Nikki?" Wading one step deeper into danger- ous waters, he said, "I don't know what the hell to do just now. You're giving me nothing, and frankly, all I'm doing is getting more pissed off."

"So this is all about you? After the night I just had?"

"No," he said, "the one thing I can be sure of is that this is all about you."

"Very glib, Rook. Excellent. Jot that in your cute little Moleskine. You can use it later. Or maybe refer to it someday when you want to remember exactly what you said to me that tore the fabric." She reached in her gym bag and came up with the keys to his loft. "Catch."

He snagged them on the downward arc. They bit into his palm when he closed his fist around them. "You're kicking me out?"

"My mess. I'll clean it up."

Rook felt the full gravity of that statement. And its broad exclusion. He searched her face but saw only a cold mask. So he pocketed the keys and left.

Nikki made it a point not to watch him walk out. Or to notice

Raley and Ochoa, who would have absorbed their encounter from across the room like it was some scene from a silent movie requiring no subtitles, and would pretend not to be gawking, even though they were.

As she flopped into the easy chair beside the piano, Nikki found herself reliving a night ten years before, in fine detail. Just like back then, dazed, empty, and terribly alone, she watched a Forensics team work that same apartment from the same perspective. Surrounded by broken glass and toppled furnishings, Nikki felt as shaken as any earthquake could cause her to feel, making the very ground under her feet suspect and untrustworthy.

The twin Murder Boards gave her no better sense of grounding as she sat alone in the bull pen before sunup, on her second cup of coffee, studying the dual case displays from a chair in the middle of the room. Nikki had been there almost three hours. Unable to sleep after ECU and Forensics wrapped and Jerzy had screwed a square of plywood over the blast hole, Heat showered and hitched a ride uptown to the Two-oh in the blue-and-white the commander of the Thirteenth Precinct had posted outside her building as a courtesy.

The boards read exactly as they had when Heat left the squad room the night before, except she had updated them with a new section for a third homicide: Don's. It took massive emotional effort for Heat to push aside—for now—the pain of his death so she could concentrate on solving it. She drew a separate box in green marker to delineate Don's area. Beneath his name and time of death, the bullets were: "Shotgun." "Unknown Male Shooter," with the sketchy physical description of height and weight, "Taxi Escape," and the words she despised writing, "At Large."

Evidence did not connect Don's killing to the others. Common sense did. That's why she put Don up there with her mother and Nicole Bernardin. Experience had taught the detective to mistrust coincidence. She knew she was the target and that the attack had come after she started digging into the other two murders. That answered one of the questions still posted up there, "Why now?" The bigger one that remained preceded it: "Why?"

That would lead to "Who?" Or so she hoped.

Nikki heard the rumble of a subway, but there was none nearby. The venetian blinds clanked against the metal window frames and the fluorescents began to sway gently in the overheads. She heard an auxiliary secretary up the hall go "Whoo!" and someone else called out, "Aftershock!" Nikki watched the blinds settle and turned back to the boards, wishing that somehow the mini-quake had made something shake loose.

This exercise of hers, patiently waiting out the Murder Board to reveal a solution or, at least, a connection, usually paid off. Far from metaphysical, there was no incense or any incantations involved. And it wasn't like playing Ouija, either. The practice was simply a means of quieting her mind and studying the puzzle pieces to let her subconscious find a fit. And, indeed, something up there was trying to speak to Nikki, but it eluded her. What was she missing? Heat began to blame herself for not having a quiet mind, but she stopped. "No self-reproach," she whispered. If Nikki Heat had one ally she needed to rely on and keep positive, it was herself.

Heat needed to keep her focus, even amid the storm.

That was the beauty of the wall Rook derided. Rook, grousing about her ability to compartmentalize when that very skill was what made her so successful at clearing cases in a whirlwind. She tried to put Rook out of her mind. What she did not need right then was distraction. Want to know what a real wall is, Mr. Rook? Check this out.

Her solitude got broken by a loyal squad. Detective Feller rolled in an hour and a half early, just behind Raley and Ochoa, whom she had said good night to at her apartment at two that morning. Randall Feller had already put out personal calls and texts to his undercover pals in the NYPD Taxi Squad to be extra vigilant looking for the missing cab with the front-end damage and two bullet holes in the windshield. So far, no sighting. Roach checked for any call backs on the advisory they had posted overnight to hospital ERs, walk-in clinics, and pharmacies about gunshot victims or bleeders purchasing first aid or painkillers in quantity.

Soon the entire squad gathered for an early showing; everyone except Sharon Hinesburg, who was late again. As they assembled around the boards for an update, Heat checked out the glass office but found Captain Irons inside, going over CompStat sheets with a red pencil. Maybe, she decided, the Iron Man had dropped off his punch at a farther corner that morning. Nikki began without her, knowing they'd manage.

Heat began with Don's murder, which they all knew about, so she gave it a quick summary. Nobody asked questions. They all knew the sensitivities and, like Nikki, were eager to move on to other matters.

Uniforms working Nicole's Inwood street said neighbors saw a carpet cleaning van there recently. "The eyewits couldn't recall a company name, but since it coincided with the search and time of death, I want Feller and Rhymer to go there for follow-up interviews. Just get what you can. Color of van, lettering, anything.

"Still waiting on toxicology," she continued, putting another question mark on the board beside it. Underneath, she erased "Fingerprints" (which was still blank, but moot now that they had positive ID) and printed "Inwood Carpet Cleaners."

Raley reported no leads off Nicole Bernardin's headhunter business. "The NAB Group is registered with Better Business and a few trade organizations, but aside from fully paid dues, not much to say. No complaints against her about executive searches and placements mainly because there seems to be no record of any. The woman gives discreet a whole new meaning."

Malcolm and Reynolds reported no fencing or stolen property receipts for a laptop belonging to Nicole Bernardin. Nikki told them to send e-mails to pawnshops and check eBay. Detective Rhymer said he was still working with the IT geeks on her Web data storage. "No hits, but they emphasize 'yet.' IT is totally intrigued by the challenge. Plus they want to know if you'll autograph your cover shot of Rook's *First Press* issue to hang."

"Sure," she said. "As long as it's not in the bathroom."

Rhymer smiled. "No, I'm pretty sure these guys will take turns bringing it home."

Nothing new from the French consulates, according to Detective Reynolds, who had also run Nicole Bernardin through Interpol. But her name didn't light anything up there. However, he did say that

Nikki was right, he did get a green light on her at the New York Road Runners Club. "She had a lifetime membership."

"Ironic," said Feller, who couldn't resist.

"Nicole participated in their summer evening training runs in Central Park, did the Fifth Avenue Mile, and a lot of 10Ks, but had no social profile there," said Reynolds. "Basically, she was a bib number."

And so it went through all their reports. Information, but nothing that led anywhere. Even Rhymer, who on his own had checked with amateur orchestras and the musicians union to see if Nicole, the former NEC violin prodigy, had any affiliations there, came up empty. All the work they did just took them nowhere; like Nicole's summer loops around the park, it all ended right back where they'd started.

As the group dispersed, Nikki found herself, by reflex, turning to Rook's empty chair to get his off-the-wall take. Before the thought of him pushed her into a tar pit of vulnerability, she got busy at her desk. In all, she counted herself fortunate that the hour had passed without gossipy whispers or needing to confront the controversy of her personal life in that bull pen. Then Detective Hinesburg breezed in and a new hour began.

"I heard all about last night. You OK?" asked Sharon, standing over her more than a bit too much. But respecting personal space was not her thing. "Had to be awful, right there in your place." She leaned down and lowered the volume only slightly. "And it was your boyfriend. Nikki, I am so sorry."

"He was not my boyfriend." Heat wished she hadn't even engaged.

"Sure, whatever you say. It had to be so traumatic. Truthfully, I didn't think you'd be in."

Heat drew back her watch cuff. "Clearly, you didn't. Where were you?"

"On the assignment Captain Irons gave me." At first, Nikki thought she was lying, but that would be too easy to check, so she moved on to annoyance that the precinct commander had gone around her, poaching squad members without consultation. But then Heat considered which one he had poached. And hadn't it been a better morning without Sharon there? Hinesburg crossed over to her desk to thunk down her monstrous purse and said, "I would have been in earlier, but you know how he's watching OT. So since I had to drive last night to Scarsdale, he told me to come in late today to make up."

Nikki's breath caught. She strode over to Hinesburg's desk and invaded *her* space for a change. "What were you doing up in Scarsdale?"

The other detective let out a low whistle. "Hoo boy. Honest. I really thought he told you."

It hit Nikki like a backdraft and made her reel. "You went to see my father? On assignment?"

Before she could answer, Heat was already on her way to the captain's office. Hinesburg called out, feebly, "Yes, but not as a suspect. Purely a person of interest."

Heat slammed his door with such force, half the building must have thought they were witnessing another big aftershock. And if they had been inside Irons's office, they would have been.

"Holy crap, Heat, what the hell?" Wally Irons had not only jolted upright in his chair Roger Rabbit–style, he'd retreated on his rollers, heels kicking at the plastic floor mat, eyes wide and mouth slack. They were good instincts to follow. Detective Heat advanced on his desk as if she intended to come right over it at him.

"What the hell, is right. What the hell are you doing, sending Sharon fucking Hinesburg to my father's home?" Heat seldom swore, and if the entrance wasn't sufficient to indicate her upset, the f-bomb was. "My father's home, Captain!"

"You need to settle yourself right down."

"The fuck I do. Answer my question."

"Detective, we all know about the stressful night you had."

"Answer me." When he just stared at her, she picked his half cup of cold coffee off the coaster and poured it on his CompStat printout. "Now."

"You are totally out of line."

"I am just starting—Wally."

She loomed there, panting as if she had run a sprint. But he could see she could easily go a few more laps, and he said, "All right. Let's talk it out. Have a seat." She didn't budge. "Come on, will you sit?"

While she pulled a chair up, he took out his handkerchief to dam the flow of creamy decaf rolling off the desktop into his trouser cuffs, all the while keeping an eye on her. "All right," she said. "Sitting. Start talking."

"I made a determination . . . as commander of this precinct," he added weakly, "to open a new line in this investigation in order to get things moving."

"With my dad?" She side-nodded to the bull pen through the glass. "With her? Come on."

"You'll show some respect, Detective."

She slapped her hand on the desktop. "Person of interest? My father? A: That man was cleared ten years ago. And B: In what world is it OK for you to send someone—anyone—to interview him without letting me know first?"

"I am the precinct commander."

"I am the Homicide Squad leader."

"Leading a stalled investigation. Look, Heat, we talked about this yesterday after this ended up in the *Ledger*. After a decade, it's time for a fresh champion."

"Uh-huh . . . Have you been polishing that quote for the next article? While you compromise my case and damage my relationship with my family?"

"My determination is that you are too involved. You have a potential conflict of interest. I think what I'm seeing here bears that out."

"Bullshit."

"I sent Detective Hinesburg because I feel her talents are underutilized."

"Hinesburg? Five bucks says she spent more time at Westchester Mall last night than she did with my father."

"And," he held up a finger as if hitting an imaginary pause button on her, "I felt we needed some objectivity, not some lone wolf on a vendetta."

"We don't need a witch hunt, either. Witch included."

"You're out of control."

"Trust me, you'd know that if you saw it."

"Like the other night in Bayside when you violated procedure and entered the hatch to that basement alone because of your obsession with this case?"

"You need some time in the field, Captain. You might understand actual police work."

"You know what you need? Some time *out* of the field. I'm benching you."

"You're what?"

"Nothing personal. Even after this . . . encounter. In fact, I'm a big enough man to see all this as your reaction to post-traumatic stress."

"Like you're qualified to know that."

"Maybe not. But the department has psychologists who are. I'm enforcing your mandated psychological evaluation following the murder of your boyfriend and your shooting of the fleeing suspect." He stood up. "Get yourself shrunk, then we'll talk about putting you back on duty. This meeting is over." But he was the one to leave. And he got out of there in a hurry.

The shrink said, "You certainly didn't waste any time making this appoint-ment, Detective." Department psychologist Lon King, Ph.D., had a friendly, low-key manner that reminded her of gentle surf somewhere tropical. "I only got your precinct commander's referral ticket this morning after your, uh, meeting."

"I wanted to get through this and get back to work, if you don't mind my being blunt."

"Blunt works here. Honesty is even better. I'll take both." He took a quiet moment in the soft chair facing Nikki's to study her intake questionnaire. She watched him for reactions but got none. His face had such a flat affect and natural calm she decided never to play poker with Dr. Lon King. Primarily, Heat considered herself fortunate to have been able to make an appointment on the same day as her stupid mandate from Irons. She hoped this meeting would be short because one of Detective Feller's pals from the Taxi Squad had just come through and located the cab Don's shooter had commandeered. It was parked under an entrance ramp to the Bruckner in the Bronx. Parts scavengers and vandals had picked it clean overnight, from medallion to copper wiring, but Forensics had it now, and she was eager to get back to see if it offered any clues to his identity. Like, did he take off his gloves and leave prints? It was then that Nikki realized King was asking her something.

"Pardon me?"

"I just asked if you have experienced any loss of concentration lately."

"No," she said, hoping the first question wasn't pass/fail. "I feel sharp."

"I deal with a lot of post-traumatic stress disorder, and I'm accustomed to police officers who are wired to prove they're invulnerable. So please know that there's no shame in anything you are experiencing or in what you share here." Heat nodded and smiled enough to signal her acceptance of that, all the while worried this man could sideline her indefinitely with the stroke of a pen. "And, to be clear, I have no interest in keeping you in treatment," he said, as if reading her mind. Or just knowing it. He continued to ask her questions, some of which she'd already covered in writing on the intake. About her sleep habits, alcohol consumption, whether she felt jumpy or frequently startled. If the shrink felt satisfied or troubled by her responses, Lon King displayed no tells.

He said, "I suppose we can stipulate the answer to one question is a yes—that you have, in your life, witnessed life-threatening events."

"Homicide detective," she answered, pointing at herself with both hands.

"What about personally, though? Outside the job?" She shared as briefly as she dared, without disrespecting the process, events of her mother's murder. He paused when she finished, then, mellow as a smooth jazz announcer, said, "At nineteen, that can be formative. Do you ever experience things that make you feel you are revisiting or reliving that tragedy?"

Nikki wanted to laugh and say, "Only all the time," but feared she might bury herself in months of off-duty shrinkage, so she said, "In the most positive way. My work puts me in contact with victims and their loved ones. Whatever intersection there is with my own life, I try to utilize to help them and my investigative work."

King didn't race over to slap a gold star on her crown. All she got was an "I see" before he asked, "And what about things that you associate with your mother's murder? Do you ever find yourself avoiding people or things that remind you of it?"

"Huh . . ." Heat slumped back against the cushion and looked at the ceiling. A second hand ticked softly on a clock behind her, and through the closed window behind him, she could hear the reassuring flow of York Avenue twelve stories below. Nikki's only answer was her avoidance of the piano in the living room. She told him that she couldn't bring herself to play it and explained why while he just listened. Another aversion, one that hadn't occurred to her until then, was the arm's-length relationship with her father. Nikki had always attributed that distance to him, but to raise it in that session could unseal Pandora's box, and so she left it at the piano, and even asked if that was a bad thing.

"There's no good or bad. We'll just talk and let a whole picture emerge."

"Great."

"Is your father still living?" Was this guy a psychologist or a psychic? Nikki filled him in on the divorce and painted a distant but cordial relationship, shading the arm's-length part as coming from her father's shoulder, not hers, which was partially true anyway. "When was the last contact you had with your father?"

"A couple of hours ago. I called him to do damage control on a mess created by my captain, who sent an investigator to question him about my mom's murder."

"So, you reached out to him." Heat gave a strong yes, mindful of the PTSD warning sign of avoiding people linked to a trauma. "And how did your dad receive it?"

Nikki recalled his bluster and the jangle of ice cubes. "Let's just say he could have been more present." The therapist didn't dwell on that but moved on to ask her about her other relationships, and she said, "Because of my work, it's hard to maintain one, as you probably know."

"Why don't you tell me?"

Truthfully, but as briefly as she could, Nikki summarized the nature of her relationships over the past few years, the longest, most recent one being with Don. She gave King the same version she had shared with Detective Caparella the night before: Combat training partner with benefits. She told him next about Jameson Rook. His only digression in the session was to ask if he was the famous writer. Nikki used that as a point of entry to describe how they had met on his ride-along the summer be-

fore and how, even though she and Rook seemed exclusive, it was unde-
clared. Nonetheless she had not slept with Don or anyone since she met
Rook.

"How are you dealing after last night's shooting?"

"It's difficult." Tears made an invasion attempt as she reflected on
poor Don, but she held them back. "Mainly, I'm trying to postpone
dealing."

"And last night, when you were with Don, was that platonic?"

"Yes," Nikki said in a blurt.

"That was an emphatic response. Is it a sensitive topic?"

"Not really. Don and I had just had a workout. At our gym. And he
came back to my place for a shower. That's when the shooting happened."

"A shower. And where was Mr. Rook?"

"Back at his place. We'd had a fight, and I . . . needed to blow off
steam." Lon King set aside the intake papers and folded his hands in his
lap, watching her. Uncomfortable with the silence, she said, "I will admit, I toyed with straying, but . . ."

"You said you and Mr. Rook hadn't declared exclusivity."

"No, but . . ."

"What do you think the—toying, as you called it—was all about?"

"I don't know." And then Nikki surprised herself by asking, "Do
you?"

"Only you do," he said. "People make their own rules about what's
faithful, or not. Just as they have their own reasons for holding to those
rules, or not." She took a page from him and, for a change, waited him
out. He obliged. "Sometimes . . . only sometimes, mind you . . . people
in crisis try to mask their pain through deflection. Try to envision a
subconscious attempt to change the radio stations in one's head to a different pain than the one he—or she—doesn't want to confront. What
did you and Mr. Rook quarrel about?"

Whatever guard she'd had up before lowered. In spite of her attitude
going in, Heat felt safe and comforted by all this. She walked him through
Rook's accusation about her defensive wall and how it sparked the fight.

"And why do you think that was so charged?"

"He's been pushing me lately in ways I don't like."

"Tell me."

"Rook's been hounding me. Insisting on dragging me back over old family issues to investigate my mom's mur—" Neither of them needed the end of that sentence to fathom the potential significance of what she was revealing. Nikki panicked. She saw herself imprisoned in Therapy World for eternity with no time off for good behavior and immediately tried to buy it back. "But you know," she said, "people quarrel in relationships. If it's not one thing it's another, right?"

"Yet, this was one thing. And not another."

As the silence crushed her, the therapist waited. And waited.

"What does it mean?" she asked.

"I can't answer that. All I can do is ask, who were you truly angry with? And, who would be most hurt if you had slept with Don?" He smiled and then looked at the clock behind her. "We're at the end of our time."

"Already?" As he picked up her papers and slid them in a file, she said, "So?"

"All these years, all these sessions, it always ends with a cop asking, 'So?'" He smiled again. "Nikki, you have a lot of loss you are coping with and more trauma than most carry in a lifetime." Her mouth sprouted cotton. "But. Having said that, I see that you are remarkably resilient and, in my view, a strong, high-functioning, centered person with what Hemingway called grace under pressure. Far healthier than most I see in your profession."

"Thank you."

"That's why I think you'll be happy with my recommendation that you return to work—after one's week's rest."

"But my work. My case . . ."

"Nikki. Look at what you've been through. You need some time to find your center. Grace under pressure comes with a price tag." He got out a pen and wrote in the file. "So that's why I'm ordering this seven-day forced leave of absence, with pay." He twisted the pen closed. "For my final disposition, it might be viewed as a healthy sign if you demonstrated an attempt to mend connections you've severed related to the trauma."

"You mean Rook?"

"That would be significant." He closed the file and said, "Let's meet a week from today to reevaluate."

"You mean, this leave of absence might extend if I don't?"

"Let's meet a week from now. Then see where you are."

EIGHT

The caller ID read "Twentieth Precinct." Nikki stepped away from the cash register to let the customer behind her go ahead while she pressed answer. "Heat."

"Roach," came the voices of Raley and Ochoa together.

"Hey, in stereo."

Raley said, "Uh, actually that technology is years away. Your earpiece is, sadly, monaural."

"Buzz killer," said Ochoa. "Detective Sean Raley, where joy goes to die."

"Did you two call to try out your morning zoo routine? Because I have news for you. Howard Stern is safe."

Ochoa led off. "Calling with an update on that taxi you shot up, figuring we're still allowed to keep you in the loop. Catch you at an OK time?"

"Sure, I'm just buying a new rug. A runner for my entry hall."

"Listen," said Ochoa, "you need any help cleaning up over there? Because Raley's got, like, no life." The pair laughed, and he continued, "Seriously, we can swing over after shift."

"Thanks, really. But I spent the rest of my afternoon sweeping and scrubbing. I'm good. Whatcha got?"

Forensics had just shipped the prelim, and Roach wanted to let her know they lifted lots of prints and were running them. To expedite things, Feller drove a mobile ID kit to the driver's house so his could be eliminated. Roach didn't sound hopeful about the rest of the fingerprints. Ochoa said, "I'm guessing the bulk are going to be from the parts scavengers. Man, they hit that cab like a school of piranha."

"Even took the security dash cam and the hard drive, so no video of our shooter."

Heat asked, hopefully, "How much blood on the seats?"

"What seats?" said Raley.

"He's still out there, Detective. You watch your back."

When she got off the phone, the clerk had already rung up her purchase, a three-by-seven Turkish wool with a color and pattern similar to the one she was replacing. Nikki paid, and he asked, "You want it delivered? We're closing for the night, but we can have it there first thing tomorrow."

Heat smiled and shouldered the roll. "It's three blocks."

Eight P.M., and traces of the departing day greened the sky to the west on 23rd Street. Window lights flicked on at a thrift store, and she stopped to admire a lamp, thinking she'd come back for closer inspection when they opened in the morning. Something reflected in the polished brass of the base moved behind her. Nikki spun.

Nobody there. When she turned back around, the roll of rug balanced on her shoulder almost whacked a passing leafleteer holding a stack of handout ads for men's suits. Relieved to avoid a Three Stooges moment, Heat rounded the corner to take Lexington home. Whether it was Ochoa's admonishment that the shooter was still out there or primal wariness as the street transitioned from shops to apartments and lost commercial light, she decided to hail a cab. Nikki raised her free hand as she walked along, but the only two cabs that passed were occupied, so she gave that up after she passed East 22nd with only two blocks to go.

Halfway to 21st, tires squealed followed by an angry horn behind her, and a woman's voice, "Asshole, it says don't walk!" Nikki turned around to check up the block, but all she saw were the car's taillights lurching west and the Chrysler Building's silvery glow a mile uptown. She continued on, but couldn't pause the streaming video of the night before replaying in her head: the footsteps of the shooter in the hoodie stomping across her rooftop; his footsteps on the planks of the scaffold; his footsteps on the asphalt of Park Avenue South. Was she just jumpy from lack of sleep or could this really be happening again? It's what fills your mind when you know somebody out there wants you dead and is looking for his next opportunity. What was she doing alone on the street at night? Heat missed the two pounds of reassurance gone from her hip after Captain Irons took possession of her service weapon. Her backup Beretta 950 sat in a desk drawer in her apartment, doing no good up there. Nikki sped up her pace.

Jaywalking across East 20th Street, she definitely heard footfalls matching hers, and when she stopped, they did, too. She pivoted, but the sidewalk was empty. It crossed her mind to lose the rug, but with her building coming in sight on the opposite side of the square, Nikki pushed it to a jog, double-timing west along the spiked wrought iron that fenced in Gramercy Park.

The notion of an ambush occurred to her. If this guy had an accomplice staking out her front stairs, she might be racing right into the jaws of a trap. She began to calculate one-on-one as better odds, especially if she surprised him with an impromptu reversal. At the corner of the park, the fence didn't cut a sharp angle but curved. As soon as Heat rounded it, she stopped and dropped.

Squatting in a crouch, Nikki waited and listened. Sure enough, the jogging footsteps approached but halted fifteen yards off. Her view was blocked by the park shrubbery hiding both of them, but she heard panting. And a man softly clearing his throat. Resting a palm flat on the flagstone sidewalk, she leaned to her left and found his distorted reflection in the restaurant window across the street. He was only a dark shape in the soft lighting of the park, but she made out his hooded sweatshirt and ball cap. She lost him when he moved forward, resuming his pursuit. Heat got ready.

He came around the corner of the sidewalk at a trot. When he did, Nikki thrust herself upward, ready to bat his face with the three-foot roll of Turkish wool. Then she recognized her pursuer as Rook.

Heat just managed to pull her swing and missed hitting him, but he startled, shouting "Whoa, no, no!," flailing his arms up defensively and losing his balance. He pitched forward, bent over in a stoop, desperately fighting gravity and losing. Rook crash landed with an "oof!" on the slate flagstones, managing, at least, to shield his face, putting his forearm between it and the sidewalk as he dropped.

"God, Rook, what do you think you're doing?"

"Protecting you," came his muffled voice spoken into the sleeve under him. He turned over and sat up. Blood streamed from both nostrils.

. . .

When they came into her apartment, she said, "Please don't bleed on the floor, I just cleaned it."

"Love the compassion. Don't worry about me. I'll be fine."

She sat him down on a bar stool with a box of tissues and washed him up with the remaining towelettes Lauren Parry had given her the night before. While she dabbed the dried blood from his upper lip and nose, she said, "Rook, think back over the past year. Haven't you learned yet not to shadow me?"

"Clearly, not. Ow."

"Sorry."

"And clearly, you haven't learned that, if you're being shadowed, it just might be the cavalry. Meaning me."

"I."

"No grammar police, OK?" He pulled a wad of tissue away from his nose to examine for fresh blood. Satisfied, he lobbed it into the trash can. "What's wrong with us, Nikki? Why can't we be like a Woody Allen movie? Two old lovers with unfinished business running into each other on a New York sidewalk?"

"You mean," she said, "instead of running into a sidewalk?"

"Is my nose broken?"

"Let's see." She reached her fingers for it, but he pulled back.

"No. Enough pain." He got up and checked his face in the teakettle. "Reflection's too distorted to tell." He shrugged. "Well, if it is broken, it'll give me character. I'll be even more rugged in my rugged handsomeness."

"Until people find out how you did it." That made him check himself out in the kettle again. While he turned away, bending to assess the damage, she said, "Thank you for trying to protect me." Then she added, "Guess you can't be that angry."

He rose upright and faced her. "Wanna bet?" But his look told her he had, at least, downgraded to a simmer.

"And I don't blame you. I know you felt blindsided."

"Why? Because you ditched me, and a couple of hours later, I find a naked dead man in your apartment? And when I dare to ask, you think you can get away with saying it's complicated and giving me the boot?"

"OK, so I guess you may still be angry."

"What if roles were reversed? What if you had come into my place and found a naked Tam Svejda with her brains on the floor? All right, maybe not so much the brains, but you get the idea."

A stillness charged by unseen toxic particles settled in the chasm between them. Nikki knew that it fell to her to break the silence, or not to. She recognized a tipping point when she saw one and waded in. "You may not agree," she began, "because of the . . . indignity of your nose injury, but tonight's unexpected encounter is sort of good timing. Today my shrink suggested I make contact with you."

"This is sounding more like Woody Allen, after all. You saw a shrink?" And then for emphasis, he added, "You?"

"Mandated. Long story involving Captain Irons, but it did get me to a session with a department therapist." Nikki drew a breath that hitched in her chest. Compartmentalization always got her through, so this was scary territory. Vulnerability meant exposure, but she opened herself to him, unarmed and unprotected. "I'm willing to explain, if you're willing to listen."

That's when the part of him she considered his essence, the part she most connected to, the part that jumped in front of bullets to protect her, softened him another degree. Yielding to his innate compassion, he held out his hand to her and said, "We'd probably be more comfortable on the couch."

As with most great fears, including imagined monsters behind a door, hers became merely life-sized once she confronted it and opened up. Rook's willingness to listen instead of interrupting her to judge, get defensive—or even to wisecrack—helped her immensely in telling him the saga of Don. After she informed him of their sexual hiatus after she had met Rook the summer before, he nodded, accepting that as fact. He even had the elegance not to ask her if they had slept together the night before. When she finished, he said one thing, and it was the best thing he ever could have.

"This must be absolute hell for you to face alone."

Nikki's tears erupted, and she threw herself from where she sat into his arms, shaking with sobs, allowing herself the unguarded emotional display without restraint. Her weeping rose from a deep, seemingly bottomless source that dredged up not just the raw hurt of the past twenty-four hours, but a decade of suppressed feelings of loss, hurt, anger, frustration, loneliness, and fear, which—until that moment—had been neatly boxed and locked away. He embraced her, cradling her into his shoulder, seeming to know that his caring silence was their strength, and that his encirclement of her with his arms signaled hope and unwavering friendship amid her catharsis.

When, after a time, Nikki was cried out, she drew herself away and they stared at each other, their gaze speaking volumes about trust and the bond they shared. They kissed lightly and parted, smiling, holding each other's gaze some more. Just as they had never declared their exclusivity, they also had never shared the love words. Right then, basking in the intimacy of some new sanctuary they had just forged, that would have been the time to say them. But neither would know if it had crossed the other's mind then in that tender, vulnerable moment. The time for voicing that came and then passed, banked for another day, if ever.

She excused herself to splash some cool water on her swollen eyes. When she came back, he helped her unroll the new rug for the entryway. After they squared it with the line of the wall, Rook stood on the curled ends to press them down flat and then took in the area. "Looks like somebody's been cleaning."

" 'Out, damned spot,' " said Nikki. "The super hung a new door and plastered the holes. Tomorrow, he's going to paint. Pretty soon it will all be back to normal."

"Like it never happened."

"But it did. And we live with that."

Rook's face clouded. "I've spent all day thinking it could have been worse. It could have been you."

". . . I know."

"Or even worse, could have been me."

"Even worse?"

"For you. Not having me around to pull your pigtails and shake my moneymaker." He danced a goofball dance in place—indeed accenting his fine moneymaker. He finished with a "Ka-ching!" and she laughed. The man could sure do that, get a serious girl to lighten up when there seemed to be no reason in hell to.

They were both hungry but wanted to get out rather than order in and spend too much more time just then in that apartment, with its recent history. Griffou down in the Village had quiet spaces and served late, so they set out for Ninth Street. Heat made sure to slip the Beretta Jetfire into her pocket along with an extra clip of .25s before they left.

At that hour, they had their pick of the four salons in the former 1800s boardinghouse that one blogger got right when she said it vibed "subterranean swank." Rook chose the Library for its tranquility and the warming company of books. After sampling their Manhattans, he surveyed the room, once frequented by Edgar Allan Poe, Mark Twain, and Edna St. Vincent Millay and wondered if the day would ever come that they lined the room with Kindles and Nooks.

She ordered the chopped salad and he got the grilled octopus, and while they ate, Rook said, "I have a thought about your forced leave. Have you considered flexing some muscle?"

"You mean deal out a sweet beat-down to Wally Irons?" she asked. "Between us, yes. But only as a fantasy."

"Not that kind of muscle. Political muscle. The power of downtown, Nikki. It's how I got my ride-along with you in the first place. You should get on the horn to that weasel at One Police Plaza. What's his name?"

"Zach Hamner? Forget it."

"You don't have to like him to use his clout. And he's made for this. You said yourself this guy looks like he pleasures himself to pictures of Rahm Emanuel."

"I never said that."

"Oh. Perhaps I reveal too much. Know any good shrinks?"

"No way am I calling The Hammer." She shook her head as much to him as herself. "Just being around that whole political cesspool is why I said no to my promotion."

"Have you considered that if you had taken it, you wouldn't be sitting on the wrong side of Cap'n Wally's Iron gate?"

"Of course I have, but the answer is still no. It's not worth the IOU it would cost me. And trust me, Zach Hamner would call in that chip. No," she repeated, "no."

"I think I get it," he said. "Then I have an alternative."

"I should have whacked you with that rug."

"Hear me out. I know you and how you hate this downtime, but, now that you're forced into it, you should do something relaxing."

"We are not going to Maui."

"No, I'm talking about continuing to work the case. Together, of course. Come on, you think I could ever imagine you relaxing in Hawaii? That's not where we're going."

She set her fork down. "Going? We? . . . Where?"

"To Paris, of course." He upended his Manhattan. "My treat. I worked it all out in the cab on the way over here."

"Oh, you did, did you?"

"Uh-huh. The stars have all lined up, Nikki Heat. First, you're sidelined, anyway. Second, it might not be the worst time for you to make yourself scarce in this city, considering your buddy with the shotgun is still at large."

"I am not running from him or anyone, ever."

"And third," he steamrolled on, "while Roach and the rest of the squad work the case here, we can go investigate the odd sock of your mom's life, which is why she gave up her dream there during that summer in 1971."

"Doesn't feel right to me."

"Neither did Boston, and look." He saw her register that and continued, "Nikki, there are precious few leads, and those you have either dead end or get screwed up by the Iron Man. The only forward movement on this case has come from going backwards. Am I right?"

"Yes . . ."

"It's back to what I keep telling you about pure effort. I may not be a cop, but in my own investigative career, I've learned you can't always force things to happen. Results have their own mind. Sometimes when you have been really, really patient for a long time, the answer is more patience."

Heat's objections began to melt away. She picked up her fork and raked together some fennel and almonds with bites of apple and pear. "I suppose you're going to say my forced leave is win-win."

"That phrase is so 1980s," he said. And then added a barb. "Like

Sting." He speared a tentacle and continued, "No, I see this more like making lemonade out of lemons. Or, more appropriately, *sauce meunière* out of lemons and butter."

The first flight they could get to Paris didn't leave until four-thirty the next afternoon, which worked fine for Nikki. Damn, she needed sleep. The trauma of Don's awful killing, the chase—correction: chases, if you counted the faux one with Rook—the myriad stresses over her dad, Irons, her forced leave, the unsolved case, and the emotional ups and downs with Rook, had all delivered body blows. Fold into that an all-nighter at the precinct the night before, and Heat checked out as soon as her head hit the pillow at Rook's, and stayed there until she awoke to a roll of thunder and rain tapping at the glass across the bedroom.

Rook was already up and dressed, flogging his MacBook for a hotel and calling to arrange a meeting with Nicole Bernardin's parents in Paris. "Want to know where we're staying?"

"No," she said, lacing her arms around his neck from behind. "I'm putting myself in your hands. Surprise me."

"All right. But it'll be hard to top the one you gave me the other night." She swatted his shoulder then poured some coffee while she got on the phone to Roach for a case update.

"What happened with the assignment I gave Feller and Rhymer to canvass Nicole Bernardin's neighbors about the carpet cleaning van?"

"Nothing at first," said Ochoa. "Her immediate neighbors had zip."

Then Raley added, "But since her house faced Inwood Hill Park, Rhymer got the idea that exercisers and dog owners might be habitual passers-by and decided to hang out awhile and see who turned up. A lot of zeroes, but they finally scored a woman who power walks Payson Avenue daily. This lady not only noticed the carpet cleaning van, she tried to hire them to do her place around the corner."

Ochoa picked up the story. "She rang the bell to ask for a brochure and said the guy got all crabby with her and said to forget it, he was booked."

Nikki said, "Did she get a description of him?"

"Negative," said Raley. "The guy never opened the door."

"That's bizarre," said Heat. "Did she remember any company name or get the phone number off the van?"

"Nope," answered Ochoa. "She didn't bother. Too pissed off."

A thought occurred to Heat. "Did she say what color the van was?"

"Maroon," Roach said in unison.

"A van that same color tried to run me and Rook down the other morning."

Raley said, "You never mentioned that."

"I never connected it until now. Put it on the Murder Board. There is still one there, I hope."

"There is, we've got you covered."

Detective Ochoa added, "Along those lines, please know we're doing all we can to get something to shake loose on this case."

Raley continued, "Don't get too excited yet, but before shift this morning, Miguel and I met up with Malcolm and Reynolds. We thought, just to double-check, we'd walk the area around Bruckner where they found the taxi your shooter jacked."

Detective Ochoa continued, "There was this pile of old tires and paint cans in the flood control drain up the block. We had some rain overnight, so I thought I'd give it a look in case the runoff carried anything there. I found a men's glove."

Heat started to pace. "What color?"

"Brown leather."

"That's what he had on," she said, seeing the gloves grip the shotgun.

"It's a long shot," said Raley, "because it's waterlogged and looks like a dog or something turned it into a chew toy. But it definitely has blood traces and gunpowder residue. Lab's running it now for prints, inside and out, as well as DNA."

"Good work, you two. Tell Malcolm and Reynolds, also."

"No," said Ochoa. "We're pretty much hogging credit on this one."

Rook could see the change in her when he came out of his office to join her. "We're still going," he said. She told him about the glove and his response was "We're still going."

"But I feel like I'm being irresponsible. Like I should stay close in case something breaks."

"You're on leave. And what are you going to do, sit outside the door to Forensics, yelling 'Hurry up' every half hour?" She chewed at the inside of her lip, unsold. "Nikki, we covered this last night. Remember

Boston? We ended up ID-ing Nicole and connecting her to your mom, big-time."

"All right," she said. "We're still going."

"Excellent. Because the real reason is those tickets are nonrefundable."

Their overnight flight got them into Paris-Charles de Gaulle at six the next morning. Both slept soundly on the plane, but as a contingency, Rook had reserved and paid for their room from the previous night so they could nap and adjust if they needed to without waiting for afternoon check-in. "Nice," said Nikki on their ride up in the elevator.

"I know it's not the George V, and the name Washington Opéra doesn't sound very French, but as boutique hotels go, this is a find." Rook told her the elegant building was the former town house of Madame de Pompadour, and Nikki couldn't help but think of her father's job when he arrived in Europe in his twenties, finding properties just like this to invest in and flip. The thought both comforted and unsettled her. She reflected on her therapist's message to reconnect to the past she had been avoiding and accepted that this would be a trip of mixed emotions that needed to be felt.

From their room, Rook opened the shutters to show her Paris's oldest bakery across the street, promising warm croissants and *pain au chocolat* every morning. "The Louvre is a few blocks that way," he said, pointing to his left. "The Opéra is to our right, and out the back of the hotel, the gardens of Le Palais Royale. Curb your dog, please."

"If we were here for sightseeing, that would all be splendid," she said. "Or does this fall under your rather loose definition of Romantic Trip While On The Case?"

"Paris? How can you talk about romance while we're in Paris? We have work to do. You've got the number of Nicole's parents, and as soon as it's nine A.M., we're calling them."

"That's a half hour away."

"Then I say we strip and knock off a quick one."

"How romantic."

"Paris, baby," he said, and they raced each other bare.

NINE

Lysette Bernardin picked up Heat's phone call sounding wary and frail, which she attributed not to age but to the soul-crushing grief Nikki had heard in the voices of so many families of murder victims over time. The old woman spoke excellent English and brightened when she learned that the caller was the daughter of her dear Nicole's best friend, Cynthia. Her husband was at a doctor's appointment for his new hip until early afternoon. Madame Bernardin gave Heat the address on Boulevard Saint-Germain near Rue du Dragon and they fixed two P.M. for a visit.

They took a taxi—a new Mercedes—to the Left Bank and had the driver drop them not far from the Bernardins' apartment so they could have some lunch before their meeting. Rook had his mind on reliving the Rive Gauche writer's experience, either at Les Deux Magots or Café de Flore. Both were crowded with tourists. Even the iconic sidewalk tables were hemmed in by rolling carry-on luggage. They opted for an open table across the boulevard at Brasserie Lipp, which Johnny Depp had told Rook also once served as a hangout for the likes of Hemingway, Proust, and Camus. "Can you imagine waiting on an existentialist?" asked Rook. "'What will you have, Mr. Camus, the steak tartare or the escargots?' 'Oh . . . What does it matter?'"

Heat checked her watch. "One o'clock here. In New York, they should be in the precinct by now." She tapped in the international code and called Raley's cell.

"Hey," said the detective. "Or should I say, *bonjour*? I was just going to call you. How's your jet lag?"

"I have been living my life jet lagged. I can no longer tell. Why were you going to call?" Heat got out her notepad, hopeful something would be worth writing down.

"I'll give you the good news first. Forensics called and said they confirmed gunpowder residue on that glove Ochoa found. Also paint particles that may match your front door. The pigment's right, but they won't know for certain until this afternoon."

Nikki covered the mouthpiece and relayed the information to Rook, then said, "OK, Rales, let's hear the bad news."

"Hang on." After some rustling and the sound of a door opening and closing, he continued, accompanied by reverb, which made her picture him seeking privacy in the back hall off the bull pen. "It's Irons. Now that the glove looks like it might bust a lead, he's pulled Team Roach off Forensics watch."

"Please, not Hinesburg."

"Not that bad, but close. Captain's taking it over himself. Lab's still working on finding fingerprints on it, but if they do, the Iron Man is poised for glory."

Inside, Nikki fumed, but kept a light touch with her detective. "I can't leave town for one day, can I?" His laugh echoed in the hall, and she said, "Look, it is what it is. Thanks for the update, and keep me posted."

The waiter had been standing by until she hung up, and when he arrived, Rook gestured to Nikki and said, "Want me to handle this?"

"No, I'll blunder through." She turned to the waiter and said flaw-lessly, *"Bonjour, monsieur. Je voudrais deux petits plats, s'il vous plaît. La salade de frisée, et après, les pommes de terre a l'huile avec les harengs mariné."*

Rook composed himself, muttered *"Deux,"* and handed the menus back. "Wow, I had no idea."

"Once again," she said.

"Full of surprises."

"I have always loved the language. They even let me skip French Four in high school. But there's no substitute for immersing yourself and speaking it with the locals."

"When did you do that?"

"On my college semester abroad. I had been in Venice most of the time, but Petar and I came here for a month before I went back to North-eastern."

"Ah, Petar. Shall we set a place for him?"

"God, drop the shoe, Sparky. So you know? Jealousy? Totally unattractive."

"I'm not a jealous guy, you know."

"Oh, right. Let's run down your list of hot buttons: Petar? Don? Randall Feller?"

"OK, now, he's different. That guy's name says it all. Randy Feller? I'm just sayin'."

"I think you're 'just sayin'' a lot."

He brooded, fumbling with his silverware, playing one-handed leapfrog with his forks, then finally said, "You named three. Is that about it?"

"Rook, are you seriously asking me my number? Because if you are, that's going to open up a ginormous subject. That's defining for a relationship. It's going to mean talk. Lots and lots of talk. And even if you're willing to go there right now and put in that work, I'd ask myself one thing, first: How many surprises can you handle in forty-eight hours?"

He saw the waiter coming and said, "You know what I think we should do? Let's just relax and enjoy whatever the hell it was you ordered."

"*Merveilleux*," she said.

Monsieur and Madame Bernardin greeted them in the foyer of their spacious apartment, a duplex comprising the top two stories of their six-floor building. In spite of the Left Bank's Bohemian pedigree, that stretch of Boulevard Saint-Germain whispered unpretentious wealth tidily wrapped in Louis XV façades. The block of apartments rose above street-level shops that were limited to elegant necessities. In this neighborhood, it would be easier to find a wine boutique or seamstress than a place to get a tattoo or Brazilian wax. The couple, in their mid-eighties, reflected the neighborhood in their attire. Both were smartly dressed in understated classics: a black cashmere pullover and tailored slacks for her; a maroon sweater vest under a butterscotch corduroy blazer *pour monsieur*. No velvet smoking jackets, but these were certainly not matching-track-suit seniors, either.

Lysette accepted the small bouquet of white lilies Nikki had bought on their walk there with a mix of thanks at the kindness of her gesture and sadness at their grave symbolism. Emile rasped a heavily accented

"This way, please," and they followed him as he hobbled to the living room and his wife disappeared in search of a vase. As they sat, he apologized for his slowness, blaming a recent hip replacement. She returned with the flowers and placed them on a corner table with some other condolence arrangements that surrounded a framed photo of their daughter. To Heat's eye, the portrait was identical to the New England Conservatory yearbook photocopy in her murder file.

"Thank you for seeing us today," said Nikki in French. "I know this is a difficult time, and we are truly sorry for your loss." The old couple facing them on the couch took each other's hand simultaneously and held it comfortably. They were both thin and small like Nicole, but seemed even more so—almost birdlike under the load of mourning their only child.

They thanked Nikki, and Emile suggested they continue in English, as they were both fluent and could see that M. Rook would like to be more included. He limped around the coffee table with a bottle of Chorey-les-Beaune to pour into the wineglasses that had been set beside a small plate of petits fours in anticipation of the visit. After a muted toast and polite sips, Lysette set her glass down, eyes riveted on Nikki. "Pardon me for staring, but you look so much like your mother," Heat heard again. "It is so strange for me to sit here across from you, who are occupying the same chair Cynthia liked to use. The sensation is as if time had . . . what is the word . . . ?"

"Warped," said her husband, and the pair smiled and nodded in unison. "We cared very much for Cindy, but I am sure you know that."

"Actually, this is all new to me. I'd never met your daughter and my mother never mentioned her to me."

"That is odd," said Lysette.

"I agree. Did my mother and Nicole have some sort of falling out at some point? Anything that might have caused them to become estranged?"

The Bernardins looked at each other and shook no. "*Au contraire,*" Emile said. "As far as we knew, their relationship was always strong and happy."

"Forgive me if this is sensitive to discuss, but I believe Nicole's murder is somehow connected to my mother's, and I hope to learn as much as I can about their relationship so I can find the killer."

"They were like sisters," said Emile. "They had their differences, though."

"It's what made up the friendship," said Lysette. "Opposite personalities that complemented each other so beautifully. Our Nicole, she was always an *esprit libre*."

Heat translated for Rook. "A free spirit." He nodded like he got it already.

"She worried us so much as a child," continued Emile. "From the moment she could walk, she was always testing things, taking risks. Climbing this, jumping over that. Just like that urban sport these days. What is it called?"

"Parkour," said his wife. "When she was seven, she gave herself a concussion. Oh, *mon Dieu*, we were so frightened. We gave her the pair of roller skates she wanted for her birthday. A week later, our little daredevil thought she would try riding them down the stairs of *le Métro*."

Her husband shook his head at the recollection and pointed to his own body to indicate Nicole's traumas. "Concussion. Knocked out a tooth. A broken wrist." Heat and Rook shared a glance, thinking the same thing: that explained the old scar. "We thought she would outgrow all this but her *esprit*, her wild side, only got more worrisome at adolescence."

"Boys," said Lysette. "Boys, boys, boys. All her energy went to boys and parties."

"And the Beatles," Emile scoffed. "And incense."

Rook shifted cheeks in his antique chair as the parents continued through the 1960s. Nikki knew this was taking a lot of time, but she didn't try to stem their oral history. It seemed important for them to tell her Nicole's story—especially considering their loss. But their narrative also gave Nikki what she wanted—not just the obvious rewarding of her attempt to dig for background to help her homicide investigation, but the opportunity to go to the places she had never gone before to learn about her mother and her world. The ceremony of sharing this moment with the family of her mom's best friend gave her a feeling of completeness about herself she hadn't expected; a sense of personal connection to things she had long avoided. If Lon King didn't reinstate her after this, that shrink could bite it.

Madame Bernardin said, "We did not know where she would go in her life until she found her passion in the violin."

"Which is how she met Nikki's mother," said Rook, scrambling to put up a stop sign on memory lane.

"The best thing that ever happened for our girl," said Emile. "She became immersed in the development of her talent in Boston and, at the same time, met a friend with opposing sensibilities to ground her."

"Nicole needed that," agreed his wife. "And I believe—if I may say so, Nikki—that our Nicole helped to open up your mother, who had such a serious nature. So full of purpose, so duty-bound to her work, rarely giving herself permission to simply have fun." She paused. "I can see this makes you a little uncomfortable, but don't be. We are talking about your mother, after all, not you."

"Although, you could be her sitting there right now," Emile added, only making Nikki feel more exposed, until Rook, thank God, jumped in brandishing his odd sock.

"That's what so curious to me," he began. "Cynthia—Cindy—had such drive and purpose and investment to succeed as a concert-class pianist. I've seen her play on video; she was astounding."

"Yes," they both said.

Rook placed his hands palms up to the heavens. "What happened? Something changed when she came here in the summer of '71. Something big. Maybe Nikki's mother didn't quit the piano, but she seemed to quit the dream. She had career opportunities back in the States and she didn't bother to go back to see them through. I just wonder, what took such a serious young woman off course?"

After thinking a moment, Lysette said, "Well, I understand, as I am sure you do, that young people do change. For some, the rigors of the serious pursuit of a goal cannot be sustained. There is no shame in that."

"Of course not," he said, "but, with all due respect, Paris is a wonderful city, but three weeks' vacation here, and she drops out?"

Lysette turned from him to Nikki to answer. "I would not say that your mother dropped out. It is more as if she took a hiatus from the pressure she put on herself and enjoyed things. Touring, visiting the museums, of course. She loved to learn new cooking. I taught her how to make cassoulet with duck confit."

"She made that for me!" said Nikki.

"So, tell me, how am I, as a cook?" Lysette chuckled.

"Three Michelin stars. Your cassoulet was always a special occasion meal." Lysette clapped her hands together joyfully, but Nikki could see fatigue descending on the old couple, and before they faded, there were some basic questions she needed to ask. The same ones she would ask the parents of any victim from her precinct. "I won't take much more of your time, but there are some details I wish to know about Nicole."

"Of course, you are a daughter but policewoman, too, *n'est-ce pas?*" said Emile. "And, please, if it helps you discover what happened to *cher* Nicole . . ." He choked up, and the couple joined hands again.

Detective Heat began with Nicole Bernardin's work. She asked if she had any professional bad blood such as rivalries or money troubles. They answered no, same as when Nikki asked if they knew of any troublesome relationships in her personal life, either in Paris or New York: lovers, friends, jealous triangles? "How did she seem to you the last time you spoke?"

M. Bernardin looked at his wife and said, "Remember that call?" She nodded and he turned to address Nikki. "Nicole was not herself. She was curt with us. I asked her if something was wrong, and she said no and would say nothing more on the subject. But I could tell she was agitated."

"When was that call?"

"Three weeks ago," said Lysette. "That was another unusual thing. Nicole always called on Sundays, just to check in. She went her last weeks without contact."

"Did she say where she was when she called?"

"An airport. I know this because when I asked her what was wrong, she cut me off and said she had to board her flight." The woman's brow fell at the memory.

Rook asked, "Did your daughter have a place here in Paris?" In preparing for the visit he and Nikki had hoped to discover an apartment to search—with the parents' permission, of course. But Nicole didn't keep one.

"Whenever she visited the city, Nicole stayed here in her old bedroom."

"If you don't have an objection," asked Detective Heat, "may I see it?"

Nicole Bernardin's bedroom had long before been redecorated and put to use as an art studio for Lysette, whose watercolor still lifes of flowers and fruit lay about in various stages of completion. "You will pardon the mess," she said unnecessarily. The room was tidy and organized. "I don't know what you wish to see. Nicole kept some clothing and shoes in the armoire, not much. You may look." Nikki parted the antique wood doors and felt the pockets of the few items hanging there, finding nothing. Same for the insides of her shoes and the lone, empty purse hanging on the brass hook. "Everything else of hers is in there," Lysette said, moving an easel to indicate a large drawer at the bottom of a built-in. Nikki found the drawer as orderly as the rest of the apartment. Clean underwear, bras, socks, shorts, and tees—neatly folded— lived in a clear plastic container. Heat knelt and unsnapped the lid to make her inspection, carefully returning everything as it had been, stacked and sorted. Beside the container sat a pair of running shoes and a bicycle helmet. She examined the interiors of both and found nothing.

"Thank you," she said, closed the drawer, and replaced the feet of the easel to the dimples they had made in the rug.

As they rejoined Emile in the living room, Rook asked, "Did Nicole keep a computer here?" When Mme. Bernardin said no, he continued, "What about mail? Did she get any mail here?"

M. Bernardin said, "Nothing, no mail." But when he said it, both Heat and Rook noticed something unsettled in the way he lingered on the thought.

"You seem unsure about the mail," said Nikki.

"No, I am quite sure she got no mail here. But when you asked me, it reminded me that someone else had recently asked the same thing."

Heat got out her notepad, making complete her transition from houseguest to cop. "Who asked you that, M. Bernardin?"

"A telephone caller. Let me think. He said it so quickly. An American voice, I think he said . . . Sea—crest, yes, Mr. Seacrest. He said he was a business associate of my daughter's. He called me by my first name, so I had no reason to doubt him."

"Of course not. And what exactly did this Mr. Seacrest ask you?"

"He was concerned a package of Nicole's might have been misdirected here by error. I told him nothing had arrived for her here."

Rook asked, "Did he describe what kind of package or what might be in it?"

"Mm, no. As soon as I said nothing had come, he got off the line quickly."

Heat quizzed him about the caller and any characteristics about his voice—age, accent, pitch—but the old man came up at a loss. "Do you remember when the call came?"

"Yes, a few days ago. Sunday. In the evening." She made a note and he asked, "Do you think it is suspicious?"

"It's hard to know, but we'll check it out." Nikki handed him one of her business cards. "If you think of anything else, and especially if anyone contacts you again to ask about Nicole, please call that number."

Lysette said, "It has been a pleasure to meet you, Nikki."

"And you," she said. "I feel like you gave me a glimpse into a big part of my mother's life that I missed. I wish I could have learned more about it from her."

Mme. Bernardin got up. "Do you know what I want to do, Nikki? I have something I'd like to share with you that you may find enlightening. *Excusez-moi.*"

Heat sat again, and in Lysette's absence Emile topped their glasses, even though neither had gone beyond the toast sip. Nikki said, "My father met my mother when she was playing at a cocktail party in Cannes. He said she had been getting by doing that and giving piano lessons. Did she start that here during the summer she visited you?"

"Oh, yes. And I am proud to say that I was instrumental in finding her employment."

"Were you involved in music?" she asked.

"Only to sing in the shower," he said. "No, no, my business was commercial and corporate insurance. Through that work I developed a relationship with an investment banker—an American who was living here who became a dear friend of the family. Nicole adored him so much she called him Oncle Tyler."

"Uncle Tyler," said Rook.

"Very good," said Emile with a wink at Nikki. For no reason other than instinct she asked his name. "Tyler Wynn. A charming man. I got a lot of business through him over the years. He was very well connected to international investors and knew anyone who mattered in Paris. And Tyler's generosity of referrals didn't just extend to me. No, no. Whenever Nicole was home from Boston, he would find her summer work as a music tutor for the children of some of his wealthy acquaintances. It was good experience for her and paid very well."

"And kept her out of trouble," said Rook.

Emile pointed a forefinger to the air. "Best of all."

Nikki had done the math and urged him on. "So this Tyler Wynn also found tutoring clients for my mother that summer?"

"Exactly. And Cindy was so good at it, soon she had appointments every day. Tyler made more referrals and one job led to another. Some of her patrons who had vacation homes would even hire your mother to come along with their family on *les vacances* to continue the tutoring. A week in Portofino, another in Monte Carlo, then Zurich or the Amalfi coast. Travel, room and board, all first class. Not a bad life for a woman of twenty-one, eh?"

"Unless your life was supposed to be something else," she said.

"Ah, once again, Nikki, so much like your mother. Both dutiful and beautiful." He took a sip of wine. "Remember what one of our philosophers once said, 'In the human heart there is a perpetual generation of passions, such that the ruin of one is almost always the foundation of another.'"

Lysette seemed newly invigorated by her mission and hurried back into the room carrying a keepsake container about the size of a shoebox covered in burgundy and white toile fabric with matching burgundy ribbon ties done into bows. "I can see I've been gone too long. Emile's quoting maxims again." She stood before Nikki's chair and said, "In this box are old photos I kept of Cynthia from her times with Nicole and also of your mother's travels. Cindy was a wonderful correspondent. If you please, I am not going to look through them with you now. I don't think I am able to endure seeing them at the moment." Then she offered the box. "Here."

Nikki reached out hesitantly and cradled it in both her hands. "Thank you, Mme. Bernardin. I'll be careful with them and return them tomorrow."

"No, Nikki, these are yours to keep. I have my memories in here." She placed a hand over her heart. "Yours are in there yet to be discovered. I hope they bring you closer to your mother."

It was a struggle. Even for the self-proclaimed queen of delayed gratification, who so wanted to rip the lid off the keepsake box in the taxi back to the hotel. But she held firm. Her fear of losing a single photo trumped her aching curiosity.

Rook gave Heat some space. He set out to find a zinc bar to serve him a stand-up double espresso to supply a much-needed caffeine bounce at the far reaches of the afternoon; she stayed in the room and pored over the unexpected treasure from the Bernardins. He returned to the hotel a half hour later with an icy can of her favorite San Pellegrino Orange and found Nikki cross-legged on their bed with rows of neatly arranged snapshots and postcards radiating out from her like beams from the sun. "Finding anything useful?"

"Useful?" she asked. "Hard to know what's useful. Interesting? Absolutely. Check out this one. She was so cute." Nikki held up a shot of her mom, striking a ditzy, laughing pose while she squeezed the bicep of a gondolier under the Bridge of Sighs in Venice. "Turn it over, she wrote on the back."

Rook flipped the snapshot and read it aloud. "Dear Lysette, Sigh!"

"My mom was a babe, wasn't she?"

He handed it back. "I'm too smart to answer a question like that about your mother. At least until we appear on Jerry Springer."

"I think you did just answer."

He sat on the edge of the bed, careful not to upset her sorting. "What's your take from all this?"

"Mostly that she had one hell of a good time. You know how in *Vanity Fair* and *First Press* you see all those photo layouts of the European rich and privileged and wonder what it must be like to live like that? My mom lived like that. At least she did one job at a time. Look at some of these." Nikki dealt out the photos like playing cards, one after another, each showing young Cynthia in a posh surrounding: on the sweeping lawn of a country estate out of *Downton Abbey*; at a lacquered grand piano with the rocky coast of the Mediterranean out the picture window behind her; on the private terrace of a hilltop manor overlooking Florence; in Paris with an Asian family under the marquee for the visiting Bolshoi Ballet; and on and on. "Apparently, for her, tutor-in-residence was like a fairy tale dream you had to wake up from, but when you did, the butler came and got your bags."

There were also pictures of Nicole and other young friends her mom's age, plus a bunch of snapshots of her mom and her pals standing individually in various locales around Europe, grinning and gesturing grandly like *Price Is Right* spokesmodels, obviously their shared joke. But Nikki remained fixated on her mom and the frozen record of her bopping around in France, Italy, Austria, and Germany. In a number of photographs she appeared posed with her host families. Most of Cindy's patrons had that look of old money, standing pompously in a circular drive or in private gardens, but mostly in predictable small-to-tall groupings of moms, dads, and impatient young musicians in bow ties or ruffled dresses in front of a Steinway grand. There was one other person in all those group pictures. A tall, handsome man, and in most of them, her mother stood close beside him.

"Who's the William Holden knockoff?" asked Rook, tapping a shot of just the man and Cynthia together outside the Louvre. He was older than Nikki's mother by twenty years and did give off the former leading man's gritty attractiveness.

"I'm not sure. There is something familiar about him I can't place." She snatched the picture from him and put it back in the proper pile.

"Whoa, not so fast." He picked it right back up. "Maybe it's the William Holden thing you recognize. . . . Or is it something else?"

"Like what?" Nikki tried to grab it away again, but he dodged her. She said, "I don't see William Holden."

"I do. I see William Holden and Audrey Hepburn. They're both straight off the movie poster for *Paris When It Sizzles*." He held the photo up to her nose. "Check it out. His weathered good looks paired with her refined innocence masking the sexy tigress inside. You know, that could be us."

Nikki looked away. "There is no sizzle in those pictures. He's too old for her."

"Know who I bet this is?" he said. "He's that Oncle Tyler who set up her tutoring clients. Yeah, this is Tyler Wynn. Am I right?"

Ignoring him, she plucked another shot from the stack and held it up. "Hey, here's one of just Mom taken right here in Paris." The developer's time stamp on the reverse read "May 1975." The photo was of her mother balanced on one foot with a hand shading her eyes, comically peering into the future. It was snapped in front of the Cathedral of Notre Dame. "I want to go there," said Nikki. "Right now."

They left the keepsake box with the hotel manager to lock in the safe and took a taxi to Île de la Cité. Darkness had fallen and the gray stoneworks of the edifice were bathed in white light, which also cast a spooky glow upon the gargoyles observing from above.

Rook knew what this was all about; she didn't have to say it. They left the taxi and hurried along silently, walking around the back of a tour group that encircled nighttime street performers who juggled flaming batons. They made their way to their destination: the center of the square that faced the front entrance of the massive cathedral. They paused, patiently waiting for a high school field trip to clear away and then approached a small piece of metal embedded in the paving stones, a shiny octagon of brass rubbed smooth by years of wear. This was the exact location in the photo of Nikki's mom. She took the picture out of her pocket to prepare herself and did what she'd come to do. A month shy of thirty-five years later, Nikki Heat stood in her mother's footsteps. Then, raising one foot off the ground, she shielded her eyes in the identical hammy pose, which Rook captured with the flash of his iPhone.

This spot of her reenactment was the famous Point Zero, the Paris milestone outward from which all distances are measured in France. This, the saying went, was where all roads began. Nikki hoped so. She just didn't know where it would lead yet.

They ate at Mon Vieil Ami, a ten-minute stroll to Île Saint-Louis. Over dinner they talked some more about their visit with Nicole's parents, which gave Rook a chance to say he didn't buy Lysette and Emile's whole theory about Cindy's taking a break from the rigors of pursuing her passion as the explanation for why she quit her dream. "You have a better theory?" Heat asked. "And does it involve UFOs, cranial needle probes, or memory-erasing light flashes from men in dark suits?"

"You know you hurt me when you mock my outside-the-box approach to case solving. Chide me if you must, but chide me gently. I'm as tender as a fawn."

"OK, Bambi," she said, "but don't look at the chalkboard, venison is the special."

After they placed their orders, Rook came right back to it. "It's still the odd sock," he said. "If someone's going to prepare her whole life like your mother did for a concert career, she doesn't just drop it. It's like an athlete training for the Olympics only to walk away from the starting blocks to become a personal trainer. Great gig, but after all that sacrifice and training?"

"I hear you, but what about what Emile said about changing passions?"

"Uh, with all due respect? *Merde.* I refer you back to my Olympics versus personal trainer theory. One's a passion, the other is a J-O-B job."

Heat said, "All right, maybe it wasn't necessarily a passion, but you saw her face in those pictures. My mom was having a ball. And probably earning just enough money to make it hard to quit. Maybe the work got to become golden handcuffs."

"Not that the subject of handcuffs doesn't titillate me, but that's also a hard sell. Responsible young woman turns into Paris Hilton in one summer? Doubtful." His salad and her soup arrived. He took a bite of tender lentils and then continued, "Do you think she had something going with this Tyler Wynn?"

Heat put her fork down and leaned over her plate toward him. "You are talking about my mother."

"I'm trying to help us—correction, help you—get an understanding of what happened over here to change everything back then."

"By going to some pretty seedy places." Her quiet tone was what unnerved him. And the steely gaze.

"Let's put a pin in it."

"Good idea."

"Besides," he said, "we already hit pay dirt with a suspect. I hope you told Raley and Ochoa to put out an APB on Ryan Seacrest."

She laughed and said, "Roach had the same response when I called them. Obviously a bogus name, but they're going to run phone records to see where that call originated last Sunday."

"It tells us one thing, for sure. Someone definitely wants to get his hands on something. And since the timing of that call came after Nicole's town house got tossed, we know he didn't find it."

"Assuming that it's the same person looking," she said.

"Well fine," he said, teasing her. "If you want to be all 'objective' in this investigation instead of leaping to conclusions, go ahead."

"Objective's kinda what I do," she said.

"Kinda," he said with a tentative edge. Her look told him Nikki knew exactly what he meant by that jab, but she let it go and concentrated on her soup.

A subtle breeze had given the night a soft spring warmth, and when they left the restaurant, Heat and Rook decided to bypass the taxis and walk back to their hotel. They strolled arm in arm over the footbridge to Île de la Cité, skirting the cathedral and the Palais de Justice until they came to Pont Neuf and stood in one of the bridge's semicircular bastions to stop the world and enjoy the spectacle of Paris at night reflected in the Seine.

"There it is, Nikki Heat, the City of Light." She turned to him and they kissed. A dinner bateau passed underneath them, and a happy couple on the top deck called out *"Bon soir"* and raised champagne flutes to them in a toast.

They mimed a toast back to the couple, and Nikki said, "Amazing. No, magical. What is it about this place? The air smells better, the food tastes like nothing I've ever had . . ."

"And the sex. Did I mention the sex?"

She laughed. "Only constantly."

"Who knows what it is?" he said. "Maybe it's Paris. Maybe it's us."

Nikki didn't answer that, only nestled against him. Rook stood holding her, feeling her breath against the soft of his neck, but at the same time he felt drawn to silently watch the hypnotic flow of the Seine.

Its dark waters streamed underneath them, a powerful force channeled between thick walls of stone revetment engineered to be impenetrable and to keep nature itself within controlled, reliable boundaries. He wondered what would happen if one of the walls ever cracked.

They didn't set an alarm. Instead Heat and Rook awoke at daybreak to pink light filtered under a thin canopy of gray clouds. Turning to each other, they smiled and said their good mornings. Rook began to slide under the sheet, but Nikki mumbled, "No, stay up here with me this time," and drew him to face her. The two made love again to the peal of morning church bells and the scent of heaven's own bakery across the street at Au Grand Richelieu. "All in all, not a bad way to start another day of homicide work," said Heat on her way to the shower.

As he had calculated, their warm pastries lasted from the bakery door to the espresso bar he had discovered the afternoon before. They found one pair of open stools at the high top counter in the window, and each drank a blood orange juice and a café au lait as they watched a businessman standing on the sidewalk turn his back to the wind and expertly roll his own cigarette.

Nikki checked her voice and e-mails. Roach, ever keen about keeping her in the loop, had closed their workday reporting that the request was in process on the phone records search for the Seacrest call to the Bernardins. The wheels of international bureaucracy turned slowly, but Detective Raley said Interpol was helping, so that was something positive anyway. Forensics had promised fingerprint test results on the found glove by morning, and Irons had told Ochoa he would check with the lab personally on his way in. Heat pocketed her phone then took it out again to double-check the time in New York, and determined it was too early to call.

Rook said, "I've been doing some further reflection." He paused, knowing this remained a touchy area. "And I think you got more than a shoe box of memories yesterday. My gut tells me we got a new lead, and it's Tyler Wynn,"

"Why am I not surprised to hear this?"

"Relax, I'm speculating in a totally new direction, seeing him in a whole other light."

"Let me guess. He's no longer William Holden, he's Jason Bateman."

"He's not a lover, he's a spy." Heat laughed. "Hear me out, Detective." He waited until she stopped chuckling and then he leaned closer to her, trying his best not to have madman eyes. "International banker has sort of a phony ring to it. Kind of like 'embassy attaché' or 'government contractor.' It sounds to me like a cover."

"OK . . . And what is the possible connection to my mother?"

"I don't know." She scoffed and took a sip of her coffee. He repeated, "I don't know."

"Of course you don't."

"I don't know!" he hissed. "Isn't this great?!!" This time his eyes had indeed widened madly. Nikki looked around self-consciously, but nobody in the café had noticed. Even the man on the sidewalk smoking the roll-your-own had turned the back of his blue suit to them. Rook startled her, grabbing Nikki by the elbow. "Oh, I know!" He snapped his fingers and pointed at her. "Tyler Wynn—air quotes—international investment banker—was using your mother just like his fake job. As a cover. Pretending to be her lover." He paused. "Notice I said, 'pretending.' Which is why Cindy quit and moved back to the U.S. when she married your dad."

Heat finished her coffee and slid a euro under the saucer. "Rook, you need to know. There's out of the box and there's out of your mind."

He worked on her the whole way back to the hotel, and one point of his logic she found hard to refute. That they came to Paris to look into the change in her mother's life, and since Tyler Wynn had been such a factor—spy or not—they'd be remiss not to see if Uncle Tyler was still around to talk to. "Or is that too sensitive an area for you?" he asked. A crafty move on Rook's part because, even if it were, the challenge aspect of his question made it impossible for her to back down.

Up in their hotel room Rook paced, spitballing how best to approach checking out Tyler Wynn. "I still have some viable clandestine contacts over here from the days I worked my Russia-Chechnya article. Also, there are a few favors I could call in at CIA and NSA. No, wait . . . Maybe we should start incrementally and make a vanilla sort of inquiry through the U.S. embassy. . . . Or possibly, Interpol. On the other hand," he rambled, going back and forth, "this is potentially important enough that we could step it up to the DCRI—that's the French equivalent of the CIA, if you didn't know." He noticed Nikki getting on her cell phone. "Who are you calling?"

She held up a finger for silence. *"Bonjour,* Mme. Bernardin? *C'est* Nikki Heat. First of all, thank you for your hospitality and for those wonderful photographs. I am so grateful to have them." She nodded and said, "You, as well. I was hoping I could ask a favor. Do you have phone number for Tyler Wynn?" Heat smiled at Rook and began writing it down.

When she hung up, he said, "Well, there's the lazy way, if you go for that sort of thing. I don't. Feels kind of like cheating."

Nikki held up the pad with Wynn's phone number. "Should I not call it, then?"

He said, "Do you want to play games or get serious about this case for once?"

Her call began in French, but whoever answered spoke English. When Rook saw her shocked reaction when she asked to speak to Tyler Wynn, he scooted from his spot standing at the window to sit on the edge of the bed beside her. "That's terrible," she said. Rook waved for her attention, mouthing "What?"s like a pestering adolescent, and she turned away to concentrate, muttered a series of "Uh-huhs," asked for an address, which she wrote down, then said her thanks and hung up.

"Come on, out with it. What's terrible?"

"Tyler Wynn is in the hospital," said Nikki. "Somebody tried to kill him."

Rook leaped to his feet and spun in a circle. "That. Is the coolest. Lead. Ever."

TEN

The taxi driver knew the place, the Hôpital Canard, in the western suburb of Boulogne-Billancourt, one of the wealthiest districts in Paris. The cabbie glanced at the couple in the backseat and asked if it was an emergency. They both answered at the same time. She said no, he said yes. Rook asked her, "And exactly what was it you told me Wynn's housekeeper said his condition was?" He cupped his ear.

"Critical gunshot."

"And that's not an emergency?"

She took his point and told the driver, "Just get there as quickly as you can."

The traffic had another idea. Along with its romance and charm, Paris also came with a morning rush hour. The driver kept surfing his radio dial in ADHD fashion, mostly to French hip-hop and electronic dance stations. The *oonce-oonce-oonce* rhythm track didn't match their cadence along the Seine. He turned down the music as the car crept by a traffic marker that read, "Bois de Boulogne, 10 km," and asked, "You have been yet to Bois de Boulogne? Very pretty for romantic walks. Like Central Park in New York." Then he pumped up the *oonce-oonce* again.

Rook said to her, "Love that name. In fact, I'm entitling my new Victoria St. Clair romance novel, *Le Chateau du Bois de Boulogne.* Which—correct me here—loosely translated means 'castle of wood in the baloney.' I predict overseas sales will skyrocket."

The hospital was just off the A-13 in a quiet neighborhood of medical and dental offices. A surprisingly small four-story modern facility, Hôpital Canard appeared more like an upscale private clinic than a big city hospital. "This is what money gets you," said Rook as they strolled past the manicured hedges and potted palms on the way to the entrance.

"Trust me, you won't see a lot of hobos expiring on the ER floor in this establishment. I'll bet they even warm the bedpans."

Nikki pointed out that flowers seemed to have gotten things off on the right foot the day before with the Bernardins, so they stopped at the small shop off the lobby. Minutes later, armed with some peonies in cellophane, they bypassed the front desk and rode the elevator to the second floor. On the way up, she said, "Not that I'm complaining, but I'm surprised they didn't ask us to sign in."

"It's the peonies. In my experience as an investigative journalist, I've learned you can get by almost any security situation unchallenged by carrying something. Flowers, clipboard . . . And it's a breeze if you're eating something, especially off a paper plate."

"Room two-oh-three," she said, consulting the note she'd made at the hotel. They turned a corner, and outside the door of 203, a uniformed *policier* rose up from his folding chair to face them. Heat elbowed Rook. "You don't have a plate of baked beans on you, do ya?"

In French, the policeman told them no visitors. Nikki replied, also in French, that she had spoken to M. Wynn's housekeeper, who assured her that it would be all right to see him. "We've come a long way," said Rook. "And we love your country."

The cop gave him a disdainful look and said, *"Allez,"* looking like he'd enjoy a bit of exercise to break the monotony, if it came to that. Heat held up her NYPD identification, a tone changer. The homegrown officer from the suburban prefecture studied the foreign credentials carefully, looking from her photo to her and back, his eyes darting under the short brim of his cap. Speaking rapidly and flawlessly like a native, Nikki explained that her mother, Cynthia Heat, had been very close to "Oncle Tyler," and that his shooting might be connected to a homicide case she was working on back home. The gendarme seemed intrigued but immovable. Until he heard the old man's weak voice coming from the open door of the room.

"Did you say . . . you were Cindy Heat's daughter?"

"Yes, Mr. Wynn," she called toward the pale yellow privacy drape. "I'm Nikki Heat, and I came here to see you."

After a pause, then a prolific hawking of phlegm, the disembodied voice said, "Let her in." The policeman's eyes flicked side to side, unprepared for this scenario. At last he regarded Nikki's ID once more, handed it to her, and stood back to let them pass. As she and Rook entered the room, they could hear the *policier* making a call on his walkie-talkie to cover himself.

For Nikki the scene behind the curtain took her right back to February in St. Luke's Roosevelt, where Rook had been clinging to life after his shooting. Tyler Wynn, frail and propped up on one side to keep the left half of his back elevated off the mattress, watched her through dazed, half-mast eyelids. Then he managed to bring a weak smile to his dry, cracked lips. "My God," he said. "Look at you. It's like I died and went to heaven and met up with dear Cindy." And then a rascally twinkle shined through. "I am still alive, aren't I?" He laughed, but that brought on deep, painful coughing. He held up his palm to signal them not to worry, and when it subsided, he drew in some oxygen from the clear tube under his nose. "Sit, please."

There was only one chair, and Rook pulled it up bedside for Nikki, carefully avoiding the batch of cables snaking from under Tyler's sheets to the array of monitors. She briefly introduced Rook as he found a path around to the foot of the bed and the windowsill where he perched. "The magazine writer," he said. "Right. Pardon me for not getting up." He briefly lifted both arms, which were connected to multiple IV drips. "Bad combination, three gunshots and a bad heart."

"You'll tell us when you need us to go, promise?" she asked.

Tyler Wynn just smiled and said, "Look at all these machines. The French sure like to make a grand spectacle of everything, don't they? Cooking, cinema, sex scandals, *les hôpitaux*. This country perfected modern medicine, but before that, I'm told, they used to operate without anesthetic. Didn't even wash their hands. So I guess, all in all, I'm lucky." He rolled his head her way on the pillow and stared. "Everybody tell you how much you look like your mom?"

"All the time. It's a compliment."

"You know it." He took her in some more and then said, "I heard you tell my personal gendarme you were investigating a homicide."

"Yes, I'm with the NYPD."

"I read that article." He cocked an eyebrow at Rook. "Looks like you got more than a byline, young man."

"No complaints," he said.

There was so much Nikki wanted to talk over with him; so many questions she wanted to get answers to in order to fill those gaps in her connection to her own mother. And there were some questions she was afraid to ask. But one look at the old man told her this wouldn't be a long visit. She made a decision to prioritize and start with the case essentials. Crude as that might be, first and foremost, she had an investigation to conduct. Heat knew all about putting her personal needs to the side. They would have to wait for later or the next visit.

"Mr. Wynn," she began, but he interrupted.

"Tyler. Or Uncle Tyler. Your mom called me that."

"OK, Tyler. I'm assuming from the guard you've been assigned that they didn't catch whoever did this to you. Do you have any idea who it was?"

"It's a crazy world. Even Europe is getting gun happy."

"Were you robbed?"

"Nope. Still got my gold Rolex. At least if the night orderly didn't steal it."

"Did you see who did it?"

He shook no. Then he told her, "That look on your face is the same one the police inspector had when he interviewed me. Sorry."

From his perch, Rook asked, "When did this happen?"

The old man's eyes found the ceiling. "Give me a minute. I was under a few days, so time is a little fuzzy, know what I mean?" Rook understood. "Tuesday night last week, late. How come?"

Heat and Rook registered the significance of that with a glance. Time zones notwithstanding, that would have been the night before Nicole Bernardin had been killed. "Gathering my facts," she said, leaving it there for now. "How did it happen?"

"Not much to describe. I'd just come back to my apartment from the late show of *Girl with the Dragon Tattoo* at the Gaumont Pathé. I got out of my car in the underground garage, and next thing, I hear three shots behind me and someone running away while I'm down on the pavement. I woke up here."

Nikki had slipped out her reporter's-cut spiral as unobtrusively as she could manage and made some notes. She asked him the questions she had asked so often in these circumstances over the years. About recent threats. No. Bad business deals. No. Romantic jealousies. "Oh, what I would give," he said. Having exhausted the usual possibilities, she sat, tapping the cap of her pen to her lip.

"I did have a few drinks after the cinema. It's possible that I drove poorly and this was some sort of road rage." It sounded flimsy. Not only was neither of them buying, it had an odor of misdirection, as if he threw it out there to try to close the subject.

"What about a hit?" asked Rook. At first, Heat objected to the baldness of his question, but she gave her reservations a second thought when she saw the animation rise in Tyler Wynn.

"I beg your pardon?"

"A contract killing. That's what it sounds like to me. Why would somebody have a reason to buy a termination? With extreme prejudice?" He used the jargon of clandestine operatives for effect. Nikki had to hand it to Rook, he walked the line beautifully, holding his ground without badgering the man. Letting innuendo do the heavy lifting. Saying, I know and you know, without speaking the words.

"That would be extraordinary, Mr. Rook," Tyler said, not denying it.

"For an international investment banker, it would be," he countered. Wynn had joined him, also playing the middle ground, so that's where Rook stayed, for the moment, and said, "It would be quite extraordinary to target a mere investment banker." The two men held a long look, the equivalent of a handshake crunch game to see who gave first. It was Tyler Wynn who blinked.

"Corporal Bergeron," he said. When the officer appeared around the yellow drape, he said, "I would like to speak privately with my friends. Would you please find some water for these flowers and close the door when you step out?" The policeman hesitated and then did as instructed.

Tyler Wynn closed his eyes to ponder for so long in the quiet, with no sound other than the soft, rhythmic beeping of his heart monitor, that they both wondered if he had fallen asleep. But then he cleared some more chest congestion and began his story. "I am going to share this with you because it doesn't just concern me, it concerns your mother." When he said those words, Nikki felt her heart jump. She dared not interrupt, only nod, encouraging him onward. "And not only can I tell from these few minutes with you, Nikki, that you would be discreet, but at this hour of my life, alone and clearly with no . . . infrastructure . . . to protect me, I have no reason to be naïve about misplaced loyalty."

Prompted by his comment about discretion, Heat capped her pen and folded her hands across her notebook. Rook remained still, arms crossed. Waiting out the beeps.

"For many years, back when I was younger and more useful . . ." He paused. Then he made the leap. "I was engaged in helping my country through covert means. Not to put too fine a point on it, I was a spy. For CIA." Rook sniffed and shifted, crossing his feet at the ankles where he leaned. Wynn tilted his head to him and said, "You had that figured out, of course. Another reason not to maintain the fiction. That's what spying is all about, you know, fiction. It's more cloak than dagger. We made up stories and lived them. And you're right, sending me to Europe as an investment banker for my legend provided me excellent camouflage. More than that, it gave me access to places I needed to gather intel. There's nothing like making people rich to open a few doors and not have anybody ask too many questions about you."

He turned back to Nikki. "I ran what headquarters in Langley nicknamed my Nanny Network. They called it that because I began with an ingenious idea. With so many influential contacts I had developed through my cover business, I began to recruit and place nannies in the homes of diplomats and other select subjects of interest, to spy on them and report back to me. The simplicity of the notion was exceeded only by the results. These nannies had incredible access to the home lives of my subjects. Once they penetrated, they not only listened, they planted bugs and, occasionally, took photographs, either for intelligence gathering or, yes, leverage. Blackmail." He smiled at Nikki. "I can see you are ahead of me. You're there, already, aren't you?"

She could feel light beads of perspiration on her chest and where the small of her back met the molded plastic chair. "I think so." Her voice sounded like someone else's.

"The director himself was so pleased by the secrets I was mining, my orders were to generate more. Remember, we're talking the seventies. The Cold War was still on. You had Vietnam. The IRA. The Berlin Wall.

Carlos the Jackal was kidnapping OPEC ministers in Vienna. SALT treaty talks were on in Moscow. The Greek monarchy got overthrown. Red Chinese sleeper cells started assimilating into the U.S. And most of the players, sooner or later, came through Paris.

"The genius of the Nanny Network was that I could expand it by plugging in more than just nannies and au pairs. I added a butler, then some cooks, and then English tutors, and, yes, Nikki Heat—music tutors. One of your mother's classmates, Nicole Bernardin, had worked out very well spying for me, and she helped me to recruit Cynthia on a summer visit."

Heat and Rook made a slow turn to each other. Neither wanted to break the thread by speaking, and they both brought their attention back to the old man. Nikki heard voices passing in the hall and hoped to learn more before the French version of Nurse Ratched came in and gave them the toss.

"Your mother's first assignment was an important one, and she excelled. In the summer of 1971 movement began behind the scenes to negotiate an end to the Vietnam conflict."

"The Paris Peace Talks," Rook said, unable to contain himself.

"That's right. I learned that the ambassador to a certain Soviet Bloc nation, a fair-weather Communist I had secretly invested some cash for, was going to host the family of one of the North Vietnamese negotiators in his home. The North Viets had a young son who wanted to keep up his piano studies." Nikki's memory raced back to the toile keepsake box and the photo of her mother with the Asian family outside the Bolshoi. "I placed Cindy in the ambassador's home as the boy's summer tutor. The kid had a great recital, and your mom passed along vital information that helped Kissinger keep a leg up at the negotiating table. You should be proud."

"I am," said, Nikki. "And it helps me understand the change that came over her when she visited here."

"You mean giving up her concert career? After a few placements there was no stopping her. She not only took tutor-in-residence assignments here in Paris, she traveled all over Europe for years, listening and reporting, listening and reporting," he repeated. "Whether it was pure patriotism or just the thrill of the work, she was one hell of a spy. She told me the sense of mission it gave her fulfilled her like nothing else could. Not even her music."

After processing that, Nikki said, "She had to be in danger a lot."

"Sometimes, yes. She thrived on that part, too. Cynthia had courage, but it was more. A focus. A singularity of purpose that saw her through everything. Preparation, contingency, execution. She covered all the bases and left nothing to chance."

He fumbled for his water cup. Nikki got up and helped him sip from his straw. "Thanks." He waited for her to sit back down. "Of course, all good things come to an end. She met your dad, got married, and quit to go back to the U.S. and raise you." His lips, moist from the water, drew into a sly grin.

"What?" asked Nikki.

"Of course, you never do retire from this business. The world was no less volatile in the mid-eighties. Just like Paris, New York City was definitely a fertile ground for intelligence-gathering. I came to Manhattan and re-recruited her in 1985."

"1985 . . ." Nikki turned her head at an angle and studied him, reaching for the same familiar connection she had tried to make but couldn't when she first saw his photograph the day before.

Tyler Wynn smiled again, but it wasn't sly this time. It was purely nostalgic. "I remember you, too, Nikki. You were five when I visited your mother, and you played the allegro from Mozart's Fifteenth Sonata for me. I even videotaped it."

"We just watched that video the other night," said Rook. Heat nodded, her affirmation not so much to agree with Rook as to acknowledge to herself the comfort she felt at being able to draw yet another line to her past.

"I can still see it now," said the old man.

"So you're saying you re-upped her mom to infiltrate people's homes in New York?"

"And thereabouts, yes."

"But you were CIA," he said. "Isn't domestic spying illegal?"

"It is if you do it right." Tyler Wynn enjoyed his own joke until his laughter made him wince. He reached on the covers beside him for the morphine button that connected to an IV bag, and thumb-pressed it twice. "Don't know if it even works on me anymore." He concentrated on deep breathing and, once he settled, finished his thought. "I have to say, your mother was just as effective in her second go-round."

Heat, at last delivered to the point she had been so eager to reach, asked him, "Tyler, was she spying for you up to the end? I mean, at the time of her murder?"

His face sobered at the memory. "She was."

"Can you tell me specifics? Anything at all that would help me find out who killed her?"

"Cindy had several projects she had been working on at that time." He raised an arm, dragging along his drip lines, tapped his temple with a forefinger, and grinned mischievously. "I still have them all right here. I've been out of the game a lot of years, but I haven't forgotten a thing. I shouldn't tell you what she had going, but I will. First of all, because time is slipping by and I may be one of the few who could help you. Or would. A lot's changed, and not for the better. The trade's lost its human factor. Nobody wants the talents of men like me, not when you have drone aircraft.

"But mostly, I'll tell you because we're talking about my Cynthia. I don't know who the son-of-a-bitch is, but I want you to fucking nail him." The surge of emotion animated him but took its toll. He pressed the oxygen tube closer to his nostrils and sucked it in while Heat and Rook waited, full of anticipation.

"I think what happened is that your mother found something sensitive and someone burned her before she could report it."

"Something like what?" Nikki asked.

"That, I don't know. Did you notice if she acted differently? Changed daily routines or patterns, like have meetings at unusual hours?"

"Right before, I can't say. I had been away at college. But she had meetings at unusual hours a lot. It became kind of a sore subject in our home."

"Occupational hazard, I'm afraid." He looked thoughtful and asked, "Did you see her try to hide something, or did you come across a key that didn't fit anything, did she get a new storage locker, anything like that?"

"No, I'm sorry, I didn't notice."

Rook joined in. "When you say someone burned her, do you mean one of her patrons, a family she was spying on, or another spy who wanted what she had?"

"All of the above. When things turn, anyone can come at you from any direction."

The potential connection Heat had been brooding over could wait no longer. "You mentioned Nicole Bernardin. Is it possible she turned on her and did this?"

He shook his head emphatically. "No. Absolutely out of the question. Nicole loved Cindy. They were like sisters. Nicole Bernardin would die for your mother. Talk to her yourself, you'll see." And then he read something on their faces. "What?"

"Tyler, I am sorry to have to tell you this," said Nikki. "Nicole is dead."

His eyes flashed wide and his jaw fell. "Nicole . . . ? Dead?"

"She was also murdered."

"No."

Heat grew alarmed at his growing distress. "Maybe we should discuss this later." She started from her chair.

"No, tell me, tell me now." He struggled to get himself up on an elbow. "Don't go, tell me. I need to know."

"All right, but please, settle back."

He didn't. Wynn's shock and disbelief got swept away in rage. "Who killed her? How? When?"

"Tyler, please," said Nikki. She moved closer to rest a hand on him, and Rook came around the other side of the bed to ease him back onto his pillows. He complied and seemed outwardly more calm, although his breathing remained labored.

"Just tell me. I'm fine. See?" He smiled a disconnected smile and dropped it. "Fair trade. I opened up for you."

Heat said, "Nicole was stabbed to death last week in New York City. The day after your attack."

Tyler Wynn squeezed both eyes shut in a full-face wince. "No . . ." he rasped and wagged his head deliriously on the pillow. Then his eyes shot open and he coughed. Between coughs he said, "No . . . They're . . . still . . . after it."

"You have to keep yourself calm now," said Rook. And then to Nikki, "Which one's the nurse call button?"

"No, not Nicole, too!" hollered Wynn, bolting up on his elbow again, gasping, the whites of his eyes visible around frantically darting pupils. The cadence of the heart rate monitor began to increase.

"I'm getting the guard," said Nikki, but when she turned, the drape billowed as the door opened and a nurse entered.

Upon seeing the patient, she hurried to him. Heat and Rook stepped back, letting her go to work, but even as the nurse attended him, Wynn moaned hoarsely and drifted backward, holding his chest. The audio alarm screeched on the monitor and the green electronic display of his heart rate spiked and fell erratically even as it gained tempo. The nurse pushed a call button. *"Code bleu, salle deux-zero-trois, rapidement. Code bleu, salle deux-zero-trois."*

Urgent voices and the sound of small rubber wheels skittering on linoleum drew closer. An arm reached out to claw the privacy drape aside. The cardiac team rushed in, a doctor and a nurse pushing the crash cart. The arriving nurse gestured an arm sweep at Heat and Rook indicating they should stay back where they stood against the window. *"Reculez vous, s'éloignier."*

The two of them stayed there, hugging the wall as the medical staff responded to the emergency. The doctor checked vitals. *"Vingt cent joules,"* he said. The cardiac nurse threw switches and twisted a dial on the cart. They heard an ascending, barely audible tone signaling the charging of the defibrillator paddles. In a measured voice, the doctor said, *"Au loin."* All stood clear of the patient as the jolt was delivered to his chest. Tyler's entire body bounced on the mattress.

Rook kept a fixed grimace, the proximity of this event to his own mortality episode hitting home. Beside him Nikki whispered, "Come on," and then, when the screen flatlined and the signature monotone of no heart activity filled the room, she urged him again. "Come on, Tyler, come on."

But the flatline tone continued stubbornly. The doctor ordered more joules of electricity. *"Au loin."* The team cleared. Tyler jerked on the mattress again. Nikki watched the tiny screen for any spike in the green line. Nothing.

Another shock was administered to his chest. The medical team didn't talk, but their eyes spoke of diminishing hope. Heat realized her fingernails were digging into her palms and unballed her fists. The doctor increased the joules again, but the next shot did nothing. As did the one after that.

Heat and Rook looked on sadly and helplessly as the man they had just met and were growing to like remained unresponsive, with the key answers to Heat's most significant questions locked inside the head he had so playfully finger-tapped just minutes before.

Following multiple attempts, first the doctor, then his team, glanced up at the wall clock. The doc wrote down the exact time. One nurse switched off the defibrillator and wound the cords of the paddles. The other reached out for the heart monitor and flipped down a toggle.

The piercing tone ceased and the flatline disappeared, leaving behind a green, horizontal ghost fading from the screen. The nurse regarded Heat and Rook sympathetically, no translation needed. Then she turned to cover the corpse of Tyler Wynn.

Slowly, delicately, the nurse drew the sheet over him. For Nikki, it felt like the steel door to a vault slamming in her face.

ELEVEN

"It seems that Paris is also the City of Lights Out," said Rook as they got into their taxi outside the hospital.

"Nice. Mr. Sensitivity strikes again."

"What? I didn't kill him. You did. You killed him."

"Would you please stop saying that?"

"But you did. You killed Uncle Tyler." He arched a brow at her. "I hope you're happy now."

Heat turned away and stared out her window at the grove of blooming horse chestnuts across the highway in Bois de Boulogne. The smooth acceleration of the Mercedes pulling onto the A-13 back to Paris created the illusion that it was not the car that was in motion but the flowering orchard of trees with their sunlit white blossoms seeming to roll past her like radiant spring clouds.

Of course she hadn't killed Tyler Wynn.

Of course part of her thought she had. The nag of responsibility tugged at her. She envisioned some Notre Dame gargoyle coming to life, and could hear its devilish voice rasping, "He died because of your visit. It was too much for him. You should have ignored the old man when he begged for more." The plainclothes detective who had arrived at Hôpital Canard to interview her in the aftermath had dismissed that notion. Naturally, he asked her what had transpired before the cardiac arrest, and Heat, avoiding specifics about her mother, shared the detective-to-detective version: Tyler Wynn knew the victims of two murders she was investigating. He engaged voluntarily, which the uniform on post had corroborated. When Wynn started showing agitation, she had tried to break it off, but that made him even more upset, so she thought the better course was to give him the information he pleaded for and then end the interview, ASAP.

"Who knew?" the French inspector said with a shrug, and handed back her credentials. "I have already spoken to the doctor, who says it was not your visit but three bullets and something called aortic valve stenosis that killed Tyler Wynn."

But Rook picked on her. Why? Because he knew Nikki well enough to short-circuit her guilt reflex with false scorn. One of the first things he had picked up on his ride-along the summer before was how cops deal with emotion by going against it with sarcasm. The first thing he had said to her after he came out of his recent coma was how pissed he was for not catching the bullet in his teeth, like the superhero he was, and spitting it back at the bad guy. Now, in the back seat of the E-320, Rook was lightening her up by accusing her with his tongue firmly in his cheek.

On the Avenue de New York they passed by the Alma Tunnel, and as Heat gazed at the perennial scattering of bouquets and melted candles offered in memory of the princess who met her fate there, she ruminated on secrets—especially the ones that died with those who were privy to them. Her reflection brought her to remind herself that in her world, every event had a cause, and coincidence was simply cause and effect, in hiding.

Until she exposed it.

The death of Tyler Wynn was, foremost, a tragedy for him and, for her, one too many deaths to witness in one week. Beyond that, its acutely untimely nature sealed a door that had only half opened to Nikki. Fulfilling the cruelest—and truest—definition of the word "tantalizing," Heat had learned just enough to torment her about everything else that remained out of reach.

Rook said, "I guess my wack job conspiracy theories aren't so wack, after all."

"Listen, pal, before you spike the ball and do your end zone salsa dance, may I remind you of what they say about broken clocks?"

"You mean that they're not only right? But beautifully right twice a day?"

"Oh, please."

"Riiight. That's such a refreshing word, isn't it? Come on, Detective, admit it. I called it. Uncle Tyler was a spy." The driver's eyes suddenly appeared in his rearview. Rook leaned forward, playing with him just like he goofed with cabbies in New York. "Tell her to admit it." The driver averted his gaze and quickly adjusted his mirror so all they could see was the widow's peak of his jet-black hair.

Rook slid back and shifted in the seat to face her. "I don't get the gloom, Nikki. Especially now. This is definitely a glass-half-full moment—unless, of course, you're Tyler Wynn." He observed a brief pause to acknowledge him but then got right back to it. "Look at all the answers you got this morning. I'd think you'd be ecstatic to learn that not only wasn't your mom's double life just your imagination, but it wasn't because she was having an affair. And—how cool is this?—she was a spy in the family like Arnold in *True Lies*. No, even better: Cindy Heat was like Julia Child in World War Two when she spied for the OSS."

"I agree, that is something."

"Damn right. The way I see it, we did Dickens one better. Paris gave us a tale of two Cindys."

This time it was Nikki who scooted up to the driver. "You want to put him out right here?"

Across the Atlantic, New York had awakened for its day by the time they got back to their hotel, and Nikki worked her phone while Rook hit the streets to forage for lunch. Detective Ochoa took her call solo. His partner Raley was tied up checking on one of the dozens of anonymous tips the squad had received since Hinesburg's leak to the *Ledger*. "It sucks, I gotta tell you," he said. "We have enough legitimate stuff to check out on our own, but since this hit the media, we're choking on tip pollution. That article slowed the whole case down."

"You're preaching to the choir, Miguel."

"I know, but you're in Paris with Rook and I want to do what I can to screw with your good time. Hey, maybe I can get Irons to bench me, then Lauren and I can go somewhere fun. There's an Elvis convention in Atlantic City. I could rock my whole Elvez gig."

"Well, before you put on your gold lamé jumpsuit, I need you to check something out for me." She swore him to silence, then gave him the short version of Tyler Wynn's connection to her mother and Nicole. After Ochoa muttered his third "Fuuuck . . . ," she said, "Wynn's shooting came the night before Nicole's murder. I want you to get on Customs and the airlines for names of passengers arriving from the Paris airports to JFK or Newark last Wednesday. Don't forget connections through London and Frankfurt, and wherever. Run the manifests through the database for any names that are on the watch list or show priors for assault or weapons busts. Do the same with Interpol."

"You think it could be the same killer?"

"I don't know what I think, but if there's any chance it was a hit by one person, it's worth clearing. I don't love the different MO, but he may have used a knife on Nicole because he couldn't travel with a gun."

"Yeah, and a gun is so hard to find in New York," said Detective Ochoa. "But I'll get rolling on it." He cleared his throat and said, "Now I guess it's on me to tell you some not so good news."

"Let's have it."

"It's the glove."

"No fingerprints?"

"Worse. No glove."

"What?"

"Captain Irons just called in from the lab. He went there this morning to bang on doors for results, and somehow, it got lost." The vacuum of silence on her end was so complete he said, "Detective Heat, you still there?"

All she said was "Somehow?"

Rook said, "Somehow?" with the same shading of disbelief when he got back to the room and she told him about it. "I don't think somehow is the reason. I think it's more like someone."

"And he's off."

"How can you say that?"

"Because I knew this would propel you into Area Fifty-one. Rook, for once, can you try doing what I do for a living and deal in hard facts instead of indulging in wild speculation?"

"Want to talk facts, Nikki? All right, fine. Exactly how often does key information go missing in an important homicide investigation?" She just stared at him. "OK, forget I even asked that. But come on, this is different. This has spook written all over it."

"Or incompetence."

"When I hear that word, I only think of one man. The man of Iron."

"Guess I'll have to wait until I get back to suss that out." She unwrapped the paper around one of the ham and cheese baguettes he'd returned with. But Rook's brain crackled too much to eat. He set aside his sandwich after a single bite and paced the room. When Nikki saw him tapping madly on the screen of his iPhone, she said, "I hope you're playing Words with Friends with Alec Baldwin, because if you're still in foil hat mode over this lost glove, let it rest."

"I'm off the glove—for now. I'm searching my contacts."

"What for?"

"You may like to play it fast and loose with the facts," he said, teasing her with her own words to him, "but as an investigative journalist with not one, but two, Pulitzers on his mantel . . ."

"Two, you say." She took another bite.

". . . I like to verify facts independently." He stopped scrolling. "Ah, here we go."

"All right, Mr. Woodward—or is it Bernstein?—what are you planning to verify?"

"I want to confirm what Tyler Wynn told us about being CIA and running your mother through his Nanny Network. To me, everything he said made perfect sense. In fact, I felt a certain vindication in his story. I don't know if you could tell that or not."

"I had an inkling. So whom are you going to verify this with?"

"An old deep-cover source of mine from when I was researching my Chechnya piece for *First Press*. His name's Anatoly Kijé. This guy's incredible. Straight out of *Tinker, Tailor*. An old school Russian spook for SVR—which is what the Russian Foreign Intelligence Service calls itself now instead of KGB. Everybody's rebranding. KGB, KFC . . ."

"Rook."

"Sorry. Anyhow, my boy Anatoly lives here in Paris, and if anyone would know about Tyler, your mother, and anything else going on in that network, he would. In fact, he may be able to shed light on those questions Tyler Wynn had the bad manners to die before he answered. May he rest in peace."

"All right. Assuming this KGB guy—"

"SVR guy."

"—knows anything, why would he share it with you?"

"Because during the course of our meetings here in Paree, let's just say Anatoly and I spent a lot of time together closing bars. We were like this." He crossed two fingers then tapped the call icon on his phone. "To this day, I can't get a hangover without thinking of him." He held up a palm to quiet her, as if she were the one doing all the talking.

"Hello, is this Imports International?" He gave Nikki a knowing wink. "Yes, hello. I would like to speak to your branch manager, please, Mr. Anatoly Kijé. Yes, I'll hold." He whispered to Nikki, "Transferring to his assistant." Then he said into the phone. "Hello? Let me see, is this Mishka? . . . No? Oh, you must be new. It's been a while. My name is Jameson Rook and I'm an old friend of Anatoly Kijé's. I happen to be in town and I was wondering if he— Rook. Jameson Rook, that's right. I'll hold—"

Rook got kept waiting on hold long enough for Nikki to finish her baguette. Long enough for him to weary of pacing and sit in the corner chair. Then he stood suddenly. "Hello? Yes?" And then a frown crossed his brow. "He did? Really. Are you sure? I'm so sorry. Yes, good-bye." He hung up and flopped back in the chair.

Nikki said, "Don't tell me he got shot, too."

"Worse. He said he never heard of any Jameson Rook."

With answers that solved at least one part of the mystery of her mother's life and no new leads to follow in Paris, Heat and Rook reserved seats for a flight home the next morning. The chaos and incompetence visited upon her elite squad had much to do with Nikki's drive to get back to New York. Captain Irons embodied the worst aspects of civil service. He always had been a paper pusher with a badge, but now, with his own command and Detective Heat out of the mix, the Ironman's blundering ways ran unchecked. Sure, sometimes evidence like gloves got lost. And media leaks wreaked havoc on cases. And occasionally, the worst detective in a squad slept his or her way to a level of responsibility that surpassed competence. But these things rarely converged all at once in a perfect storm of serial bungles. Even if her leave remained in force, Nikki reasoned that proximity would at least give her a fighting chance to stem the damage before the case of her life got trashed.

True to form, Rook suggested that they try to unplug from work for their final night in Paris. Nikki asked, "You mean, like try not to be too mindful of the fact that we watched a key witness die before our eyes this morning?"

"There ya go," he said. "And if it helps, I'm not above digging up the old 'Tyler would have wanted it that way' chestnut. And judging from those photos in that keepsake box, he wasn't one to let a good time go to waste."

Heat agreed to the mental night off. In fact, she welcomed it—but only if Rook let her treat him to dinner for their REWOTC (Romantic Evening While Off The Case). "Even for me, these acronyms are starting to blur," he said. "But you're on."

She took him to Le Papillon Bleu, a hidden treasure on a side street in Le Marais where locals dined by candlelight on fresh mussels and clams from Port du Belon while they listened to accented American jazz performed live. A stunning young French reincarnation of Billie Holiday sang "I Can't Give You Anything But Love" with a voice that almost made them forget Louis Armstrong's version. Well, almost.

They ordered aperitifs, and after Rook surveyed the menu and pronounced the place quite a find, Nikki gave him the unasked-for assurance that it was her first time there. "You mean this hasn't been boyfriend tested, boyfriend approved?"

"On the contrary," she said. "Of course, I had heard all about Le Papillon Bleu, but ten years ago, as a student, I didn't have enough money to eat in a place like this."

He took her hand in his across the crisp white linen. "So this qualifies as a special occasion."

"Count on it."

They walked off their meal wandering hand in hand past the quaint shops of Le Marais. With the jazz singer's "Our Love Is Here to Stay" and "Body and Soul" still floating in their heads, they ended up at the Place des Vosges, an immaculately maintained square surrounded on four sides by historic brick-faced homes with elegant blue slate roofs. "This place looks like the rich uncle of Gramercy Park," she said as they followed the path into the garden.

"Yeah. But without the sneak attacks by rug-wielding cops." As soon as he said that, they heard a shoe crunch on gravel behind them and she turned abruptly. A lone man hobbled along the sidewalk outside the park on a bad leg and continued on, whistling to himself. Rook said to her, "You need to relax. Nobody's going to bother us. Not on our big ROTC."

"ROTC?"

"Hey, I give. At this point, I'm just throwing out capital letters in any order."

They had the park to themselves, and she led him to a bench under the trees, where they sat in the shadows together, nestling against each other. The city traffic floated like distant white noise, merely blocks away but buffered by the uniform row of stately buildings surrounding the square and the gentle splash of fountains. As they so often did, without a word or a signal, they leaned into each other at the same time and kissed. The wine and the warm April evening scented by night blooms and his taste released Nikki from the weight of her cares and she pressed herself against him. He encircled her with his arms and their kiss grew in its intensity until they both parted lips, breathing hard as if suddenly remembering that, to live, they also needed air.

"Maybe we should take this back to the hotel," he whispered.

"Mm-hm. But I don't want to move. I want to freeze this moment." They kissed again, and while they did, he unfastened the top button of her blouse. She reached for his lap and held him. He moaned, and she said, "You know, I don't think my New York credential would help me beat an indecent exposure."

"Or a lewd act in public," he said, slipping his hand in her bra.

"OK, I know we can make this much more interesting back in our bed. Let's do it."

They crossed through the park in silence, arms slung around each other's waist. As they walked, he felt her shoulders and biceps tauten slightly. He said, "As long as you insist on thinking about the case, why don't you tell me what's on your mind? Maybe we could find some kinky way to incorporate it into foreplay. With handcuffs, of course."

"You could tell?"

"Please. I'd like to think I'm more to you than diverting wit and arm candy. But it's OK if you're preoccupied, I know this is big."

"Sorry. Something from today keeps bugging me. Something I know

I've overlooked, and I'm reaching for it but I can't grasp what it is. That's not like me." Her reply was only partially true. Nikki did have a feeling of missing a step and it did pester her. But she only offered him that as a cover to avoid the deeper, more personal issue she had been mulling all day.

Rook yanked her hip to bump his, to shake her up. "Give yourself a break. You've had a lot coming at you." The nod she gave in the dark read to him as noncommittal, so, as they strolled on, he continued, "I mean, beyond the obvious mill you've been through this past week, some of the things you learned about your mother . . . ? Those are going to take you a while to digest."

"Yeah, I know." She felt her throat constrict and swallowed hard, which didn't seem to do much good. How could Rook know her so well, be so attuned as to see through her armor? To get it—that it wasn't really the murder case per se she was stuck on at that moment. But he didn't know the depth of it. Rook couldn't know that right then, she wasn't walking through a storybook park across from Victor Hugo's home, holding him while he hummed "Stardust" off-key. In her mind, she was back in that hospital room feeling relief that her mother had been working as a spy to serve her country, only to have the rug pulled from under her by the words she couldn't shake.

She could still see Tyler Wynn regarding her from his pillow. The old CIA man saying her mother was one hell of a spy. And how "the sense of mission it gave her fulfilled her like nothing else could. Not even her music."

Nikki completed the rest of the thought herself: Not even me.

Tires screeched. Light blinded her and shook her from her reverie. She and Rook were getting ambushed—boxed in at the street corner— sandwiched between two dark Peugeot 508s with blacked-out windows and their high beams frying them.

Rook moved quickly and instinctively, sliding to step in front of her. But footsteps approached from behind them, too. Heat pivoted to see the man from before, the whistler, rushing toward them, his bad leg miraculously healed. Four others—two muscle men from each car— converged from both sides, grabbing for them. By reflex, she reached for her hip. But her gun was back in New York.

In a flash, two of them enveloped Rook and dragged him to one of the vehicles while a third man appeared from the passenger seat and pulled a cloth sack over his head. Heat dodged the first of the other pair when he reached for her, but the one coming up from behind, the whistler, bagged her head, also. Disoriented and surprised, she felt the powerful arms of the other two goons wrap her up in a bear hug and lift her feet off the sidewalk. Nikki kicked air, squirmed, and hollered, but the big men had her overmatched.

They bundled Heat into the backseat of the other car and wedged her between their wide shoulders when they got in. Her shouts mixed with the scream of rubber on pavement as the Peugeot accelerated. The car had started roaring up the block, when she felt a sharp stab in her upper arm.

TWELVE

When Heat woke up, she couldn't move her body. She tried to figure out where she was. It was too dark to see, but she knew that she was lying on her side, nearly fetal. Her knees felt cramped, pulled up to her chest as they were, but when Nikki tried to extend her legs, she couldn't; the soles of her shoes were up against a solid wall. A shiver ran through her. This was exactly the position in which she had found Nicole Bernardin inside her mother's suitcase.

Her arm itched where the needle had pierced her, but when she tried to reach for it to give it a scratch, something stopped her. Heat didn't need to see to know what caused that. She was handcuffed.

To find out how much range of motion she had, Nikki gave the cuffs a tug. And then came a bizarre sensation that made her wonder if she was hallucinating under whatever drug they had injected her with. The handcuffs . . . tugged back.

"Oh, good, you're awake," said Rook. "Can you do me a favor? Your right elbow is digging into my ribs."

Still foggy from her sedation, it took Nikki a moment to process all this. Wherever she was, Rook was there, too, wedged beside her. Or under her. Or a bit of both. She drew in her right arm as close as she could to her body. "How's that?"

"Heaven."

"Rook, do you know where we are?"

"Not sure. They gave me something to knock me out. I felt a little prick."

"Would you stop?"

"Sorry. I think it, I say it. Anyway, judging from the scent of steel-belted radial, I'm guessing we're either spooning the Michelin Man or we're locked in the trunk of a car."

Heat detected neither motion nor an engine idling. Then she tried to envision the space as best she could with no light. "Do you know if these cars have inside trunk releases?"

"I don't. Not sure whether French safety regulations mandate them or not," he said.

"Let's feel around for anything like a lever we can pull. Spare me the jokes, please." They both tried to move their hands but were snagged. "Rook. Are we handcuffed to each other?"

He didn't answer but paused. Then he gave her cuffs a jerk. "Awesome."

She ignored him and ran her fingers over her wrists to assess the situation. "Feels like the chain of my cuffs is looped through the chain of yours. Is that biting into your skin?"

"A little, but not so bad. I had actually fantasized about a furry number with some leopard print, but I'll take it."

"Shh, listen."

From outside came the sound of a car slowly approaching over gravel and squeaking to a halt. They heard footsteps and muffled voices then the chirp of a remote followed by the thunk of the latch popping. The sudden rush of fresh air smelled like grass and woods. Hands reached in to unlock their cuffs, and they got hoisted out by the same men who had captured them.

Standing on unsteady legs, Heat shielded her eyes from the high beams of the Mercedes and tried to build an escape plan. Rook got set down beside her and rubbed his wrists. She could sense him making calculations, too.

It didn't look promising. Only two of them, unarmed and weakened by their injections, in some unknown woodland at night, versus four brawny thugs who had already demonstrated pro skills and were also probably carrying. Then there were however many more stood by in that idling car. Nikki waited there, inhaling the BO and cheap cologne of her captors, and decided to ride it out, hoping an opportunity would present itself—and that this wasn't the same crew that handled Tyler Wynn.

She flashed a be-cool palm at Rook, and he dipped his head in acknowledgment. Then both turned their attention as the passenger door of the Mercedes opened and another big fella got out. This one opened the back door for a shorter, thickset man in a snap-brim cap who moved around to stand in silhouette before the headlights while his bodyguard waited a yard to the side. The man removed his cap and said, "You wanted to talk to me, Boy-O?"

"Oh. My. God," said Rook. "Anatoly!"

The man in the headlights took a step forward with his arms wide, and Rook rushed toward him, which made Heat tense up, but nobody tried to stop him. The two men embraced, unleashing a volley of back-clapping, laughing, and saying, "You dog" and "No, *you* dog," repeatedly to each other.

When the effusiveness of their reunion settled down, Rook called out, "Nikki, it's Anatoly. See? He really does know me." He put an arm around the other man's shoulder. "Come on, there's someone I want to introduce you to. This is—"

"Nikki Heat, yes, I know."

"Course you do," said Rook. "Nikki, say hi to my old friend, Anatoly Kijé."

The Russian extended a hand that felt callused to her shake. The Mercedes driver killed the engine and dialed down to parking lights, and as her eyes adjusted, Heat got a better look at Kijé. He had the squat, blocky physique and weathered bulldog face that would have fit well on the reviewing stand beside Brezhnev at a May Day Parade in Red Square. His hair, unnaturally black for a man his age, was fronted by a jelly roll lacquered by enough spray that his hat had not made a dent. Under a coarse hedge of artificially black brows his eyes were playful, those of a perennial ladies' man. Nikki had seen many guys like him in the States, but instead of snatching people off city streets they installed custom pools and stone decks on Long Island and in Jersey. She wondered, did they also clean carpets?

"It is a pleasure to meet you."

"You sure went to enough trouble," she said. "If you had just called, we could have met you at a café."

"I apologize." The spy made a slight bow and then gently released her hand. "This is what you call abundance of caution. It is how, in my line of work, one lives to be sixty years old."

She said, "You mean as an importer and exporter?"

"Ah," he said with a laugh, pointing at her. "I like this one, Boy-O. She has some stones, yes?"

"Oh, yes."

Anatoly checked his watch and made a quick survey of the woods. "Tell me, Jameson, so we don't press our welcome here tonight. What did you need to discuss with me? Another article you will get a prize for and I get nothing?" He laughed.

Rook said, "I'm looking to verify some details about an old network that may have been run here in Paris. Now, you know my rules, Anatoly. I won't compromise national secrets or jeopardize anyone's life, but that shouldn't be a problem because I believe this particular operation is inactive."

"Let me make a guess." He smiled at Heat as he spoke to Rook. "That it might have something to do with the work done by the mother of your friend here."

"Wow. Clairvoyant," Rook said.

"I had some idea. And why waste time dancing when we can get right to business." There was a noise in the woods, probably just a branch falling, but Kijé caught the eye of one of his bodyguards, and a pair of them slipped into the night to investigate.

"So my mother was involved in clandestine work of some kind," said Nikki, trying to bring him back to the subject.

"Most definitely. I first became aware of her when I was stationed here in '72 as an agricultural liaison at the Soviet embassy."

Rook fake-coughed, "KGB."

"Always a wise guy, this one. I love it." He shadowboxed at Rook's gut, then turned back to her. "Does that answer what you wanted to know?"

"Depends. On how much you're willing to tell me." She held his gaze in a way that said I want more and you know it. "And seeing what you put us through getting here . . ."

"Everything's a trade-off, isn't it? The price of my peace of mind is to help you find yours. What else would you like to know?"

"My mother was murdered."

"I am truly sorry."

"It was ten years ago in the USA. But you already know that, don't you?" He didn't reply. She said, "I'm trying to find out if it was connected to her spying."

"Nikki Heat, let us not insult each other's intelligence. You already believe it is connected. What you want from me is to tell you how." He paused and said, "I honestly don't know."

"Anatoly Kijé?" she said. "Boy-O? Please do not insult my intelligence. You know."

"I know rumors. That's all. And, if true—if," he said, pointing a finger in the air for emphasis, "it could have come back upon her in a very unfortunate way."

Rook said, "Come on, what did you hear?"

Anatoly became distracted momentarily as the two bodyguards returned from their perimeter check and signaled all clear. Slightly more relaxed, he said to Nikki, "There were rumors that your mother became a double agent."

Heat was already shaking her head emphatically. "No. She would never do that."

"Well, she wouldn't do it for me, and believe me, I tried." A twinkle shined in his roguish eyes. "But people do turn. Some for ideology, some for revenge, some are blackmailed. Most, I find, simply do it for the money. The real answer is always found not in the heart but in the bank." Heat still shook her head in denial, but he pressed on. "You asked the question, *dorogaya moya*. The perception, true or not, about your mother hinted that she had some 'extracurricular' contacts and activities."

"But I'm telling you," said Nikki, "she never would have gone to work for anyone but the United States."

"People don't always align with another government. There are other entities, you know. The last decade has become a new era for tradecraft." The gruff Russian spook, who had no doubt ordered (and probably even administered) his fair share of back alley beatings and terminations, took on a wistful look at the mention of this new era. She could envision how an old-school spy like him would be an inconvenient fit among the more outwardly refined operatives who ate sushi, did yoga, and hacked what they needed from underground computer nerve centers.

But Kijé survived, if uncertainly. The bloated hide of his face told her he coped with his unsure future in the world order by cracking open a bottle of Stoli. Heat was more interested in the information she needed. "What do you mean by other entities?"

"I would say, ask Nicole Bernardin. But you can't, can you?"

"What do you know about Nicole Bernardin?"

"I know that, just like your mother, Nicole became involved with people outside the strict margins of her government's scope."

Rook jumped in again. "For argument's sake, what if her mother had turned?" He could almost hear the adrenaline rising in Nikki's veins, so he added, "Or if it just looked like she had—would CIA act on that?"

"Not likely," said the Russian. "Well, not on American soil."

"Who would?" asked Heat, aware of the possibility it could have been the man standing right in front of her.

"Kill her?" He shrugged. "As I said, these are changing times. It wouldn't have to be a government at all, would it?"

"Could it be the same as whoever hit Tyler Wynn?" asked Rook.

"Who knows? Either way, it's a sad lesson about the nature of the trade. You can never really retire. I, myself, tried retiring once. It went poorly. That is why I have to meet people like this." He gestured to the forest and the night.

"Even old friends?" asked Rook.

"You kidding, Boy-O? It is old friends who can be the most lethal of all."

Nikki said, "You must know some of the projects my mother was working on. Nicole, too."

She had conducted enough interrogations to tell by the way his eyes rose in his lids, to ponder, that he did know, and he was weighing how much to reveal to this friend of Jameson Rook—and daughter of a CIA operative. Then she lost his attention.

Kijé cocked an ear to the darkness. Soon the bodyguards did, too, straining at the horizon as wolves did for signs of food. Or danger. Heat and Rook also listened, and soon heard them muttering, "*Вертолёт.*" Rook translated for her, but by then, Nikki heard it herself. Helicopter.

She tried to draw Kijé back to her, but the ignition of his Mercedes was already turning over. "What are some of the extracurriculars you're talking about?" His bodyguard opened the back door of the car and held it open for him.

The little bear pumped Rook's hand and gave him a fast back slap. "Boy-O, until next time, right?" And then he bowed to her. "Nikki Heat."

Doors started slamming on the two Peugeots behind them as the other guards saddled up. Nikki's frustration mounted as the clock ran out for the second time just when she was so close to getting an answer. Kijé hurried to the side of his car. "Anatoly, please. At least give me a direction."

"I told you. Check the bank," he said and ducked to get in the back-seat.

"I already got that. Give me more to go on. Please?"

He stopped and his head rose up over the open door. The Russian said to her, "Then think of what else I told you. Ask yourself about the new era." That would be all she got.

The bodyguard shut Anatoly's door and took the shotgun seat for himself. All three cars drove a semicircle around them, kicking up a rooster tail of dust. The trailing Peugeot slowed to leave a gap for Kijé's Mercedes to fill in the hammock spot of the convoy, and then they sped away with their headlights doused.

Heat and Rook tasted the fine cloud of dirt that swirled around them, illuminated by moonlight and shrouding them in a radiant fog. When it began to vanish, Nikki saw a reflection on the ground near them and found their cell phones stacked there, each with the battery removed to disable GPS tracking. As they reinstalled them and powered up, the heli-copter passed and continued on, seeming uninterested and unhurried. Nikki paused to watch it fly, eclipsing the Paris moon. She noticed that at least it was half-full.

Nikki Heat saw the next night's half moon rise behind Terminal 1 at JFK when she and Rook piled into the backseat of the town car he had or-dered for their ride to Manhattan. In spite of Nikki's misgivings about leaving New York for Paris, Rook had been right. The brief trip had moved both cases forward. Not enough for Nikki—never enough for

Nikki—but the tantalizingly incomplete information she'd gotten over there would fill critical spaces on both Murder Boards. What nagged at her was where to go next. One avenue Heat knew she needed to explore pained her, but she took the step to address it right that moment.

"Hey, Dad, it's me," she said when Jeff Heat picked up. To put a cheerier spin on things she added, "What are you doing at home on a big Saturday night?"

"Screening my goddamned phone calls so I don't get any more ass-hole reporters calling for interviews."

"Oh, no. Has it been that bad?"

"All hours. Worse than the freakin' telemarketers. Hang on." She heard ice cubes tink against glass and painted the mental picture of her father situated in his easy chair command post taking the edge off it all with another Cape Codder. "Even that bimbo from the *Ledger* showed up at my front door the other morning. Must have snuck in behind one of the residents before the gate closed. Those jerks have no regard for privacy."

"Yeah, we all know reporters are scum." Rook whipped his head her way. Then, on quick reflection, the journalist nodded his agreement. "Listen, Dad, are you going to be around tomorrow? I wanted to swing by to talk some more. I've learned a few things I think you'd be interested in knowing about Mom." That, along with asking him to go over the box of photos Lysette Bernardin gave her, presented a valid excuse to drop by. But her real plan was to use the occasion to broach another subject best left for face-to-face. They agreed on a time for the visit and said good night. Nikki tapped end, feeling bad for not being straight with him about her ulterior reason for wanting to talk. She wondered if her mother had felt those kinds of misgivings when she withheld information from them. Then she wondered if Rook had been right, after all, about becoming her mother in that regard, too.

Detective Ochoa had left a recent voice mail from his number at the Twentieth Precinct. "Surprised to find you in the pen tonight, Miguel," she said.

"Someone has to take responsibility for this case while you and Rook drink wine and eat snails, know what I mean?"

"Well, I'm done slacking. We're back in town and I'm ready to bail you boys out of whatever mess you made of things."

Detective Raley popped onto the extension and said, "Did you bring me anything?"

"You're working, too, Sean? I only hope I can get back in there soon enough to watch Captain Irons's head explode when he sees the OT report."

"Hey," said Raley, "the Iron Man actually made an appearance here himself tonight."

"Irons? On the weekend?"

Ochoa said, "Yeah, he came in with Detective Hinesburg about an hour ago. The two of them closed the door to his office and listened to some audio recording on his speaker phone and rushed out like they were in a big hurry."

Raley said, "I told Ochoa they were probably calling Moviefone for the show times of *Hot Tub Time Machine*," which made them all laugh, but any Irons activity raised a yellow flag for Heat, more so if it involved Sharon Hinesburg.

They ran down the day's developments for her. "I finally got confirmation from French authorities on that call the Bernardins said they got last Sunday evening from the mysterious Mr. Seacrest," Detective Raley began. "It came to their number as an international call, but unfortunately, it was a burner cell, so that trail ends there."

Heat's disappointment mixed with relief that Emile Bernardin's story about the call checked out. Of course, she would have preferred that it lead her to Seacrest, but in the end, upholding the credibility of Nicole's parents pleased her. "Did the glove turn up?"

"Negative," said Ochoa. "If you promise not to tell, we have a Plan B there."

"Tell me first and then I'll tell you whether or not I'll promise that."

Ochoa paused then said, "Detective Feller is going off-road. Even though Irons put himself in charge of anything that even smells like it will break the case . . ."

"Including the glove," added Raley.

"... Feller is calling in some old IOUs to do some indy snooping at Forensics to see what he can scare up about the fate of that thing."

Raley said, "You know what Feller is like. All that time on the street with those swinging dicks in the Taxi Unit? He's not wired to color inside the lines."

"So he's ignoring his commander's direct orders?" asked Heat.

"Yup," they said in unison.

"It's a good thing I'm on forced leave. I'd have to do something about that."

When she hung up, Rook said, "Who's dissing Wally Irons, and when can I shake his hand?" But before she could answer, he noticed they were pulling off the expressway at the Van Dam exit. "Excuse me, driver? Aren't we taking the Midtown Tunnel?"

"Closed down. They shut it for earthquake repairs."

Nikki looked out the back window but saw no cones, no flashing lights or portable orange construction advisory signs. "Are you sure?" The traffic behind them stayed on the LIE and flowed onward, at speed, toward the toll plaza at the mouth of the tunnel.

The driver crossed Van Dam and made a U-turn onto a side street fast enough to pin her shoulder against Rook's, then hooked another turn onto a service road leading into an industrial zone of double- and single-story auto body shops and warehouses.

Rook asked, "Don't you want the BQE to the Williamsburg Bridge?"

But the driver didn't reply. The power locks snapped down, and he made another sharp turn into a driveway and through the open double wide door into the receiving area of a trucking fulfillment depot. The driver got out, leaving them in the car as the steel double doors rolled down behind them, putting the whole place in darkness. Once more, Heat reached for her hip, found it empty, and cursed to herself.

"I'll tell you one thing," said Rook's voice in the dark. "This is the last time I use this car service."

A single fluorescent lamp blinked on and cast sickly blue light down on two men in business suits who descended the ramp slanting from the back of a cargo trailer across the warehouse. They walked calmly but purposefully in matching cadence to their car. The ghosty illumination of the overhead tube caused the whiteness of their shirts to pop in contrast to their suits and ties. As they neared, the one in the brown suit held up his ID and slapped it against the window for them to see.

It read, "Bart Callan, United States Department of Homeland Security."

Heat and Rook sat on folding metal chairs in the cargo trailer watching a pair of lab technicians in white coveralls at the deep end of the hold swab the exterior of their luggage with wipes that they placed in portable infrared scanners. After each cloth got electronically sniffed, it was then sealed in an evidence-grade plastic zip bag. The techs had followed the same procedure with the swabbing pads they had run over their hands and shoes. "Not being one to jump at criticizing the federal government," said Rook, "but aren't you supposed to do that *before* we get on the plane?"

Agent Callan turned from the scanning table and strode over to him. He looked like he did triathlons because marathons got too easy. "You can save the snappy one-liners for your next appearance on Anderson Cooper, Mr. Rook. Although you won't be commenting on this meeting there or anywhere, as it is classified. I have a paper for you both to sign." He slipped his hands into his pockets and rocked on his heels, body language for stud in charge.

Heat turned to appraise Callan's partner, who sat to the side, observing. There was something the other agent didn't like in the knowing way Nikki smiled at him, and he averted his gaze. She turned back to the alpha. "What is this about, Agent Callan? I'm sworn law enforcement. You have no reason to detain me."

"I guess you don't get to make that determination, Detective Heat." His tone was matter-of-fact, not threatening. He seemed too secure in himself to bully. He had the sort of authority that came from personal dedication instead of ego. But he also clearly enjoyed dealing the hand from his own deck. "I have some questions I want answers to. We'll see how satisfied I am and how soon, and we can talk about getting you on your way."

Rook couldn't resist. "Good, because I want to get to the Apple store in SoHo before it closes, to see what this new iPad device is all about."

Nikki gave Callan one of those shrugs that says *What are ya gonna do?* and the agent acknowledged it with his first hint of a smile. He leaned a hip against the metal task table he had set up as a work space inside the trailer and picked up a file. "Two days in Paris. That's what I call whirlwind."

"You said you had a question," was all Nikki gave back.

"You going to wrestle with me, Detective?"

"Your meeting, Agent."

Rook rubbed his palms together. "This is so cool. It's like a mixed martial arts smackdown. We even have folding chairs."

A standoff followed while Callan assessed her. For Nikki's part, she normally wouldn't give so much push-back to a fed, but it felt instinctively right. Aside from lingering annoyance at their kidnapping, she had a protective motive about her mother since hearing the rumor that she might have gone double. And frankly, there was too much she didn't know. Heat figured that by making the DHS man do some work, she might gain more than she gave.

Bart Callan shifted techniques from chatty open-ended to business-specific. "I want you to tell me who you saw and what you did while you were in Paris."

"Why?" asked Rook.

"Because I'm asking. And I'm asking her."

To see what she could draw out of Callan, she said, "Maybe if you could narrow it down for me. Is there someone or something you're interested in? We packed a lot into two days."

This had become a chess match between two experienced interrogators, and Agent Callan knew his game had to play up to hers. He tried a new tack, to see how she reacted to being dwarfed by a larger force. Paranoia was a primary tool for bumping interview subjects off base. Casually turning a page in the file, he read, "Subject B: 'I didn't kill him. You did. You killed him.' Subject A: 'Would you please stop saying that?' Subject B: 'But you did. I hope you're happy now.'" Heat fought making eye contact with Rook because she knew that was the rise Callan wanted. The agent continued, "Subject B: 'I'd think you'd be ecstatic to learn that not only wasn't your mom's double life just your imagination, but it wasn't because she was having an affair. And—how cool is this?—she was a spy in the family like Arnold in *True Lies*. No, even better: Cindy

Heat was like Julia Child in World War Two when she spied for the OSS.'"

"How dare you," said Heat. She regretted her blurt instantly but couldn't help herself. The introduction of her mother was bait and she had chomped it.

Agent Callan rolled on, picking at the sore spot. "Subject A: 'I agree, that is something.'"

"I knew that cabdriver was skeevy," said Rook. "What did he do, record us all the way from the hospital?"

The DHS agent smiled and turned to another page. This one, from Brasserie Lipp. "Subject B: 'Let's run down your list of hot buttons: Petar? Don? Randall Feller? . . . You named three. Is that about it?' Subject A: 'Rook, are you seriously asking me my number?'" Callan riffled a few more pages and gave Heat and Rook a once-over. "You really think that's all we have?"

By then Heat had settled down and distanced herself from the personal intrusion to regain ground. "Well, then if you have all you need, you don't need us."

"I want to know about all your meetings. What were you doing in the Vincennes Forest last night?"

"So. You don't have as much as you make out," she said.

"I am seeking your cooperation. We're wearing the same uniform, Detective."

"If we're on the same team, you give me something. Like, for instance, what was Nicole Bernardin doing before she was killed and who was she doing it for?"

"Not playing that game," said Callan.

"Who wanted her dead?"

"Give it up, Heat."

"Who's Seacrest?"

"I ask the questions." He used his command voice, but the tell was all over his face when she mentioned the name. A micro flinch of increased vigilance.

"Are you Seacrest?"

"This dog won't bark."

"Then we'll talk when it does," said Heat. This was the hardest of hardball, but with the stakes she was playing for, Nikki would bare-knuckle it to the bitter end. The agent seemed to get that, and shifted to Rook.

"I'll ask you. Who did you see and what did you discuss?"

"Those are private matters. I am hereby claiming the protection of my rights as a journalist under the U.S. Constitution."

He switched back to Heat. "So, for the record, you are refusing to cooperate with an official national security investigation?"

"Of course I'd cooperate with an official investigation," she said. "But an official, bona fide investigation would walk through the front door, not resort to carjacking and intimidation. This is official? All I see is a rented warehouse and two cowboys in a trailer with a science kit. If this is official, Agent Callan, go through channels at One Police Plaza and I'm all yours. Otherwise, it's you, me, and a throwdown with some folding chairs."

Agent Callan closed the file and tapped his thigh with its edge while he chewed the inside of his mouth. He glanced at his partner, who only nodded. "Very well," he said. "Go." But as they collected their luggage, he added, "Oh, and Rook. You can claim protection under the Constitution. But let me warn you. Considering what you two are messing in, you may find that protection sorely lacking."

They decided to eat in that night. Heat wanted to work and they both craved some of Rook's famous pasta carbonara. As Nikki pored over notes at the dining table in his loft, Rook got to slicing and dicing on the other side of the counter. "Do me a fave?" he asked. "Careful where you step. My little Scotty dog statuette that lives on the table by the couch may be an earthquake casualty. It's MIA—Missing in Aftershock."

"Oh, poor Scotty . . . I'll keep an eye out." She bent and walked the area without finding it, and ended up in the kitchen. "Mm, bacon smells great. How soon?"

"When the water boils. And please, do not watch that pot."

Too late. She was already reaching for the lid. "Seems like a lot of water."

"On the Food Network, Alton Brown specifically says not to cook pasta in less than a gallon." He took the lid from her and replaced it.

"Why don't I grate my Parmigiano-Reggiano while you relax and find a killer. Deal?"

While he cooked, the squeak of her marker on the whiteboard they had nicknamed Murder Board South mixed with the chop of his chef's knife on the Boos Block. "Pop quiz, Rook. What have we learned from our DHS carjacking?"

"You mean, besides that automobile travel with you is repeatedly fraught with peril? We've learned that we are on to something. Otherwise, you don't get that kind of attention."

"Including eavesdropping on our conversations and tailing us in Paris. You did recognize Callan's partner, didn't you?"

He looked stumped but tried to cover. "Uh, sure. He . . . I have no idea."

"Wake up, Rook. He was the guy in the blue suit outside the café the other morning acting like he was killing time rolling his own cigarette. Did you see how he looked away tonight when I made him?"

"Ah . . . sure I did," he lied.

"Homeland Security is nervous about something. And for all their snooping, our interrogation tells me whatever that is, they still haven't cracked it."

"No kidding. Every question he asked told us what they don't know. And did you see his face when you mentioned Seacrest? And what's with the swabs?" He looked through the steam rising from the pot to see her circling "DHS Swabs?" on the whiteboard. "So what's got them operating at DEFCON One?"

"I don't know, but I say, let's keep doing what we've been doing because it's working."

He fanned the spaghetti in the roiling water and gave her a self-satisfied grin. "You mean like going to Boston and Paris?"

"Yes," said Nikki. "Those were great ideas I had, weren't they?"

"Brilliance," said Rook, "brilliance."

Jeff Heat's socks matched, which pleased his daughter, who wasn't ready to witness his decline just yet. Maybe the advance overnight notice had given him a chance to better prepare for the visit this time. But while he sat beside her on the couch in Scarsdale that afternoon, going through the box of old photos, she noticed that even with the pressed khakis straight from the dry cleaners, a springy pastel sweater, and a fresh shave, her dad looked many years older than his age.

Every time he paused on a photograph, Nikki would ask, "Anything?" and he would shake no but hesitate again before dropping it in the discard pile. It didn't take long for Nikki to understand what was happening. Jeff Heat was not recognizing any of her mother's contemporaries; he was stopping to dwell on the shots of the woman he had fallen in love with. The divorce had made Nikki overlook the possibility that he would enjoy those shots. But why not? They were not only part of his life, they might have been from the best part. She made a mental note to get some of the pictures scanned and make an album for him.

"Here's one I recognize. Eugene Summers. He's the butler now on that asinine TV show," he said, holding up a group shot of her mom, Tyler Wynn, and a young man who now, decades later, had his own hit reality series playing himself as a manservant to the young slacker of the week. "Think I even took this picture."

"I love that show. You know Eugene Summers?" asked Rook.

"Not really. Just met him once over in London. Liked the guy at first, then he kept correcting everything I did. He even took the handkerchief out of my suit pocket and refolded it. Can you believe that?"

"Cool," said Rook, earning a withering glance from Nikki.

"Why were you in London, Dad?"

"Your mother, why else? Cindy had a tutoring job there the summer of '76. What a time to be stuck there. Worst heat wave in decades. And a drought. And how crazy to be in England during the Bicentennial of kicking their royal asses." He tossed the picture of Eugene Summers into the discards.

Nikki, who had seen the photo but hadn't made the connection to Summers, set it aside as a reminder to contact the reality star. "Do you remember who she was tutoring?"

Her father laughed. "Sure as hell do. The kid of some big millionaire brewer over there. Good beer, too. Durdles' Finest. That's how I remember." He licked his lips, which made her sad. "Largest exporter to Ireland. No wonder the SOB was rich. If you can't sell beer in Ireland during a heat wave, hang it up."

His attention waned as they reached the bottom of the toile-covered box, which he did without making any other identifications, except the numerous shots of Nicole Bernardin. "Sorry I couldn't be any more help," he said.

Nikki repacked the photos, taking her time to be careful with them, but also, in truth, to procrastinate. There was a difficult subject she would be broaching soon. But first, she had a question. "People I've talked to asked me if Mom had something she tried to hide."

"Her other life," he said with a scoff. "If she was spying for the CIA like you say, great. But it still shut me out. And, by the way, just 'cause she was spying doesn't mean she wasn't also having an affair with that . . . ," he gestured to the box that Nikki had just put the lid on, "smooth operator, Wynn. Maybe he was the attraction." She didn't have anything to say to that and considered the best course would be to nod and leave it for him to work out his anger his own way. The CIA news hadn't been the cleansing tonic she had hoped for. Part of what he said, she had to admit, made sense. Spying and an affair weren't mutually exclusive. In her own relief—and, perhaps, wishful thinking—Nikki hadn't thought to question it as he had. Perhaps because they had different agendas. She was seeking to absolve Cindy Heat; he wanted reinforcement of the injustice he'd suffered.

Rook had been trying to stay out of the way, but he spoke up to help steer things back on topic. "Nikki, wasn't it more like something physical they were talking about hiding?"

"That's right. Dad? Did you ever see Mom trying to hide an object or did you find something around that didn't make sense?"

"Like what?"

"I'm not sure. It could be a key, a videocassette, a blueprint, an envelope. The fact is, I don't know. But did you ever stumble on something that made you say, what the heck is this?"

She heard him sucking his teeth, and his eyes got the same downcast look she'd seen when he admitted he had hired that private investigator to follow his wife. Her father excused himself then returned from his bedroom after five long minutes of drawers and cabinet doors opening and slamming. "This is the thing I found that made me hire Joe Flynn."

Rook said, "Joe Flynn. He was your PI?"

Jeff Heat nodded and handed Nikki the small velvet bag. As she took it from him, she experienced the kick in her chest she always got when a dead case felt like it might be getting some legs. Rook felt goosed, too. He slid forward on his armchair and tilted his head up as she opened the drawstring. "It's a charm bracelet," she said as she shook it out into her palm. Rook got up and stood beside her father to get a better view. It was simple, not very expensive. A gold plated link chain with only two charms on it: the numerals one and nine. "Who's it from?" she asked.

"I never knew."

"Didn't Mom tell you?"

"I, ah, never told her I had it. I was too ashamed. And she never asked about it. So when the private detective said things were all clear on the affair front, I decided not to tempt fate, you know?"

"Sure, I get that." Heat turned the numbers over to inspect them but saw nothing unusual. "Do you mind if I keep this?"

"Take it." And then he whisked a hand at her like a broom. "Take it away." Nikki studied her father and didn't see age anymore, but the toll of secrets. Then she wondered what her mom's face would look like if she were alive.

"Oh, listen, one more thing before we go." Nikki stepped into the awkward subject with a light touch, trying to ignore how much her duplicity made her feel like her mother's daughter. But the difficult question had to be asked, especially after the Russian had made such a point of it the other night in the Bois des Vincennes. "You held on to all of your bank records, right?"

"Yeah . . ." Even though his financial background made him a records pack rat, Jeff Heat's reply carried a timbre of uncertainty that was about as straightforward as her question. Reminding herself that the information she sought was to clear her mother of the double agent rumors, Heat pressed on with the anvil she had to drop.

"Any chance I could see them?"

"May I ask why?" She saw more than wariness in him. It was more like something she had seen so often in suspects during interrogation: fear of discovery. But he wasn't a suspect, he was her father. Nikki didn't want to break him down, she only wanted information. So she went right for disclosure.

"I want to know if Mom had any accounts that were separate from yours. Secret, sort of like this." Heat held up the velvet pouch with the charm inside. "An account you didn't know about until you stumbled on it."

The silence that followed got broken by the ringing phone on her father's side table. Nikki could see that the block letters on the orange field of the caller ID read, "NYLedger." Her dad saw it, too, and waited out the four rings without answering. By the time the phone had dumped silently to voice mail, he'd come to a decision and said, "It is like that damned bracelet. I asked her about it. I said, why the separate account, and she said for mad money, independence. It's the thing that first got my gut twisting that there really might be another man." The way he looked at her broke Nikki's heart. "Do you really need this?"

Heat nodded grimly. "It may help me find her killer," she said, hoping that would end up being the only significance of the secret account.

He gave it a moment of thought then wordlessly disappeared again to the back hall, this time to the second bedroom. Rook gave Nikki an affirming smile that did little to make her feel any better. When her dad returned moments later, he carried a brown cardboard accordion file with an elastic strap around it. He didn't come to Nikki with it, though. He stood by the front door and waited. The two of them joined him there and he gave her the file.

"Thanks," she said.

"Tell me something, Nikki," he said in a low, hollow voice. "What makes you any different than that other cop who came here to disrespect me?" He swept an arm toward the phone with its blinking message light. "Or those reporters?"

Her eyes began to sting. She spoke the truth, and meant it. "The difference is that I'm trying to help."

It offered him no comfort. Her father said, "I think it might be a good idea for you to give me some space for a while." Then her dad retreated to the back hall so they could let themselves out.

Their usual ride would have been in Heat's motor pool Crown Victoria, but since she was stuck on leave, they had taken a car Rook had rented. That's how he ended up as the lucky duck to endure the stop-and-go braking of the Sunday caravan back to Manhattan by weekend day trippers. He had prepared himself for a silent, moody ride but Heat had immersed herself in full work mode. Rook considered the emotional slap Nikki had just gotten from her father and, reflecting on her emotional wall, was glad for her sake that she had the capacity to seal herself on the good side of it, if only temporarily.

From the passenger side, Heat made a quick pass of the bank file, eyeballing the sparse amount of paperwork and monthly statements in it. "These are incomplete," she said. "My mom only carried a balance of a few hundred dollars, with just enough activity to keep the account active, but the statements abruptly come to an end without any sign of the account being closed."

"When's the last statement you see?"

"October 1999. The month before she was killed." She got out her phone and did some scrolling until she came to Carter Damon. As she listened to his phone ring, she wondered if the former lead detective on her mom's case would be too pissed to talk to her after their last encounter. "Detective Damon," she began her voice mail, using his former rank as an olive branch, "Nikki Heat. Hope I'm not disturbing you on the weekend, but I wanted to ask you a question about the old case and challenge your memory about a bank account." She left her cell number and hung up.

For guilty pleasure and to cement their return to the good old USA, they turned in the car then went to a local favorite of Rook's called Mudville9 for an early dinner of barbecue wings and Prohibition Ale. They chose a table near the TV showing the local news, so they could catch up on the progress of the earthquake cleanup, which, the scrolling text under the official in the hard hat said, was 95 percent complete, with a price tag in the millions. Rook dipped a fry in his extra Buffalo Wow sauce and started to ask Nikki how he'd look in a hard hat. "Not for safety, mind you, but as a fashion choice." But she had become so suddenly riveted to the screen that he turned back around to see what had caught her attention.

A blazing headline graphic filled the top of the wide screen: BREAK-ING NEWS: POLICE ARREST KILLER IN FROZEN MURDER CASE.

THIRTEEN

Rook asked the bartender to turn up the volume on their TV so they could hear the breaking story, which didn't go down so well with the *Sunday Night Baseball* fans, but he and Nikki didn't care. They stood under the big screen, their wings forgotten and growing cold on the table behind them, as they gaped up at the New York cable news channel.

The reporter stood outside a length of caution tape in a city street and spoke to the camera. Underneath him the graphic read: "Live, from Hell's Kitchen." Pressing the earpiece to his ear, he nodded, picking up his cue from the anchor. "Thanks, Miranda. Yes, a major break in a case that has been the talk of New York this week, ever since the frozen corpse of an Inwood woman, the victim of a fatal stabbing, was found inside a suitcase on a food delivery truck." He turned and gestured behind him, and the camera slowly zoomed to show the front entrance of a tan brick apartment building, where an NYPD uniform stood guard. "You can see it's quiet here now on West Fifty-fourth Street, but that's the doorway of the building where, minutes ago, officers and detectives of the NYPD stormed the apartment of an alleged killer."

Next came recorded footage of Captain Irons standing with his gut to the crime scene tape, in his glory, with his name plastered on the screen and a sea of microphones pointing at him. "Our suspect's name is Hank Norman Spooner, age forty-two, a self-employed apartment sitter. Mr. Spooner was apprehended without incident by myself and Detective Sharon Hinesburg from my precinct, the Twentieth, as well as officers assisting from Midtown North."

Rook said, "This gets better every minute." Heat didn't respond; she just stood transfixed as Irons answered one of the questions shouted at him from the press frenzy.

"The suspect came under our scrutiny this weekend after one of my team received an anonymous phone call expressing regret for the murder of Nicole Bernardin last week, as well as for the death of another victim, Cynthia Trope Heat, in 1999." Nikki flashed back on Roach's account of the giddy Saturday night appearance of Irons and Hinesburg listening to an audio recording behind closed doors. Reporters shouted more questions all at once. "That's right," answered the captain, "the caller implicated himself in both murders and said he couldn't live with it anymore. His call contained sufficient detail about both crimes that we felt assured he was our man and, upon tracing him to this address, made tonight's arrest. He is currently in custody up in the Twentieth Precinct, and is in the process of making a formal confession. May I say that the citizens of New York City will sleep better tonight, knowing we have taken this individual off the streets, and I am proud to have led the team that brought this case to a safe and swift conclusion. Thank you."

Heat's cell phone rang. It was Ochoa. "What about a heads-up?" she snapped. Not even a hello.

"Hey, I'm just hearing about it myself. Captain iced us all out. Except for Hinesburg, nobody had a clue. I'm calling you first off to make sure you knew. I guess you did."

"Oh, Miguel, I'm sorry I flared."

"No sweat. It blows, we all get it. I'm heading in now to see what's what and do as much damage control as I can. I'll keep you posted."

"Do," she said and hung up. Nikki threw down enough cash to cover the check and tip and started for the door. Rook was already holding it for her.

On the walk back to his loft, he said, "I wonder how many items on the Kama Sutra menu Big Wally scored by mentioning Hinesburg on TV."

"Save it, Rook."

"Hey, I'm pissed, too. This is how I cope."

"Then cope with your inside words. I'm not up for conversation now." But then after three strides, she said, "He's screwing the whole thing up. No, worse than that. What scares the hell out of me is that he's just getting started screwing it up. I'm out of there less than a week, and he's not only got the wrong guy but he's potentially doing irreparable harm to these cases."

"Then stop him."

"How?"

They waited at the crosswalk, and he stepped to face her eye to eye. "You know how."

"No," she said. "I told you I would never do that."

"Then, fine. Let Wally be the bull in the china shop while you watch it on TV." The light turned and he walked on. She caught up with him.

"I hate you."

"Inside words," he said.

The next morning, Heat arrived ten minutes early for her seven o'clock coffee meeting with Zach Hamner, hoping to use the time before he showed to quell the upset she felt at stooping to see the weasel. But when she walked into the café near One Police Plaza, he was already finishing off a combo breakfast consisting of a Denver omelet, home fries, bagel and cream cheese, juice, and an espresso. Hamner didn't rise when she came in, just gave her a nod and pointed to the chair across from him. "You're early," he said, checking the time on his BlackBerry.

"I can wait outside and you can finish your meal." She had told herself on the subway ride downtown that she wouldn't be snarky with him, but Zach Hamner made it hard to resist. The NYPD senior administrative aide to the deputy commissioner of legal affairs liked to swing his dick, and Nikki figured it got all its length from his title. Every transaction, large and small, was a power play to him, and forcing her to come all the way down to the Cort Café, for a conversation they could have easily completed the night before on the phone when she'd called him, constituted a command appearance to prove who swung the longest rope.

Zach pretended to be oblivious to her annoyance. "No, I can eat while we talk. Coffee?"

"No, thanks."

He finished his bagel, making her wait out his chew while he surfed new e-mails on his phone. Heat conceded that Zach "The Hammer" Hamner had cause to be unhappy with her. And, clearly, this ceremony of disrespect was payback for the political capital she'd cost him two months before. That was when she'd stunned the Police Commission by declining the promotion he had engineered for her to take command of the Twentieth Precinct.

When he took his sweet time to flick a sesame seed off the sleeve of his charcoal pin-striped suit, she almost walked out. In these few short minutes of proximity, the viscousness of his world—a power broker's bazaar of trades and leverage—brought back the agony that had sent her fleeing from the bump in rank. This was why Heat had refused to call him when Rook mentioned it the week before. But now, with Irons in danger of blowing up her mother's case, Nikki knew she had no choice but to suck it up and acquiesce.

And so did Zach Hamner.

He set his BlackBerry to the side and said, "So. Trouble on Eighty-second Street?"

"As I said last night on the phone, I'm on mandated leave at the worst possible time. Captain Irons engineered that, and now that I'm sidelined, he's bigfooting both of my investigations and putting them at risk."

"And one of them's your mother's homicide, right?"

He knew that already, but she played along and swallowed it. "That's why I'm asking for your help."

"I tried to help you once before and that didn't go so well."

"Let's be honest, Zach, you would have been helping yourself with my promotion, too."

"Enlightened self-interest. You can't hitch your wagon to a star without creating one." He flashed a mirthless grin and let it drop. "I misjudged you, Heat. You pissed on me in public."

Fulfilling her role in the transaction, she said, "I'm truly sorry if I caused you trouble," and watched him process those words: the entire reason for the trip.

"OK, then," he said, satisfied to get the deference he wanted. "Wally Irons. Tough one. They love him at One PP. His CompStats are stellar."

"Come on, Zach. His CompStats versus The Hammer?"

He liked the sound of that. "Your cell phone charged? Good. Stay aboveground this morning so I can reach you."

"Thanks for this."

"Oh, hey, listen," he said. "Let's understand ourselves here. You'll get a chance to thank me. The bill will come due someday." He slid the check for his breakfast across to her. "And it'll be a lot more than just this." Then he left without a good-bye.

Two hours later Detective Heat might have entered the bull pen of the Twentieth Precinct to applause, but she got ahead of that. Nikki had called Roach and told the two of them to pass the word to keep her return low-key. Zach Hamner warned her that Irons had to choke down the orders from the top of the food chain and not to rub his nose in it. But The Hammer had worked his magic getting her reinstated, with the sole face-saving bone thrown to the captain that she agree to return for a follow-up with the shrink for the blowup in his office. "That's all I have to do?"

"For them," Zach had said. As if she needed to be reminded of his banked IOU.

She dug in immediately by having Hank Norman Spooner brought up from his holding cell to Interrogation One while she read the confession he'd written the night before. The suspect also had a rap sheet that she studied. In the nineties he had worked as a security guard but got dismissed following complaints for petty thefts in the offices he patrolled and for stalking several females in the apartment buildings he'd been hired to protect. Spooner did probation and suspended sentences for those and had been served with several orders of protection. He also had a peeper charge in Florida from when he had worked as crew on a cruise ship, which had constituted his sporadic employment for much of the prior decade. He did ninety days plus probation for that; otherwise, no other jail time.

Nikki asked Detective Rhymer if anyone had checked Spooner's cruise dates against the murders, and when he said no, she gave him that assignment and wondered how the hell Wally Irons could have gone on TV and called this an investigation.

The inevitable confrontation with her precinct commander came as she put her old friend, the Sig Sauer, in the lockbox in the hall outside Interrogation One. "Welcome back, Heat." She spun the combination and turned to the voice. There he stood with Detective Hinesburg at his elbow.

"Captain." Brevity, she thought, was face saving's best friend.

"What's going on here? I understand you called my prisoner up."

"Yes, sir," said Heat, keeping things deferential. "I have a few questions to ask him. I also have one for you. Any news on that missing glove?"

"Nada. And I've been a thorn in the butt of Forensics."

Detective Hinesburg chimed in. "Immaterial now, isn't it? Now that we've got our man."

Hinesburg's stupidity might have been amusing to Heat in a *Real Housewives* sort of way if the detective didn't do so much damage. "And what about the guy I shot who wore that glove? Does 'our man' have any bullet holes, or did you notice?"

"No," Sharon said, "I'd definitely notice that."

Irons interceded on behalf of his detective-slash–secret girlfriend. "Obviously, we're not talking the same person, Heat. Which is telling me your shotgun shooter is probably from another case altogether. An old grudge. Like maybe a holdout from that death squad that tried to get you in Central Park last winter."

Detective Heat could see this was going nowhere good and looked to move things along. "Guess we'll see. Excuse me."

"Hang on," said Irons. "We already got a signed confession, why you going in there?"

She held up Spooner's file. "Captain, with all due respect, everything in his confession is public knowledge. Every detail has appeared in magazine articles like Rook's one about me, news reports, news leaks . . ." Nikki managed not to look at Hinesburg, whom she was certain had also sourced the numerous follow-up stories to her first leak. The latest reports had even given away critical media hold backs, such as the railroad grime on Nicole's clothing and the matching precision stab wounds in the backs of her mother and Bernardin.

Irons waved both palms at her. "Whoa, let's get to this flat out, Detective. Published or not, this guy confessed to it all. And you should be happy 'cause it takes your dad off the list. So what's on your mind, going in there? Is it our job to get the guilty off, or to get them off the street?"

"It's our job to get the truth. And that is precisely what I have in mind. Because if this man is lying to get his moment of fame, or whatever, the killer is still out there. Now let me do my job. Because if you arrested the wrong guy, would you rather find out now or when the DA throws your case out at a press conference?"

Nikki loved watching Wally's eyes widen at that notion. "OK, Heat. You've got one shot. Take it. I'll be watching."

Hank Norman Spooner's eyes lit up when Detective Heat entered the air-lock door into the interrogation room. A smile that felt a little too grand to Nikki greeted her as she took her seat across the table from him. She said nothing, just let first impressions enter, unfiltered. These always proved valuable, and to absorb them, she shut out everything else: the stakes of the case; the upheaval of the week-plus since the freezer truck; the audience of Irons and others behind the mirror. For Nikki Heat, it always came back to Beginner's Eyes.

He hadn't shaved but still managed to appear clean-cut. His sheet put him at forty-two, but she would have subtracted seven years. Attribute that to the slight build and the boyish face. And the hair. Neatly trimmed and parted, it was red. Not red in the bright sense but softer. Auburn. The day's growth of whiskers had a blonder hue, making them disappear on his cheeks which, she noticed, had begun to blush as she studied him. And he still smiled that too-friendly, too-familiar grin. His teeth had some yellow in them, and he knew it, judging by the way he kept his upper lip. His hands were folded on his lap under the table, so they would have to be read later. To Nikki, hands were the best tells, second only to the eyes. His stayed on her, expressing what she could only call bliss. And the eye contact was good. Like the smile, too good. Her beginner's impression got borne out by his opening sentence.

"I can't believe I'm meeting the real Nikki Heat."

Hank Spooner was a fan.

She decided not to acknowledge that and maintained a clinical distance, turning her attention down to his file. The fan card could be played later, if needed. What she wanted right then was to listen and to learn. If this was indeed the killer, Nikki wanted to pick up the bits of information that would tell her that. If he wasn't, she needed to pay attention for the inconsistencies to get to that, too. Heat did what she did in every interview: set aside her bias and paid attention.

"I have some clarifications I need regarding your statement."

"You got it."

"But first, I want to understand your background."

"Name it, Detective."

"You had some trouble on one of your jobs as a security guard."

"It was really a misunderstanding." His manacles clanked as he brought his hands up to gesture. She wasn't surprised to see that his nails were immaculate, and his slender fingers were clean and lightly freckled like the skin under his eyes.

"These charges say you stole from the offices you guarded and stalked women in the apartments you patrolled."

"As I said, all a misunderstanding. I did borrow some electronics, you know, computers and a printer, but intended to return them."

"And the stalking?"

He put a hand over his heart. "I learned the hard way, when you are a lowly apartment security guard, it's best not to ask residents on a date."

"You had three restraining orders."

"That's what I mean about the hard way." He fixed her with his grin again, and she put her nose back in the manila folder.

"And for about ten years you've worked on cruise lines?"

"That's right. Well, off and on."

"What sort of work?"

"Bit of this, bit of that. I worked casino operations staff doing slot maintenance. Also did some time on deck operations. You know, prepping chairs, handing out towels, lifeguarding."

"You got fired from your cruise in 2007."

"Only because I refused to accept a reassignment to work as bartender. I have a severe citrus allergy." Heat looked up to stare at him at length for the first time. He fidgeted under her fixed gaze and explained himself. "That's right. And you try to mix a drink on a tropical cruise that doesn't have a lemon, orange, or lime."

"Never heard of that," she said.

"That was the reason, no lie. As a kid, I almost died from anaphylactic shock, so I said no way, and they fired my ass."

Nikki mulled that over and went back to the rap sheet. "I thought you'd been put ashore because you were caught spying on a female guest."

"That was on another ship. And all I did was check her stateroom for fresh towels. Her word against mine, and who do they believe? The paying guest or the grunt in the white uniform?"

"And how have you made ends meet between cruises?"

"I do some dog walking, a lot of apartment sitting. Oh, and I have a blog now."

"Blogging? How well does that pay?"

"Not so much yet. But I'll get there. I'm also on Twitter. I hear I've gone bat shit with followers since I got arrested."

Easing into a new phase, she smiled at him and said, "You're going to be pretty famous yourself, I guess, Hank."

"Think so?" He beamed upon hearing his name from her. "Not like you, Detective Heat. And you're not even on social media."

"Not my thing."

"You should do it. You'd trend off the hook. Seriously, you're a real hero. I'll bet I've read everything there is about you." Nikki pulled out his confession and, from its contents, bet Hank Spooner had indeed become quite the expert.

"So you say you killed Cynthia Heat?"

"Your mother."

"How did you kill Cynthia Heat?"

"It's in there."

"Tell me."

"I stabbed her. One time. In the back."

"Where was she?"

"In her apartment near Gramercy Park."

"Where in the apartment?"

"In the kitchen. She was making pies."

"Nicole Bernardin. How did you do that?"

"I stabbed her."

"How many times?"

"Once. Same way. In the back."

"And where was Nicole?"

He paused slightly. His first hitch. "Waiting for a train."

"Where?" The railroad connection had been leaked in one of the articles and this was her attempt to shake him with detail.

"Larchmont."

"PD up there says no blood on the platform."

"It's in there," he said with a gesture to the confession. "I said she was buying a ticket at the machine near the parking lot. And it's rained a lot since then." He gave her a satisfied look as if he had seen through an attempt to trip him up.

Over the next hour, Heat tried to knock him off his declaration either by misstating things he'd written or by rapid-firing questions about details out of order, knowing that most liars adhere to sequence as their means of sounding credible. He nimbly adjusted to everything she threw at him, and Nikki pictured Irons behind the glass, gloating. Spooner had just finished describing the front of her building in Gramercy Park when she said, "We have more to talk about, but I'm going to get something to drink. You thirsty, Hank?"

"Well, sure," he said with that smile nearing adoration.

As she passed through Observation One, Irons rose from a chair. "What's going on? Aren't you satisfied yet?" She just smiled and stepped out the hallway door, so he turned to Raley and Ochoa. "She always like this?"

"Always," said Roach.

Hank Spooner perked up again when Heat returned a few minutes later with two cans of soda. She popped the tops, took a sip of hers, and set the other in front of him. He just stared at it. "Something wrong?" she asked.

"Do you have anything else?"

"Sorry Hank, this isn't McDonald's. What wrong with it?"

"Nothing, unless you're trying to kill me." He slid the orange Pellegrino as far away as he could reach. "I told you. I have a bad citrus allergy. One sip of that, and I'm in the hospital or dead."

"Oh, sorry. Wasn't thinking. I love them. Keep my own stash in the fridge here." She picked up his can and her own and walked toward the door.

"You're good," he said. When she turned and gave him a puzzled look, he continued, "The orange soda. You were just testing to see if I was lying about my citrus allergy." He gave her a wink. "Nice one."

"Busted," she said.

When she entered the Observation Room again, Irons said, "Well, are you satisfied he's our killer?"

"No."

"How can you not be? His story's solid as a rock."

"So what? Like I said, it's a story anybody could have put together from public knowledge."

"But like *I* said, the man confessed."

"Sure, because he's got some sort of fame psychosis or stalker agenda he's working out and I'm the lucky object of his desire. Leave that to the shrinks. He's lying, and I can prove it."

"How? He answered all your questions."

"True, but there's one hold back on this case that didn't get leaked. And it's my own. Whoever killed my mother took a can of soda from our fridge right afterward and gulped it down." She held up the orange San Pellegrinos. "It was one of these. Sixteen percent real citrus juice." As it registered on Irons and he turned to gawk at Spooner through the glass, she said, "You can book Allergy Hank on whatever you want, but my mom's murder? Forget it."

Captain Irons stood gaping through the ob window at his prize suspect when she left.

Detectives Raley and Ochoa were at their desks when Heat came back into the Squad Room, and she corralled them to the back hallway, out of earshot of the rest of the bull pen, and closed the door. "Sorry to go all Deep Throat, but I need this handled with discretion."

"Want me to get Sharon Hinesburg so she can join us?" said Ochoa.

"Do," she said. "And let me put Tam Svejda from the *Ledger* on my speaker phone." After they had a good laugh, Heat opened up the accordion file of bank documents her father had given her. The two detectives' faces sobered as Nikki briefed them on the account her mother held in secret from her dad. "I can't go into the significance of it, but I need someone I can absolutely trust to quietly—but thoroughly—trace its activity. Especially in November 1999."

"Done," said Raley, taking the documents from her.

"And if he blabs," said his partner, "I'll cap his ass."

"He would," agreed Raley.

The three emerged from the back hall, and Nikki found Rook camped at his squatter's desk off to the side of the bull pen. He pointed to the shield and Sig on her hip. "Nice to see you wearing your tin again and packing, Sheriff."

"Feels right," she said. "Not quite Paris, though."

"Look at it this way. Not as much dog crap to step in."

"Elegant. You're a wordsmith *and* a poet."

Heat called together a quick Murder Board roundup. Detective Rhymer reported that his checks with the cruise line showed Hank Spooner had not been away at sea during either killing he confessed to. Even though Nikki had eliminated Spooner from her mother's murder, she decided to go beyond thorough and assigned Detective Hinesburg to make sure he got held in custody until his whereabouts could be verified for the night of Nicole Bernardin's stabbing. Then she sent Sharon on a field trip to Westchester County to survey the Larchmont train station herself and to show pictures of both Nicole and Spooner around. The alibi check went to Malcolm and Reynolds.

Heat very much wanted to bring the squad up to speed on the information she and Rook had learned about her mother's and Nicole's CIA activities, but her tight little ship had sprung too many leaks. She had already confided in Ochoa, so her work-around would be to also brief Raley, Feller, Malcolm, Reynolds, and Rhymer individually—not the transparency Nikki liked to operate in, but that's what happens when the boss is sleeping with a team member with a Bat Phone to the Metro desk at a tabloid.

After the meeting broke, Nikki listened to a call-back message from Eugene Summers, the young man in the 1976 London picture with her mother and Tyler Wynn. When she asked Rook if he wanted to come along with her to meet him for lunch, he got so excited that he shook his moneymaker right there in the bull pen.

"God, will you look at me back then?" said Eugene Summers as he examined the old snapshot of himself. "Good lord, and the width of that tie. Margaret Hamilton could land her broom on it and still have room for three flying monkeys." He handed the photo back to Nikki. "I loved your mother, you know. Those were great years, and Cindy was absolutely special."

Nikki thanked him for saying so, while he took a sip of iced tea, avoiding eye contact with the other lunchers at Cafeteria who recognized him from the cable TV show that had made the real-life butler a breakout sensation in his sixty-first year. After decades as a professional manservant in Europe, Eugene had gotten a call from a studio head he had served during a summer in London, who had an idea for a TV show like *Arthur*, pairing the fastidious and urbane Mr. Summers with various unruly young celebrity stoners. Thus was born *Gentlemen Prefer Bongs*, whose success transformed Eugene into America's ex officio arbiter of taste and propriety in everything from grooming to etiquette to wine pairing.

In his message, when he had called her back from his Chelsea loft, Summers seemed thrilled to have heard from Cindy Trope's little girl and agreed to meet for lunch. Rook couldn't have been happier, too. Not only was he addicted to the series, but on the way to the restaurant, he had said to Nikki, "What do you think the odds are this is going to be one of those cases where the butler did it? Because I could sell that story to any magazine in the country just for the headline."

Of course, when they met at his table, Nikki heard the obligatory praise about how much she resembled her mom. Rook, who regularly hobnobbed with Hollywood A-listers and blockbuster music icons, just grinned like a dope as he shook hands with the reality star. Heat prayed he wouldn't embarrass her by asking her to take a photo of the two of them.

They began on a somber note with Eugene's condolences to Nikki for the loss of her mother, and his disbelief at the deaths of Nicole and, now, Tyler Wynn. "I got a call about Tyler when I woke up Sunday morning. I'm still reeling." He made a brave face and sat tall. "However, I am reminded of the words of Oliver Wendell Holmes, who said, 'Good Americans when they die, go to Paris.'"

Nikki found it interesting that he was still in the loop. "May I ask who told you about Wynn's death?"

"Not by name. Let's say a mutual acquaintance."

"Were you and Tyler Wynn close?" she asked.

"Once. But we hadn't seen each other, oh, in ages. But he's a man you hold in your heart."

Heat said, "I guess this leads us to where I want to start. Were you part of this Nanny Network of Tyler's that my mother was in?"

"Not that I don't want to cooperate, Detective, I do," said Summers, "but you put me in an awkward position."

"You took an oath not to divulge secrets?" asked Heat.

"Oath or not, I'm preternaturally discreet. It's not just professional, I have personal standards." Then he saw her disappointment. "But despair not. For Cindy's daughter, I can bend the rules. I'll speak in generalities. Or use non-denial denials. For example, to the question you just asked, my answer is that I'm sworn not to say. And that tells you exactly what you want to know, doesn't it?"

"Good enough," said Nikki.

Summers noticed Rook absently playing leapfrog, as he often did, with his knife and spoon, and fixed a chastening look on him. Rook ceased and said, "Wow, just like the show. Did you see, Nikki? I just got the Summers Stare." Then he pleaded to the TV butler, "Give me the catchphrase. Come on, just once? Please?"

"Very well." Summers arched a brow and delivered a haughty "How uncouth."

"Effing awesome." Rook laughed with glee but settled when he saw Nikki stare, and said, "Continue. Please."

Heat formulated a question according to the rules. "Let's say—*if* you had been in this network—would you recall the names of some of the enemies whose homes became infiltrated?"

"*If* I had working knowledge of that network I'd probably take a wild guess and suppose that not everyone spied on was an enemy. Intelligence-gathering is often back channel, so the subjects of surveillance might just as likely be diplomats or businesspeople ripe with information. Or merely social friends of an enemy."

"And what about my mother? If you had been in a position to know, would you know the names of the subject homes she infiltrated?"

"Sorry. If I had known such information I didn't retain it. And that's flat-out true. I would have had my own full plate."

"What about when this picture was taken in London? Was she there to spy on her patron family?"

"Again, I can't say."

"Same for Nicole Bernardin?"

"Afraid so."

Rook said, "Can I play this word game, too? You said *if* you had known such information, you didn't retain it. *If* you were in a position to find out what a fellow spy was working on, how would you guess that you—or *someone*—would do that?"

"Well played, Mr. Rook."

"I have a headache," he said.

"I would imagine, like any close friends in their twenties moving about Europe, social contact would be important. No Twitter back then. So systems probably developed. Mail and phone calls would be out of the question due to surveillance, so I would *guess* . . . ," he paused and winked, "that enterprising kids would communicate their whereabouts and sensitive information through a series of unorthodox secret mail stashes. Let's call them drop boxes."

"A drop box," repeated Rook. "You mean like a loose brick in the town square with a chalk mark on it?"

The famous butler pinched his face into a sour grimace. "Oh, please. That is so Maxwell Smart."

Nikki asked, "How, then?"

"I suppose," he said with another wink, "that each member might have had his or her own signature drop and might find unique means to communicate its secret location so the bad guys couldn't figure it out."

Images surfaced in Heat's mind of her mom's and Nicole's ransacked apartments. Plus the phone call to the Bernardins from a Mr. Seacrest looking for a package. "If you had such knowledge, would my mother or Nicole have drop boxes other than in Europe? Let's say—hypothetically—here in New York?"

"That I wouldn't know. I would have left the network by then—*if* I had been in it in the first place." Another wink, why not?

"When might that have been, if you'd left it?" Rook asked.

"Late nineties." Then he added with a chuckle, "*If.*"

"Would you have still been in Europe when her mother was killed?"

"That's where I was when I heard the news, yes." Summers thought some more and said to Rook, "Did you just ask me for my alibi?" Then he turned to Nikki. "Is that what this was for? To check me out as a suspect?"

"No, not at all," said Heat.

"Well, it feels like it to me. And I have to say, as someone who came here out of respect and in good faith, that I am insulted. If you wish to speak with me again, it will be along with my attorney. Excuse me." Heads in the restaurant turned from red pear salads and chicken and waffles as Eugene Summers scraped the feet of his chair from the table and stormed out.

Rook leaned down and plucked the butler's napkin off the floor. He held it up and said, "How uncouth."

Nikki flipped to a fresh page in her spiral and made a note to have someone check the whereabouts of Eugene Summers on the murder dates. If only to dot the i on the if.

Heat had just finished double-parking her Crown Victoria on West 82nd with the other double-parked undercover cars outside the precinct, when Lauren Parry called her on her cell phone. "Got a second, Nikki?" Her voice sounded constricted and low. Something was up. Nikki waved at Rook to go inside ahead of her and leaned on her car. "This is not a good news call, Nik," said her pal, the medical examiner. "I really, really have to apologize."

"What's up?"

"It's the toxicity test on Nicole Bernardin. It's ruined."

"You're going to have to help me here, Lauren. I've never heard about a tox test getting ruined. What's that mean?"

"Just what it sounds like. Something went wrong in the lab. You know how we put blood and fluids through tests using gases to screen for chemicals and toxins in the system of the deceased?"

"If you say so."

"Well, that's what we do. And somehow, the gases got screwed up. The supply of pressurized gas canisters that got delivered was contaminated, and now we cannot lab Nicole's body chemistry. I feel awful. Nothing like this has ever happened before."

Nikki said, "Don't beat yourself up. Unless you are the one responsible for gas delivery. You aren't, are you?"

Lauren didn't chuckle. Instead she said a sulky "No."

"Then when you get your gas supply situation cleared up, just run her tox test again from other samples."

"I can't, Nikki, that's the thing. This morning Nicole Bernardin's body was cremated at the request of her parents and sent back to France."

In spite of Heat's disappointment and frustration, she reacted to her friend with a feather touch. Nikki told Lauren not to dare to take it personally, and that she would be in contact later about a follow-up investigation since this had a fishy quality, particularly in light of the lost glove at Forensics.

Detectives Rhymer and Feller were her free team at the moment, so when she got into the bull pen Heat told them she wanted to see them immediately for an assignment. But then she saw the light blinking on her desk and checked her voice mail first.

The message was from Lysette Bernardin calling from Paris, in tears. Between her anguish and her accent Nikki had to strain to understand her message at first, then it suddenly became chillingly clear. Mme. Bernardin and her husband Emile wanted to know how this could happen. How in the world could someone cremate their daughter's body against their wishes?

FOURTEEN

etective Ochoa came to Heat to thank her for not assigning him the toxicity lab investigation at OCME. "Even though Lauren and I are in a relationship, I want you to know I could deal, if you put me on it. But the doc takes a lot of pride in her work, and she's wicked upset right now. I'm just as glad to have Feller and Opie handle it so I can just be her shoulder, know what I mean?"

"I get it, Miguel. Hey, look at me, working my own mother's case. I think we both know how to shut out our personal feelings."

He frowned. "Didn't say I could do that. But good for you." And then before he walked on, he added, "I guess."

Nikki gathered the troops to get some new assignments rolling. Her squad made a smaller circle with Hinesburg away in Larchmont and Detectives Feller and Rhymer off covering OCME, but Heat was eager to regain momentum her first day back, so she decided not to wait for a full house.

On the walk from his desk, Detective Raley put his hand up and said, "I just got some news you might be interested in." Nikki's heart skipped, fearing he might slip and make a public report on the bank account she had asked him to keep low-key, but Sean Raley knew better than that. "For the last few days, I've been surfing traffic cam archives along East Twenty-third and I finally scored a hit." He handed her a color still. "This is at Third Ave, just after that maroon van tried to snowplow you and Rook."

"This is the van." She could see Rook craning, so she held it up for all to see.

Rook said, "Sure is. Too bad the cam didn't get a shot of the driver."

"I know," said the King of All Surveillance Media. "And the plate's a stolen. But check out the side of the van. Righty-O Carpet Cleaners.

208

Don't get too excited, the name's bogus. So's the phone number." He consulted his notes. "It's listed to some business called the Pompatus of Love."

Rook said, "Oh, right, that hotline where sex goddesses fulfill your wildest fantasies. As long as you have a valid major credit card." He caught Nikki's look and added, "Or, so I've read."

Raley tapped the photo with his pen. "I'm betting this is the same van that was parked outside Nicole Bernardin's when her place got tossed."

"Let's find out," said Heat. "When Feller and Rhymer get back, have them run the pic up to Inwood to show their power walker eyewit. If it's a match, put it out as an APB. Nice work, Sean." She smiled and added, "It's good to be king." As Heat posted the shot of the van on the Murder Board, she said, "Malcolm and Reynolds."

"Yeah, I see our initials up there beside 'cremation,'" said Reynolds.

"I want you to find out where that order came from. Now, I don't need to tell you this is about as serious as it gets. Not just because somebody messed with our case, it's a desecration that brought tremendous heartache to a bereaved family." The partners could read how deeply Nikki felt this and managed to say they'd handle it without adding their usual gallows humor. The embargo didn't last long.

Detectives Feller and Rhymer came into the bull pen from OCME, and Malcolm said, "Hey, look who's back. The gas masters."

Reynolds jumped in, "That was fast. What, you both have a tail wind?"

And they were off for several rounds of gas ribbing. Nikki knew better than to fight a room full of guys lapsing into locker room adolescence, so she waited them out, clocking one minute on her watch. "OK, OK, now I'd like to hear their report."

Ochoa said, "Hey, guys? I think she wants to move on. That is, if you *culos* are done venting."

Following a chorus of "whoas," Feller and Reynolds reported that the contaminated gas didn't end up at the coroner's by mistake. They explained that the medical examiner's toxicity lab receives scheduled deliveries of pressurized gas tanks from an outside supplier for its tests. But the morning of Nicole's lab workup, the delivery truck got stolen and used by someone to deliver the tainted supply of canisters.

"How come nobody reported the truck stolen?" asked Rook.

"Because it showed up back in the lot with its original load an hour later," said Rhymer. "They figured it for a joy ride."

Feller added, "And when the real driver made his usual delivery, it was a different shift at OCME, so they just unloaded it and kept them as spares. Nobody said anything." He shrugged. "Flaw in the system."

"That someone exploited and sabotaged Nicole's tox test," added Heat.

Rhymer asked, "Why would someone go to all that trouble?"

"Same reason they'd order the cremation of the body," said Rook. "To hide something in the results." He saw they weren't looking at him like he was so nutty this time, so he continued. "But what?"

"And who?" asked Heat. "I want to find out who."

"I'll take point on that." The roomful of detectives turned to see Captain Irons in the doorway. "Heat, your crew has its plate full. I'm going to handle this one personally." Then he left, leaving no room for debate.

Feller said, "Guess after his Hank Spooner screwup, Wide Wally is trying to prove his worth."

"Or pull his weight," said Ochoa. "Good luck with that."

Much as she didn't care for his leadership, Heat didn't abide public contempt for a precinct commander. "A little respect, all right?" That was all she needed to say to shut that down.

Detective Rhymer asked her, "What do you suppose is going on here, Detective? First the missing glove, then the bad gas, then the body gets cremated."

"It's no coincidence, we all know that." She and Rook made eye contact, both thinking the same thing: that the hand of CIA, Homeland Security, or even some clandestine foreign agency might be orchestrating this. Nikki wondered if this was the time to share what she'd learned in Paris with the rest of the group. Then Raley spoke up, and the decision got made for her.

"Does anybody else think it's weird that we never got a match on Nicole Bernardin's fingerprints? I mean, here she was, a foreign national without prints on file?"

Malcolm joined in. "Odd, indeed. Especially since back in 2004 the feds changed immigration regs to make even permanent legal residents get printed. So how did Nicole skip that biometric documentation?"

"And no alien registration number, either," said Raley. "All those years in this country, and no A-card? I bet you know what this means, Detective Heat."

She tried to decide: Close it off, or share? Sharing would allow this bright group that was so eager to help her weigh in with ideas. But what a risky step, even with Hinesburg and Irons out of the building. Closing off discussion would be safe but potentially obstructive. Nikki stalled in the middle ground to buy time. "I have some thoughts, but I'm not sure I should go into them."

"Why not?" asked Reynolds.

Rook said, "It's need-to-know. Eyes-only."

"Nicole Bernardin was a spy?" asked Raley, not at all as a question.

Heat turned to Rook and shook her head. He said, "What gave it away?"

"Eyes-only? Clever . . . Max."

"Sorry about that, Chief."

Heat held up her hands to the squad, the palms separated by inches. "I was this close to telling you anyway. So now I'm this close." She brought them together. "But with all the leaks around here lately, I need your pledge that this stays in this group and doesn't go beyond you." Every single one, without prompting, raised his right hand.

So Nikki made a leap of faith.

Sometimes risks pay off. If Heat had not opened up to her squad, she never would have found herself in Midtown with Rook an hour later waiting for an elevator in the lobby of the prestigious Sole Building and feeling her first excitement at a potential lead since spotting Nicole Bernardin on her mother's old recital video.

Nikki had given her detectives the cut-down version, editing out the Russian kidnapping, the Homeland Security encounter, and the most private parts. Nikki was not prepared to give up family secrets—especially not the nasty rumor that her mother had turned traitor at the end. Roach might piece that together if anything came of the hidden bank account, but she'd deal with that then. Meantime, filling the squad in on the Nanny Network, Tyler Wynn, and the CIA had given them plenty to digest. She'd finished by admonishing them again not to share and also to make sure to tell her immediately if anyone contacted them about the case.

Feller asked, "You mean CIA? FBI? One PP?"

"I mean anyone." Nikki didn't explain further, and as surely as she had in her Paris photo reenactment at Point Zero, she once again found herself in her mother's footsteps, becoming cagey and strategic rather than open.

One practical advantage of her briefing was that she could now make assignments, like having Rhymer check out the alibi for the reality TV butler, Eugene Summers. But beyond mechanics, it also allowed her to mine the thoughts of her team, even if only for validation of her own ideas. Reynolds said, "First place I'd go is to those folks your mother spied on." Which Heat, of course, had already considered.

"The problem is, where to start?" she said.

Rook opened his Moleskine to a dog-eared page. "I did some research on the North Vietnamese family from that box of photos—the family whose son your mom tutored before the Paris Peace Talks. The dad was prominent, so he was on Wikipedia. Both parents died in the eighties, and the son has been in a monastery since."

"Not that Wikipedia isn't the investigative journalist's best friend, Rook," said Randall Feller, putting a bit of stank on it, "but my gut says we're smarter to focus in person on her mom's most recent activity before the murder."

"Agreed." Detective Malcolm swung one of his work boots up on a chair back. "I'd say fuck it to the old gigs and start with her U.S. spy work. The old European stuff is going to be hard to trace and you're going to end up doing a lot of wheel-spinning, sifting through forty years."

His partner Reynolds said, "True that. Old scores are harder to trace and not likely to carry motives unless they are some mighty epic grudges. I'd start with those last targets she was snooping."

Heat, already feeling better for their input, said, "Yeah, but how do you do that if you don't know who her clients were?"

Rook got the lightbulb look and jumped up. "I know how."

And he did.

The elevator let them out into the forty-sixth-floor offices of Quantum Retrieval. The receptionist was ready for them and ushered Heat and Rook to the corner office so immediately that they were still clearing their ears from the elevator ride when she gestured them in to meet the CEO.

"Joe Flynn," he said with a broad smile to go with his self-assured handshake. After Heat and Rook declined bottled waters, Flynn motioned them to the mission decor conversation area away from his desk.

Before Rook sat, he took in the view of Rockefeller Center below. The skating rink had long been defrosted and switched over to café tables that he watched being set for dinner. "Nice digs. Business must be good."

"Smartest move I ever made was to quit staking out adulterers at seedy motels and make the jump to insurance recovery. That was my quantum leap." He paused to let them make the connection to his company name. Flynn looked tan, fit, and rich, like a doctor from a primetime medical drama. Rook didn't like the way the sexy insurance investigator was appraising Nikki, and he sat close to her on the couch. "First piece of stolen art I recovered took me one week and paid me as much as I'd made in three years of gumshoeing errant spouses. . . . Plus the ones who weren't having affairs," he said pointedly to Heat. He flashed her some teeth Rook bet came courtesy of the Brite Smile off Fifth Avenue.

She said, "So you recall that my father hired you once for a case."

"It was ten years ago, but Heat's not that common a name. Plus you look just like your mother. And that's a major compliment, in this humble man's view."

Rook, who hadn't bargained for this when he came up with the brainstorm of contacting Joe Flynn for leads, tried to quell the ex-PI's bald flirtation by jerking the leash into business. "Cynthia Heat's murder is still under investigation."

"Saw that in the *Ledger*," he said. "And all over TV last night. I thought you had your killer."

"We're keeping things open for now," said Heat. "We need to go deeper."

"I like going deeper," said Flynn, prompting Rook to slide even closer to her. It didn't seem to faze the other man. "Can I do that for you, Nikki?"

"I hope so. Do you still have records of your surveillance and any other checks you made on the people she was spending time with back then?"

"Well, let's just see." Flynn picked up an iPad from the table beside him and started flicking the screen. He caught Rook watching and said, "You should get yourself one, man, they're amazing. They gave me one of the betas after I recovered a stolen prototype. Some goof left it in a bar, if you can believe that." He tapped the glass and said, "Here we go. Summer–fall 1999. Piano tutor, right?"

"That's right," she said.

"Got it." He looked up at her. "I'd normally ask for a warrant, but since this hits close to home, let's not stand on ceremony this time. All right with you, Detective?"

"Quite."

He tapped the screen again. "Copy's being printed for you now. Leave me your e-mail and I'll also attach the file for you."

She handed him a card. "My phone number's on there, too."

"But the e-mail," said Rook, "that's all you need, right? For the attachment."

"Right," said Flynn. "So you think one of these people may have killed her?"

"Hard to know. Let me ask one more question. You were hired to check for infidelity. Did you observe anything else? Arguments? Anybody threatening my mother? Did she do anything or go anywhere out of the ordinary that you didn't log because it wasn't strictly part of your assignment?"

He tugged his ear as he thought. "Not that I recall. Been a number of years, but I'll keep thinking. If I come up with anything, I'll sure phone you."

"Great."

"Anything else?" he asked. "And I mean anything."

"Yes," said Rook stepping between them. "Do you validate?"

Rook's hide was still chapped over Joe Flynn's come-ons to Nikki when they got back to the precinct. "That guy obviously clocked too much time chasing lotharios and degenerates. You hang out at enough hot sheet motels, sooner or later the bedbugs are going to bite." Heat ignored his grousing and made a list of the handful of names in Flynn's file of her mother's tutoring jobs during his surveillance and apportioned background checks on them around the squad. She didn't post the list on the Murder Boards; this wasn't for everybody.

Meanwhile, other results started coming in. Eugene Summers alibied out. Customs confirmed from passport records that he had indeed been in Europe in November of 1999. And the night of Nicole Bernardin's death, TV's most famous butler had been in LA on a location shoot at the Playboy Mansion. Also, Malcolm and Reynolds had buttoned down Hank Spooner's whereabouts in the kill zone. At the time he had confessed to stabbing Nicole in Larchmont, New York, his credit card placed him in Providence, Rhode Island, running an arcade tab at Dave & Buster's until midnight. The detectives e-mailed Spooner's mug shot to the manager, who confirmed he'd been there until closing, pestering waitresses.

Armed with Flynn's short list and some background checks on them to read overnight so she could start interviews the next day, Heat and Rook killed the lights in the bull pen and set out for his loft for some takeout and study.

At that time of night, the half hour before Broadway curtain, it was impossible to get a southbound cab, so they surrendered and took the subway. When their train made its stop at 66th, both of them twisted in their seats to see how repairs were going on the tiles damaged by the quake. Work had stopped for the day but, as they pulled away, behind the caution tape and sawhorses, the mosaic of acrobats and divas was well on its way to restoration. That's when Nikki turned back and noticed the man watching her. The tell had been his eyes, which darted away when she saw him.

She didn't say anything to Rook. Instead, two stops later, when the man in the rear of the car remained in her periphery, Heat nonchalantly got out her cell phone and typed a note and held her screen on her lap for Rook to see: "Don't look. Back of car. Gray suit, white shirt, black beard. Watching us." Rook, not the best at following instructions, surprised her by not looking. Instead he pressed his thigh against hers in acknowledgment and hummed a low, "Mm-hm."

The man stayed in position through numerous stops. At Christopher Street, Nikki used the bustle of passengers getting off and on to sneak a peek. When she did, she noticed a bulge in his suit coat at the hip. Heat typed, "Carrying." That made Rook make a quick scope. As soon as he did, the man stood.

Heat watched him by not watching, using her periphery but letting her hand fall casually across her lap, ready to draw.

At Houston, the man stepped off without a glance.

"What's your take?" said Rook.

"Maybe nothing. Maybe undercover transit cop watching me because I had a bulge, too."

"Then why did he get off?"

"Guess we'll never know," said Nikki, rising herself as the train slowed at Canal Street. "Ours, right?"

They came up the stairs to the sidewalk and instinctively kept their heads on swivels. The intersection, where West Broadway and Sixth Avenue converged, was busy, as usual, but the sidewalk was clear. Then Rook said, "Heat. Blue Impala."

Nikki followed his gaze across Sixth and spotted the man from the subway in the passenger seat of the blue Chevy as it pulled up. "This way," she said, and they both made a sharp turn in the opposite direction, not running, but striding quickly to get some cover behind the line of mail trucks parked beside the post office. As they passed the third truck in the line, another man stepped out from in front of it, blocking the sidewalk. Nikki reached for her hip.

"I wouldn't," the man said. He held his hands open to show they were empty, but they could also see he wasn't alone. Two other men flanking them on the sidewalk held hands on holsters inside their coats. Footsteps from behind told them they were surrounded. The setup was perfect for an ambush—a dark, windowless street—and Heat kicked herself for taking the bait. She kept her hand on her gun, too, but didn't draw.

"You've been running a check on me, Detective. I want to know why." He let his hands fall to the sides of his tailored suit and sauntered closer. With his shaved head and goatee he resembled Ben Kingsley. But not the *Gandhi* Ben Kingsley. Menacing, like the *Sexy Beast* Ben Kingsley. That's when Heat recognized Fariq Kuzbari, security attaché to the Syrian Mission to the UN, standing before her.

"I have some questions to ask you, Mr. Kuzbari. Why don't you come to my precinct during business hours tomorrow instead of a street at night? I imagine you must have the address."

He chuckled. "That creates numerous complications. I have diplomatic immunity, you see, therefore this arrangement saves you a great deal of frustration."

"Immunity, huh? How would your ambassador like to explain why the head of his secret police and his armed detail accosted a New York cop on an American street?"

"Feisty."

Rook said, "You don't want to know."

Kuzbari spoke something in Arabic to his entourage, and they dropped their hands off their guns. "Better?"

Heat assessed the situation and took her hand off her Sig. His brow lowered. "Now, what kind of questions?"

She thought of pressing for the station-house interview but he had a point. A stall or, worse, a no-show, wouldn't help her. "They're about a homicide case I'm investigating."

"How would such a matter be of any concern to me?"

"A woman was murdered in 1999. She was a piano tutor to your children. And she was my mother."

If Kuzbari made any visual connection from Cynthia to Nikki, he didn't let on. "My deep condolences. However, again, I must ask how this involves me."

"She had been in your home twice a week the summer before she was killed. She traveled with you for five days to a resort in the Berkshires, Mr. Kuzbari."

"These are all true facts, as I recollect them. Yet, if you are trying to assign some motive to me by implying I had some sort of relationship with your mother, you would be wasting your time as well as mine." Nikki wasn't suggesting anything like that, since Joe Flynn had pretty much ruled out an affair, but her experience as an interviewer told her not to say anything, to see where Kuzbari would go. "As for that week in the Berkshires—Lenox, as I recall—it was hardly a romantic getaway.

I was there in my capacity of providing security to the ambassador at a symposium, and I stayed with him. Your mother roomed in a separate bungalow with my wife and children and another family attending the conference."

"May I ask who they were?"

"Why, so you can harass them for no reason, as well? Detective Heat, I sympathize with your interest in settling this score, but I am confident I will be of no service. So, unless you have anything else, let us adjourn to continue our lives."

Before she could reply, he turned and disappeared between the parked mail trucks. They heard a car door slam, then the rest of his group vanished, leaving Heat and Rook alone on the sidewalk.

Rook said, "At least no bags over our heads this time."

The next morning Heat and Rook walked down Fulton toward the South Street Seaport to visit another one of her mother's tutoring clients. This time, barring surprise ambushes, they had an appointment. As Rook paused to read the plaque on the Titanic Memorial, Nikki said, "I've been thinking about our encounter with Fariq Kuzbari. If it made me feel like I'm swimming into deeper waters on this case, imagine how Carter Damon felt."

They moved on and Rook said, "You're not excusing that loser, are you?"

"Never. I just understand why, being the mediocre lead he was, he probably felt overwhelmed and checked out."

"And what about Kuzbari? After a pushback like he gave us, do you just cross him off your list?"

"No. And I make that call, not he. But I have a gut feeling that says Kuzbari's not worth the focus, so I am going to concentrate on the other names on Flynn's list, for now. I can always brace him again later, if I need to."

"Did you just say you had a gut feeling? Detective Heat, are you starting to pick up someone's bad habits? Are you thinking like a writer?"

"Lord, take my gun and shoot me now. No, forget gut. You want to hear my rationale? Fine. Even if Kuzbari were implicated, it's not likely he would have done the killing personally. He has a crew of suited goons to do that, so I'm certain he'd alibi out. Also, he'd be tough to investigate because of his diplomatic protection. Not impossible, but it would draw time and energy. Meanwhile, I have three others to interview, and we both know the clock is ticking before Captain Irons works his magic again. No, Rook, this is triage. So let's not call this my gut. Let's say I am . . . accessing instincts born of experience."

"Spoken just like a writer."

A custodian in rubber boots hosing cobblestones on the mall shut off the nozzle to let them pass as they arrived at the main entrance to Brewery Boz. The landmark brick mercantile building not only had been restored to serve as the British company's U.S. flagship brewery, it catered to tourists with a Dickens-themed pub. The owner and chief brewmaster, Carey Maggs, met them in the lobby, and the legendary English reserve went right out the window when he saw Nikki. "Bloody hell," he said in his Mayfair accent. "You look just like your mum."

Maggs had good reason to do a double-take at the sight of her. In London back in 1976, when Carey was eight years old, Nikki's mother had been employed by his beer magnate father as his piano tutor. After he'd emigrated to America in 1999, Carey Maggs had passed the torch by hiring his childhood piano teacher to tutor his own son. "That's the circle. The circle of life," said Rook.

"Don't need to tell me about history repeating. Here I am making suds just like my father did back in the UK," Maggs said as he led them on a tour of his brewery. The humid air in the massive facility was tinged with enough yeast and malt to taste them; equal parts inviting and off-putting at that early hour. As they passed giant vats and containers with their sprouts of coiled tubing and pipes, Carey Maggs described the process in brief, and how they performed all processes on-site, from malting, to mashing, to lautering, fermenting, conditioning, and filtering.

Rook said, "I don't know why, but I thought these would all be copper."

"Stainless steel. Doesn't impart taste to the brew and it's easy to clean and sterilize, which is critical. Those vats over there are copper-plated on the outside, but that's just for aesthetics because they face the showcase window of the pub."

"Impressive. Your father must be proud of you for continuing the legacy," said Nikki.

"Not so much. We part company on the business model. Dad named his signature beer after the town drunk in a Dickens novel, *The Mystery of Edwin Drood.*"

"Durdles," said Heat, recalling her own dad's longing for it.

"Right. Well, my dear father seemed to forget that Charles Dickens was all about exposing social injustice and corporate greed. So now that I run the company, I've not only expanded our Dickens brand to pubs and beer gardens, I donate half our profits to Mercator Watch. That's a foundation that monitors international child labor abuse. I call them GreedPeace. You heard of it?"

"No," said Rook, loving the nickname, "but now that you gave me a title, I have an article to pitch *Rolling Stone.*"

"The way I see it, how many million is enough when half the world is starving or doesn't have water to drink? Of course, that's all too radical and socialistic for the old man, but he's just a big Scrooge. Now, how's that for irony?" Carey laughed and finger combed the unruly curtain of brown hair that had fallen over one side of his forehead. "Sorry about prattling on. You didn't make the trip here this morning to listen to this."

The three of them took seats on red leather bar stools in the empty pub, and Nikki said, "Actually, I do have some serious business to discuss. I'm investigating my mother's murder, and since you knew her so long, maybe you can help provide some information."

"Of course. Now I feel even worse for blathering on. Whatever I can do." Then his eyes widened. "I'm not a suspect, am I? Because that would pretty much suck, especially considering how I felt about her. I mean, Cynthia was wonderful."

She didn't tell him whether he was a suspect or not because she hadn't decided. Instead, Nikki moved forward with her questions. She'd prepped carefully, knowing an interview like this would be tricky because she faced the challenge of not revealing that her mother had been a spy. So Heat decided to proceed as she would with any other interrogation of an eyewitness or person of interest and see what shook out: nervous behavior, inconsistencies, lies, or even new clues. "Think back, if you can, to the month leading up to her killing," she began. "November of '99. Did you see any changes in my mom's behavior?"

He thought it over and said, "No, not that I recall."

"Did she confide any worries? Seem agitated? Mention anybody who was bothering her, threatening her?"

"No."

"Or say that she felt like she was being followed?"

He thought and wagged his head. "Mm, nothing of that sort, either."

And then Heat tried to ascertain if her mother had been snooping his home. "During that last month she worked for you, did you or your wife ever get a feeling that things in your house were disturbed?"

His brow was puzzled. "Disturbed in what way?"

"Any way. Items in disarray. Items out of place. Items missing."

He shifted on his bar stool. "I'm trying to makes sense of this, Detective."

"You don't have to, just think back. Did you ever come into a room and find something was moved? Or gone?"

"Why would that be? You asked me if she was agitated. Are saying your mother had developed some mental problem and gone klepto?"

"I'm not saying that. I'm just asking if things were disturbed. Do you need to think about it?"

"No," he said. "I don't remember anything like that."

"Let me ask about other people who may have been in your home back then."

"You do realize that was ten years ago plus."

"I do. So I'm not talking about plumbers or deliverymen. Houseguests. Did you have anyone staying with you?"

"Hello. You think somebody we knew might have killed her?"

"Mr. Maggs, it would be helpful for you not to keep guessing what I'm trying to learn and just focus on the question."

"Brilliant. Carry on."

"I just want to know if you had any houseguests. Overnight, weekends?" Heat had circled a notation in Joe Flynn's surveillance log that a man, about thirty, had been at the Maggs residence that week just before the PI got pulled from his stakeout by her dad. "Anyone stay in your apartment with you while my mom was there giving lessons?"

He shook his head slowly as he thought. "No, I don't think so."

Rook said, "That was right around Thanksgiving. No friends or relatives came to stay with you the week before Thanksgiving?"

"Of course, that is not one of our traditional UK holidays, so let me give it a fair bit." He made a steeple of his fingers and pressed them to his lips. "Well, now that I think it over, it comes to me that a college mate of mine did arrive and stayed with us that week. Your mentioning Thanksgiving jogs my memory because the kids were going to be off school. We were planning to leave that weekend for London and he was going to mind our flat while we were chocks away." Maggs recognized the implications and grew unsettled. "But if you're thinking he had anything to do with it, no. I couldn't believe that, not him."

She turned her spiral to a fresh page. "May I have the name of this friend?" Carey closed his eyes slowly and his face went slack. "Mr. Maggs, I am going to ask you again to give me the name."

In a voice that had gone strangely toneless, he said, "Ari. Ari Weiss." Then he opened his eyes. He looked as if the admission had hollowed something out of him.

Nikki spoke quietly, but persistently. "Can you tell me how I could get in touch with Ari Weiss?"

"You can't," he said.

"I have to."

"But you can't. Ari Weiss is dead."

"Confirmed," said Rook, hunched toward the screen at his desk back in the precinct. Heat crossed over to him as he referred to it. "Obituary for Ari Weiss, MD, says the graduate of Yale School of Medicine and Rhodes Scholar—which is probably how he met up with Carey Maggs, up at Oxford—died of a rare blood disease called babesiosis. It says here, that is a malaria-like parasitic disorder which, like Lyme disease, is usually tick-borne, although it can come from transfusion, blah, blah."

"Rook, a man's dead, and all you can say is, 'blah blah'?"

"Nothing against him. It's just I'm one of those people who hears about rare diseases delivered by ticks and I start scratching and checking my temperature every five minutes."

"You're a prize package, Rook. Lucky me." She hitched a thumb at the obit on his screen. "Meanwhile, a potential lead hits another dead end. When did he pass?"

"2000." Rook closed the webpage. "That eliminates him as a suspect for Nicole Bernardin's murder, anyway."

Nikki tried to stay upbeat in the face of yet another lead coming to an apparent dead end. She was making a mental note to do some of her own research later on Ari Weiss, when Roach startled her.

"Detective Heat?" Nikki turned to see the partners standing before her, looking grim.

"Tell me," she said.

"We'd better show you," said Ochoa.

As she and Rook followed Roach across the bull pen, Raley said, "I scored this a few minutes ago, but I waited for Sharon Hinesburg to clear out for her two-hour lunch." He sat at his desk and keyed some strokes on his computer keyboard.

Ochoa said, "It's the statement for November 1999 on your mother's separate account at New Amsterdam Bank and Trust." The monitor filled with a financial PDF. Raley rolled his chair back so Nikki could lean in to read it.

Rook bent over beside her to look and let out a low moan. Heat turned away, her face drained of color.

As if to confirm the reality she feared, Detective Raley said in a hushed voice, "According to this, your mom received a two-hundred-thousand-dollar deposit the day before she was killed."

"Detective, do you have some idea what this means?" asked Ochoa.

Nikki didn't reply. Because she would have had to say that it meant it looked like her mother had sold out her country.

Her head became light. Heat turned back to see the document again, hoping she had been mistaken, but the image clouded before her eyes. Small trembles made her hands start to shake, and when she crossed her arms on her chest to hide them her whole body began quaking from the inside, radiating out to her joints. As her legs grew weak, she heard

Rook's voice, sounding like it came from the end of a tunnel, asking if she was all right. Nikki turned away to cross to her desk but changed her mind when she got halfway across the room and wove unsteadily out of the bull pen, smacking her thigh into a chair or maybe a desk on the way out.

When she got to the street, fresh air didn't help. Nikki's head still cycloned in a whirl of panic. Even in the bright morning light her vision remained fogged by a deep blue haze, the way condensation forms on a shower door. She rubbed her eyes, but when she opened them again the mist had crystallized, making her view a solid sheet of blue ice. Behind it, shadowy figures moved, seeming familiar to her, but unrecognizable. A face looked back at her through the frost. It looked like her own, through a clouded mirror. But it might have been her mother's.

She didn't know which.

Somewhere behind her, Heat heard her name being called. She ran.

She didn't know where.

Rubber squealed and a truck horn blasted. Defensively, Nikki put out her palms and touched the hot grill of a semi as it skidded to a stop. She stayed on her feet, but the jolt fractured the veneer of ice she was looking through enough for her to see how close she had come to getting hit by a truck.

Nikki turned and bolted through traffic on Columbus Avenue, running somewhere, anywhere.

Away.

FIFTEEN

A statue of Theodore Roosevelt on horseback fronts the entrance of the American Museum of Natural History across from Central Park. Surrounding the famous bronze, a dozen titles listing the achievements of the great president are carved into the stone wall of the parapet: Ranchman, Scholar, Explorer, Scientist, Conservationist, Naturalist, Statesman, Author, Historian, Humanitarian, Soldier, and Patriot. Before these words sits a line of granite benches arranged for contemplation.

When Rook caught up with Heat, she was on the Statesman bench, doubled over, hyperventilating.

Nikki saw his shoes and pant legs before he spoke, and without raising her head, she just whispered, "Go." He ignored that idea and sat on the bench beside her. Neither said anything for a time. She kept her face to the ground; he rested his palm on her back. It rose and fell with her breathing.

He reflected how, just a few short nights before, the two of them had held each other on the Pont Neuf in Paris while he'd contemplated the thick stone walls channeling the Seine. And Rook recalled wondering what would happen if one of them ever cracked.

Now he knew.

And he set about shoring up the damage.

"It's not conclusive, you know," he said as soon as her breathing leveled off. "It's just a bank deposit. You can project the bad thing if you want, but sounds to me like you'd be breaking one of your own rules if you jumped to a conclusion without hard evidence. That's my job."

Not a chuckle from her, not even a scoff. Instead, she folded her arms across her knees and rested her forehead on them. Finally, she spoke. "I wonder if it's worth it. Seriously, Rook, maybe I should just shut it down. The whole investigation. Leave the past in the past, keep all the bad stuff, I dunno . . . frozen in time."

"Do you really mean that?"

"It's not unthinkable, and that's a first." Nikki sighed and her breath hitched. Then in a small, plaintive voice, she said, "But then I keep telling myself I'm doing this for her."

"Are you?"

"Why else?"

"I don't know. Maybe you're doing it for yourself because you need to find out the part of her then that's part of you now. That's the best reason I can think of to keep going." He paused and added, "Or you could just throw in the towel because it got difficult, like Carter Damon did." Heat sat up and glowered at him. "Hey," he said, "I'm pulling out all the stops here."

"No kidding. Comparing me to that washout? Not too manipulative."

"I have my moments." He looked past her to the Teddy Roosevelt equestrian statue that loomed over Central Park West. "He was a force of nature, wasn't he? Did you know he was once NYPD commissioner? They told him the department was hopelessly corrupt and lazy. TR turned it around in two years. You remind me of him. Although you'd have to work on the mustache."

Nikki laughed. Then she grew pensive and stared deeply into him, seeing something there precious and infinite. Finally she stood. "Time to get back to work?"

"If you insist. And if you're crazy enough to keep going, I'm crazy enough to follow."

Algernon Barrett was the next name on the list of wealthy tutoring clients Nikki had gotten from the PI who'd tracked her mother, and when Heat pulled up to the gate of his business, she asked Rook if they had the wrong address. Located on a dead-end street of cement factories and auto scrap yards in the Bronx, Barrett's Jamaican catering company, Do The Jerk, appeared anything but prosperous. "Know how they say not to judge a book by its cover?" asked Rook, stepping around weeds on their walk up the fractured walkway to the front entrance. "Do judge a caterer by his cockroaches."

However, as they waited in the small lobby that seemed suited more to a car wash, Rook drifted to the windowed double doors giving onto the food preparation plant and said, "I take it back. You could eat off the floor in there and not be a rodent."

They paced twenty long minutes before the receptionist answered a phone buzz and led them down a dingy, Masonite-paneled hall to the owner's office. Algernon Barrett, a whip-skinny Jamaican with an impressive set of Manny Ramirez dreds cascading from under his knit cap, didn't get up. He remained seated behind his massive desk, peering around an accumulation of spice bottles, unopened UPS cartons, and horse racing magazines scattered there, making no effort even to acknowledge them. In fact, with his designer sunglasses on, it was hard to tell if he was even awake. But his attorney certainly was. Helen Miksit, a former star prosecutor who had quit for private practice and carved an equally strong reputation on the opposite side of the aisle, sat in a folding chair beside her client. The Bulldog, as she was known, didn't extend any courtesies, either.

"I wouldn't bother sitting," she said.

"Nice to see you again, too, Helen." Nikki extended her hand, which the lawyer shook but without rising.

"Your first lie of the morning. Trying to remember the last time we crossed paths, Heat. Oh, right, the interrogation room. You were putting the pins to my client Soleil Gray. Right before you badgered her so much she killed herself." That was untrue; they both knew the famous singer had jumped under that train in spite of Nikki's words, not because of them. But the Bulldog was all about living up to the nickname, so to argue the point would only feed the beast.

In his own form of defiance, Rook grabbed two folding chairs that faced the big screen showing a cable poker tournament and swung them around for him and Nikki. "Whatever," said Miksit.

"Mr. Barrett, I'm here to ask you some questions about the time that my mother, Cynthia Heat, was your daughter's music tutor."

The Bulldog crossed her legs and sat back. "Ask away, Detective. I've advised my client not to answer anything."

"Why not, Mr. Barrett? Do you have something to hide?" Heat decided to press. With this attorney in the mix, niceties would be ignored and/or crushed.

He sat up in his chair. "No!"

"Algernon," said Miksit. When he turned to her, she just shook her head. He sat back again. "Detective, if you want to know about Mr. Barrett's top shelf line of Caribbean-inspired jerk rubs and marinades, great. If you want to inquire about franchising one of his Do The Jerk gourmet trucks, I can see you get an application."

"That's right," he said. "See, I operate a profitable company and mind my own business, yeah."

"Then why the expensive lawyer?" asked Heat. "You need protection for some reason?"

"Yes, he does. My client is a new citizen and wants the protection afforded every American from undue pressure by zealous police. We 'bout done here?"

"My questions," said Nikki, "are part of a homicide investigation. Would your client prefer to conduct this interview down at the precinct?"

"Your call, Heat. My meter runs the same wherever I am."

Nikki sensed Barrett was hiding behind counsel because he had a volatile emotional side, and she tried to get a rise. "Mr. Barrett. I see you've been arrested for domestic violence."

Barrett whipped off his glasses and sat bolt upright. "That was long ago."

"Algernon," said the Bulldog.

Heat pressed on. "You assaulted your live-in girlfriend."

"That's all been cleared up!" He tossed his glasses on the desk.

"Detective, do not harass my—"

"With a knife," said Heat. "A kitchen knife."

"Don't say anything, Mr. Barrett."

But he didn't back down. "I did my anger management. I paid for her doctor. Got that bitch a new car."

"Algernon, please," said the lawyer.

"My mother was stabbed with a knife."

"Come on. Things get crazy in the kitchen!"

"My mother was stabbed in her kitchen."

Helen Miksit stood, towering over her client. "Shut your fucking mouth."

Algernon Barrett froze with his jaw gaping and sat back in the chair, pulling on his shades. The Bulldog sat, too, and crossed her arms. "Unless you want to charge my client formally, this interview has concluded."

Back in the car, they had to wait out the long convoy of Barrett's gourmet trucks clearing the lot as they deployed for the streets of New York. Rook said, "Damn lawyer. That guy was going to be a talker."

"Which is exactly why the lawyer. The too-bad part is that I wanted to try to pull some information out of him before I got to the knife, but she made me change it up." With only one name remaining on the list of her mother's clients, the elation Nikki had felt at scoring these leads began to feel like an unfulfilled promise.

"Well, it wasn't a total loss," said Rook. "During all the drama, I pocketed this jar of Do The Jerk Chicken Rub." He pulled out the spice bottle and showed it off.

"That's theft, you know."

"Which will only make the chicken taste better."

A half hour later, they'd just pulled off the Saw Mill Parkway on their way to Hastings-on-Hudson to visit the last person on the list when Heat got an excited call from Detective Rhymer. "It may not be anything, but it's at least something." He said it with just enough of his Southern roots coming through to make him indeed sound like Opie. "Remember sending me to IT to chase down whether Nicole Bernardin used Internet cloud storage?"

"Are you seriously asking if I'd forget having to autograph my magazine cover photo to, um . . . inspire them?"

"Well, it worked. They haven't found a storage server yet, but one of my geeks had the idea of using the electronic fingerprint of her cell phone to track her mobile Internet searches through location services. Even though we never found her physical phone, they were able to backtrack her billing and dig out the address of her account. Don't ask me how they do all this, but I'm sure it's why they enjoy sitting alone in rooms day and night, touching themselves."

"Rhymer."

"Sorry. They managed to score one hit for a HopStop search she made."

"What's HopStop?"

"A website that gives you directions when you tell it where you want to go. It gives you subway, bus, taxi, and walking info, including distances and times. Am I making sense?"

"You could star on *Big Bang Theory*. What was she searching?"

"Directions to a restaurant on the Upper West Side."

"When?"

"The night she was murdered."

"Drop whatever you're doing, Opie. Go now to that restaurant. Go right now and show her picture, learn everything you can."

"Feller and I are en route as we speak."

"If this pans out, I suppose I'll owe IT, big time."

Rhymer said, "Maybe a lipstick smooch to go under the autograph."

"OK, now you're creeping me out," she said, then hung up.

As Heat turned off the rural two-lane, her tires crunched the long pebble drive leading to Vaja Nikoladze's Victorian country house, and the sound of barking dogs rose from a kennel behind a stand of rhododendrons in the side pasture. She parked beside the blue hybrid, nosing up to the split-rail fence that separated the driveway from the back field. When they got out, Heat and Rook paused to admire the green sweep of meadow leading down toward the line of hardwoods whose foliage shimmered under the midday sun. They couldn't see it, but between those trees and the cliffs of the Palisades just beyond, the Hudson River flowed.

Rook said, "Look out there where the field ends. Is that the most realistic scarecrow you've ever seen, or what?"

"I'm going with 'or what?' That's no scarecrow. That's a man."

And, just as she said it, the stock-still figure in the distance began walking toward them. He moved steadily through the meadow, with a dancer's grace and economy, in spite of his trail boots and heavy Carhartt jeans. The man never looked behind him or to the side. But they never had a sense he was looking at them, either, even though a broad smile cut across his face when he drew near. His hands, which he had been holding cupped in front of his belt buckle, as if in casual prayer, rose up to his chin and a single forefinger extended. He was signaling them to remain quiet.

When he was one yard away, Vaja Nikoladze stopped and whispered in an accent that sounded Russian to their ears. "One moment, if you please. I have her on a sit-stay." Then he rotated. Turning his back to them to face the meadow, he raised one arm straight out to the side, held it there for five seconds, and then swung his palm swiftly to his chest.

The instant he did, a very large dog began bounding across the pasture to him at full speed. He held his place as the Georgian Shepherd, about the size and color of a small bear, charged at him. At the last moment, and without so much as a hand signal to command it, the dog stopped and dropped to an alert sit, her front paws aligned with the toes of his boots. "Good girl, Duda." He bent to pet her broad face and scratch under her ears as her tail wagged. "Now, go to place." Duda stood, turned, and trotted, cutting a straight line for the kennel, and went inside.

"How awesome is that?" said Nikki.

"She has promise," he said. "With more training, she may be a winning show dog." He stuck his hand out. "I am Vaja. You are Nikki Heat, yes?"

Because it was such a warm spring day, he invited them to sit on the gallery that wrapped around the back of the house. They declined his pitcher of iced tea and settled into teak rocking chairs while he perched up on the rail to face them. His dangling feet not only made Nikoladze appear shorter in spite of his elevation, but boylike instead of the fifty Heat made him to be.

"Up in town at the institute they told us to find you here," began Nikki. "You're taking a personal leave?"

"A brief one, yes. I'm mourning the loss of one of my dogs. Fred would have been the first Georgian Shepherd to win Best in Show at Westminster, I believe."

"I'm sorry," said Heat and Rook, nearly in unison.

He made a pained smile and said, "Even show dogs get sick. They are only human, yes?" Nikki observed that his Georgian accent grew thicker in sadness.

Rook must have had the same thought and said, "So you're from

Georgia. Spent some mighty good times in Tbilisi on an assignment not long ago."

"Ah, yes, I enjoyed your article very much, Mr. Rook. Insightful. But the times were not so good when I defected. We were still under the boot of Moscow."

"That was when?" asked Detective Heat. The mention of defecting from a Russian satellite and its potential clandestine implications snagged her interest.

"1989. I was twenty-eight and, not to be boastful, one of the leading biochemists in the Soviet Union. Such as it was then. You know, yes, that there is much bad blood between Georgian people and Russians?"

"Yes," said Rook. "Lots of actual blood."

"Mostly Georgian. And Moscow, they wanted my talent put to use for war, so it was double insult. I was young, and no family to worry about, so I left for freedom, you see. Soon, I was fortunate to get fellowship at the Spokes Institute here."

"And just what is the Spokes Institute?" she asked.

"You call it think tank, I guess. Although, many days, there is more talking than thinking." He chuckled. "But our mission is policy study to demilitarize science. So is good fit for someone like me. Plus the fellowship grant gives me time to follow my passion for breeding the next prize-winning show dog." He laughed again, then fell off into brief melancholy, no doubt at the memory of Fred.

Heat had questions to ask concerning his defection but used this lull to transition to her business. She asked Vaja if he'd been following the murder cases in the news, and he confessed he had been preoccupied lately with losing his poor dog. But Nikoladze had heard of the suitcase murder because of its spectacular nature. Heat told him, in addition to Nicole Bernardin's killing, she was also investigating her mother's. Then she asked the same basic questions she had that morning at the brewery about the events surrounding Cynthia Heat's tutoring in his home back in 1999: her mother's state of mind; her sense of agitation; whether she was being followed or bothered; if there were things upset or missing in the house.

Vaja said, "I would much like to help you with your questions, but unfortunately, I don't have enough information to share. You see, your mother only came here to tutor twice."

"Your child gave up?" asked Rook.

The scientist looked down at him from his perch on the railing with amusement. "My child? I assure you that would be most unlikely."

Nikki asked, "Who, then?"

"My protégé."

"A protégé from the institute?"

"No." Nikoladze hesitated but continued. "He was someone I met at a dog show in Florida. He also came from Tbilisi." Heat sensed his discomfort at the subject and understood why, but knowing that often the host household was not the target for her mother to spy on but could be the link to an acquaintance who was, she started troweling away layers.

"He showed dogs, as well?"

Vaja lowered his eyes and said, "No, he was groomer's assistant." Then, as if he'd decided to surrender, he let it out. "We had much in common. He and I hit it off, so I invited him to come here to learn from me about breeding and training the dogs. I also got him the piano lessons, but he was not serious enough."

Rook said, "The piano's not for everyone."

"Serious enough about me."

Nikki took out her notepad. "May I ask the name of this protégé?"

With a sigh, Vaja said, "This must be my time for emotional pain, old and new." Nikki thought, You're preaching to the choir on that one, pal. She uncapped her pen to prompt him. "His name is Mamuka. Mamuka Leonidze." Mindful of the language difference, he spelled out the name for her.

"Do you know where Mamuka is now?" she asked.

"Ten years ago he left for Canada to join Cirque du Soleil as an acrobat. After that, I do not know." Then he added, "If you find him, tell me, I'm curious."

Vaja escorted them to their car, which gave Heat a chance to walk the conversation back to the topic of his defection. "Do you ever have contact with representatives of foreign governments?"

"All the time, of course. The Spokes Institute is a global think tank."

"I mean outside your policy work. Any government contact?"

"Only to report my address as a legal alien."

She and Rook hadn't conferred, but he was right there with her and asked, "What about spies? Secret police?"

"Not since I left Georgia." But then he reconsidered. "Well, they did come to me a little bit after I first got here, but by the mid-nineties, after Shevardnadze was ousted, they started to leave me alone."

"Who?" asked Nikki.

"You want names? This is just like back in Tbilisi but no concrete room."

Rook said, "I'll give you one, then. Anatoly Kijé, you know of him?"

"You mean the Soul Crusher? Everyone knew of him back then. But since I left? No."

"One more name," said Heat. "Tyler Wynn."

"No, afraid I don't know that one."

The low rumble of a diesel shuddered the air as the Amtrak Adirondack passed a quarter mile away along the banks of the Hudson, heading up to Albany. Heat slid into the front seat and asked Vaja to call her if anyone else contacted him about this case. He nodded and said something, but she couldn't hear it because the train horn blasted and he got drowned out by all the yelps and howls answering it from within the dog kennel. The soundless movement of his mouth felt to her like the perfect image for the empty motion of pursuing these leads.

Back on the road, Rook expressed his frustration another way. "Seems like our sexy insurance investigator's list is a lot like he is. Sizzle without the steak. Or, more to the point, tan without the sun. Did you see those goggle marks?"

"Come on, Rook, it's not Joe Flynn's fault these didn't pan out yet."

"Did you say 'yet'?" He saw her tenacious look and said, "Got it."

She gave it some gas and resolved to practice what she preached to her squad. When you ground out, you don't quit. You go back. Dig harder. Do the work. After putting in some more study of these people and reviewing their interviews, Heat had a feeling she'd be seeing some of them again.

. . .

Nikki's cell phone buzzed with a text when she passed through the precinct lobby with Rook. "Finally," she said. "A message from Carter Damon."

"What's it say?"

"Nothing. Well, not nothing. It's a partial. He must have lost service or hit send by mistake." She held the screen out to him. All it said was "I am" and the rest was blank.

"Hm, 'I am . . .' Let me guess—'the walrus'? 'Such an asshole for not calling you back'?" The duty sergeant zapped the security lock and Rook pushed the door open to let her go first.

Heat was texting back to Damon, telling him to call, when Detective Raley snagged her as she came into the bull pen. "I've got something I want to show you before Irons and his maiden came back." She looked past his shoulder and could see a financial statement up on his monitor. Sensitive, following her hasty exit earlier, Raley asked, "You OK with this, Detective?"

Rook sidled up close to her. She steeled herself and said, "Whatcha got?"

"After you left this morning, I did more tracking and found new information on your mom's account. Don't know why, maybe it was a data entry screwup, or it didn't get posted until after the Thanksgiving holiday, but New Amsterdam Bank filed the rest of her November, '99 transactions in December. Check it out."

Nikki leaned in once again, feeling steadier this time, and read the statement. "It says here the two hundred thousand dollars got withdrawn, as cash, the day after the deposit." She stood up and turned to Rook, who was still at her elbow. "That would have been the same day she was killed."

"Remember in the hospital, Tyler Wynn asked if you saw your mom hide anything? Could it be the money someone was after?"

"Could be, but think about it, Rook. Ten years, three killings? Isn't that a lot of carnage for two hundred grand?"

"Depends," said Ochoa from his desk. "I know guys who'd gut you for a ham sandwich."

Raley killed the screen on his monitor and said, "Heads up" just as Captain Irons strolled in.

"Heat? A minute?" Instead of leading her to his office, he beckoned her aside to her own desk and stood there until she joined him. "I don't know who you've been pissing off, but I got a call from the deputy mayor's office saying there's a complaint about you harassing people on this vendetta of yours."

"First of all, sir, it's a case, not a vendetta. And, second, have you ever been on an investigation that didn't bruise someone's toes along the way?"

"Well . . ."

Seeing him standing there, stumped, reminded Heat that the ex-administrator was pretty much experience-free when it came to working the street. "It happens. Who complained?"

"They didn't tell me. They just wanted to know if you had a plan or if you were just beating bushes with a stick, and I couldn't answer because I'm kind of out of the loop." Behind him, Roach mouthed "Kind of?" and Heat had to look away so she wouldn't laugh. "That's gonna change, pronto. I'm going to study your latest Murder Board postings and then I want a full and detailed briefing so I can dig in."

"But sir, what about tracking down the driver of the truck that delivered the tainted gas to OCME? I thought that was your priority."

"Not to worry. I delegated that to my secret weapon. Sharon Hinesburg." Irons strode over to the Murder Boards and camped out with his hands in his pockets as he read them, manifesting Heat's nightmare scenario. Nikki snagged Rook by the elbow, pulled him into the back hall, and shut the door.

"Cone of Silence, huh? Can you hear me, Chief?"

"Grow up, Rook. We need to do something."

"Who do you suppose complained? Fariq Kuzbari? Oh, I know! I bet it was Eugene Summers. That snarky butler can dish it out, but he can't take it."

"My money's on The Bulldog, Helen Miksit, but that doesn't matter. What does matter is keeping Irons from meddling in the case more than he already has."

"How do we do that?"

"No, it's how *you're* going to do that. I need you to distract him."

"You mean be the rodeo clown again?"

"Yes, put on your red nose and big shoes. Try teasing him with a bogus interview for an article. It worked before."

"True, although past results are no guarantee of future performance." She just stared at him. "Perhaps I spent a little too much time watching TV in my rehab."

Irons looked annoyed when Rook stepped right between him and the board he was reading. "Got a minute, Captain?"

"I'm a little busy, as you can see."

"Oh, sorry. I just had some thoughts about that article I'm working on, but no problem. Later's fine." He'd stepped away precisely two paces before Irons gripped his shoulder.

"Be more comfortable in my office, I think." He led Rook to his glass box.

Detectives Feller and Rhymer came back from their trip to the restaurant Nicole Bernardin had gotten Web directions to from HopStop. "Got a hit," said Opie as they joined Nikki at her desk.

"Harling and Walendy's Steakhouse up at Ninety-fourth and Broadway. Had to wait for the assistant manager to come in for his shift, but he definitely ID'd our vic," said Feller. "Said Bernardin came in about seven P.M. The reason he noticed her was because she took up a table drinking nothing but club soda for a half hour waiting for someone and never ate dinner."

Heat asked, "Did he say why not? Did she get a call or something and leave?"

"No, she met a guy there," said Rhymer. "He came in, sat down, they talked about five minutes. She goes, but he keeps the table and has a bone-in rib eye."

Nikki frowned. "They actually remember his order?"

"Even better. They got their picture taken with him while he ate it." Feller held up a framed photo of waitstaff and a chef posed around the table of a familiar face grinning at a rib eye and giant baked potato. "Got this off their wall in the bar."

"Is that who I think it is?" asked Heat.

"None other," said Rhymer. "Lloyd Lewis, treasure hunter."

"May I see that?" she asked.

He handed it to her. "OK, but be careful. The man's a legend."

Nikki said, "It's a photo."

"Of a legend," Rhymer repeated with emphasis.

"He's been like this all afternoon," said Feller.

Heat studied the picture briefly then handed it back, pretending to drop it just to watch Rhymer freak. He didn't disappoint. "Let's get Lloyd Lewis in here and talk to him."

"We'll have to wait," said Feller. "His agent says he's on a secret adventure somewhere on the Amazon."

"A secret adventure. How cool is that?" said Rhymer.

"Gimme a golll-ee, Opie," said his partner. "Give it up. Just once for ol' Randy."

As Heat and Rook got on the elevator to his loft that evening, she held up her cell phone. "Carter Damon texted me back. 'Apologies for not returning your call. . . . Came across an old case file you'll find very interesting.' He wants me to meet him for coffee." As Nikki replied, the elevator started to shake.

"Incoming," said Rook, and they both hopped back out into his lobby. "Getting sick of those. If I liked aftershocks, I'd move to LA, where I could at least die tan."

When she came out from the bedroom a few minutes later, he handed her one of the Sierra Nevadas he'd opened. They clinked necks, and he said, "What have you got there?"

Nikki held up the velvet pouch. "The charm bracelet my dad stole from my mom."

"You make it sound so underhanded."

"Go ahead, defend him, you who shoplifts jerk spice rub." She shook the bracelet into her palm and examined the two charms, spinning the gold plated numerals between her thumb and forefinger, wondering what the one and nine meant. If anything.

Rook sipped more of his pale ale. "I've been mulling our visit with Vaja today. Know what I think? I'm thinking Mamuka was a spy."

"Maybe," she said.

"This is too weird. Isn't this where you tell me to put on my Area Fifty-one foil hat? That I think everyone is a spy?"

"Yeah. But tonight, you get a free pass for taking one for the team."

"Did I ever. Five minutes in the same room with Wally Irons, I want to eat my own flesh just for the distraction. Thanks to you, I'm stuck having dinner with him to discuss his view of modern urban law enforcement. Can't you at least come along and goose me under the table?"

"Inviting as that sounds, I've got my coffee meet with Damon."

"Fine, do legitimate case work while I pretend to be taking notes from that gas bag."

"Stop whining, Rook. This can't be the first time you pretended to interview someone you had no plans to include in an article."

"True, but they were supermodels or smokin' hot actresses and there was the potential for sex afterward. Not that I ever took one of them up on it." And then he grinned. "Two of them, yes. One, no."

Nikki shook her head and then put the bracelet on her wrist and held it to the light. She studied it some more, then took it off. When she picked up the pouch, he said, "Before you put that away, humor me. Did you notice whether your mom, or Nicole, or anyone else was wearing that bracelet or one like it in any of the old photos?" She gave him a look of approval but he seemed wary. "Does this reaction mean my free pass is still in effect and you're only humoring me, or did I just have an actual good idea?"

"I'm going to go get the box, what do you think?" She disappeared down the hall but then came back out empty-handed. "It's gone."

"What's gone?" He followed her back into his office. She pointed to a file drawer.

"I put the box in there. It's gone." He started to reach for the handle and she stopped him. "Don't. In case we need to dust for prints."

"Are you sure they aren't somewhere else?"

"Those pictures were important to me, I know just where I put them. And that drawer has a big empty space where they were this morning when I closed it."

Taking care not to touch anything, they made a quick survey of the loft. Everything seemed in place, and there was no sign of a forced entry from the door or the windows. "Maybe I should cancel my dinner with Wally."

"Nice try. We both have things to do. Let's lock up and have evidence collection sweep it in the morning. We can sleep at my place tonight."

Rook thought that one over a moment. "OK, but if anybody knocks on your door, you're answering it."

Heat arrived at Café Gretchen first, and even though the April air in Chelsea that night carried a brisk chill, in memory of Paris she defiantly chose one of the open sidewalk tables and ordered a latte while she waited for Carter Damon. Nikki was glad for her few moments of solitude, but they were anything but relaxing. The theft of the photos had unnerved her. She also wondered why Damon needed to see her on short notice. Maybe his guilt over basically phoning in his investigation had gotten to him and he wanted to make up for it. She tried to let go of her edginess by watching the evening strollers up on the High Line across Tenth Avenue from her.

The High Line represented everything Heat loved about New York: a bold idea done big and done right, and open to everybody. The half-mile, unused elevated railway spur had been a rusting urban eyesore for years until someone got the absurd notion to transform it into a linear aerial park. They cleaned it up, incorporated the rail tracks into the pedestrian walkway, added benches at vista points, then lined it, beginning to end, with diverse greenery including tall grasses, sumac, birches, and meadow plants. It had just opened the summer before, but already it had become such a pedestrian Mecca that the city was at work constructing an extension scheduled to be completed by the next summer.

Nikki scanned up and down the sidewalk. No Carter Damon yet. The waiter delivered her latte, and she watched the steam rise and curl sideways above the thin cuff of foam rimming the espresso. She raised the cup for a sip. It was still too hot to drink, so she pulled it back to blow on it.

And when she did, she saw the red laser dot appear on her cup.

SIXTEEN

The porcelain cup exploded in Nikki's hand. She immediately dropped for cover behind the planter beside her chair and reached for her gun. When she did, she found the cup handle still in her fingers and let it fall to the pavement. Her shirt front was warm and wet. She felt for a wound, but the liquid was latte, not blood. She wondered, How did he miss with a laser sight?

The answer came when she turned to make sure nobody behind her had taken the slug. Patrons inside the café were oblivious to her but were reacting to something else: An aftershock large enough to make the overhead lamps sway and send the stacked glassware behind the espresso bar crashing onto the back counter. Also large enough to throw off the aim of a sniper.

Heat popped up for a fast recon. As soon as she did, the red dot traced across the planter toward her, and she gophered down just as the shot rang out and the bullet kicked up a spray of potting soil. But she had seen the source of the laser.

"Man, did you feel that?" asked the waiter as he stepped out the door.

"Get inside," she shouted. His smile dropped when he saw the Sig Sauer in her hand. "Get everyone down. Away from this window." He started to back up. "And call 911. Tell them, sniper on the High Line, shots fired. Officer needs help." He hesitated. "Now."

She chanced another peek and saw a dark form break from his position in the tall grasses and run north on the elevated path. Heat vaulted the planter to the sidewalk and dodged traffic across Tenth to go after him.

As she ran, Nikki kept an eye upward to make sure he didn't stop to take another shot at her. She raced along the sidewalk past an hourly-rate parking lot and came to the public staircase leading up to the High

Line at 18th Street. She powered up the four zigzag flights and emerged topside, crouching, panting, gun braced.

Then she spotted him in the distance.

Her sniper had a good head start and was already crossing over West 19th. A strange familiarity came over Heat as she followed him—the night chase, the rifle he cradled—it all took her right back to her pursuit of Don's killer. She kicked up her speed, sprinting, all-out, so this one wouldn't get away.

Nikki lost a step dodging a couple standing in the path beside a park bench. When she blew past, the woman said to her boyfriend, "What's going on? She has a gun, too." Heat told them to call 911, hoping Dispatch could track her progress. Maybe backup would be there to cut the shooter off where the High Line terminated in one block, and he'd come down the stairs.

But he didn't take them.

When Nikki rounded a bend in the path, she caught his silhouette climbing over the top of the chain link fence to the construction zone for the park's extension. The perp spotted her, too. He dropped to the ground, setting up for a shot. But unslinging the rifle took time. She stopped and braced against a light post to take aim.

He rolled in the dirt behind a pile of gravel and disappeared. Seconds later she spotted him. With his rifle slung across his back, he blasted through an opening in a debris curtain that hung from a crane.

Following him through that drape made her too vulnerable. If he was waiting for her on the other side, she'd be a big target. So when Heat got over the fence, she opted to lose a few seconds to pick her way around to the side of it rather than roll through the partition in the middle.

She crept through at the edge and paused. Where was he?

Then Nikki heard feet running away on crushed cinder.

Even in daytime, the work zone for the High Line's new segment would have been challenging—an obstacle course of uneven dirt, piles of rebar, and stacks of old wooden crossties that had been ripped up and tossed aside for removal. But at night, it was plain treacherous. The only light in that section bled up from the street below. Everything on top where she ran became shadow and form, darkness and outline—including her perp.

When her eyes became better adjusted, Nikki pressed her speed but paid for it. She whiffed a massive pothole in the concrete and stepped right into it. Only a small crosshatch of rebar on one side of the hole kept Heat from falling right through it to the street below.

Nikki hated backing off her speed but resigned herself to a more careful pace and eased her sprint to a jog. Weaving around loose rocks and sharp metal, she approached the new section's termination at 30th Street, the end of the line. Heat cranked it down to a walk. That's when she saw the red dot cross the sawhorse beside her, then rise up her pant leg.

She dove behind a large plastic tub stenciled as "Clean Soil" and waited for the shot. It never came.

Heat rolled in the dirt. On the other side of the container, she came up in a brace. She spotted her sniper.

He was too far away to get an accurate shot. Plus he wasn't aiming at her anymore. He back-slung his rifle again, vaulted the ornate deco railing, and balanced his heels on the edge.

She started for him. "NYPD, freeze!"

He turned and stared right at her, then looked down—and dove.

Nikki reached the spot where he had leaped and looked in amazement. Immediately below her stood the Trapeze School of New York, housed in a giant, inflatable white dome. Her perp had soft landed on it like it was a kid's bouncy castle.

And fled.

Heat swung a leg over to follow but stopped when she saw him disappearing into a taxi across the street. She tried to get the medallion number, but it was too far away and it sped off too quickly.

Back at the sniper's hide overlooking Café Gretchen, the tech from Evidence Collection knelt to show Heat the compressed earth and trampled grasses where he had fired at her. "Get the best casts you can of those footprints," she said, thinking back to the work boot of whoever had ransacked Nicole Bernardin's apartment. "See if they're size eleven."

She stood up and arched her back. "You OK?" asked Detective Ochoa.

"Yeah, just a little sore. Took an unexpected step into a pothole up there during the chase."

"You're lucky that's all that's sore." Ochoa held up two plastic evidence bags, each containing a shell casing. "No shortage of stopping power here."

Heat curled her right hand to form a circular hollow in her palm and closed one eye to peer through it like a sniper's scope down at the café. Another ECU tech was busy inside the yellow tape excavating a slug from the planter beside her chair. Nikki felt a chill and turned back to Ochoa. "I don't want the same thing to happen with this brass that happened to the glove."

"Already with you. I'm taking these to the print lab myself and sitting with them all night, if I have to." He started to go but took a step back. "No more close calls, OK?"

"I'll try. Meanwhile, I'll never complain about an earthquake again."

Back down at street level, Heat found her waiter in the back of the café. When she handed him the money for her latte and tipped him, he said, "You're kidding, right?" And then he looked at her and saw that she wasn't.

A gleaming black Crown Victoria pulled up to the curb when she stepped back out front. Rook rolled out of the passenger seat and hugged her. "Now that I know you're alive, thank you for interrupting my dinner. Seriously. Bless you."

Wally Irons hauled himself from behind the wheel and ambled around the car to the sidewalk. "Heat, you're going to give me a heart attack."

"No, I think the mud pie will get you first, Captain," said Rook.

Irons chuckled and said to her, "Jamie's been like this all night. What a kidder." Then he frowned. "In all seriousness, Detective, in light of recent events that I shouldn't need to remind you of, what the hell are you doing exposing yourself to such a risky meet, alone and at night?"

"I appreciate your concern, sir, but I am working a case, and that's not going to stop at sundown. Plus, my meeting was with someone I knew, who happens to be an ex-cop, so it didn't seem like a risk to me."

"Now what does it seem like?" asked Rook.

"A setup."

"Who's the ex-cop?" asked Irons.

"Carter Damon. He was lead on my mother's case."

"Oh yeah, I remember him. From the Thirteenth." Irons surveyed the crime tape and the fractured planter beside Nikki's tipped-over chair. "Let me ask you this. He ever show up?"

"No, sir."

"You find that curious?" He inclined his head to Rook and muttered, "You should be getting some of this down." Rook just winked and tapped his forehead with his finger.

Nikki said, "I found it curious enough to call the One Twenty-second in Staten Island to send some uniforms to drop by his house."

"Already? Quick thinking," said Irons, which only made her fume. She was so close to insubordination, it was lucky he spoke again before she could. "They get him?"

"No. And there's an accumulation of mail and newspapers at his door."

"Want me to put out an APB for Carter Damon?"

"Already done, sir."

"Well, then." The captain stood jangling pocket change, then pulled back his cuff to see his watch. "You know, Rook, since everything's in hand here, we could—"

"Thanks the same, but you've already given me a lot to think about for one night. And I should probably hang out with Detective Heat."

"Sure thing," he said. The captain waited an awkward moment then got in his car. After he put it in gear, he powered down the passenger window and called across the front seat, "Alert me, twenty-four-seven, if there are any developments." Then he drove off.

"Who talks like that?" said Heat.

"A man hoping to be quoted."

She hated leaving Rook, so warm and naked under those sheets the next morning. He didn't make it any easier. "Sure, use me and go to work. I feel so cheap." And then he added, "There's a twenty on the dresser. Get yourself something nice." That's when the pillow landed on his face.

Before Nikki got into the shower, she did her ritual check of personal electronics. She came back into the bedroom holding her cell phone. "Rook, listen to this. I got a text from Carter Damon at four-fifteen this morning. It says, 'Heat. I am so sorry.'"

"For setting you up to be killed?" He looked at the text and handed the phone back to her. "Who says manners are dead?"

Nikki had already put in a good two hours when Rook strolled into the bull pen at nine. "Just got word from Detective Malcolm on Nicole Bernardin's cremation," she said. "Order came in from a mortuary that went out of business last year."

"Let me guess. Seacrest Mortuary?"

"No, but I hear what you're getting at. How bad is it, Rook, when even your wack conspiracy theories are nothing compared to this case?"

"Guess I just need to get wackier." He handed her a Starbucks. "Here. Now try not to get a bullet hole in this one."

"You know, I'm not one to give anyone the finger, even in jest, but I'm considering breaking my rule. You're just that special." She took the cup and saluted him with it. "What's the story in Tribeca?" she asked.

"Fingerprint techs were still dusting my loft when I split. They'll be most of the morning, but basically, they're telling me not to hold my breath. Except for one set of yours, from opening it, there are no prints to get off the filing cabinet."

"Wiped?"

"With extreme prejudice—a phrase that now seems apt. Same with the front doorknob and the door to the office. No prints even to lift."

"I'm trying to reconstruct the pictures in that box to figure out what someone would want, but I'm drawing a blank. I should have kept them in a safe."

"Like that would have stopped these guys." He sat on her desk and she pried a sheet of paper from under one of his cheeks. "Carter Damon ever get back to you?" She shook no. "Send flowers? Edible Arrangement? A bullet with your name on it?" This time she did sneak him the finger. He smiled. "There's hope for you yet, Nikki Heat."

"I tried calling Damon. No answer and his voice mail box is full. I put Malcolm and Reynolds on checking his gym, his barber, the usuals. They also ran his ATM and credit cards for activity. Nothing. He's off the grid."

"You think he might have just set you up, or was he your sniper?"

"At this point, anything's possible. But why? Because I pissed him off at lunch at P.J. Clarke's? And why the text apology?" Her phone rang. It was Detective Ochoa.

"Tell me the lab did not lose that brass."

"No, Raley and I camped out to make sure of that. In fact, I'm calling because we scored some nice, juicy prints and we have an ID on them."

"That's fantastic," she said. "Bring him in."

"I'm not thinking he's your man."

She slumped back in her chair. "Let's hear it."

"Raley, you on?"

His partner came on, conferenced in. "Yeah, so here's the deal. I met with the guy we ID'd. He runs an indoor gun range in the Bronx. He's a decorated combat vet with a stellar record. Nice guy, too."

"None of that rules him out as our sniper."

"True, but this does. He got paralyzed by an IED in Iraq and he's in a wheelchair."

"Then how did his prints get on those shell casings?" Nikki pondered that for a moment. "Sometimes these shooting ranges recycle spent brass and reload them. Your vet friend. Does he sell reloads?"

"Uh, yeah, in fact I saw a sign. You think our sniper bought his ammo from him?"

"I'm hoping so, Rales. I'm also hoping his name shows up in his sales records."

Shortly after Rook relocated to his squatter's desk to type up some of his field notes from the previous day's interviews, Sharon Hinesburg came in and turned on her computer. At first, Nikki tried to ignore her, but the scent of a fresh mani-pedi made her cave. She picked up the sheet of paper Rook had been sitting on and stepped over to her. "Good morning, Detective," she said.

"We'll see." Hinesburg opened her desk drawer carefully so she wouldn't trash her new manicure.

"Listen, I've got everyone else deployed so I need you to run a check on someone for me." She handed her the page. "His name's Mamuka Leonidze. He may be out of the country. Notes are all here."

Hinesburg flashed a brief, condescending smile. "Sorry. I already have an assignment, direct from the precinct commander. The OCME gas truck?"

"And how's that going, Detective?"

"Slow." She handed the sheet of notes back. "Give it to Rook. He's not doing anything. He's just writing."

The administrative aide called across the pen, "Detective Heat, Feller on your line. Says it's important."

Heat let go the standoff with Hinesburg for the moment and grabbed the call. "You've got to be kidding," she said, loud enough to get Rook to saunter over while she scrawled an address. "Be there in fifteen." She hung up, tore the top sheet off the notepad, and said to him, "They found Carter Damon."

"Where?"

"Floating in the East River."

Lauren Parry had already set up shop on the East River piers off the FDR when Heat arrived. The traffic control uniform moved the sawhorse and waved her and Rook through, and she parked her Crown Vic between Randall Feller's and the white OCME van. Detective Feller, who was a hundred yards out on the elbow of the L-shaped pier with Lauren and the body, spotted Heat and walked to the parking area to meet her. When he arrived, he pulled off his wraparounds and hooked the sunglasses by the temple in the V of his T-shirt. He wore a sober look, a stark contrast to his customary crime scene grabass face. Heat picked up on the change in him right off.

"Tell me what you know," she said.

With years in the street and an orderly mind, he didn't need to consult notes. "Harbor Unit hauled him out of the drink about an hour ago. A pilot for the helicopter service that leases the pier spotted him on approach and radioed it in." Nikki could see the small blue airport shuttle chopper tied down on the pad at the end of the wharf, farther out in the channel. "Harbor said they'd been on the lookout for a floater. Middle of the night, a motorist called Bridges and Tunnels to say he saw somebody go off the Brooklyn Bridge."

"Kersplat," said Rook, getting a reproachful glance from Nikki.

"The eyewit says he wasn't alone, someone was up there with him."

"Did he say there was a struggle, or was Damon a jumper and somebody tried to stop him?"

"Unclear. Detective Rhymer is en route to get that statement now. Should be a solid witness, though. A cardiologist driving in for an early surgery at Downtown Hospital. Opie will brace the doc soon as he finishes his operation."

Like Nikki, Rook must have also been thinking of suicide and the apology text she'd received at four-fifteen A.M. "What time did this come down?" he asked.

"About four-thirty."

"Let's go check in with Lauren," said Heat, and she started to walk out onto the pier. Feller and Rook kept up and she asked, "Any note on him?"

"No but one thing you need to know, and it's big. He'd been shot."

That stopped Nikki in her tracks. The other two stopped with her. Rook said, "I wonder if he was shot by the sniper who tried to get you last night."

Detective Feller said, "Definitely not."

"You sound mighty certain," said Heat.

"Because I am. Detective, I know who shot him."

"You know who shot Carter Damon?" Feller nodded. "Who?"

"You."

SEVENTEEN

The two bullet holes in Carter Damon had Nikki Heat's name on them. The medical examiner had already cut the shirt off his corpse, and both upper-body entry wounds matched with the rounds she'd put in him the night of Don's killing.

Lauren Parry squatted in a catcher's stance on the deck of the pier, where his body had been placed by the Harbor Unit, and indicated the wounds with the tip of her stick pen, beginning with the one in the left side of his neck where it met the shoulder. "Let's start with this one here."

"That's from the shot I got off through the passenger window of the taxi."

"When I do the postmortem, my money says this one was nearly fatal. You were on the curb, as I recall from your Shooting Incident Report, so this would have come down at an angle, probably getting awfully close to the subclavian vein or the jugular, or both. If you'd outright hit one of those, he'd have died in minutes, if that long. So, I'm thinking a tiny nick, and assume he did a lot of slow bleeding over the past few days. But I'll know better down in B-Twenty-three," she said, referring to the autopsy room number.

Heat knelt on one knee beside her and pointed to the second wound, the one on his chest. "What are those marks around the entry hole?"

"Good eye. Those marks you see are from sutures. They must have torn open when he hit the water coming off the bridge." She put her face an inch from the wound. "Uh-huh. I see thread fragments."

"But we checked ERs," said Nikki. "No reports of him, anywhere."

Rook said, "Are you saying this guy stitched himself up? Talk about macho. Take that, Chuck Norris."

Lauren said, "I highly doubt he did this himself. This is a professional-looking job." Then, when she saw Nikki duck over the other bullet hole, she added, "I couldn't see any evidence of work done on the other wound."

"Why one and not the other?" asked Detective Feller.

"The other wound is high-risk because of proximity to veins and arteries. Whoever took care of him knew to leave it alone."

"So," Nikki said, "Damon got some kind of aid, but off the books." She stood and stretched her back. "And he wasn't dead when he went in the river?"

"Doubtful. See all the bruising here?" Lauren traced her finger along the discoloration on his face and chest. "That seems consistent with impact when he hit the water. And I just saw evidence of clotting where the sutures tore on wound two. That wouldn't happen if he'd been dead. I'll be able to check for mast cells to confirm when I get back to my microscope. Also, I'll check his lungs in the post. If he was alive, he'll have river water in them."

As the detectives and Rook left for their cars, Lauren held Nikki back to speak in confidence. "I'm still stressing Nicole Bernardin's messed-up tox test."

"Obviously not your fault, Laur. And Irons is on it now."

"Is he? I had Security pull our surveillance tapes so they didn't get recorded over, but when I called Captain Irons to arrange getting them, he said to call Detective Hinesburg and I never got a call back."

"Typical," said Heat. "I'll put Raley on it. He's King of All Surveillance Media, you know."

"What about Irons? Won't that piss him off?"

"Doctor, as long as he's out of my way, I truly don't care."

The atmosphere in the bull pen was crackling when Heat walked in, and she called a squad meeting to kick up the momentum. But first, she had to clear a few gnats out of the way. Lon King had left Nikki a message reminding her to make a shrink appointment. She balled up the note and trashed it. Dealing with the Iron Man wasn't quite as easy.

The captain found her in the kitchen while she was getting coffee. "Detective Heat, I assume, since Carter Damon is off the boards, we can now close this case out and release our overtime personnel?"

"How is it over? He was one player, the way I see it."

"He killed your Navy SEAL friend, right? He probably did the lady in the suitcase, too."

"Probably isn't the same as proving. And there's still my mother."

"So you don't think it's convenient he was lead on that case?"

"Good question," she said. "If you'll excuse me, Captain, I'm going to do my job and investigate it." She left him standing in the kitchen without a glance back.

Detective Heat still had plenty of questions troubling her. With Sharon Hinesburg off God knew where, and Irons in the kitchen making toaster waffles, she was able to share them with her brain trust gathered at the Murder Boards. In the green square she had created for Don's case, Nikki printed "Carter Damon" in block letters and said, "OK, we solved Don's killing."

"We? More like you and Mr. Sauer," said Detective Malcolm, kicking off a small round of applause that she quelled with one glance.

"But," she continued, "one solve opens a slew of other questions."

Raley said, "Sure, because Don wasn't the target, you were."

"Correct. So we're right back to, why come after me?"

"Simple," said Reynolds. "You were digging into your mother's case."

"But I was always digging into that case. Does anyone here doubt a week went by that I didn't check into it?" Nobody challenged that. "And why would he be the one to come after me?" She turned and wrote under Carter Damon's name: "What stake in murders?"

"I know why he came after you," said Rook. "You lit up the radar. Not just by digging into your mother's case—you were digging way back in her case. That upset somebody. If not Carter Damon, somebody he worked with."

"Or for," said Feller, finding himself in rare agreement with the writer. "I mean, Damon was a blunt instrument. Guys like that follow instructions, take their pay, and spend Saturdays waxing the car."

Ochoa said, "I agree. It can't be just one dude. And Carter Damon sure didn't take those shots at you up on the High Line."

Detective Rhymer came in from interviewing the eyewitness from the Brooklyn Bridge. "What did you get?" Heat asked before he even sat.

"Mixed. Dr. Arar was driving in from Park Slope this morning at four-thirty. He was mid-span when he thought he saw someone ahead

tossing a garbage bag over the side. Then he got closer and saw the garbage bag had arms and legs. So he hit the brakes just as the guy went
over. He says he stopped and honked his horn at the person tossing him
over, and when he did, she started running the opposite way."

"Hold on," said Heat. "She? Your eyewit says the other person was
a woman?"

"He has no doubt."

"What's the description?"

"Five-nine or -ten, athletic build, dark clothing, hat."

"Did he see her face? Can we work up a sketch?"

"That's the mixed part. He says it was too dark, and she didn't turn
to look at him. Just put her head down and booked."

Malcolm asked, "How does he know for sure it was a woman?"

"I asked him the same thing. He said he's a doctor, and he knows a
woman when he sees one."

"I always check for Adam's apples," said Feller. "Avoids a lot of awkward surprises when you get them home."

When their ribbing died down, Raley asked Heat, "What about
your sniper last night? Is it possible you were chasing a female instead
of a male?"

Nikki said, "I don't know. I never saw the Adam's apple," and started
her next round of assignments. She sent Malcolm and Reynolds out to
Staten Island to assist the 122nd Precinct in its search of Carter Damon's
house. Among the rest of the unit, she divvied up checks of his phone
records and financials. To be thorough, she had Feller check the four
people on Joe Flynn's piano tutoring list for alibis during her High Line
attack. Rhymer got the task of re-canvassing ERs and pharmacies now
that they knew Damon had received some sort of medical aid.

"Happy to," said Opie, "but didn't we cover that base last week?"

"We did, and now we can do it again—but with a photo of Carter
Damon to e-mail them." She capped her marker and said to the group,
"This is a good time to remind all of you: Do not get complacent. I
know it feels like we're starting to get traction with some hot leads, but
this can just as easily go the wrong way if we don't stay sharp and do
the donkey work. That's the way we'll bring these cases home."

When the squad had deployed, Heat dispatched a uniform to First

Avenue to pick up the OCME security cam data Lauren Parry had secured. Nikki would hold it for Raley to scrub after he'd run Damon's
financial checks. Or she might even drop it in Sharon Hinesburg's lap,
if the diva detective ever made an appearance.

Nikki phoned Lauren to let her know to expect the video pickup.
"Oh, this isn't a call to say, 'Come on, girl, hurry up, what's taking so
long with my autopsy?'"

"No way." Heat paused then said, "Well, since you brought up the
autopsy . . ."

Her friend chuckled and told Nikki this was good timing, she had
just completed it. "First off, yes to water in the lungs. Carter Damon was
breathing when he went in. Also, around the torn sutures, I did find mast
cells, white blood cells, and lymphocytes. That's what I look for under
the scope when I want to know if a live body was trying to heal itself."
Nikki heard a page of notes turn on Lauren's end and the medical examiner continued, "Here's an interesting wrinkle. Not only had that chest
wound been sutured, whoever did it removed the bullet. Not the most
elegant job, but good enough. So we're dealing with a reasonable degree
of competence."

"What about the neck?"

"Minor graze of the jugular. Toldja! Who's better than me?"

Nikki said, "You need to spend more time with people. Preferably
living."

"Too much work. Anyway, that slug was still lodged there. Of course,
I saved it for ballistics, but I'm sure it'll match the nine-millimeter from
your gun."

Rook came back to loiter on her desktop when she'd hung up. "Know
what I can't shake out of my brain since the pier this morning? Small
thing, but, ask yourself—What was the odd sock about Carter Damon's
body?"

"I regret the day I ever taught you about odd socks."

He ignored her and said, "Give up? I'll tell you: No old scar from
getting shot when he was a rookie. Remember he told us about that at
lunch?"

"Maybe you just didn't see it."

"I didn't see it because there wasn't one."

"Well, I happen to know he's still on a mat down at the ME's. Want me to call Lauren back to check?"

"You don't have to. I had one of the administrative aides call down to Personnel."

"Rook. You used one of our aides to make a call for you?"

"I had to, since Personnel has this 'thing' about civilians accessing confidential police records. Anyway, Carter Damon never got shot. Why would the guy lie about that?"

Rook was right, it was a small thing. But Heat knew small things often made critical jigsaw fits, and noted it on the Murder Board, although Rook complained she had written it in tiny letters.

That afternoon, through the buzz of phone conversations from detectives making rounds and lunch orders getting delivered because nobody wanted to take a break, came a holler from Rhymer at his desk. "Got one!" Opie sounded like he'd hooked a big fish. In a sense, he had.

Heat drove Rook and Detective Raley up to the Bronx as fast as she could get there. Having rolled through every yellow light and punching the accelerator when they were about to turn red, she double-parked in front of Price It Drugs and hustled inside.

The pharmacy sat three blocks from where Carter Damon had abandoned his jacked taxi the night Nikki shot him. In addition to blast e-mailing Damon's photo to ERs and drugstores in all the boroughs, Detective Rhymer had gotten a map and worked the phones in concentric circles radiating out from the dumped cab. The first walk-in clinic he'd called came up zip. His next try was a small drugstore on Southern Boulevard near Prospect. The owner, who was elderly and not so big on e-mail, had missed the earlier alerts but pegged Damon by the detective's description. He confirmed it when Rhymer faxed him his photo.

Diligent as she was eager, Detective Heat showed her copy of Carter Damon's photo to the owner to double-check in person. "Yes, that is him," said Hugo Plana, also reaffirming that the wounded Damon had staggered in just before closing at midnight, the night of the shooting. "He came in on his own, but I don't know how," said the old man. He took off his bifocals and handed the photo back to her. "He was a mess. Blood here and here." Hugo pointed to the two bullet wounds Heat had given the ex-cop. "I asked him if he wanted me to call an ambulance and he shouted at me, 'No!', like that. Then he told me he wanted some gauze and some scissors and antiseptic to dress the wounds. He started to pass out, so I helped him to one of the chairs over there in the prescription waiting area."

"How come you didn't call the police?" asked Rook. "Guy came into my place like that, I'd sneak a call, no matter what he said."

The old man smiled and nodded. "Yes, I understand. But, you see, we are a small, independent pharmacy. A family business. In this neighborhood, I see a lot of folks in bad shape. My goodness, it's unbelievable. Sometimes a fight, sometimes a turf war—sometimes, I don't want to know. When they come for help, I help. I'm not here to ask too many questions or to bust them. They trust me. They're my neighbors."

Heat asked, "So did you get the supplies he wanted?"

"I did. I put a bag together, and when I finished, he was out of it. His head kept dropping down and up. I offered to call an ambulance again but he refused. Then his cell phone rang and he asked me if there was a hotel nearby. I told him the Key Largo is on the corner, and he told me to help him to his feet. Then he gave me a bunch of cash, took the shopping bag, and left."

"Do you know who called him?" asked Rhymer.

Hugo shook his head. "It just sounded like someone was coming to meet him and needed to know a place."

The lobby of the Key Largo was dark and carried the stink of every scuzzy hotel Nikki had ever investigated—a mix of stale mustiness, harsh cleansers, and dead smoke. The floorboards creaked under the soiled carpet leading to the front desk. Nobody was there, and a plastic sign with missing moveable clock hands said, "Back in . . ."

Nikki called a hello and got no answer. Rook said, "Wow, they've re-created the elegance and charm of Key Largo right here in the Bronx. Makes me feel like I'm Bogey and you're Bacall." He tapped the service bell with his palm. It did not ding. Then, to Rhymer's amusement, he examined his hand with a frown and wiped it on the thigh of his pants. Heat was about to call out again when her phone vibrated. It was Malcolm checking in from Staten Island.

"Have something juicy for you, Detective Heat." Nikki turned away from the desk and started to pace. "The squad from SI is still going over Damon's house, but Reynolds and I discovered he rented a public storage unit one town over in Castleton Corners. Guess what's inside."

"Just fucking tell her, man," said Reynolds in the background. Heat agreed.

"A van," he said, making her heart quicken.

"Maroon?" she asked.

"Affirm. And the lettering on the side? 'Righty-O Carpet Cleaners.'"

"You guys did great." But Heat held the brake on her excitement and went practical. "Now, please tell me you're both gloved up."

"Yes, ma'am, we are the Blue Hands Group."

"Excellent. Have you touched anything?"

"No, just shined a light in the rear window to make sure there was nobody in there, alive or dead. It's clear."

"Now here's what I want you to do. Step out of there and stay out. Leave the door up where it is, don't touch the handle again. Just stand guard and get the Evidence Collection Unit on this with a fine-toothed comb. And when I say ECU, I want Benigno DeJesus and only Benigno DeJesus. No screwups."

"Got it."

"And Mal? You and Reynolds rock."

Heat had just finished filling in Rook and Rhymer when the front desk clerk, a large middle-aged white woman with bleached cornrows, emerged from the back, followed by a trail of cigarette smoke. "Booking a three? That's a fifty-dollar damage deposit." She plucked the be-back sign off the counter and pulled some keys from a cubby behind her. When she turned back, she was looking at Nikki's shield.

The clerk's name was DD, and they followed her down the second-floor hallway, stepping over numerous duct tape repairs to the carpet. "Think again, DD," said Nikki. "Are you sure you didn't see anyone else come up here to visit him?"

"I don't see anything, anytime, anyhow. People come and go."

Rook asked, "What about another person staying with him, you'd have to know that, wouldn't you?"

"Technically. But come on." She stopped mid-hall and gestured to the joint with both arms spread out as a woman in bright yellow hot pants and a halter passed them on the way to the elevator. The picture made it hard to argue. "Dude paid up two weeks in advance in cash. Alls I care about."

They stopped at a door at the end of the hall with a "Do Not Disturb" dangling from the handle. Wondering about site contamination and forensics, Nikki asked, "Has housekeeping been in here?"

"Yuh, right," DD scoffed and pointed at the sign. "No little chocklits on his pillow." Then she rapped twice and said, "Yo, manager." When she slid the key in, Nikki motioned her back. She and Rhymer rested their hands on their holsters and went in first.

"Holy fuck," said DD, summing it up for all of them. She backed away and said, "I gotta call the owner," and rushed out.

Blood covered everything. The bed, especially the pillow and head end of the top sheet, was a dry lake of deep rust. A pile of towels on the floor beside it was likewise saturated in red. The desk, which had been moved to the middle of the room, was covered by the ripped-down shower curtain. On one end of that vinyl sheeting, there was yet another pool of blood that had separated over time, with amber at the edges and deep maroon in the center of the stain. Cinnamon red, like drippings from a candle, clung to the sides of the shower curtain where blood had leaked and made small puddles in the rug, which also looked dried. Clumps of bloody gauze decorated the floor there beside their torn, discarded sterile packaging.

Rook said, "I haven't seen this much blood in a hotel since *The Shining.*"

"Looks like I found my ER," said Opie.

"And makeshift ICU," said Heat. She left Detective Rhymer in charge of the scene, hoping that, in the middle of all that, Forensics could get some prints and find out who administered to Carter Damon.

When Nikki came back from the Bronx with Rook, Roach was waiting and pounced on her at the door of the bull pen. They led her to their side-by-side desks, where they had organized a briefing. "Bank, first," said Detective Raley. "Turns out Carter Damon had a money trail of his own." He opened a file on his monitor and clicked through pages of bank statements as he talked. "Look here. A three-hundred-thousand-dollar deposit went into his account the Monday after your mom got killed. And then, see here? Smaller sums—twenty-five grand—every six months thereafter."

The shocking conclusion was too obvious not to draw—that a member of the fraternity, an NYPD detective, might have killed her mother by contract and then been retained to screw with the investigation's progress. Obvious or not, Nikki fought the instinct to close her mind by racing to that conclusion just yet and asked, "How long did he get the payments?"

"Till last month. Then, big change." He brought up the next page. "Another deposit for three hundred thou, two weeks ago."

Nikki looked at the date. "That's the day we found Nicole Bernardin in the suitcase."

"And the same day we met ex–Homicide Detective Carter Damon for lunch," added Rook. "Was that a payment for doing Nicole, or for trying to kill you?"

"Or both?" wondered Ochoa. "Phone records tell a story, too." He gave Heat a copy of the printouts he had researched. Rook read over her shoulder.

"I highlighted three major calls of interest. Bottom of page one, note that Damon made two international calls to a disposable mobile number in Paris. One the night Nicole was killed—to refresh your memory, that would have been two nights before we found the suitcase— and the second call to Paris, same burner cell, right after meeting you and Rook for lunch."

Nikki took a moment to quiet her mind and said, "All right, just trying this on. Let's suppose, for argument's sake, the first call to Paris was about killing Nicole Bernardin. Either to get the order or confirm that he'd killed her. What's the second call about, do you think?"

Rook said, "Maybe Damon was calling in the hit man who killed Tyler Wynn. He could have been your sniper last night."

"Yeah, but we checked incoming passengers from Paris through U.S. Customs, remember?" said Ochoa. "No knowns on the watch list."

"So?" said Rook. "Maybe whoever it was came in through another port of entry, like Boston or Philadelphia. Or isn't on a watch list."

"Let's keep thinking on this," Nikki said.

"Did Damon make any calls to the Bernardins in Paris?" asked Rook. "Any chance he was the elusive Mr. Seacrest?"

Detective Ochoa shrugged. "No record. But that call came from a burner, remember?"

Heat turned to the next page of Ochoa's printout. "What's this call here?"

"It's not the call, it's the timing. Check it out. Carter Damon made this one immediately after he hung up on his Paris call following your lunch with him."

Raley said, "If it's like Feller said, and Damon was a blunt instrument, looks to me like maybe somebody told him what to do, and he did it."

"Miguel, I assume you ran the number," said Nikki.

"You assume correctly. No wants or warrants on the party he called. The number is listed on Second Ave to a Salena Kaye."

Heat and Rook whipped their heads to each other. He said, "Salena!? That's my naughty nurse!"

The gumball on the roof of the Roach Coach reflected in Heat's rearview mirror as they ran a convoy, Code Two, across Central Park and uptown to Salena Kaye's address on Second near 96th Street. Nikki chirped her siren crossing Fifth Avenue as she came out of the transverse. As she steered onto Eighty-fourth, Heat checked her mirror to make sure Raley had kept up, and Rook said, "Well, now I know why Carter Damon lied to me about getting shot. He was just BSing me into swapping rehab stories so I'd give him Gitmo Joe's name. He must have tracked him through my agency and had him replaced by his girl Salena."

"I'm right there with you." Nikki blasted her horn and jerked her wheel to pass a delivery truck that had dead-stopped her lane. Turning uptown, she continued, "Damon placed her with you to keep tabs on the case. Think of it, Rook, she saw Murder Board South, our case notes, and everything before she left." Nikki couldn't resist, and added, "Smiling those big white teeth the whole time."

Rook caught her needle and countered, "She gave one helluva massage, too."

She pulled to the curb at Ninety-sixth and threw it in park. "Time to pay a house call on a naughty nurse." But when Rook got out, she said, "Oh no, you stay here."

"Why? Is this payback for what I said about the massage? I was thinking of you the whole time, I swear."

She joined up with Raley and Ochoa at the front steps to the apartment building. "Not going to debate this. Stay in the car, I mean it."

"What is he, like, six?" said Ochoa on the way in.

"You flatter him," said Raley.

Up at the apartment door on the fifth story, Raley knelt beside the lock, holding the key from the super at the ready. Heat and Ochoa flanked him with guns drawn. "Salena Kaye, NYPD, open up," she called. No answer. Heat gave Rales the nod and he keyed the lock. Nikki turned the knob and pushed, but the door hit something solid, a piece of furniture, and stopped.

"Mine," said Ochoa. He backed up and gave the door a flying kick with his foot. It opened only a few inches. "Together, pard," he said, then he and Raley hit the door with both their shoulders, and they were in.

"Bedroom, clear," said Ochoa.

"Kitchen, clear," called Heat.

Raley came out from the bathroom and holstered. "Not in the bathroom, either."

Detective Ochoa said, "She busted out of here in a hurry. The drawers are open and there's a half-packed duffel on the bed."

Nikki saw the open window. On her way out the door she shouted, "Fire escape. One of you go high. I'll take the street."

Heat blasted out the lobby stairs and raced through the vestibule onto the sidewalk. Rook was standing beside the Crown Vic, pointing. "A car service picked her up."

"Get in," she said.

"I saw them take a left on Ninety-seventh."

"Buckle up," she said and lit the gumball.

As they rounded the corner, he got out his cell phone. "I also got the medallion number of the car." He got Dispatch for the car service. "I'm declaring a police emergency, I need to know the drop route for your car number K-B-four-one-three-one-nine." At Lexington he pointed frantically to make a left, and she did. He asked for the plate number and wrote it down. "Appreciate the assist," he said and hung up. "JFK, via Midtown Tunnel."

"You did that a little too easily," she said, reaching for her radio mic.

"Hey. Investigative journalists have their tricks, too."

Detective Heat called in to alert the duty officers at the tunnel entrance to detain a black Lincoln Town Car and gave the plate number Rook had gotten. Nikki still kept her speed up and, just after they crossed 42nd Street, Rook said, "There! Right lane, passing the Pret A Manger."

One bleep of the siren, and the sedan pulled over and stopped. She called for backup and opened her door. "Stay," she told Rook.

The windows were not tinted and the backseat appeared empty. She approached in the blind spot with her Sig up and threw open the rear door.

No one in the backseat.

Nikki opened the front passenger door and that was empty, too. The driver still had his hands up as she holstered her weapon. "Where's your passenger?"

"The lady told me to let her out right after the pickup. I dropped her way back at Sixty-sixth, up near the Armory." Heat looked uptown, feeling hopeless. "I told her she paid for an airport run and she said to keep going there."

"Do me a favor, sir, pop your trunk," she said, knowing it was futile.

She allowed Rook to accompany her back up to Salena Kaye's apartment this time. Raley and Ochoa were gloved up, going over the living room when she came in. She handed Rook an extra pair from her case.

Raley said, "Just heard from Detective Rhymer up at the fleabag. We shot him a text pic of Salena Kaye from the photo over there." He indicated the picture frame on the bookshelf beside the TV. "He said to tell you DD—you'd know who that is—positively ID'd Salena as the woman who was visiting Carter Damon's room during his stay."

What should have been joy at making that key connection to Carter Damon slid into the pit as Nikki's heart sank at losing her suspect. It must have shown on her. "Pretty slick move, ditching you like that," said Ochoa.

"Tell me," said Heat. "I really thought we had her."

Raley cleared his throat. "Maybe we could just follow the scent of tea tree oil."

"Hilarious," said Rook. "What happened to the whole brotherhood of Roach Blood thing?"

"We talked it over. We want our blood back."

Nikki just let them riff and walked the rest of the apartment. Losing Salena didn't cancel out the day of progress, but it absolutely left a bad taste. Before the gloom could seep in, she decided to get busy. "You guys get the bedroom yet?"

"Not yet," said Roach.

The duffel was still open at the foot of the bed, so Heat started there, figuring what Salena Kaye would pack to take with her meant the most to her. The outer pockets contained makeup and toiletries bagged in TSA portions. The end zipper section held a blow dryer and brushes. The main compartment was half-filled with a pair of sandals, a bikini, some Victoria's Secret underwear, on the daring side—no surprise—and a pair of jeans. She carefully lifted that stack out to set on the bedspread and let out a "Yesss!" to the empty room.

Underneath the clothing, Nikki had found her stolen keepsake box of photos.

EIGHTEEN

In a rare and blatant move of tactical Irons avoidance, Nikki Heat skipped going back to the station house after completing the search of Salena Kaye's apartment that evening. The last time she had called in, Detective Feller told her that the captain was in his glass box highlighting CompStats but had regularly scoped the bull pen to check her desk. Whatever he wanted, it would have to wait. Nikki had a date with the keepsake box.

After confirming that the APB had gone out on Salena Kaye and satisfying herself that Malcolm and Reynolds had the forensic examination of Carter Damon's van covered, she took her reclaimed photos and cabbed down to Tribeca to meet up with Rook at his loft.

He had gone there an hour before to keep an appointment with a locksmith, and when Heat arrived, Rook handed her a shiny brass key to fit his new deadbolt. "I'd like to think a new lock makes a diff," he said, "but the way things have been going, I might as well just leave the front door wide open and slap Post-its where to find the good stuff."

"One good thing," she said. "Now that we know it was Salena, we don't need to worry that Forensics didn't find any prints."

"Maybe they didn't score any fingerprints, but they did find my little Scotty dog under the couch."

"Yay, Forensics."

"It must have gotten knocked off the table and rolled under there when Salena planted this." He held up a small black box with a wire dangling from it.

"A bug? So she not only had access to our Murder Board and stole these pictures, she planted a bug?"

"Now I'm all paranoid about things I might have said." And then he added with a sly grin, "During the massage, I mean."

"I've heard you in your ecstasy, Rook. I'd be paranoid, too." Then Heat set up shop at the dining room table, opening the lid of the keepsake box and poring over the photos.

The first pass through was to eyeball for jewelry. If that bracelet with the one and the nine charms held any meaning, the first clue would be to see if her mother, Nicole, or anyone else in the pictures wore it or something similar. But after scrutinizing every picture, they had seen no similar bracelets or jewels of unusual note.

Next she set about arranging the pictures in separate piles. When Rook couldn't detect a pattern to her stacks, he said, "Pardon me if I'm in violation of using your registered trademark, but what are you doing, looking for an odd sock?"

"No, actually I'm looking for the opposite of that. I'm playing around with various sequences and configurations to see what matches instead of what doesn't. Just letting instincts dictate piles. For instance, these are turning out to be a bunch of poses with tutor patron families. I'll make that one stack."

"Got it," he said. "And these here . . . What, solo shots of your mother and a piano at various homes?"

"Right, there you go." Nikki continued sorting and resorting, creating categories of pictures including poses with Tyler Wynn and her mom, Oncle Tyler with Nicole, Tyler with other groups, and then the last stack of remainders—constituting all the solo shots of members of the Nanny Network in those comical, goofy poses, gesturing like spokesmodels.

Rook went over to the counter to pour some hot water through two Melitta filters of French roast, leaving her to spread that last stack out across the table. She found herself drawn to these more by feeling than reason. What were these pictures telling her? She tried rearranging them by date stamp on the backs. The sequence didn't teach her anything. She made another order by geography. She stared at that grouping for a while and felt nothing coming back. Then Heat tried something uncomfortable for her: She let go of Cop-Think and went back to something more primal.

She let Nikki, the seasoned investigator, think like Nikki, the little girl. And when she did, she thought of how her mom used to love to make her laugh by striking those very same *Price Is Right* model poses at home. Or to Nikki's greater mortification, in the aisle of a super-market or at Macy's. She called it "styling," and little Nikki would giggle or groan with embarrassment depending on where her mom styled. The funniest places were at home, safely away from the eyes of schoolmates—or anyone, for that matter. Cynthia would sweep her graceful arms and delicate wrists in front of the oven. Then she'd open the door to style the interior. And then do the same for the fridge, opening the crisper and styling a head of lettuce. "Styling," her mom had said, "is what you do when it's not polite to point."

A new idea triggered by that old memory dawned on Heat. She looked at one photo, then another. Sure, this could have been some run-ning gag or inside joke within the network; the early version of how people nowadays text cell shots of food in the shape of presidents, or forced perspectives of themselves pretending to hold up the Gateway Arch or cradling the Hollywood sign in the palm of a hand.

But what if it wasn't a joke?

What if her mother and Nicole Bernardin and Eugene Summers and her other friends weren't just goofing but were doing something else? What if they were using what appeared to be a sophomoric joke as cover for something more serious?

If styling was what one did when it was impolite to point, what if they were pointing at something?

She called Rook over to the array on the table and shared her idea. "Go with me on this," she said then tapped the first shot. "Check it out. Here's our butler, Eugene, in front of the Riesenrad Ferris wheel in Vienna back in 1977. He's holding the camera in one hand to take his own picture, and with the other, he's styling toward that booth of tourist brochures." She went to the next. "Here's young Nicole in 1980 in Nice. She's at the out-door flower market, but look, she's gesturing to a service locker near the entrance. And even in this one . . ." She picked up the picture of Cynthia in Paris—the same one Nikki had used for her reenactment to stand in her mother's footsteps. "In this one, Mom's styling toward that wooden book vendor's stall. See it, the one that's over on the side of the square near the Seine?" She set the photo down with care. "I think these are signals."

"Hey," said Rook, "I definitely think you're on to something, but I'm the foil hat guy, remember? How do we find out for sure?"

"I know how." Heat opened her notebook and flipped pages until she found the cell number she wanted.

Eugene Summers gave her a chilly reception, obviously still harboring bruised feelings following the slight he'd felt from Rook at lunch. But the butler was, in the end, a man of manners. He took a break from shooting *Gentlemen Prefer Bongs* out in Bel Air to find a private place to answer her question. He didn't even play the what-if game. "You cracked the code, so I might as well tell you. Especially since it's a dead protocol anyway. You're absolutely correct. We'd adopted those modeling poses as our own little Nanny Network secret language. In fact, it was your mother who came up with the idea of styling. She'd say, 'Styling is what you do—'"

"'—when it's not polite to point,'" said Nikki, doubling him. And then she asked, "Tell me one more thing. What were you pointing to?" Heat believed she had cracked that one, too, but needed to hear it from him, and without prompting.

"Remember I told you about drop boxes? We'd use these pictures as a means to secretly show each other the locations of our various hiding places."

Feeling a wave of exhilaration starting to lift her, she thanked Summers and hung up just as Rook returned to join her from his back office. He came into the great room brandishing the jumbo magnifying glass from his desk that had been decommissioned to the role of paperweight. "I knew this impulse buy would come in handy someday." He held it over one of the photos of Nicole Bernardin.

"I already saw this," said Heat. "Taken somewhere here in New York, right?"

"Have a closer look and see where."

Nikki leaned over and peered through the lens. Rook moved it off the image of Nicole and aligned it on the background. When Heat saw the enlarged sign come into focus behind Nicole, she shot her eyes up at him and said, "Let's go."

When Heat and Rook got to the Upper West Side, they both felt thrust into a replay of their photo moment at the Notre Dame Cathedral when Nikki had put one foot on the brass marker at Point Zero and he'd framed the shot. Only this was not a sentimental reenactment of her mother's pose. They were restaging one by Nicole to learn its message and, hopefully, find a killer.

"We want to be somewhere around here," Nikki said, circling on the sidewalk near the street corner. Using the old picture for reference, Heat moved closer to the phone booth. "This it?" Rook stood a few feet away, looking at her image on his iPhone screen. He fanned the fingers of his left hand, directing her to shift a few inches to the side, and she did.

"Set," he said. Then Nikki rotated and, behind her, saw the small green sign Rook had magnified in the background of Nicole's photo: "W 91st ST."

"All right, so we had the charms on the bracelet reversed," said Rook. "It's nine and one, not one and nine. But what do you suppose Mademoiselle Bernardin was pointing to?"

Nikki studied the photo again and struck Nicole Bernardin's spokesmodel pose. "This here, this is what she's going for." Nikki's styling indicated a subway grate, about the surface area of a coffee table, recessed in the concrete.

"Why would she be pointing here?" asked Rook. "It's just a ventilation grate." The ground rumbled, and a rush of air came up to warm their faces through the screening as a subway passed below and continued onward. Rook said, "Son of a— I know!" He bent over and tried to look through the mesh. "It's not the grate, Nikki, it's what's down there. Oh, this is cool." His face lit up. "This is cray-cray cool."

"Rook. Shut up and talk to me."

"There's an abandoned subway station down there. Holy crap, I did an article on it for the *Gotham Eye* when I was freelancing after J-school. Fifty years ago the city closed the station when the extension of the new platform at Ninety-sixth Street stretched all the way down to Ninety-third and made this stop obsolete. They just sealed off this station and left it to rust. If you look out the window of the One train, you can still see the old ticket booth and gates when you roll by. It looks spooky, all frozen in time. In fact, the MTA old-timers still call it the Ghost Station." Rook paused while another train sped under them, quaking the ground. "Ghost Station. Not a bad hiding place for something like a drop box, if you ask me."

Rather than mock him for spinning another wild theory, Nikki recalled Nicole Bernardin's forensic results that reported grime consistent with a railroad environment on the soles of her shoes and on the knee of her pants. So instead of tweaking Rook, she asked one question. "How do we get down there?"

"Beats me. I remember my PR guide from the transit authority said when they dismantled the sidewalk entrance, they sealed off the stairs with concrete slabs. Guess they also put in these vents."

Nikki got on one knee and tried to pull the grate open. "Won't give." Then she got up, looked around, and pointed to the center divider in the middle of Broadway. "There's another grate out there behind that fence, see?" Heat took a step out into the street without checking traffic. A horn blasted. Rook grabbed her arm and jerked her back just in time; she had almost gotten clipped by a passing gypsy cab.

"You OK?" he asked.

"Fine. Close one, thanks."

"No, I mean are you OK-OK?" He studied her and she knew what he meant. It wasn't like her to be reckless. It wasn't her nature to let impatience drive her.

Heat dismissed him. "All right, fine, we've got the walk now, let's use it." She didn't wait for him but hurried to the median that divided the uptown and downtown flows on Broadway. When Rook caught up, she led him between the evergreen shrubs and tulips to the wrought iron fence surrounding the grate, which was much larger than the one on the sidewalk.

Rook reached both arms through the bars and tried to lift that grate. It wouldn't budge, either. Another train passed underneath, even louder than the one before, and it blew more wind up at them. "This one must be right above active tracks." He turned up to her and said, "The one back on the sidewalk would be over the station itself." But Nikki was already on her way back to it, dodging traffic.

When Rook rejoined her, Heat had both knees on the sidewalk and had her head down, peering through a hole in the grate. "Come see. There's just enough light from the street lamp to make out the stairs." She rocked back to give him room.

He shut one eye to focus and spied the deteriorated concrete steps littered by cigarette butts, plastic straws, and all colors of gum that had fallen through the grate over the years. "That's it, all right." Then he scanned the grate. "It wouldn't have these hinges if it wasn't designed to open. Look. Here's how it's locked." He pointed to a hole in the grid, about the size of a quarter, with a hex head bolt screwed into it.

"Got it." She squeezed her fingers into the hole and tried to turn it. "That puppy's on tight. If we could just unscrew that bolt, we could get in."

"You're kidding," he said. "You're seriously thinking of busting this thing open and climbing down there tonight?"

"Damn straight."

"I like the way you think. But can't we call the MTA or Parks and Rec and see if we can have them open it?"

"After office hours?" She shook her head. "Besides, by my estimation, after we got all the red tape cleared and signed all the insurance waivers, we'd be doing our climbing using walkers." And then she added, "And since when did you become the cautious thinker?"

"Maybe because you're scaring me. You look like you could use a choke chain tonight."

"I'm tired of waiting. Ten years, Rook. And now I feel like I'm this close." She tried the bolt head again with her bare fingertips, knowing it was useless. "I don't want it to slip away."

Rook felt the fire in her and said, "We're going to need a tool to get that off."

"That's the Rook I know."

He surveyed the area as if he'd miraculously find one to improvise, which would have been just that, miraculous. Nikki pointed across Broadway and said, "Oh, man, talk about a cruel irony." Maybe a hundred feet away sat a locksmith shop with its lights off. "All locked up for the night."

"We could call them." When Rook read her impatience, he said, "No, we are not going to break in there. I may not always know where to draw the line, but burglary feels like a good place to start."

She kicked at the grate with her toe. "If Nicole did get down there, she either had a key or she knew another way in."

"What we need is a hex wrench to turn that bolt. Or, if it won't turn, one of those handheld rotary cutters to saw off the head," said Rook. "Those guys on *Storage Wars* use them all the time. They go through padlocks like buttah."

"Is there an open hardware store at this hour?"

"No, but I know the next best thing. Remember JJ?" he said, referring to the building super of a gossip columnist whose murder they had solved.

"JJ, as in Cassidy Towne's JJ?"

"He's just down on Seventy-eighth. The man owns every tool imaginable."

Even though it meant waiting a half hour, Heat agreed their best plan was for Rook to hop down to JJ's. She would stay there and canvass the area for alternate points of entry. When he got in his taxi, he said to her, "Feels like we're getting somewhere, doesn't it?" She just shrugged and watched his cab drive off. Nikki had gotten somewhere too many times before only to have it be nowhere.

But this did feel different. Not just the recent surge in leads, but something else. Detective Heat—cautious, measured, mistrustful of haste—felt herself propelled forward as if by some unseen hand, nudging her. There had been flashes of that sensation before on this case. Like when she bailed down the hatch in that living room floor in Bayside. Or chased Don's killer into an exposed stairwell without backup. Or let herself get set up for a night meet under the High Line. Unguarded feelings like these were foreign to her and were usually unsettling—disturbing enough to be walled off.

What was different? she wondered. Was she suffering poor judgment from PTSD, after all? Or was she starting to see her precious emotional compartments as obstacles instead of allies and going with her gut more? Or was there truly some unseen force guiding her?

Or was she just plain obsessed with this case?

Whatever it was, touring in circles and zigzags along Broadway that night, literally searching for a doorway to the past, Nikki had a sense of homing in, and caution had lost its voice. Which was why, when she descended the subway stairs to the 96th Street station and found herself all alone in it, she walked as far south as she could on the platform to see just how close it came to the abandoned station at Ninety-first. Nikki gripped the stainless steel guardrail and used it to lean out over the tracks and peer into the tunnel. It was dark, except for two red lights shining back at her in warning. She couldn't see the Ghost Station, but its platform was probably only a block and a half away from where she stood. She listened and, hearing no rumble, wondered if she could make it on foot before a train came.

And then Heat stopped wondering and jumped.

She kept to the center of the two main tracks, giving wide berth to the third rail on the outside right that powered the trains with six hundred fifty deadly volts. The ambient light from the station behind her faded with each stride she took away from it, and soon Nikki faced total darkness. Farther from the platform there would be less litter and fewer broken bottles to step on, but she still needed to see. Especially to watch out for uneven footing or unexpected obstacles to trip her. This was not the place to fall, or worse, break an ankle or get a foot stuck. The idea made her shudder. Reason told her to give it up and go back; to go through channels and get the MTA to arrange a special stop and shuttle her to the station the next morning. To Nikki, the next morning seemed forever away. She got out her cell phone and turned on the flashlight application. She smiled to herself because she could almost hear Rook smart-assing, "Subway spelunking? There's an app for that." Rook. She should call him and let him know where she was. But she'd wait until she got there. If there was any signal underground.

Her phone threw decent enough light for her to continue, but as soon as she switched it on, she heard voices behind her at the platform. She quickly turned it off and pressed herself against the tunnel wall and listened, hoping some well-intended Samaritan wouldn't risk his life trying to rescue her.

Nikki felt a draft of air on her neck and craned upward to see if there was a ventilation grate overhead, but there wasn't. Then she realized the movement on her neck wasn't air but fur. She swept her hand and felt the rat fill her entire palm as she brushed it off. When it thudded onto the ground, she couldn't see it, but she could hear it skitter off. She stepped away from the wall, switched the flashlight app back on, and got hustling toward 91st.

Moving as quickly as she dared, Nikki hopped puddles and stepped up and over crossties, which seemed to get higher because the dirt bed between rails in that section had become deeper. From the faint light ahead, she thought she might be getting closer to the Ghost Station and that, perhaps, it had a few service bulbs going. But to her alarm, the light grew swiftly brighter and the ground began to tremble lightly. Then a headlight pierced the blackness in the tunnel far ahead and made the rail tops shiny as they traced twin lines right toward her. Nikki was in the worst place: between platforms with a train coming.

She got ready to jump the third rail to the center track, but just as the thought came to her, a downtown express raced along those, closing off her escape. Nikki didn't know how far ahead the platform was, but behind her felt like a long way, so she started running toward the on-coming train, vaulting crossties as if on an obstacle course at an NFL training camp. The headlight grew larger and more piercing. The low, distant tremble became a thundering rumble. Air, displaced by the forward motion of the subway, gusted into her face.

The headlight also lit up the Ghost Station that she neared on her left. But was it close enough to beat the oncoming train?

While she was distracted calculating her distance to the platform, the toe of her shoe snagged under a crosstie she'd misjudged and Nikki began to tumble forward. She wondered if the soil depression under the tracks was deep enough to let the train ride over her if she fell.

Nikki never had to find out. She righted herself. Gasping, she lurched for the edge of the platform. But it was too tall for her to jump up on. The train was seconds away. Its blazing headlight turned the tunnel into day. That's when Nikki saw the metal service ladder recessed into the concrete. She pitched herself at it and grabbed the railing.

Heat rolled onto the deck of the platform just as the Uptown One roared by, kicking up a swirl of wind and a clatter more deafening than she'd experienced in all her years in New York. She was lucky to be alive to hear it.

The train moved on, and the air and noise stilled fast in its wake. Two blocks away, its brakes screeched as it pulled into the station she had just left. Nikki rolled over and sat to regain her breath from the excruciating whack she had given her kneecap on her scramble up the ladder. When she tested it with her fingertips, it didn't feel broken, although the sting told her some skin would be missing. She used her phone flashlight to look for blood on her pants but didn't see any. Just a smudge of railroad grime on the knee, identical to Nicole Bernardin's.

Heat rose to her feet. She swept her light around the Ghost Station and saw a study in contrasts. One the one hand, design and equipment from the early part of the last century, left as it was the day the station had been sealed: a deco ticket booth; a vintage disposal machine for chopping tickets after entry; overhead fixtures for individual bulbs instead of fluorescent tubes; rows of scalloped ceiling accents; an ornately wrought banister descending the stairs from the capped sidewalk entrance; a scrolled iron gate that the station agent lifted for passengers exiting the trains; and a terra-cotta panel with "91" in relief on it, set into the wall to designate the station. But the romance of frozen time had been offset by its defilement.

Nearly every surface in the station wore a coat of graffiti: the wall tiles; the banisters; the support pillars. Soda cans as well as broken wine and beer bottles littered the ground, collected in corners, and rested next to a plastic cooler on the decaying concrete stairs. The doors to both restrooms had been broken off and taken. Nikki didn't venture inside either one but could see and smell the violations inside the battered, tagged stalls.

This was the handiwork of the Mole People, she assumed. The Moles were the stuff of urban legends in the New York underground, which told of tribes of misfit subcultures that had organized to rule these tunnels. In reality, they were just tag artists making their marks or homeless who survived in the musty darkness. There had been a TV drama called *Beauty and the Beast* Nikki watched when she was in grade school that was about a lion man living below like that, but she had never seen dear, urbane Vincent with a spray can and a bottle of fortified wine.

A noise behind her made her turn and switch off her light. As her eyes adjusted to the muted street glow filtering down through the grates she and Rook had investigated, Nikki figured she must have heard the approach of another train. This one raced downtown on the opposite side of the tunnel from her. She waited until it passed before she lit up her phone again. She didn't want to chance being seen and reported. She had work to do.

Nikki began old school, just like the station. She looked for footprints. A thick layer of soot and dust coated everything down there, and if Nicole Bernardin indeed had been there before she was killed, Heat just might find hers. She squatted down and held her light close to the floor. Slowly, patiently, she swept the beam just inches above it, alert for any disturbance or telltale shape that she might follow to the hiding place. The problem was that so many Moles had used the platform that the footprints were myriad. She made one more pass, this time walking the station floor in a stoop, seeing if any smaller, female prints emerged, but none did.

Next, she searched the ticket booth, which only took seconds. It had long ago been trashed and gutted. As she'd expected, both restrooms presented no hiding places when she examined them, too. The cooler on the stairs was empty, as was the inside of the ticket shredder, whose door had been pried off and left on the ground. She even inspected the bottom of the sidewalk grate itself, in case that was, literally, where Nicole had been styling. It wasn't.

Unable to accept defeat, Nikki ignored her frustration and thought. Again she put herself in her mother's shoes, asking herself, if she had been Cynthia Heat, and had been directed to find the drop, would Nicole expect her to search for footprints in the dust?

No.

Then what? How would Nicole let her know exactly where to look?

By giving her a clue.

And she had—the bracelet with the numeral charms.

Nikki looked up at the nine and the one embedded in the wall.

Could it be?

It was too high for her to reach, so Nikki surveyed the place for something to stand on. She climbed back up the steps, came down with the plastic cooler, and set it on the ground to use as a stepstool.

Nikki's phone vibrated in her hand, startling her. The caller ID said it was Rook. Damn, she forgot to call Rook. She pushed accept and said, "Hey, guess what? I made it down here, and I—" Her ear filled with the dropped-call beep. She tried to redial him but the lone reception bar faded out and she got the "No Signal" display.

Carefully balancing herself on the cooler, Heat reached up and ran her fingers along the flamboyantly scrolled edges of the "91" faceplate. It felt loose.

It moved.

Nikki set her phone on the ground, positioned the light to shine up the wall, and got back on the cooler, stretching out so that the fingertips of each hand were on either side of the faceplate. Her arms ached from the awkwardness of her position, but she kept prying, feeling the panel coming looser from the wall with her effort.

As she struggled, tugging at one side and then the other, Nikki envisioned her mother working on the same panel ten years before. What did Cynthia Heat find, she wondered, and was it what had sealed her fate? And what about Nicole Bernardin? If Nicole had placed something here in her drop box so many years later, what could that be? And who did she leave it for? And why was it worth killing her over?

Just then the faceplate popped out of the wall and Nikki fell backward off the cooler, landing hard on the floor, still clutching it.

"I'll take it from here," said the man's voice behind her.

Nikki rolled to her knees and reached for her gun, but before she could get to her holster, she got blinded by a strong flashlight beam and heard the action slide on a pistol. "Touch it, and you'll die right there," said Tyler Wynn.

Heat dropped her hand to her side. "Lace your fingers behind your neck, please." She did as he told her and squinted beyond the light to try to the see the old man as he stepped forward from the top of the ladder onto the platform.

"You're every bit as good as your mother, Nikki. Maybe better." He swung the light out of her eyes and shined it up on the wall where a tan leather pouch sat inside the recess she had exposed. "Thanks for finding this for me. I've gone to a lot of trouble to retrieve it."

"You mean like faking your death?"

"Miraculous recovery, wouldn't you say? Do you know I actually paid that doctor extra to zap me with low voltage just to be convincing?"

He trained the beam back on her face. "Don't look so disappointed. One thing you learn in the CIA. Nobody is ever really dead for certain."

"I know one woman who is. And you killed her."

"Not personally. I had hired help do that. In fact, I think you two know each other." He called over his shoulder to someone Nikki couldn't see. "You'd better get up from there, unless you want to get run over. The next train is due any minute."

She heard footfalls on the metal rungs and a silhouette came up from the tracks behind Tyler Wynn, who said, "Take her gun."

And when the other man stepped forward into the light and Heat saw who it was, her heart punched all the air from her chest.

NINETEEN

"Petar."

It was all Heat could manage to say. She had no breath for more, as if the oxygen had been sucked from the tunnel. But those two hoarse syllables spoke volumes. She whispered her old lover's name as both a question and an answer. And the weight she gave the word articulated a sour array of feelings suspended from it on sharp, cutting hooks:

Betrayal. Sadness. Shock. Disbelief. Blindness. Anger. Hatred.

Petar's face displayed no shame or regret as he moved toward Nikki. His eyes met hers and she saw in them something like amusement. No, arrogance.

Heat thought of going for her gun. Even if Tyler Wynn hit her, she might get off a shot at Petar. He was armed, too, but holding his Glock sloppily. She could do it.

"I wouldn't," said the voice behind the flashlight. Tyler Wynn, the living ghost in the Ghost Station, had read her. So much for making the play.

Petar took her Sig.

"Good." Tyler stepped a little closer. "I've seen so many people try something stupid when emotions take over."

Nikki twisted to look up at Petar. "You killed her? Fuck you."

All Petar did was take a step back while he tucked her gun into this waistband. He looked past her in pure dismissal. To him, she was just a chore.

"I said, 'Fuck you.'"

"You two will have time to air things out after I leave. Petar, get the bag, please."

Petar stepped behind her, and Nikki could hear him sliding the cooler back under Nicole's drop box. She tried to wall out her torment and get strategic. Petar would need to pocket his gun to reach up for that pouch. If only she weren't on her knees, she might have a shot at catching Wynn with a surprise kick. He had read her before, so she covered with conversation. "Was it you that Carter Damon called on the burner cell to get the green light to kill Nicole?"

"That was for logistics. Petar did the actual work."

"And he called you again. Was that to set up the visiting nurse to spy on us?"

"I am a creature of habit. Once you run a Nanny Network, it's hard to stop."

She didn't ask permission, just kept her hands behind her neck and eased up off the ground onto her feet as she spoke. "I really thought Carter Damon killed my mother."

"No, he was there after, for cleanup." Petar fell off the cooler behind her and swore. She noticed Wynn become alert and didn't make her move. When Petar stepped up on it again, he relaxed and continued, "Detective Damon was quite an asset until the very end when he got a dying man's conscience and tried to text you."

"The interrupted text," she said, inching closer.

"Yes, we caught him trying to reach out to you to make amends. Bad for his health, it turned out."

"The Brooklyn Bridge?"

Wynn nodded. "His attempted confession gave me the idea of staging his suicide with another text taking responsibility for the murders. Seemed win-win."

Nikki said, "More like win Wynn," pointing at him. And when she extended her arm to do that, she used it as a feint to lunge for him.

The old man anticipated her and quickly got her in a choke hold, pressing the muzzle of his gun against her temple. "What? Do you want me to shoot you? Well, do you?" Nikki stayed still. "I will if I have to, but I'd rather not. In fact, I've been thinking train mishap. More ambiguous to the police than a bullet, but I'm happy to improvise, if you force my hand." He pressed the muzzle harder against her flesh. "This gun is a throwdown I can easily plant at Rook's loft. Do the math on that before you make me shoot you with it. Understood?" He didn't wait for an answer. He just shoved her away.

Petar came down from the drop box and handed him the leather pouch. Tyler whispered instructions to him. She picked up "after the next train," but the rest was lost in the racket as a downtown subway rushed through on the far side of the tunnel.

Heat battled to keep her head under the crush of emotions coming down on her. Self-anger dominated. She found herself sucked back to Paris, in the Place des Vosges, where she had felt unsettled about something she couldn't articulate. Now, waiting to be killed in the Ghost Station, the nagging thought defined itself, albeit a bit late. As usual, it was the odd sock.

"I should have known," she said to Wynn. She shook her head, unhappy with herself. "I should have smelled it back at the hospital when your 'dying words' were urging me to nail the bastards who killed my mom, that's what you said."

"I did."

"But I never asked myself, if you were CIA and were so passionate about avenging my mother's death, why didn't you do it yourself? You had ten years and all the resources."

He smiled. "Don't feel bad. I've fooled more experienced players than you, and for much longer." A train began to approach them from downtown. Blocks away, but the soft rumble drifted up the tunnel. Nikki's chest seized with sudden urgency.

"Why did you have my mother killed?"

"Because I didn't fool her. When she found out I had gone independent in the interval between Paris and when I reactivated her in New York, she had to go. She just had to. Up to then, she thought working for me meant she'd still been working for CIA. Then she found out who I was really working for and, unfortunately for her, what the project was."

"You killed her for that?"

"Your mother's sense of mission is what killed her. She was just like you."

They stood as statues when an uptown train raced through, rattling the station and making the hair on their heads lift and swirl. The moment it passed, Petar took out his gun. Tyler Wynn holstered his under his sport coat and climbed down the ladder to the tracks. "Should have four to six minutes before the next train."

"You'll have plenty of time," said Petar, switching on his Mini Maglite. "Catch you after."

Nikki watched just Wynn's disembodied head move along the platform as he walked the tracks. "Tyler." He stopped. "What's in the pouch?"

"You'll never know."

"Wanna bet?"

Wynn said, "Shoot her, if you have to." Then started his walk back to the 96th Street station.

Heat made up her mind she would kill Petar.

That's how she would survive. The only question was, would she enjoy it? And what would that make her if she did?

Alive. That was all she cared about. The morality of how she felt, she would gladly sort out in her old age.

She had already figured out their plan. It wasn't hard to. The next train would rocket past in four to six minutes, and the idea was for her to be in front of it when it did. So she had five minutes, give or take, to get it done.

"So there's no way to call this off?"

Petar didn't engage. He stood silently, close enough to be accurate with his Glock but distant enough to be out of reach if she made a run at him. At the moment, their plan was better than hers.

"A head start for old times' sake?" Still no reply. He watched her but without looking at her.

It was hard for Nikki to even see Petar as the same man she had fallen for. She had not gone to Venice in the summer of '99 seeking romance but passion of another kind: her love of theater. Other students interning at the Gran Teatro La Fenice had asked her out, and she had a series of first dates, but nothing serious. Until the night at the Ai Speci wine bar when she met an earnest-looking Croatian film student visiting the city to shoot a documentary on Tommaseo, the renowned Italian essayist. Within a week, Petar Matic had moved out of his hostel into her apartment. After Venice, they spent a month touring Paris before she returned to Boston to start her fall semester at Northeastern. He surprised her by sliding into her booth one morning in the student union, saying that he missed her so much, he'd enrolled there himself.

"Just tell me one thing, you owe me that," she said, still trying to engage him. "Did Tyler actually go to all the trouble to find out who I was dating and then recruit you to kill my mother?"

That got a reaction from him. He snorted and shifted his weight back onto one of the support pillars. "You like to flatter yourself? Go ahead."

"I'm not flattering myself, I'm just trying to figure out Tyler's approach. 'Hello, young man, would you be interested in earning a few extra dollars murdering your girlfriend's mom?'"

"See, that's where your head's up your own ass. Nikki, do you honestly believe our relationship was ever about romance?" Heat felt herself absorbing yet another emotional shock but kept the conversation going, kept pushing.

"Sure felt like it to me."

He laughed. "It was supposed to. Come on, do you think we met in Venice by accident? Like it was Kismet? It was a job, man. The whole thing was a setup."

"You mean like 'accidentally' running into me and Rook in Boston? Was that to find out what I knew?"

"No, I was just tailing you. Or was, until fucking Rook spotted me. My assignment in Venice was to get in your pants and work that to get close to your mom."

"To kill her?"

"Not at first. To find out some things."

"And then kill her." Nikki gritted her teeth, fending off her own fury to stay focused on getting him distracted.

"Yeah, kill her. Like I said, it was a job. I'm good at it."

"Except for the suitcase."

"Right. I fucked that up. I used that old piece of shit to carry papers from your mom's desk and forgot all about it. Hey, it was ten years, I'm allowed one."

"That's not all you screwed up."

"What's that supposed to mean?"

"The High Line. You were the sniper, weren't you?"

"And?"

"And you blew the shot."

"I didn't blow the shot. There was an earthquake."

"Then you blew the second shot."

"No way."

"And the one you could have taken at the end of the line. I saw the laser dot. But instead, you jumped."

"You're crazy."

"You bet I am." Nikki took a step toward him.

"Stay where you are."

She took another step. "I want you to shoot me."

"What?" He shined the light in her eyes and raised his gun, but she took another step. "I'm warning you, stop."

She moved closer. "You seem to be real good at slipping knives in women's backs. Can you put one of those bullets in me? No you can't. Come on, Pet. Face-to-face. Right here. Bring it on. I'll even make a better target for you." She moved closer yet.

But he took a step back and bumped into the support pillar he'd been leaning on. A sound like the low roar of the sea floated up the tunnel. The train was coming. Right on time. He wagged the gun, gesturing her to step to the edge.

Heat stood firm.

"Go on. Let's not make this harder than it has to be."

"For whom, Petar?" She took one more stride closer. They were only three feet apart, and for the first time, she could look into his eyes. And he, into hers.

"Now," he shouted.

"Do you really think I'm going to make this easy for you? Stand with my back to you so you can give me a shove?"

His eyes darted away, then returned.

The roar grew into a rumble. The concrete platform vibrated.

"You killed my mother. You lied about loving me. Take me out of my misery, you son of a bitch!"

"I'll do it," he said.

Nikki smiled and spread her arms before him, daring him to go ahead.

And then she heard the whine of a small power tool and metal grinding. Sparks showered down through the ventilation grate at the top of the stairway, falling into the dark tunnel like fireflies.

Petar turned to look at them.

Nikki made her move.

She threw herself toward him, leaping inside the danger circle of the gun on his right side. Her arms were already up from her "go ahead and shoot me" gesture, and as she brought her body next to his, her right hand was in position to lock onto his wrist to aim the gun away. At the same time, Heat brought her left elbow up over his shoulder and spiked it into his nose.

He cried out but managed to keep his grip on the pistol. Heat delivered a sharp knee to his quad. With her right hand still clamping his wrist, she wrapped her left on top of the Glock and began to twist the barrel inward to point back at him.

Petar must have had some combat training, too. He surprised her by suddenly dropping his butt to the floor, pulling her off balance. Nikki fell forward and hit the deck on top of him, still clutching his gun wrist, but her other hand had come free of the Glock.

He tried to head butt her nose. She slipped it and went for the gun again with her free hand, but he pulled it away.

She called out to Rook, but he couldn't hear her over his grinding.

Nikki leaped back to her feet. Keeping her joint lock on his wrist, she yanked his arm to full extension and smacked it, trying to break the elbow. But Petar jerked his arm back defensively, just enough for her blow to hit his forearm instead. She didn't disable the joint, but the punch did loosen his hold on the Glock. It dropped to the floor.

Heat dove for it, but the gun landed just beyond her reach, skimming across the deck. Scrambling to snatch it, she reached the edge of the platform just as the pistol tumbled over the side onto the tracks below.

She almost went over after it. But bright light grew in the tunnel. The train raced toward her, seconds away.

Heat shouted for Rook again.

The sparks continued to fall.

Petar got to his feet. He reached for her Sig Sauer in his waistband.

Nikki scoped the platform in the light from the train. No cover for her.

The Sig came out.

The train broke the mouth of the station.

Petar brought it up to aim.

Heat made a choice.

She dove over the side.

Nikki stretched herself out lengthwise and hunkered as flat as she could in the grimy ditch between the rails. In the two seconds before the lead car got to her, she flashed on news stories she'd seen on subway commuters who had fallen on the tracks and survived that way. And those who hadn't; it all depended on the terrain.

Heat had never been in a tornado, but that's what it felt like to her. A ten-car cyclone of howling wind and screaming steel. The ground quaked, her body shuddered. She screamed a scream that nobody heard.

On the hike to get there, Nikki had cursed the deep depression in the railroad bed. It had created an obstacle course, making her climb up and over the crossties. Now she hoped that trenching would save her life. She pressed her face hard against the soil and emptied her lungs to make her torso smaller. The tiny breath she dared take made her mouth taste of stagnant water and rust.

Unable to count the cars, they seemed to go on forever. Hundreds more than ten. Which car, she worried, would be the one with the protruding bolt that would carve her open? Or have the dangling loop of chain to snag her and decapitate her?

Then, sudden silence. Except for the grinding of Rook's power tool, above.

Nikki didn't wait. She rolled under the edge of the platform and looked for the Glock in the dim spill from Petar's Maglite. She swept the area but couldn't see the gun. Only more plastic soda bottles and old spray cans left by taggers.

The flashlight beam hit the tracks. He was searching for her body.

Heat didn't call to Rook again. She scrunched herself further underneath the lip of the platform and waited quietly. The concrete felt cold on her back where her flesh touched it. The bottom of one of the cars must have sliced her coat and blouse.

The light grew more intense directly in front of her. That put Petar right over her head. "Nikki?" he said tentatively. She had never hated the sound of her name so much as in his mouth just then. Heat readied herself. Made sure of her footing. Waited for his next "Nikki," and then sprung.

She popped up and twisted to square herself with Petar where he knelt, peering over the edge of the platform, and sprayed his eyes with aerosol paint. He screamed and put his hand to his face, dropping his flashlight but not the Sig. Nikki tossed the spray can and reached up for him with both hands. Clawing him by the shirtfront, she hauled him over the side, letting go of him midair. He landed shoulder-first on the railroad bed and screamed again.

Nikki went for him, reaching for her handcuffs, but he rolled over onto his back and swung a beer bottle at her. It connected with her jaw hard enough for her to see stars. She staggered back, dazed, and sat down clumsily, just breaking her fall by putting one hand behind her.

Petar got up. His hands were empty. He wanted the Sig. Nikki had heard it hit the ground when he landed but couldn't see it in the bad light, either.

He tried to boost himself up on the platform to get his flashlight, but it was too high. Petar had gotten to the metal ladder but had only cleared two rungs when she grabbed him again to pull him back down with her. He didn't resist. Instead, he tried to pile drive her, letting himself be pulled and falling on top of her.

When they landed in a heap, he didn't go for the ladder again. He tried to make a run for the station at 96th.

Without good light, he misjudged the height of the crossties and tripped, once again, landing between the rails. He hauled himself up to his feet but too slowly. Nikki hopped on him, throwing a blindside tackle. He spun himself on the way down, making her take the brunt of the landing. The wind got knocked out of her, and she ached for air so she could go after him. But he wasn't running. Petar had her by the lapels of her coat. He was dragging her. When Heat turned her head and could see where, she was inches from the third rail.

In seconds he would drop Nikki on it and she'd take six hundred fifty volts.

Heat kicked a leg up into his crotch. They were too close together for her to generate the swing power to drop him, but it hurt enough to make him moan and loosen his grip. The back of her head hit the ground an inch from the hot rail.

He staggered away.

A downtown express was coming on the center rails. Petar started for those tracks. He was going to try to beat it across and put the train between them to give himself a chance to get away. Nikki stopped him before he got there.

She slammed a fist behind his ear and his knees buckled. He grabbed a metal beam with one hand to support himself and used it to swing his body around to strike back. But his own momentum carried him into her next blow, a fist to the temple. His eyelids fluttered and he started to lose balance.

The express train was fast approaching behind him. Heat pulled him up and slammed him against the steel beam. He took a looping swing at her. She tilted her head to dodge it and hit him with another punch in the nose. And then another. Blood gushed out his nostrils, mixing with the blue spray paint on his face.

As the telltale rush of wind from the oncoming train pushed into the tunnel, he lolled his head north, turned glazed eyes over his shoulder at the approaching headlight, and then back to her with resignation. He regarded her with the look of a man prepared to receive his fate. They both knew there were no witnesses.

This perfect moment was Heat's chance to avenge her mother. The stuff of both dreams and nightmares.

Nikki gathered him up by his armpits and yanked him clear of the post, balancing him on weak legs as the first car broke the entrance to the Ghost Station.

He closed his eyes and waited for the push.

But when the speeding train got there, she threw him to the ground away from it. With his face in a puddle in the ditch, Nikki pulled his hands behind his back. She said, "Petar Matic?" And then Detective Heat paused before she gave voice to the words she had waited a decade to speak. "I am arresting you for the murder of Cynthia Heat." She swallowed hard and continued, "You are also under arrest for the murder of Nicole Bernardin."

After she put the cuffs on her prisoner and read him his rights, Heat looked up, choking back tears, and saw that Rook was still sawing at that bolt. Nikki took a moment to wipe her eyes and watch the sparks fly.

In spite of the late hour, when Heat stepped into the Observation Room on her way into Interrogation One, she found that, in addition to Rook, a small audience of detectives had come in to the precinct that night. Roach had made the trip, as had Rhymer and Feller. Malcolm and Reynolds would have been there, but they were still on Staten Island working Carter Damon's van with Forensics. She felt all their eyes on her. They knew what this arrest meant. They also knew the ordeal she had suffered through that night, and this was a turnout for their team leader. But cops being cops, the show-up itself was the message of support. They weren't going to express any sentiment.

To make sure of that, Ochoa said, "Real nice of you to get dolled up for us, Detective. Special."

Heat resembled the cover of one of those commando video games. She hadn't changed clothes, plus her face and hands were scuffed and filthy. In the hallway coming from the bull pen she had pulled a wad of grape chewing gum from the back of her hair. "Been a tad busy."

Nikki stepped up to the magic window to look in on Petar Matic, who sat alone, in shackles, at the conference table on the other side. "Surprised you didn't waste the asshole when you had the chance," said Detective Feller. "Him and you? Nobody would ever know."

"I would. Besides, he's worth more alive. I want to know the whole story. Everything he did. Everyone he worked with. Who else he might have killed."

"And where's Tyler Wynn," said Rook.

"Especially that."

When Heat went into the box and sat across from Petar, she could see the fight all over him, too. The only difference was he'd been changed into jailwear. He bore more than his share of cuts, bruises, caked dirt, and dried blood. He even still wore the stripe of blue paint Nikki had tagged his face with. In his orange coveralls, he looked like he'd gotten ejected from a Florida Gators game.

The two stared at each other in frosty silence. Nikki didn't like what she saw. Not just that she saw the man who had stabbed her mother to death and killed at least one other woman. Or that she saw the ex-lover who had called their relationship a job, merely a means to an end. What Nikki didn't like was in the eyes. His submissive, resigned, defeated eyes from his takedown in the subway were history. Petar Matic had always been a strategic thinker, and his eyes told her he had done some brainstorming since they brought him up from the tunnel in handcuffs.

"You should have killed me when you had the chance," he said.

"A lot of people around here think the same thing."

"Why didn't you?"

"I'm not the jury. I'm just the cop. At the end of the day, I have to stand for something. You do, too. We both know what that is."

"The ever-righteous Nikki Heat. Saint and soldier." He leaned forward over the table and smiled. "Too bad lover doesn't make the list."

When she felt her face flush, Nikki reminded herself to separate. Petar was going to try for any leverage he could get, especially messing with her head to gain an advantage. She tried to ignore the emotional stab—and the fact that, even if her squad had left the Ob Room to work the assignments she had just given them, Rook stood on the other side of that mirror. She drew a slow breath to get her focus back. "Tell me exactly when you got the contract to kill Cynthia Heat."

"Very good. So professional to depersonalize. Your specialty."

"Who approached you about it?"

"See? You remain focused on the work, as always."

"I want some answers."

He grinned. "I want a deal."

"You don't have anything to deal with. I already know you killed my mother and Nicole Bernardin."

"Says who?"

"You."

"When?"

"Tonight in the subway."

"Prove it."

Petar smiled his grin again, only bigger and more self-assured. It was the attitude she had seen in his eyes when he'd disarmed her earlier in the night's drama. It was the arrogance that had made her consider killing him then. For a moment, as she knew she might from that day on, she wondered if she should have.

They both knew that this interrogation was not perfunctory. As a homicide detective, Heat recognized that any case required solid proof for the DA. Which was why she had just assigned detectives to search Petar's apartment as well as his office at the TV show he worked for. In addition, they'd run his entire life through a sifter for any evidence they could find. And that was just the start.

But Petar was trying to seed her with doubt. Nobody else had heard him admit to the murders any more than anyone else would know if she had shoved him in front of that train. If she couldn't find physical proof that would stand up in court, Petar Matic would walk. Keenly aware of those stakes, he played his ace card. "I have something you want, you know."

If she blinked and showed interest she would lose ground, and that could be the beginning of the unraveling of this case. So Heat remained stoic. She betrayed no tells and said nothing.

"And maybe it's not just information about your mother's killing. Or the other one." He tossed it off as if these murders were just inventory items to be noted then dismissed from reflection. "Something is coming. It's big and it's bad. This has been in the works for ten years—if that period creates a context in any way for you." His allusion to the decade that bookended the two stabbings was his way of teasing her interest without admitting guilt. Petar was smart. Nikki had to be smarter.

Without taking the negotiation bait, she said, "If you know something about a pending crime, you are obligated to share that information."

"Sound advice, Detective. Maybe I will." He flashed her his arrogant grin again and said, "I guess that depends on the right arrangement."

Irons was in the Ob Room with Rook when she came through the air lock from Interrogation. The captain rushed over to Nikki. "You're not really going to bargain with this creep, are you?"

Heat glanced up at the wall clock. "What are you doing here after midnight, Captain?"

"I heard you nabbed our man and I wanted to be here." She noticed he was freshly shaved and dressed in his duty uniform, with extra starch in the white shirt. Wally had taken time to get himself camera-ready. "You've got him to rights, don't you?"

"Not that simple. He told me he murdered both victims, but it's my word against his, unless we button him down hard. Even beyond that, there are things we need to know that his cooperation will bring to light."

Irons scoffed. "Sure. And long as you're letting him call the tune, why don't you just spring him?" And when he remembered who else was in the room, he said to Rook, "Don't print that."

"Never heard it, Captain."

"Petar is not going to spring anywhere, sir. I just think the prudent course is to take a breath, bide our time, and confer with the DA first thing in the morning."

Irons said, "You just want to drag this out so you can satisfy your own personal curiosity about every little detail and loose end about your mother."

Heat said, "Listen to me, Captain, nobody wants to see this guy sent away forever more than I. But that means getting it right so he doesn't walk because someone got hasty and sloppy. We have him. Our job now is to make it stick." Irons started to interrupt, but she plowed right over him. "And what if he's not posturing? What if he does know something that will help us arrest conspirators and prevent someone else from getting killed? Do you call that just a loose end?"

She didn't wait for Irons's permission. Nikki opened the door to the hallway where a pair of uniforms waited on post. "Take my prisoner down to Holding."

It felt like any normal workday in the bull pen, except it was coming up on two A.M. on the biggest night of Heat's career as a detective. Nikki had Ochoa hitting the phones, extending her initial APB on Tyler Wynn to CIA, DHS, and Interpol, as well as making sure the spy's name and image made all airport checkpoints plus Amtrak police and Port Authority

PD. She'd sent Feller and Rhymer to search Petar's apartment with special instructions to quarantine all documents, receipts, photos, and computer data. Detective Hinesburg was MIA again, so Heat put Detective Raley on scrubbing those OCME security tapes that had been sitting around to see if they could get a face to go with the gas truck driver who'd sabotaged the toxicology test. No detail of the case existed in isolation for her anymore. Every thread they could eventually connect to Petar would keep him from walking.

Rook came over to Nikki's desk when she hung up her phone. "Malcolm and Reynolds checked in while you were on your call, so I took the message for you. Let's see if I got all this. They said they're glad you're not dead. . . . At least I think that's what they said." He shrugged. "Oh, well. And then they gave me an update on the Forensics work at Carter Damon's storage unit. How'm I doing?"

"Ass like yours, you could be my personal secretary anytime. What's up with the van?"

"They found a set of work boots in it. Size eleven, same as the kind that stomped through Nicole's apartment. Lab will check them for a carpet fiber match."

Nikki moved over to the Murder Boards, where she made a notation for the boots next to the other data for the Bernardin apartment. "What else?"

"Traces of blood in the cargo area inside the van. Malcolm said he knew you'd be all over that, and assured you that DeJesus is handling that personally." He waited while she logged "Blood/DNA" on the board, and then he continued, "Finally, they have good lifts off all surfaces and door handles. They're running fingerprint IDs now."

When she capped her marker, he asked, "So who were you on with so long?"

"Prefecture of Police in Paris, France."

"That's a toll call, you know."

"Worth every penny." He followed her back to her desk and she picked up her notes. "Get this. No record of any attack on Tyler Wynn. No record of his death. No record of him being in the Hôpital du Canard. No record of him leaving the country."

Rook stroked his chin. "Were we even there?"

"No. Not according to hospital records or detectives in Boulogne-Billancourt. They never spoke to us. It never happened." She tossed her notes on the desk.

"How are you bearing up?"

"It's like a Road Runner cartoon. I'm fine, as long as I don't stop and look down." She touched his arm. "And how about you? How's your poor wrist after grinding on that bolt half the night?"

"Hey, five more minutes and I would have cut through that thing. How do they make it look so easy on *Storage Wars*?"

"Real life is never like TV," she said.

"Especially reality shows."

Nikki's phone rang and she picked it up. "Homicide, Detective Heat." The color left her face. She dropped the phone on her desktop and rushed to the door.

Rook chased after, "What's wrong?"

"Everything."

Heat didn't wait to use the lockbox. She just handed her Sig to the guard as she raced into Holding. Sprinting past cells of drunks, burglars, and public urinators, she arrived at the back where the isolation cell door stood open and three officers in blue gloves knelt over Petar.

He had pitched forward off his bunk and lay sprawled on his back with a fresh, open gash in his forehead where his head had smacked the concrete. His eyes bulged in their sockets, and his skin was deep purple with crimson webs of capillaries coloring it. His tongue looked blue enough to be called black and protruded from his open mouth from a pool of froth that capped a trail of pungent, bloody vomit that ran down his neck and onto the floor. The crotch of his orange coveralls was drenched with his urine and his bowels had released in death.

The officers rose up from him. One ran out, clutching his mouth. Nikki found herself taking an unconscious step back and bumped into Rook. One of the uniforms said, "We tried to CPR him, but he was gone by the time we got the cage unlocked."

"Did anyone see what happened?" she asked.

She was speaking to the officers, but one of the other prisoners said, "He just got his dinner and started retching something fierce." The prisoner added a demonstration, but Nikki turned away to survey the cell.

A food tray sat on the floor with an empty plastic juice bottle tipped on its side. Nothing else had been touched. "Nobody gets near him until the ME," said Heat. "And nobody in here eats or drinks anything until we know what poisoned him."

"And who," said Rook.

TWENTY

Nikki splashed more cold water on her face and rose up to see herself in the mirror above the women's room sink. Her lips began to turn downward and tremble, and she looked away, only to force herself to go back for a brave stare, but the trembling only grew and grew and her eyes were rimmed with tears. Before they could roll down her cheeks, she bent to the faucet again and scooped more water onto herself.

Unlike with his handler's faked death in Paris, Detective Heat had the means and cause to verify that Petar Matic had indeed expired. A call to her friend, Lauren Parry, brought the medical examiner from a sound sleep to the holding cell in less than forty-five minutes. Dr. Parry's prelim squared with the eyeball evidence. Poison, introduced through an innocuous, half-pint plastic bottle of apple juice. Strong stuff, too. In all her years, Lauren had never seen such a ferocious attack by an outside toxin. "This dose—of whatever the hell it turns out to be when we lab it—was designed to put him down fast and hard. Full organ shutdown with no chance of resuscitation. Better believe I'll be double-checking the seals on my moon suit when I do his postmortem."

Petar's postmortem.

Heat dried her face with some paper towels and held them to her closed eyes. Behind the lids she was thirteen, on a school ski trip to Vermont where she had lost her way on the trail and skied onto a steep incline that had iced over. When she fell that day, she had lost her gloves and a ski that had spun sideways down the ice and clattered off a precipice into a gulch she couldn't see. The gloves had stopped yards below, but to go for them she would risk following the ski.

Alone and in peril, Nikki had clawed her fingernails into the ice, trying to pull herself to safety. All she had to do was make it ten feet up the incline and grab hold of a rock. Halfway there, her fingertips lost purchase and she slid back to where she had begun. Sobbing, and with skin raw from ice burn, she found the strength to draw herself up the slope again. Almost there, reaching out for the chunk of stone which sat just inches from her grasp, she lost her grip again. The slide took her farther down, all the way to her gloves, which fell over the cliff when she skidded into them.

Heat opened her eyes. She was in the precinct restroom. But she was still on that frozen slope.

"Got something for you on our poisoned food," said Detective Feller when she came back into the bull pen. "The delivery kid from the deli where Holding places our orders got spiffed a twenty at his bike rack by someone who said they'd handle this one."

"Excellent. Did he give you a good description?" she asked.

"Yes, and when I heard it, I showed him this." Feller held up the APB pic of Salena Kaye on his cell phone. "Positive ID."

"I'll see that and raise you one," said Raley, coming through the door clutching a photo print. "Just pulled this still from my surveillance screening of the OCME cams. Check out who dropped off the bad gas at the loading dock." He held up the shot for them all to see: Salena Kaye in a delivery uniform and baseball cap.

Rook joined them from his desk and said, "That is one naughty nurse."

"Yeah," said Raley. "Too bad this surveillance tape has been sitting around unscreened for a couple of days. If we'd only seen this day before yesterday, we might have gotten her before she rabbitted."

"Or got Petar," added Feller.

"Refresh my memory," said Rook. "Who was it who said he wanted to take point on the gas truck, personally? Then delegated it to his secret weapon?"

Nikki took the still from Raley and walked it into Irons's office and shut the door. Less than three minutes later, the captain must have decided not to summon the press, after all. He grabbed his coat and left in a hurry.

Exhausted, but unwilling to go home with things in such flux, Heat spent the night at the precinct. Rook came in at daybreak with a latte and fresh change of clothes for her. "Did you get any sleep?" he asked.

"Ish," she said. "Tried to grab a few winks in one of the interrogation rooms, but, you know." She took a sip of her coffee. "My dad's an early riser, so I called him a little while ago to fill him in, so he wouldn't hear it on the news first."

"How'd he take it?"

"Closed, as ever. But at least he didn't screen me out when he saw the caller ID, so that's a start."

Rook thought back to the brittle exit from her father's condo after she had asked him for the bank statements. "You're either stronger than I thought you were or a glutton for punishment."

"Aside from all the personal crap? I really thought I had this case locked down." She led him to the twin Murder Boards. Both were brimming with new notes she had made on them in the predawn hours. "I thought once I nailed the killer, I'd be done. But Petar ended up—well, he ended up just the consolation prize."

"You know, Nikki, that's the tragedy of all this. I was feeling that your old boyfriend and I were just starting to bond." He looked at her innocently. "What, too soon?"

"A little," she said, but smiled in appreciation of his usual effort to try to make her laugh, in spite of. "This nerve's still a bit exposed. But don't give up, OK?"

"Deal."

She contemplated one of the boards with a bleak sigh. "This one . . ." Nikki tapped Tyler Wynn's name, now featured prominently. "He called the orders. Because of him, my mother died, Nicole died, Don died."

"Carter Damon, also."

"Right. And why?" She shook her head. "Damn, I really thought I'd be done."

Most of the squad gathered early. Clearly, sleep was not anybody's priority. Roach came in a little later, but only because they had paid a visit to the MTA headquarters on the way in to check surveillance video from the 96th Street station. "They're making dubs for us now," said Detective Raley, "but we logged Nicole Bernardin going over the platform toward the Ghost Station with the leather pouch and then coming back without it the same night she died."

"Any idea what was in it?" asked Rhymer.

"None. I never even touched it."

Detective Feller joined them. "Any guess who Nicole left it for?"

Heat bobbed her head side to side. "I would only be guessing." Although Nikki did have one idea she would keep to herself.

Detectives Malcolm and Reynolds came into the bull pen with fresh news from Forensics. The blood traces in the cargo hold of Carter Damon's van matched Nicole Bernardin's type. "They're running it at the DNA lab for confirmation," said Reynolds. "But I'd bet we hear a ding, for sure."

Malcolm added, "Carpet fibers match positive for Damon's work boots. And, even though there's more fingerprints on that vehicle than an airport lap dancer, they also managed to isolate three big hits: Damon, Salena, and Petar."

Behind them they heard raised voices and a door slam and all turned toward the glass office to see Captain Irons in a muffled shouting match with Detective Hinesburg, whose mascara had raccooned down the sides of her cheeks. "Trouble in the diorama," said Feller.

"You guys didn't see this morning's *Ledger*?" asked Reynolds. "*Metro* column was all about wondering how a prisoner could die in custody."

Ochoa said, "All the papers are on that."

"Yeah, but Tam Svejda has a source who says one of the detectives dropped the ball on identifying Salena Kaye from surveillance video."

"And we know who that source is, don't we?" said Feller. "The survivor."

Ochoa agreed. "Hey, if Wally'd knock a kid over to get on camera, why wouldn't he save his ass by throwing Sharon Hinesburg under the bus?"

"Or, in this case, under the pressurized gas truck," added Rook.

Heat cleared her throat. "Much as you know I love forming a gossip circle, maybe we could keep our heads in the game and get back to work?" But as they all returned to their desks, her own gaze drifted to the glass office and she secretly hoped if Hinesburg didn't get transferred, at least she'd get a nice, fat suspension.

Rook joined her. "I'm going to head out. I have some work of my own to do. Outside stuff. No big deal."

"Liar. You're going to work this up as your next article, aren't you?"

"All right," he said, "as long as you're forcing my hand, my editor at *First Press* e-mailed me to say that they're going to do a major launch for a new online version of the magazine and think an exclusive on this case would be a perfect cover story to premiere on the new website."

"And you know how much I loved the last article."

"I promise, nothing about your sexual prowess, strictly facts."

"Pants on fire."

"Let me put this another way," he said. "Would you prefer I do the article of record, or Tam Svejda?"

She didn't hesitate. "Get crackin', writer boy."

"You won't be sorry."

"I already am."

"Can I buy you lunch later?"

She lowered her eyes from his. "You go on. I've got something to do around lunchtime." When he studied her, deciding whether to ask what it might be, she said, "Go on. I'll see you at my place after work tonight."

When she got to the door, she put her ear to it and heard nothing inside. Nikki rapped lightly to make sure the place was empty, and when nobody answered, she quietly slipped in and twisted the lock on the knob.

Taking care not to disturb Detective Raley's screening notes that were stacked in neat piles along the counter in front of the monitor, she sat behind the console in the little closet he had converted to his surveillance media kingdom. Heat smiled when she saw the cardboard Burger King crown she had awarded to him in a squad meeting after he had found the security cam footage of a gigolo's street abduction last winter. Then she took a memory key out of her pocket, plugged it into the USB port, and put on the earphones.

Nikki didn't know how many times over ten years she had listened to the audio of her mother's murder. Perhaps twenty? First, she had made a crude dub of it by holding a dictation recorder beside the answering machine before Detective Damon could take the mini cassette from the apartment. The quality was poor so, when she became a detective, Heat wrote herself a pass into the Property Room and got the phone cassette copied as a digital file. That WAV sounded much cleaner, yet with all the times she had listened to it, straining to analyze the muffled voice of the killer in the background, she had never gotten closer to identifying it.

She always did it in secret because she knew it would seem ghoulish to anyone who didn't know she was only doing a clinical playback. This was a search for clues, not an obsession with reliving the event. That's what she told herself, anyway, and felt it to be true. Her focus was on background, not foreground. She especially hated hearing her own voice on it, and always—every single time—stopped the audio just before it picked up her coming into the apartment and screaming.

That was too much to bear.

Of all the times she had listened to it, though, this was the first time she had knowing that the muffled voice was Petar's.

Homicide 101. In any murder case, the likely killer is close in. You clear husbands, wives, exes, common-laws, estrangeds, children, siblings, and relatives before you move on to the other likelies. Beyond her father, they looked for boyfriends in her mother's life but not in Nikki's. But then, who was the lead investigator but Carter Damon, Petar's accomplice-after-the-fact and obstructionist-for-hire.

Nikki listened again and yet listened anew. She heard the familiar small talk with her mother about spices, the checking of the fridge, her screams, and the dropped phone. The mumbled voice of a man. She paused and played it back. And then she played that section back again and again.

At straight-up noon, Heat sat on the twelfth floor, in the tranquil room on York Avenue, at the session she'd booked that morning with Lon King, Ph.D. Nikki told the department psychologist about her history with the recording and that, for the first time ever that day, when she listened to it, she heard Petar.

"And why is this something you want to focus on, this recording?"

"I guess to ask if I could have been in denial."

"That's always possible, but I wonder if your curiosity goes deeper."

"See, this is the part I hate."

He smiled. "They all do, at first." Then, he continued, "I don't care how resilient you are, Nikki, you have a lot to deal with here."

"That's why I called you."

"I'm certain you are not only reliving trauma and loss, but also experiencing a profound sense of anger and betrayal. Not to mention confusion about your own choices and instincts. As a detective, about crime. As a woman, about men."

Nikki sat back and rested her neck against the cushion. As she stared at the unblemished whiteness of the ceiling, she tried to wish away the confusion, to grab the handle on the sense of order she'd held just a day before. "I feel like I had the rug pulled. Not just on the case, but on what I thought my own life was. What I thought love was. It makes me worry about what I can trust."

"And for you, I know trust is paramount. Mistrust feels . . . well, it's chaotic."

"Yes," she said, but it came out in breath without resonance. "Which is what I feel now. I always envisioned solving my mom's murder would be clean and neat. Now all I feel is . . ." She swirled a finger like a cyclone.

"I'm sure. Especially with the betrayal of your intimacy. But could part of it also be because your life has been so defined by this case you don't know who you are if it's over?"

She sat up to face him. "No, it's upsetting because it still isn't over and I don't want to let my mother down."

"You can't. She's dead."

"And the man who ordered it is still out there."

"Then you will do what you have to do. I know that just by your unique definition of a leave of absence." She nodded in agreement but without humor. "I'd ask you to try to keep scale on this, as overwhelming as it all is. Mistrust feeds on itself. It's like a virus. You can't do your work—or live your life—second-guessing your instincts. You'll become the proverbial deer, frozen in the headlights. Who do you trust the most, Nikki?"

"Rook."

"Can you discuss this with him?"

Nikki shrugged. "Sure."

"Openly?" She hesitated, which answered his question. "My experience with cops in this room is that grace under pressure is great in a moment. As a lifestyle it takes a toll. It's the stoicism. You are alone."

"But I'm not now. I'm with Rook."

"How much of you?" He didn't make her answer but let the softly ticking second hand behind her fill some space before he continued.

"At one time or other, if we're lucky, we struggle with how much of ourselves to reveal to one another. At work. In friendships. In relationships. You and Don kept the struggle physical without revealing or sharing. That worked because of parity. Neither of you wanted to go deeper. That won't be so in all relationships. You may want to reveal more of yourself than someone else. But, from what you've told me, the opposite is true. So—long term—the issue will have to be confronted at some point if Rook needs more intimacy than you are willing to give. It may turn him away. Not now, but someday, that reckoning will come. And you will let him in, or not. You will be vulnerable with him, or not. And you will experience the consequences, based on your choice. I hope the choice you make fulfills you."

Nikki stepped out onto the sidewalk from her session bearing more questions than solutions, but one thing in life looked brighter. The yellow Wafels & Dinges gourmet food truck had parked for its lunchtime business that day a block up York Avenue. She waited in line, vacillating between sweet and savory and went for a mashup: de Bacon-Syrup wafel, and ate it on a bench under the Roosevelt Island Tram. When Nikki finished, she sat a while to watch the red gondolas of passengers float overhead and ride out over the East River, and wished the weight of her cares could be packed into a sealed capsule and borne away into the sky on steel cables. It didn't work. That became clear when Agent Bart Callan, Department of Homeland Security, sat beside her.

"You should try de Throwdown," he said. "It's the wafel that beat out Bobby Flay's."

"Don't you guys have e-mail? Instead of ambushing me, how about a nice OpenTable invitation next time?"

"Like you would respond."

"Try me, Agent Callan. As I said last meeting, come in through the front door, I'm very cooperative by nature."

"Unless cornered."

"Who isn't?"

"I need to know everything you learned from Tyler Wynn and Petar Matic. If you can tell me what was in that drop box, that would be helpful, too."

Heat took her eyes off the tugboat churning upriver under the Queensboro Bridge and regarded the agent. Peel away the military zeal and the aggravating habit of surprise appearances, he seemed like an OK guy. Then self doubt about her trust instincts raised a caution flag. "You must have One PP on speed dial. Use it."

He shook no. "Not optimal. This is too sensitive, too big. If this goes into the bureaucracy chain, there's no containment."

"Then why involve me?"

"Because you are already involved. And you don't have a big mouth." He grinned. "I learned that the other night in the warehouse." She returned his smile and he held out his hand. At first, Nikki thought he wanted to hold hers, but he took her lunch garbage, and she blushed at her misunderstanding. He tossed her plate and fork in the can beside him and then pivoted on the bench to face her. "Detective Heat, I can assure you of one thing. The case we are working is developing into a matter of the highest national security. Maybe if I disclose to you, it will make you feel better about sharing with us."

"I'm listening."

"It's a short story. Nicole Bernardin, who was once CIA, reached out to us about a month and a half ago to say that she had come upon highly sensitive documentation of something urgent she needed to share. We did thorough checks on her background with Central Intelligence as well as her more recent history working with Tyler Wynn in his new—let's call it, independent—capacity. We made arrangements for her to get the information to us, but someone killed her before she could tell us where to find it."

Heat said, "If you want to know about the drop box, I found it, but I never saw what she had stashed."

"What did it look like?"

"A tan leather pouch with a zipper on top. The kind merchants use to take their cash to the bank."

He squinted, envisioning it, and said, "Thank you for that."

"You can thank me by answering this. If you knew Tyler Wynn had switched sides, why didn't you arrest him? Especially if he was into something endangering national security?"

"Exactly for that reason. Come on, Heat, you know what it's like to keep a suspect on a leash. We never picked up Wynn because we didn't want to blow his cover before he led us to whatever he's involved with."

"And how many people have died while you held this leash, Agent Callan?"

He knew what she was getting at and said, "For the record, Intelligence had no information Tyler Wynn had gone rogue at the time of your mother's death. In fact, her murder is where this investigation began. I was FBI back then, and I was the designated contact for your mother." That made Nikki turn to face him. "That's right, I knew her," he said. "In a scenario that played out very close to Nicole Bernardin's, your mother had reached out to us, voicing suspicion about a developing security threat on U.S. soil. We seeded her with two hundred thousand bucks to bribe an informant to get the proof and she was murdered the night she got it."

Nikki watched a tram float overhead as she digested the news. If Callan was telling the truth, that money wasn't her mother's Judas pay-off, after all. She brought her eyes down to meet his, and he said, "So there you have it. That's the story."

"Except for what sort of domestic plot she uncovered that, apparently, has been sitting on your radar all these years."

"That's classified."

"Convenient. And meanwhile, Tyler Wynn has been roaming free. Excuse me, on your leash."

Agent Callan ignored the shot. Part of that double-locked military demeanor, nothing appeared to knock him off mission. "A lot of people have asked you this, but I'm going to ask again, and I hope you will be straight with me. Do you have any idea what your mother received from that informant?"

"No."

"And you have no thoughts about where she might have hidden it?"

"No. Wherever it is, she hid it very well."

"You found Nicole Bernardin's drop."

"I told you, I don't know. Don't you think I've been through this on my own a million times?"

After a crisp nod, he got to his point. "I want you to cooperate with me on this."

"I have been. Are you listening?"

"I mean moving forward."

"I work for NYPD."

"I work for the American people."

"Then use your speed dial to call an American downtown at headquarters, then I'm all yours. Otherwise, thanks for the visit."

She was almost to York with her hand up for a cab when he walked toward her, trying out any leverage he could bring to bear. "Think about this. Doesn't the fact that someone can reach one of your prisoners and kill him while he's in custody tell you something about how serious this threat could be?"

"I can't help. I simply don't have anything to give you."

"I could help you get Tyler Wynn."

Or, thought Nikki, keep me from getting him if it didn't serve your purposes. She said, "Thanks for the tip on the wafel," and got into her taxi.

Heat got back to her apartment that evening and Rook got up from his MacBook at her dining room table to greet her with a deep kiss. He folded his long arms around her and they melted into each other where they stood. After they held each other a moment, he said, "You're not falling asleep on me, are you?"

"Standing up? Are you calling me a horse?"

"Neigh," he said, and she laughed for the first time that day.

"So stupid." She laughed again because it was stupid. And welcome. She cupped a hand on his jaw and caressed his cheek.

When he asked her how she was managing, she told him the truth. That the day had been a struggle and that she craved a warm bath. But after he mentioned he'd made a pitcher of Caipirinhas, the bath went on hold and the glasses came out.

They settled on the couch and she filled him in on her meeting with Bart Callan. "So that was your mysterious lunch engagement, DHS?"

For a moment, she thought about telling him about her shrink session but felt too spent to open up that topic and let it go. But then Nikki considered what Lon King had said about her reticence to reveal herself—his version of the wall speech—and she said, "No, I saw my shrink."

"So you've gone from calling him 'the' shrink to 'my' shrink? That's new."

"Let drop it, OK?" Baby steps, she thought, baby steps.

But he persisted. "I think it's good for you. If ever there was a time, Nikki. For the Petar baggage alone, if not for Don."

"Speaking of Don," she said, seizing an alternate topic to steer the conversation elsewhere. "I'm planning to fly to San Diego day after tomorrow. His family is holding a memorial at the navy base."

"I'd like to go with you, if that's all right."

Nikki's eyes widened in surprise. "You'd do that?" Rook's smile said yes, and she leaned forward and kissed it, beautiful to her as it was.

They snuggled for a moment, and after just the right amount of stillness, he said, "But if Petar has a funeral? I'm busy." The shock and poor taste of it made her laugh the way only Rook could, making the unsayable funny because it wasn't unthinkable.

Then her brow darkened. He knew what that was about. She didn't need to say anything. "I know it's disheartening. You solve this huge case only to have it lead to another dead end. We'll find out what's behind this. Just not now."

"But suppose what both Petar and Bart Callan said is true, that something big is coming that needs to be stopped?"

"At this point, I don't know where to go with that. And from what you said about Agent Callan, the feds don't either. Obviously Tyler Wynn is the key. It's all about whoever he's working for now. What did my friend Anatoly say that night in Paris? That it's a new era and that when spies turn it's not for other governments but—what did he call them— 'other entities'?"

She rubbed her face in her palms. "It all feels bigger than me right now."

"Nikki? That's all right." Rook put a hand on each of her shoulders and turned her to him. "You don't have to be the one-person crime task force. You've already done a great job. Right now you could plant the flag, declare victory, and move on. Nobody would fault you." And then he added, "I'll be with you, either way."

Everything rolled up in that sentence warmed her to the core, and Nikki said, "That helps, thanks." She set her unfinished drink on the coffee table. "Would you be terribly offended if I took that bath and just spent some alone time here tonight?"

"You want to cocoon?"

"Desperately. I need it."

"You've got it."

Rook packed up his laptop and notes into his backpack, and after they kissed at the door, he said, "Think about this tonight in your jammies."

"OK."

"One thing that's made this worth the trip: At least you learned your mother wasn't having an affair. And she wasn't a traitor. In fact, your mom was a hero."

"Yeah, you know what F. Scott Fitzgerald said, though. 'Show me a hero . . .' "

" '. . . I'll write you a tragedy.' "

"Plus," she said, "noble cause or not, I still feel pissed that she shut me out of so much of her life. Intellectually, I can say I want to forgive her, but the truth is, I don't feel it. Not yet."

"I understand," said Rook. "Listen, I'm no shrink, but if I were, what I'd suggest is that maybe the best you can do in the meantime is find some way to connect with her and see where that goes."

She floated in the indulgent warmth of lavender-scented water until the next track loaded on her boom box: Mary J. Blige, testifying to "No More Drama." Nikki sang along at first, belting it out, but then became an audience of one receiving the message of the Queen of Hip-Hop Soul about standing for yourself, ending the pain and the game. Nikki had heard the song many times, but—like the answering machine recording that documented her mother's stabbing—that day, it came to new ears. Especially the part about not knowing where the story ended, only where it began.

Sitting cross-legged on the couch with a hot cup of chamomile and wet hair dampening the terry shoulders of her robe, Nikki traced her mother's life story into her own. She tried not to dwell on the blemishes Cynthia Heat's secret life had created. Of course there were the absences that bred longings and fears, but more impactful were the learned traits that Nikki had so elegantly carried into her own life and selectively employed: caution, secretiveness, isolation. These could be her never-ending story, if she allowed it. The shrink had cautioned her to accept that her mother was dead, but Nikki knew her mother's story would live on through her and that her mother still resided in her heart, as she always would.

Still, Nikki sought the beginning of a story. One that fastened itself to the many good things received from her mother that so outweighed the rest. Or, at least, they would, if she chose no drama.

In her living room in the solitude of the night she owned, Heat's choice was to reflect on virtues and gifts. On the independence she'd gained from the upbringing her mother gave her. The sense of wonder, of imagination, of standards, and character, the value of hard work, of goodness itself, and the power of love. The new story she began went on like that, a tale of glasses that grew from half-full to brimming the more she composed it. It told her that laughter transcended, forgiveness healed, and music enkindled the coldest of hearts.

Music.

Nikki stared at the piano across the room.

Her mother had played it beautifully and shared its wonder with her. Why had it gained so much power in silence?

A flutter rose in her breast as she recalled Rook's parting words about finding some way to connect with her again. The flutter became dread, but she chose courage and stood anyway. As she crossed the rug to the baby grand, her dread melted away and became something that buoyed her as she lifted the bench's seat to take out the top booklet of sheet music. *Mozart for Young Hands.*

It was the first time in ten years she had opened that bench; even longer since she had held that book. Nikki was certain it had been lost.

She had been nineteen when she last lifted the cover on the Steinway. Nikki hesitated, not to falter but to mark the new passage.

The hinges on the cover creaked as she opened it and exposed the keys. Her fingers trembled with the anticipation of every one of her childhood recitals as Nikki sat, opened the music book to the first page, pumped the pedals for feel, and then began to play.

For the first time in a decade, music from that cherished instrument filled the apartment, and it came out of Nikki by way of Cynthia. Music is sense memory; however, it's muscle memory, too, so she misstruck a few keys, but that only made her smile as she began Mozart's Sonata Number Fifteen. Her play, which felt so rote and halting at first, slowly became more fluid and graceful. She fumbled, though, when she got to the bottom of the page and had trouble coordinating the turn with her fingering. Or maybe it was the tears that had clouded her vision. She wiped them away and prepared to resume, but stopped.

Nikki frowned and looked at the sheet music, confused. She leaned forward to the booklet on the stand and saw strange pencil marks in her mother's handwriting between the notes.

Her mom had always told her that Mozart considered the space between the notes music, too, but these were not music notations that she recognized, but something else.

But what?

Heat snapped the light up one more notch and held the music book under its brightness to study the marks. To her eye, they appeared to be some sort of code.

She began to rock slightly on the bench and the floor felt like it shook. Nikki thought she was experiencing another aftershock. But then she looked around her.

The rest of the room sat perfectly still.

ACKNOWLEDGMENTS

I participated in a mystery authors panel at the New York Public Library recently, and, as usual, it was the opening question. An aspiring novelist in the front row wanted to know about my habits. Did I write in the morning or evening? Use a pen or a keyboard? Auto spellcheck on or off? I gave my standard answer: I don't have any habits. In fact, as I sit here now at dawn's first light, filling my Hemingway Montblanc (medium nib) with Noodler's Baystate Blue, a stack of thirty crisp, blank, annotation-ruled, twenty-two-pound Levenger sheets ready on my slant-angle editor's desk, I've got to ask, where does a question like that even come from?

Not saying I do, but if I actually did have any habits, they'd probably stem from the fact that, if I'm doing it right—if I *am* hanging it all out there riding the bucking back of an untamed story—my little rituals would be the only things under my control. Writing a mystery is a bit like a trip to Atlantic City. Even though you've been there before, you can never be sure what will happen. You go sleepless for days, try crazy shit you wouldn't otherwise dream of, and, when you're through, you're left with nothing. Oh, and all that great sex was in your imagination.

The only way through—Atlantic City or a novel—is never to go it alone, and I'm running with a posse that would put the *Hangover* boys to shame. It all starts and ends with Detective Kate Beckett, who has shown me that luck is a lady cop, and has a little experience herself waking up with a Bengal tiger. Her colleagues from the 12th Precinct, Javier Esposito and Kevin Ryan, know something about doing AC, and have made me feel like a brother. The brother they cherry-bomb in the outhouse, but a brother, nonetheless. I also owe thanks to Captain Victoria Gates, who kept me around in spite of seeing me for the stunted adolescent miscreant I am.

Dr. Parish has been a patient, if eye-rolling, medical examiner, enduring my ghoulish puns, gallows humor, and high jinks. I am also fortunate to have been around to discover that Lanie sings the blues.

My mother, Martha, has given me the primer on how to get myself into trouble—elegantly, while my dear daughter, Alexis, has shown me someone has to be the grown-up of the family. Thank God it doesn't have to be me.

Nathan, Stana, Seamus, Jon, Molly, Susan, Tamala, and Penny bring life, truth, and heart, day and night. How the hell do they make it look so easy?

The crew in the Clinton Building at Raleigh Studios knows me better than I know myself, and to them, for the imagination, belief, and cold deli takeout, a sincere tip of the Montblanc cap.

Thanks to Terri Edda Miller, I never have to wonder who's beside me or worry what's behind me. May every journey continue to be a safari-level adventure for us.

Jennifer Allen still makes me swoon and then catches me when I fall. It shall be ever thus.

To Gretchen Young, my editor . . . one dice roll, and look, we're still at the table, giddy and ignoring the three-dollar buffet. Thanks to Gretchen and everyone at Hyperion, including Allyson Rudolph. I'm also continually thankful for the care and support of Melissa Harling-Walendy and the team at ABC.

Thanks to Sloan Harris, my literary agent at ICM. I feel I am the luckiest author in the world after all these years of his faith and kind guidance.

Whether it's hanging in Vegas, doing the AC, or working the green felt in a certain Tribeca loft, a big thanks to Connelly, Lehane, Patterson, and, in spirit, Cannell, for keeping my poker skills sharp.

My friend Alton Brown taught me to boil water, and Ellen Borakove at the Office of the Chief Medical Examiner in New York City showed me how to breathe through my mouth to fool my brain. My appetite is better thanks to both of them.

As for Andrew, what can I say to adequately draw the picture? I began as an admirer, became a colleague, and now proudly call him friend. He's got them all beat because Andrew has more than talent. He is also brave. This man is not afraid to double down. And, I suspect, like his cohort Tom, he cares.

About the mission. About getting it right. And dearly, about the fans. Let it ride, fellas.

RC

New York City, June 2012

A Series of
Unfortunate Events

BOOK THE FIFTH

THE AUSTERE ACADEMY

by

Lemony Snicket

Illustrated by
BRETT HELQUIST

EGMONT

www.unfortunateevents.com

First published in the USA 2000
by HarperCollins Children's Books
First published in Great Britain 2002
by Egmont Books Limited
239 Kensington High Street, London W8 6SA

Published by arrangement with
HarperCollins Children's Books,
a division of HarperCollins Publishers, Inc.,
New York, New York, USA

Text copyright © 2000 Lemony Snicket
Inside illustration copyright © 2000 Brett Helquist
Cover illustration copyright © 2002 Brett Helquist

The moral right of the cover illustrator
has been asserted

ISBN 1 4052 0871 6

10 9 8 7 6 5

A CIP catalogue record for this title is available from
the British Library

Printed and bound in Italy

BOOK THE FIFTH

THE AUSTERE ACADEMY

For Beatrice –
You will always be in my heart,
in my mind,
and in your grave.

THE AUSTERE ACADEMY

CHAPTER One

If you were going to give a gold medal to the least delightful person on Earth, you would have to give that medal to a person named Carmelita Spats, and if you didn't give it to her, Carmelita Spats was the sort of person who would snatch it from your hands anyway. Carmelita Spats was rude, she was violent, and she was filthy, and it is really a shame that I must describe her to you, because there are enough ghastly and distressing things in this story without even mentioning such an unpleasant person.

It is the Baudelaire orphans, thank goodness, who are the heroes of this story, not the dreadful Carmelita Spats, and if you wanted to give a gold medal to Violet, Klaus, and Sunny Baudelaire, it would be for survival in the face of adversity. Adversity is a word which here means "trouble," and there are very few people in this world who have had the sort of troubling adversity that follows these three children wherever they go. Their trouble began one day when they were relaxing at the beach and received the distressing news that their parents had been killed in a terrible fire, and so were sent to live with a distant relative named Count Olaf.

If you were going to give a gold medal to Count Olaf, you would have to lock it up someplace before the awarding ceremony, because Count Olaf was such a greedy and evil man that he would try to steal it beforehand. The Baudelaire orphans did not have a gold medal, but they did have an enormous fortune that their parents had left them, and it was that fortune Count Olaf tried to snatch. The three siblings survived living with Count Olaf, but just barely,

and since then Olaf had followed them everywhere, usually accompanied by one or more of
his sinister and ugly associates. No matter who
was caring for the Baudelaires, Count Olaf was
always right behind them, performing such das-
tardly deeds that I can scarcely list them all: kidnapping, murder, nasty phone calls, disguises,
poison, hypnosis, and atrocious cooking are just
some of the adversities the Baudelaire orphans
survived at his hands. Even worse, Count Olaf
had a bad habit of avoiding capture, so he was
always sure to turn up again. It is truly awful
that this keeps happening, but that is how the
story goes.

I only tell you that the story goes this way
because you are about to become acquainted
with rude, violent, filthy Carmelita Spats, and
if you can't stand reading about her, you had
best put this book down and read something
else, because it only gets worse from here.
Before too long, Violet, Klaus, and Sunny Baudelaire will have so much adversity that being

shoved aside by Carmelita Spats will look like a trip to the ice cream store.

"Get out of my way, you cakesniffers!" said a rude, violent, and filthy little girl, shoving the Baudelaire orphans aside as she dashed by. Violet, Klaus, and Sunny were too startled to answer. They were standing on a sidewalk made of bricks, which must have been very old because there was a great deal of dark moss oozing out from in between them. Surrounding the sidewalk was a vast brown lawn that looked like it had never been watered, and on the lawn were hundreds of children running in various directions. Occasionally someone would slip and fall to the ground, only to get back up and keep running. It looked exhausting and pointless, two things that should be avoided at all costs, but the Baudelaire orphans barely glanced at the other children, keeping their eyes on the mossy bricks below them.

Shyness is a curious thing, because, like quicksand, it can strike people at any time, and also, like quicksand, it usually makes its victims look down. This was to be the Baudelaires' first day at Prufrock Preparatory School, and all three siblings found that they would rather look at the oozing moss than at anything else.

"Have you dropped something?" Mr. Poe asked, coughing into a white handkerchief. One place the Baudelaires certainly didn't want to look was at Mr. Poe, who was walking closely behind them. Mr. Poe was a banker who had been placed in charge of the Baudelaires' affairs following the terrible fire, and this had turned out to be a lousy idea. Mr. Poe meant well, but a jar of mustard probably also means well and would do a better job of keeping the Baudelaires out of danger. Violet, Klaus, and Sunny had long ago learned that the only thing they could count on from Mr. Poe was that he was always coughing.

"No," Violet replied, "we haven't dropped anything." Violet was the oldest Baudelaire, and usually she was not shy at all. Violet liked to invent things, and one could often find her thinking hard about her latest invention, with her hair tied up in a ribbon to keep it out of her eyes. When her inventions were done, she liked to show them to people she knew, who were usually very impressed with her skill. Right now, as she looked down at the mossy bricks, she thought of a machine she could build that could keep moss from growing on the sidewalk, but she felt too nervous to talk about it. What if none of the teachers, children, or administrative staff were interested in her inventions?

As if he were reading her thoughts, Klaus put a hand on Violet's shoulder, and she smiled at him. Klaus had known for all twelve of his years that his older sister found a hand on her shoulder comforting—as long as the hand was attached to an arm, of course. Normally Klaus would have said something comforting as well, but he was feeling as shy as his sister. Most of the time, Klaus could be found doing what he liked to do best, which was reading. Some mornings one could find him in bed with his glasses on because he had been reading so late that he was too tired to take them off. Klaus looked down at the sidewalk and remembered a book he had read called *Moss Mysteries*, but he felt too shy to bring it up. What if Prufrock Preparatory School had nothing good to read?

Sunny, the youngest Baudelaire, looked up at her siblings, and Violet smiled and picked her up. This was easy to do because Sunny was a baby and only a little bit larger than a loaf of bread. Sunny was also too nervous to say anything, although it was often difficult to understand what she said when she did speak up. For instance, if Sunny had not been feeling so shy, she might have opened her mouth, revealing her four sharp teeth, and said "Marimo!" which may have meant "I hope there are plenty of things to bite at school, because biting things is one of my favorite things to do!"

"I know why you're all so quiet," Mr. Poe said. "It's because you're excited, and I don't blame you. I always wanted to go to boarding school when I was younger, but I never had the chance. I'm a little jealous of you, if you want to know the truth."

The Baudelaires looked at one another. The fact that Prufrock Preparatory School was a boarding school was the part that made them feel the most nervous. If no one was interested in inventions, or there was nothing to read, or biting wasn't allowed, they were stuck there, not only all day but all night as well. The siblings wished that if Mr. Poe were really jealous of them he would attend Prufrock Preparatory School himself, and they could work at the bank.

"You're very lucky to be here," Mr. Poe continued. "I had to call more than four schools before I found one that could take all three of you at such short notice. Prufrock Prep—that's what they call it, as a sort of nickname—is a very fine academy. The teachers all have advanced degrees. The dormitory rooms are all finely furnished. And most important of all, there is an advanced computer system which will keep Count Olaf away from you. Vice Principal Nero told me that Count Olaf's complete description—everything from his one long eyebrow to the tattoo of an eye on his left ankle—has been programmed into the computer, so you three should be safe here for the next several years."

"But how can a computer keep Count Olaf away?" Violet asked in a puzzled voice, still looking down at the ground.

"It's an *advanced* computer," Mr. Poe said, as if the word "advanced" were a proper explanation instead of a word meaning "having attained advancement." "Don't worry your little heads about Count Olaf. Vice Principal Nero has promised me that he will keep a close eye on you. After all, a school as *advanced* as Prufrock Prep wouldn't allow people to simply run around loose."

"Move, cakesniffers!" the rude, violent, and filthy little girl said as she dashed by them again.

"What does 'cakesniffers' mean?" Violet murmured to Klaus, who had an enormous vocabulary from all his reading.

"I don't know," Klaus admitted, "but it doesn't sound very nice."

"What a charming word that is," Mr. Poe said. "*Cakesniffers.* I don't know what it means, but it reminds me of pastry. Oh well, here we are." They had come to the end of the mossy brick sidewalk and stood in front of the school. The Baudelaires looked up at their new home and gasped in surprise. Had they not been staring at the sidewalk the whole way across the lawn, they would have seen what the academy looked like, but perhaps it was best to delay looking at it for as long as possible. A person who designs buildings is called an architect, but in the case of Prufrock Prep a better term might be "depressed architect." The school was made up of several buildings, all made of smooth gray stone, and the buildings were grouped together in a sort of sloppy line. To get to the buildings, the Baudelaires had to walk beneath an immense stone arch casting a curved shadow on the lawn, like a rainbow in which all of the colors were gray or black. On the arch were the words "PRUFROCK PREPARATORY SCHOOL" in enormous black letters, and then, in smaller letters, the motto of the school, "Memento Mori." But it was not the buildings or the arch that made the children gasp. It was how the buildings were shaped—rectangular, but with a rounded top. A rectangle with a rounded top is a strange shape, and the orphans could only think of one thing with that shape. To the Baudelaires each building looked exactly like a gravestone.

"Rather odd architecture," Mr. Poe commented. "Each building looks like a thumb. In any case, you are to report to Vice Principal Nero's office immediately. It's on the ninth floor of the main building."

"Aren't you coming with us, Mr. Poe?" Violet asked. Violet was fourteen, and she knew that fourteen was old enough to go to some-body's office by herself, but she felt nervous about walking into such a sinister-looking build-ing without an adult nearby.

Mr. Poe coughed into his handkerchief and looked at his wristwatch at the same time. "I'm afraid not," he said when his coughing passed. "The banking day has already begun. But I've talked over everything with Vice Principal Nero, and if there's any problem, remember you can always contact me or any of my associates at Mulctuary Money Management. Now, off you go. Have a wonderful time at Prufrock Prep."

"I'm sure we will," said Violet, sounding much braver than she felt. "Thank you for everything, Mr. Poe."

"Yes, thank you," Klaus said, shaking the banker's hand.

"Terfunt," Sunny said, which was her way of saying "Thank you."

"You're welcome, all of you," Mr. Poe said. "So long." He nodded at all three Baudelaires, and Violet and Sunny watched him walk back down the mossy sidewalk, carefully avoiding the running children. But Klaus didn't watch him. Klaus was looking at the enormous arch over the academy.

"Maybe I don't know what 'cakesniffer' means," Klaus said, "but I think I can translate our new school's motto."

"It doesn't even look like it's in English," Violet said, peering up at it.

"Racho," Sunny agreed.

"It's not," Klaus said. "It's in Latin. Many mottoes are in Latin, for some reason. I don't know very much Latin, but I do remember reading this phrase in a book about the Middle Ages. If it means what I think it means, it's certainly a strange motto."

"What do you think it means?" Violet asked.

"If I'm not mistaken," said Klaus, who was rarely mistaken, "'Memento Mori' means 'Remember you will die.'"

"Remember you will die," Violet repeated

quietly, and the three siblings stepped closer to one another, as if they were very cold. Everybody will die, of course, sooner or later. Circus performers will die, and clarinet experts will die, and you and I will die, and there might be a person who lives on your block, right now, who is not looking both ways before he crosses the street and who will die in just a few seconds, all because of a bus. Everybody will die, but very few people want to be reminded of that fact. The children certainly did not want to remember that they would die, particularly as they walked beneath the arch over Prufrock Prep. The Baudelaire orphans did not need to be reminded of this as they began their first day in the giant graveyard that was now their home.

As the Baudelaire orphans stood outside
Vice Principal Nero's door, they were
reminded of something their father
said to them just a few months
before he died. One evening, the
Baudelaire parents had gone
out to hear an orchestra play,
and the three children had
stayed by themselves in
the family mansion. The
Baudelaires had something
of a routine on nights like
this. First, Violet and Klaus

would play a few games of checkers while Sunny ripped up some old newspapers, and then the three children would read in the library until they fell asleep on comfortable sofas. When their parents came home they would wake up the sleeping children, talk to them a little about the evening, and send them off to bed. But on this particular night, the Baudelaire parents came home early and the children were still up reading—or, in Sunny's case, looking at the pictures. The siblings' father stood in the doorway of the library and said something they never forgot. "Children," he said, "there is no worse sound in the world than somebody who cannot play the violin who insists on doing so anyway."

At the time, the Baudelaires had merely giggled, but as they listened outside the vice principal's door, they realized that their father had been absolutely right. When they first approached the heavy wooden door, it sounded like a small animal was having a temper tantrum. But as they listened more closely, the children realized it was somebody who cannot play the violin insisting on doing so anyway. The sounds shrieked and hissed and scratched and moaned and made other horrible sounds that are really impossible to describe, and finally Violet could take it no longer and knocked on the door. She had to knock very hard and at length, in order to be heard over the atrocious violin recital going on inside, but at last the wooden door opened with a creak and there stood a tall man with a violin under his chin and an angry glare in his eyes.

"Who dares interrupt a genius when he is rehearsing?" he asked, in a voice so loud and booming that it was enough to make anyone shy all over again.

"The Baudelaires," Klaus said quietly, looking at the floor. "Mr. Poe said to come right to Vice Principal Nero's office."

"*Mr. Poe said to come right to Vice Principal Nero's office,*" the man mimicked in a high, shrieky voice. "Well, come in, come in, I don't have all afternoon."

The children stepped into the office and got a better look at the man who had mocked them. He was dressed in a rumpled brown suit that had something sticky on its jacket, and he was wearing a tie decorated with pictures of snails. His nose was very small and very red, as if somebody had stuck a cherry tomato in the middle of his splotchy face. He was almost completely bald, but he had four tufts of hair, which he had tied into little pigtails with some old rubber bands. The Baudelaires had never seen anybody who looked like him before and they weren't particularly interested in looking at him any further, but his office was so small and bare that it was difficult to look at anything else. There was a small metal desk with a small metal chair behind it and a small metal lamp to one side. The office had one window, decorated with curtains that matched the man's tie. The only other object in the room was a shiny computer, which sat in a corner of the room like a toad. The computer had a blank gray screen and several buttons as red as the pigtailed man's nose.

"Ladies and gentlemen," the man announced in a loud voice, "Vice Principal Nero!"

There was a pause, and the three children looked all around the tiny room, wondering where Nero had been hiding all this time. Then they looked back at the man with the pigtails, who was holding both hands up in the air, his violin and bow almost touching the ceiling, and they realized that the man he had just introduced so grandly was himself. Nero paused for a moment and looked down at the Baudelaires.

"It is traditional," he said sternly, "to applaud when a genius has been introduced."

Just because something is traditional is no reason to do it, of course. Piracy, for example, is a tradition that has been carried on for hundreds of years, but that doesn't mean we should all attack ships and steal their gold. But Vice Principal Nero looked so ferocious that the children felt this was a time to honor tradition, so they began clapping their hands and didn't stop until Nero took several bows and sat down in his chair.

"Thank you very much, and welcome to Prufrock Preparatory School, *blah blah blah*," he said, using the word "blah" to mean that he was too bored to finish his sentence properly. "I'm certainly doing Mr. Poe a favor in taking on three orphans at such short notice. He assured me that you won't cause any trouble, but I did a little research of my own. You've been sent to legal guardian after legal guardian, and adversity has always followed. 'Adversity' means 'trouble,' by the way."

"In our case," Klaus said, not pointing out that he already knew what the word "adversity" meant, "'adversity' means *Count Olaf*. He was the cause of all the trouble with our guardians."

"He was the cause of all the trouble with our guardians," Nero said in his nasty, mimicking way. "I'm not interested in your problems, quite frankly. I am a genius and have no time for anything other than playing the violin. It's

depressing enough that I had to take this job as vice principal because not a single orchestra appreciates my genius. I'm not going to depress myself further by listening to the problems of three bratty children. Anyway, here at Prufrock Prep there'll be no blaming your own weaknesses on this Count Olaf person. Look at this."

Vice Principal Nero walked over to the computer and pressed two buttons over and over again. The screen lit up with a light green glow, as if it were seasick. "This is an advanced computer," Nero said. "Mr. Poe gave me all the necessary information about the man you call Count Olaf, and I programmed it into the computer. See?" Nero pressed another button, and a small picture of Count Olaf appeared on the computer screen. "Now that the advanced computer knows about him, you don't have to worry."

"But how can a computer keep Count Olaf away?" Klaus asked. "He could still show up and cause trouble, no matter what appears on a computer screen."

"I shouldn't have bothered trying to explain this to you," Vice Principal Nero said. "There's no way uneducated people like yourself can understand a genius like me. Well, Prufrock Prep will take care of that. You'll get an education here if we have to break both your arms to do it. Speaking of which, I'd better show you around. Come here to the window."

The Baudelaire orphans walked to the window and looked down at the brown lawn. From the ninth floor, all the children running around looked like tiny ants, and the sidewalk looked like a ribbon somebody had thrown away. Nero stood behind the siblings and pointed at things with his violin.

"Now, this building you're in is the administrative building. It is completely off-limits to students. Today is your first day, so I'll forgive you, but if I see you here again, you will not be allowed to use silverware at any of your meals. That gray building over there contains the classrooms. Violet, you will be studying with Mr.

Remora in Room One, and Klaus, you will be studying with Mrs. Bass in Room Two. Can you remember that, Room One and Room Two? If you don't think you can remember, I have a felt-tipped marker, and I will write 'Room One' and 'Room Two' on your hands in permanent ink."

"We can remember," Violet said quickly. "But which classroom is Sunny's?"

Vice Principal Nero drew himself up to his full height, which in his case was five feet, ten inches. "Prufrock Preparatory School is a serious academy, not a nursery school. I told Mr. Poe that we would have room for the baby here, but we do not have a classroom for her. Sunny will be employed as my secretary."

"Aregg?" Sunny asked incredulously. "Incredulously" is a word which here means "not being able to believe it," and "Aregg" is a word which here means "What? I can't believe it."

"But Sunny's a *baby*," Klaus said. "Babies aren't supposed to have jobs."

"*Babies aren't supposed to have jobs,*" Nero

mimicked again, and then continued. "Well, babies aren't supposed to be at boarding schools, either," Nero pointed out. "Nobody can teach a baby anything, so she'll work for me. All she has to do is answer the phone and take care of paperwork. It's not very difficult, and it's an honor to work for a genius, of course. Now, if either of you are late for class, or Sunny is late for work, your hands will be tied behind your back during meals. You'll have to lean down and eat your food like a dog. Of course, Sunny will always have her silverware taken away, because she will work in the administrative building, where she's not allowed."

"That's not fair!" Violet cried.

"That's not fair!" the vice principal squealed back at her. "The stone building over there contains the cafeteria. Meals are served promptly at breakfast time, lunchtime, and dinnertime. If you're late we take away your cups and glasses, and your beverages will be served to you in large puddles. That rectangular building over there,

with the rounded top, is the auditorium. Every night I give a violin recital for six hours, and attendance is mandatory. The word 'mandatory' means that if you don't show up, you have to buy me a large bag of candy and watch me eat it. The lawn serves as our sports facility. Our regular gym teacher, Miss Tench, accidentally fell out of a third-story window a few days ago, but we have a replacement, who should arrive shortly. In the meantime, I've instructed the children just to run around as fast as they can during gym time. I think that just about covers everything. Are there any questions?"

"Could anything be worse than this?" was the question Sunny had, but she was too well mannered to ask this. "Are you kidding about all these incredibly cruel punishments and rules?" was the question Klaus thought of, but he already knew that the answer was no. Only Violet thought of a question that seemed useful to ask.

"I have a question, Vice Principal Nero," she said. "Where do we live?"

Nero's response was so predictable that the Baudelaire orphans could have said it along with this miserable administrator. *"Where do we live?"* he said in his high, mocking tone, but when he was done making fun of the children he decided to answer it. "We have a magnificent dormitory here at Prufrock Prep," he said. "You can't miss it. It's a gray building, entirely made of stone and shaped like a big toe. Inside is a huge living room with a brick fireplace, a game room, and a large lending library. Every student has his or her own room, with a bowl of fresh fruit placed there every Wednesday. Doesn't that sound nice?"

"Yes, it does," Klaus admitted.

"Keeb!" Sunny shrieked, which meant something along the lines of "I like fruit!"

"I'm glad you think so," Nero said, "although you won't get to see much of the place. In order to live in the dormitory, you must have a permission slip with the signature of a parent or guardian. Your parents are dead, and Mr. Poe tells me that your guardians have either been killed or have fired you."

"But surely Mr. Poe can sign our permission slip," Violet said.

"He surely can *not*," Nero replied. "He is neither your parent nor your guardian. He is a banker who is in charge of your affairs."

"But that's more or less the same thing," Klaus protested.

"That's more or less the same thing," Nero mimicked. "Perhaps after a few semesters at Prufrock Prep, you'll learn the difference between a parent and a banker. No, I'm afraid you'll have to live in a small shack, made entirely of tin. Inside there is no living room, no game room, and no lending library whatsoever. You three will each have your own bale of hay to sleep on, but no fruit. It's a dismal place, but Mr. Poe tells me that you've had a number of uncomfortable experiences, so I figured you'd be used to such things."

"Couldn't you please make an exception?" Violet asked.

"I'm a *violinist*!" Nero cried. "I have no time to make exceptions! I'm too busy practicing the violin. So if you will kindly leave my office, I can get back to work."

Klaus opened his mouth to say something more, but when he looked at Nero, he knew that there was no use saying another word to such a stubborn man, and he glumly followed his sisters out of the vice principal's office. When the office door shut behind them, however, Vice Principal Nero said another word, and he said it three times. The three children listened to these three words that he said and knew for certain that he had not been sorry at all. For as soon as the Baudelaires left the office and Nero thought he was alone, he said to himself, "Hee hee hee."

Now, the vice principal of Prufrock Preparatory School did not actually say the syllables "hee hee hee," of course. Whenever you see the

words "hee hee hee" in a book, or "ha ha ha,"
or "har har har," or "heh heh heh," or even "ho
ho ho," those words mean somebody was laughing. In this case, however, the words "hee hee
hee" cannot really describe what Vice Principal
Nero's laugh sounded like. The laugh was
squeaky, and it was wheezy, and it had a rough,
crackly edge to it, as if Nero were eating tin cans
as he laughed at the children. But most of all,
the laugh sounded *cruel*. It is always cruel to
laugh at people, of course, although sometimes
if they are wearing an ugly hat it is hard to
control yourself. But the Baudelaires were not
wearing ugly hats. They were young children
receiving bad news, and if Vice Principal Nero
really had to laugh at them, he should have been
able to control himself until the siblings were
out of earshot. But Nero didn't care about con-
trolling himself, and as the Baudelaire orphans
listened to the laugh, they realized that what
their father had said to them that night when
he'd come home from the symphony was wrong.

There *was* a worse sound in the world than somebody who cannot play the violin insisting on doing so anyway. The sound of an administrator laughing a squeaky, wheezy, rough, crackly, cruel laugh at children who have to live in a shack was much, much worse. So as I hide out here in this mountain cabin and write the words "hee hee hee," and you, wherever you are hiding out, read the words "hee hee hee," you should know that "hee hee hee" stands for the worst sound the Baudelaires had ever heard.

The expression "Making a mountain out of a molehill" simply means making a big deal out of something that is actually a small deal, and it is easy to see how this expression came about. Molehills are simply mounds of earth serving as condominiums for moles, and they have never caused anyone any harm except for maybe a stubbed toe if you were walking through the wilderness without any shoes on. Mountains, however, are very large mounds of earth and are constantly causing problems. They are very tall, and when people try to climb them they often fall off, or get lost and die of starvation. Sometimes two countries fight over who really owns a mountain, and thousands of people have to go to war and come home grumpy or wounded. And, of course, mountains serve as homes to mountain goats and mountain lions, who enjoy attacking helpless picnickers and eating sandwiches or children. So when someone is making a mountain out of a molehill, they are pretending that something is as horrible as a war or a ruined picnic when it is really only as horrible as a stubbed toe.

When the Baudelaire orphans reached the shack where they were going to live, however, they realized that Vice Principal Nero hadn't been making a mountain out of a molehill at all when he had said that the shack was a dismal place. If anything, he had been making a molehill out of a mountain. It was true that the shack was tiny, as Nero had said, and made of tin, and it was true that there was no living room, no game room, and no lending library. It was true that there were three bales of hay instead of beds, and that there was absolutely no fresh fruit in sight. But Vice Principal Nero had left out a few details in his description, and it was these details that made the shack even worse. The first detail the Baudelaires noticed was that the shack was infested with small crabs, each one about the size of a matchbox, scurrying around the wooden floor with their tiny claws snapping in the air. As the children walked across the shack to sit glumly on one of the bales of hay, they were disappointed to learn that the crabs were territorial, a word which here means "unhappy to see small children in their living quarters." The crabs gathered around the children and began snapping their claws at them. Luckily, the crabs did not have very good aim, and luckily, their claws were so small that they probably wouldn't hurt any more than a good strong pinch, but even if they were more or less harmless they did not make for a good shack.

When the children reached the bale of hay and sat down, tucking their legs up under them to avoid the snapping crabs, they looked up at the ceiling and saw another detail Nero had neglected to mention. Some sort of fungus was growing on the ceiling, a fungus that was light tan and quite damp. Every few seconds, small drops of moisture would fall from the fungus with a *plop!* and the children had to duck to avoid getting light tan fungus juice on them. Like the small crabs, the *plop!*ing fungus did not appear to be very harmful, but also like the small crabs, the fungus made the shack even more uncomfortable than the vice principal had described it.

And lastly, as the children sat on the bale of hay with their legs tucked beneath them and ducked to avoid fungus juice, they saw one more harmless but unpleasant detail of the shack that was worse than Nero had led them to believe, and that was the color of the walls.

Each tin wall was bright green, with tiny pink hearts painted here and there as if the shack were an enormous, tacky Valentine's Day card instead of a place to live, and the Baudelaires found that they would rather look at the bales of hay, or the small crabs on the floor, or even the light tan fungus on the ceiling than the ugly walls.

Overall, the shack was too miserable to serve as a storage space for old banana peels, let alone as a home for three young people, and I confess that if I had been told that it was my home I probably would have lain on the bales of hay and thrown a temper tantrum. But the Baudelaires had learned long ago that temper tantrums, however fun they may be to throw, rarely solve whatever problem is causing them. So after a long, miserable silence, the orphans tried to look at their situation in a more positive light.

"This isn't such a nice room," Violet said finally, "but if I put my mind to it, I bet I can invent something that can keep these crabs away from us."

"And I'm going to read up on this light tan fungus," Klaus said. "Maybe the dormitory library has information on how to stop it from dripping."

"Ivoser," Sunny said, which meant something like "I bet I can use my four sharp teeth to scrape this paint away and make the walls a bit less ugly."

Klaus gave his baby sister a little kiss on the top of her head. "At least we get to go to school," he pointed out. "I've missed being in a real class-room."

"Me too," Violet agreed. "And at least we'll meet some people our own age. We've only had the company of adults for quite some time."

"Wonic," Sunny said, which probably meant "And learning secretarial skills is an exciting opportunity for me, although I should really be in nursery school instead."

"That's true," Klaus said. "And who knows? Maybe the advanced computer really can keep Count Olaf away, and that's the most important thing of all."

"You're right," Violet said. "Any room that doesn't have Count Olaf in it is good enough for me."

"Olo," Sunny said, which meant "Even if it's ugly, damp, and filled with crabs."

The children sighed and then sat quietly for a few moments. The shack was quiet, except for the snapping of tiny crab claws, the *plop!* of fungus, and the sighs of the Baudelaires as they looked at the ugly walls. Try as they might, the youngsters just couldn't make the shack into a molehill. No matter how much they thought of real classrooms, people their own age, or the exciting opportunity of secretarial skills, their new home seemed much, much worse than even the sorest of stubbed toes.

"Well," Klaus said after a while, "it feels like it's about lunchtime. Remember, if we're late they take away our cups and glasses, so we should probably get a move on."

"Those rules are ridiculous," Violet said, ducking to avoid a *plop!* "Lunchtime isn't a specific time, so you can't be late for it. It's just a word that means 'around lunch.'"

"I know," Klaus said, "and the part about Sunny being punished for going to the administrative building, when she *has* to go there to be Nero's secretary, is completely absurd."

"Kalc!" Sunny said, putting her little hand on her brother's knee. She meant something like "Don't worry about it. I'm a baby, so I hardly ever use silverware. It doesn't matter that it'll be taken away from me."

Ridiculous rules or not, the orphans did not want to be punished, so the three of them walked gingerly—the word "gingerly" here means "avoiding territorial crabs"—across the shack and out onto the brown lawn. Gym class must have been over, because all the running children were gone, and this only made the Baudelaires walk even more quickly to the cafeteria.

Several years before this story took place, when Violet was ten and Klaus was eight and

Sunny was not even a fetus, the Baudelaire family went to a county fair in order to see a pig that their Uncle Elwyn had entered in a contest. The pig contest turned out to be a bit dull, but in the neighboring tent there was another contest that the family found quite interesting: the Biggest Lasagna Contest. The lasagna that won the blue ribbon had been baked by eleven nuns, and was as big and soft as a large mattress. Perhaps because they were at such an impressionable age—the phrase "impressionable age" here means "ten and eight years old, respectively"— Violet and Klaus always remembered this lasagna, and they were sure they would never see another one anywhere near as big.

Violet and Klaus were wrong. When the Baudelaires entered the cafeteria, they found a lasagna waiting for them that was the size of a dance floor. It was sitting on top of an enormous trivet to keep it from burning the floor, and the person serving it was wearing a thick metal mask as protection, so that the children could only see their eyes peeking out from tiny eyeholes. The stunned Baudelaires got into a long line of children and waited their turn for the metal-masked person to scoop lasagna onto ugly plastic trays and hand it wordlessly to the children. After receiving their lasagna, the orphans walked further down the line and helped themselves to green salad, which was waiting for them in a bowl the size of a pickup truck. Next to the salad was a mountain of garlic bread, and at the end of the line was another metal-masked person, handing out silverware to the students who had not been inside the administrative building.

The Baudelaires said "thank you" to the person, who gave them a slow metallic nod in return. They took a long look around the crowded cafeteria. Hundreds of children had already received their lasagna and were sitting at long rectangular tables. The Baudelaires saw several other children who had undoubtedly been in the administrative building, because they had no silverware. They saw several more students who had their hands tied behind their backs as punishment for being late to class. And they saw several students who had a sad look on their faces, as if they had been forced to buy somebody a bag of candy and watch them eat it, and the orphans guessed that these students had failed to show up to one of Nero's six-hour concerts.

But it was none of these punishments that made the Baudelaire orphans pause for so long. It was the fact that they did not know where to sit. Cafeterias can be confusing places, because there are different rules for each one, and sometimes it is difficult to know where one should eat. Normally, the Baudelaires would simply eat with one of their friends, but their friends were far, far away from Prufrock Preparatory School, and Violet, Klaus, and Sunny gazed around the cafeteria full of strangers and thought they might never put down their ugly trays. Finally, they caught the eye of the girl they had seen on the lawn, who had called them such a strange name, and walked a few steps toward her.

Now, you and I know that this loathsome little girl was Carmelita Spats, but the Baudelaires had not been properly introduced to her and so did not realize just how loathsome she was, although as the orphans drew closer she gave them an instant education.

"Don't even *think* of eating around here, you cakesniffers!" Carmelita Spats cried, and several of her rude, filthy, violent friends nodded in agreement. "Nobody wants to have lunch with people who live in the Orphans Shack!"

"I'm terribly sorry," Klaus said, although he wasn't terribly sorry at all. "I didn't mean to disturb you."

Carmelita, who had apparently never been to the administrative building, picked up her silverware and began to bang it on her tray in a rhythmic and irritating way. "Cakesniffing orphans in the Orphans Shack! Cakesniffing orphans in the Orphans Shack!" she chanted, and to the Baudelaires' dismay, many other children joined right in. Like many other rude, violent, filthy people, Carmelita Spats had a bunch of friends who were always happy to help her torment people—probably to avoid being tormented themselves. In a few seconds, it seemed like the entire cafeteria was banging their silverware and chanting, "Cakesniffing orphans in the Orphans Shack!" The three siblings stepped closer together, craning their necks to see if there was any possible place to which they could escape and eat their lunch in peace.

"Oh, leave them alone, Carmelita!" a voice cried over the chanting. The Baudelaires turned around and saw a boy with very dark hair and very wide eyes. He looked a little older than Klaus and a little younger than Violet and had a dark green notebook tucked into the pocket of his thick wool sweater. "*You're* the cakesniffer, and nobody in their right mind would want to eat with you anyway. Come on," the boy said, turning to the Baudelaires. "There's room at our table."

"Thank you very much," Violet said in relief

and followed the boy to a table that had plenty of room. He sat down next to a girl who looked absolutely identical to the boy. She looked about the same age, and also had very dark hair, very wide eyes, and a notebook tucked into the pocket of *her* thick wool sweater. The only difference seemed to be that the girl's notebook was pitch black. Seeing two people who look so much alike is a little bit eerie, but it was better than looking at Carmelita Spats, so the Baudelaires sat down across from them and introduced themselves.

"I'm Violet Baudelaire," said Violet Baudelaire, "and this is my brother, Klaus, and our baby sister, Sunny."

"It's nice to meet you," said the boy. "My name is Duncan Quagmire, and this is my sister, Isadora. And the girl who was yelling at you, I'm sorry to say, was Carmelita Spats."

"She didn't seem very nice," Klaus said.

"That is the understatement of the century," Isadora said. "Carmelita Spats is rude, filthy, and violent, and the less time you spend with her the happier you will be."

"Read the Baudelaires the poem you wrote about her," Duncan said to his sister.

"You write poetry?" Klaus asked. He had read a lot about poets but had never met one.

"Just a little bit," Isadora said modestly. "I write poems down in this notebook. It's an interest of mine."

"Sappho!" Sunny shrieked, which meant something like "I'd be very pleased to hear a poem of yours!"

Klaus explained to the Quagmires what Sunny meant, and Isadora smiled and opened her notebook. "It's a very short poem," she said. "Only two rhyming lines."

"That's called a couplet," Klaus said. "I learned that from a book of literary criticism."

"Yes, I know," Isadora said, and then read her poem, leaning forward so Carmelita Spats would not overhear:

*"I would rather eat a bowl of vampire bats
than spend an hour with Carmelita Spats."*

The Baudelaires giggled and then covered their mouths so nobody would know they were laughing at Carmelita. "That was great," Klaus said. "I like the part about the bowl of bats."

"Thanks," Isadora said. "I would be interested in reading that book of literary criticism you told me about. Would you let me borrow it?"

Klaus looked down. "I can't," he said. "That book belonged to my father, and it was destroyed in a fire."

The Quagmires looked at one another, and their eyes grew even wider. "I'm very sorry to hear that," Duncan said. "My sister and I have been through a terrible fire, so we know what that's like. Did your father die in the fire?"

"Yes he did," Klaus said, "and my mother too."

Isadora put down her fork, reached across the table, and patted Klaus on the hand. Normally this might have embarrassed Klaus a little bit, but under the circumstances it felt perfectly natural. "I'm so sorry to hear that," she said. "Our parents died in a fire as well. It's awful to miss your parents so much, isn't it?"

"Bloni," Sunny said, nodding.

"For a long time," Duncan admitted, "I was afraid of any kind of fire. I didn't even like to look at stoves."

Violet smiled. "We stayed with a woman for a while, our Aunt Josephine, who was afraid of stoves. She was afraid that they might explode."

"Explode!" Duncan said. "Even I wasn't afraid as all that. Why aren't you staying with your Aunt Josephine now?"

Now it was Violet's turn to look down, and Duncan's turn to reach across the table and take her hand. "She died too," Violet said. "To tell you the truth, Duncan, our lives have been very topsy-turvy for quite some time."

"I'm very sorry to hear it," Duncan said, "and I wish I could tell you that things will get better here. But between Vice Principal Nero playing the violin, Carmelita Spats teasing us, and the dreadful Orphans Shack, Prufrock Prep is a pretty miserable place."

"I think it's awful to call it the Orphans Shack," Klaus said. "It's a bad enough place without giving it an insulting nickname."

"The nickname is more of Carmelita's handiwork, I'm sorry to say," Isadora said. "Duncan and I had to live there for three semesters because we needed a parent or guardian to sign our permission slip, and we didn't have one."

"That's the same thing that happened to us!" Violet cried. "And when we asked Nero to make an exception—"

"He said he was too busy practicing the violin," Isadora said, nodding as she finished Violet's sentence. "He always says that. Anyway, Carmelita called it the Orphans Shack when we were living there, and it looks like she's going to keep on doing it."

"Well," Violet sighed, "Carmelita's nasty names are the least of our problems in the shack. How did you deal with the crabs when you lived there?"

Duncan let go of her hand to take his notebook out of his pocket. "I use my notebook to take notes on things," he explained. "I plan to be a newspaper reporter when I get a little older and I figure it's good to start practicing. Here it is: notes on the crabs. They're afraid of loud noises, you see, so I have a list of things we did to scare them away from us."

"Afraid of loud noises," Violet repeated, and tied her hair up in a ribbon to keep it out of her eyes.

"When she ties her hair up like that," Klaus explained to the Quagmires, "it means she's thinking of an invention. My sister is quite an inventor."

"How about noisy shoes?" Violet said suddenly. "If we took small pieces of metal and glued them to our shoes? Then wherever we walked would make a loud noise, and I bet we'd hardly ever see those crabs."

"Noisy shoes!" Duncan cried. "Isadora and I lived in the Orphans Shack all that time and never thought of noisy shoes!" He took a pencil out of his pocket and wrote "noisy shoes" in the dark green notebook, and then turned a page. "I do have a list of fungus books that are in the school library, if you need help with that tan stuff on the ceiling."

"Zatwal!" Sunny shrieked.

"We'd love to see the library," Violet translated. "It sure is lucky that we ran into you two twins."

Duncan's and Isadora's faces fell, an expression which does not mean that the front part of their heads actually fell to the ground. It simply means that the two siblings suddenly looked very sad.

"What's wrong?" Klaus asked. "Did we say something that upset you?"

"Twins," Duncan said, so softly that the Baudelaires could barely hear him.

"You *are* twins, aren't you?" Violet asked. "You look just alike."

"We're triplets," Isadora said sadly.

"I'm confused," Violet said. "Aren't triplets *three* people born at the same time?"

"We *were* three people born at the same time," Isadora explained, "but our brother, Quigley, died in the fire that killed our parents."

"I'm very sorry to hear that," Klaus said. "Please forgive our calling you twins. We meant no disrespect to Quigley's memory."

"Of course you didn't," Duncan said, giving the Baudelaires a small smile. "There's no way you could have known. Come on, if you're done with your lasagna we'll show you the library."

"And maybe we can find some pieces of metal," Isadora said, "for noisy shoes."

The Baudelaire orphans smiled, and the five of them bussed their trays and walked out of the cafeteria. The library turned out to be a very pleasant place, but it was not the comfortable chairs, the huge wooden bookshelves, or the hush of people reading that made the three siblings feel so good as they walked into the room. It is useless for me to tell you all about the brass lamps in the shapes of different fish, or the bright blue curtains that rippled like water as a breeze came in from the window, because although these were wonderful things they were not what made the three children smile. The Quagmire triplets were smiling, too, and although I have not researched the Quagmires nearly as much as I have the Baudelaires, I can say with reasonable accuracy that they were smiling for the same reason.

It is a relief, in hectic and frightening times, to find true friends, and it was this relief that all five children were feeling as the Quagmires gave the Baudelaires a tour of the Prufrock Library. Friends can make you feel that the world is smaller and less sneaky than it really is, because you know people who have similar experiences, a phrase which here means "having lost family members in terrible fires and lived in the Orphans Shack." As Duncan and Isadora whispered to Violet, Klaus, and Sunny, explaining how the library was organized, the Baudelaire children felt less and less distressed about their new circumstances, and by the time Duncan and Isadora were recommending their favorite books, the three siblings thought that perhaps their troubles were coming to an end at last. They were wrong about this, of course, but for the moment it didn't matter. The Baudelaire orphans had found friends, and as they stood in the library with the Quagmire triplets, the world felt smaller and safer than it had for a long, long time.

If you have walked into a museum recently—
whether you did so to attend an art exhibition
or to escape from the police—you may have
noticed a type of painting known as a triptych.
A triptych has three panels, with something
different painted on each of the panels. For
instance, my friend Professor Reed made a triptych for me, and he painted fire on one panel, a
typewriter on another, and the face of a beautiful, intelligent woman on the third. The triptych is entitled *What Happened to Beatrice* and I
cannot look upon it without weeping.

I am a writer, and not a painter, but if I were to try and paint a triptych entitled *The Baudelaire Orphans' Miserable Experiences at Prufrock Prep*, I would paint Mr. Remora on one panel, Mrs. Bass on another, and a box of staples on the third, and the results would make me so sad that between the Beatrice triptych and the Baudelaire triptych I would scarcely stop weeping all day.

Mr. Remora was Violet's teacher, and he was so terrible that Violet thought that she'd almost rather stay in the Orphans Shack all morning and eat her meals with her hands tied behind her back rather than hurry to Room One and learn from such a wretched man. Mr. Remora had a dark and thick mustache, as if somebody had chopped off a gorilla's thumb and stuck it above Mr. Remora's lip, and also like a gorilla, Mr. Remora was constantly eating bananas. Bananas are a fairly delicious fruit and contain a healthy amount of potassium, but after watching Mr. Remora shove banana after banana into his mouth, dropping banana peels on the floor and smearing banana pulp on his chin and in his mustache, Violet never wanted to see another banana again. In between bites of banana, Mr. Remora would tell stories, and the children would write the stories down in notebooks, and every so often there would be a test. The stories were very short, and there were a whole lot of them on every conceivable subject. "One day I went to the store to purchase a carton of milk," Mr. Remora would say, chewing on a banana. "When I got home, I poured the milk into a glass and drank it. Then I watched television. The end." Or: "One afternoon a man named Edward got into a green truck and drove to a farm. The farm had geese and cows. The end." Mr. Remora would tell story after story, and eat banana after banana, and it would get more and more difficult for Violet to pay attention. To make things better, Duncan sat next to Violet, and they would pass notes to one another on particularly boring days. But to make things worse, Carmelita Spats sat right behind Violet, and every few minutes she would lean forward and poke Violet with a stick she had found on the lawn. "Orphan," she would whisper and poke Violet with the stick, and Violet would lose her concentration and forget to write down some detail of Mr. Remora's latest story.

Across the hall in Room Two was Klaus's teacher Mrs. Bass, whose black hair was so long and messy that she also vaguely resembled a gorilla. Mrs. Bass was a poor teacher, a phrase which here does not mean "a teacher who doesn't have a lot of money" but "a teacher who is obsessed with the metric system." The metric system, you probably know, is the system by which the majority of the world measures things. Just as it is perfectly all right to eat a banana or two, it is perfectly all right to be interested in measuring things. Klaus could remember a time, when he was about eight years old, when he had

measured the width of all the doorways in the
Baudelaire mansion when he was bored one
rainy afternoon. But rain or shine, all Mrs. Bass
wanted to do was measure things and write
down the measurements on the chalkboard.
Each morning, she would walk into Room Two
carrying a bag full of ordinary objects—a frying
pan, a picture frame, the skeleton of a cat—and
place an object on each student's desk. "Measure!" Mrs. Bass would shout, and everybody
would take out their rulers and measure whatever it was that their teacher had put on their
desks. They would call out the measurements
to Mrs. Bass, who would write them on the
board and then have everybody switch objects.
The class would continue on in this way for the
entire morning, and Klaus would feel his eyes
glaze over—the phrase "glaze over" here means
"ache slightly out of boredom." Across the room,
Isadora Quagmire's eyes were glazing over too,
and occasionally the two of them would look
at one another and stick their tongues out as if

to say, *Mrs. Bass is terribly boring, isn't she?*

But Sunny, instead of going into a classroom, had to work in the administrative building, and I must say that her situation was perhaps the worst in the entire triptych. As Vice Principal Nero's secretary, Sunny had numerous duties assigned to her that were simply impossible for a baby to perform. For instance, she was in charge of answering the telephone, but people who called Vice Principal Nero did not always know that "Seltepia!" was Sunny's way of saying "Good morning, this is Vice Principal Nero's office, how may I help you?" By the second day Nero was furious at her for confusing so many of his business associates. In addition, Sunny was in charge of typing, stapling, and mailing all of Vice Principal Nero's letters, which meant she had to work a typewriter, a stapler, and stamps, all of which were designed for adult use. Unlike many babies, Sunny had some experience in hard work—after all, she and her siblings had worked for some time at the Lucky Smells Lumbermill—but this equipment was simply inappropriate for such tiny fingers. Sunny could scarcely move the typewriter's keys, and even when she could she did not know how to spell most of the words Nero dictated. She had never used a stapler before, so she sometimes stapled her fingers by mistake, which hurt quite a bit. And occasionally one of the stamps would stick to her tongue and wouldn't come off.

In most schools, no matter how miserable, the students have a chance to recuperate during the weekend, when they can rest and play instead of attending wretched classes, and the Baudelaire orphans looked forward to taking a break from looking at bananas, rulers, and secretarial supplies. So they were quite distressed one Friday when the Quagmires informed them that Prufrock Prep did not have weekends. Saturday and Sunday were regular schooldays, supposedly in keeping with the school's motto. This rule did not really make any sense—it is, after all, just as easy to remember you will die when you are relaxing as when you are in school—but that was the way things were, so the Baudelaires could never remember exactly what day it was, so repetitive was their schedule. So I am sorry to say that I cannot tell you what day it was when Sunny noticed that the staple supply was running low, but I can tell you that Nero informed her that because she had wasted so much time learning to be a secretary he would not buy any more when they ran out. Instead Sunny would have to make staples herself, out of some skinny metal rods Nero kept in a drawer.

"That's ridiculous!" Violet cried when Sunny told her of Nero's latest demand. It was after dinner, and the Baudelaire orphans were in the Orphans Shack with the Quagmire triplets, sprinkling salt at the ceiling. Violet had found some pieces of metal behind the cafeteria and had fashioned five pairs of noisy shoes: three for the Baudelaires and two for the Quagmires so the crabs wouldn't bother them when they visited

the Orphans Shack. The problem of the tan
fungus, however, was yet to be solved. With
Duncan's help, Klaus had found a book on
fungus in the library and had read that salt might
make this particular fungus shrivel up. The
Quagmires had distracted some of the masked
cafeteria workers by dropping their trays on the
ground, and while Nero yelled at them for
making a mess, the Baudelaires had slipped three
saltshakers into their pockets. Now, in the brief
recess after dinner, the five children were sitting
on bales of hay, trying to toss salt onto the fungus
and talking about their day.

"It certainly is ridiculous," Klaus agreed.
"It's silly enough that Sunny has to be a secretary, but making her own staples? I've never
heard of anything so unfair."

"I think staples are made in factories,"
Duncan said, pausing to flip through his green
notebook to see if he had any notes on the
matter. "I don't think people have made staples
by hand since the fifteenth century."

"If you could snitch some of the skinny metal rods, Sunny," Isadora said, "we could all help make the staples after dinnertime. If five of us worked together, it would be much less trouble. And speaking of trouble, I'm working on a poem about Count Olaf, but I'm not sure I know words that are terrible enough to describe him."

"And I imagine it's difficult to find words that rhyme with 'Olaf,'" Violet said.

"It is difficult," Isadora admitted. "All I can think of so far is 'pilaf,' which is a kind of rice dish. And that's more a half-rhyme, anyway."

"Maybe someday you'll be able to publish your poem about Count Olaf," Klaus said, "and everyone will know how horrible he is."

"And I'll write a newspaper article all about him," Duncan volunteered.

"I think I could build a printing press myself," Violet said. "Maybe when I come of age, I can use some of the Baudelaire fortune to buy the materials I would need."

"Could we print books, too?" Klaus asked.

Violet smiled. She knew her brother was thinking of a whole library they could print for themselves. "Books, too," she said.

"The Baudelaire fortune?" Duncan asked. "Did your parents leave behind a fortune, too? Our parents owned the famous Quagmire sapphires, which were unharmed in the fire. When we come of age, those precious jewels will belong to us. We could start our printing business together."

"That's a wonderful idea!" Violet cried. "We could call it Quagmire-Baudelaire Incorporated."

"*We could call it Quagmire-Baudelaire Incorporated!*" The children were so surprised to hear the sneering voice of Vice Principal Nero that they dropped their saltshakers on the ground. Instantly, the tiny crabs in the Orphans Shack picked them up and scurried away with them before Nero could notice. "I'm sorry to interrupt you in the middle of your important

business meeting," he said, although the youngsters could see that the vice principal wasn't
sorry one bit. "The new gym teacher has arrived, and he was interested in meeting our
orphan population before my concert began.
Apparently orphans have excellent bone structure or something. Isn't that what you said,
Coach Genghis?"

"Oh yes," said a tall, skinny man, who
stepped forward to reveal himself to the children. The man was wearing sweatpants and a
sweatshirt, such as any gym teacher might wear.
On his feet were some expensive-looking running shoes with very high tops, and around his
neck was a shiny silver whistle. Wrapped around
the top of his head was a length of cloth secured
in place with a shiny red jewel. Such things are
called turbans and are worn by some people for
religious reasons, but Violet, Klaus, and Sunny
took one look at this man and knew that he was
wearing a turban for an entirely different reason.

"Oh yes," the man said again. "All orphans

have perfect legs for running, and I couldn't wait to see what specimens were waiting for me here in the shack."

"Children," Nero said, "get up off of your hay and say hello to Coach Genghis."

"Hello, Coach Genghis," Duncan said.

"Hello, Coach Genghis," Isadora said.

The Quagmire triplets each shook Coach Genghis's bony hand and then turned and gave the Baudelaires a confused look. They were clearly surprised to see the three siblings still sitting on the hay and staring up at Coach Genghis rather than obeying Nero's orders. But had I been there in the Orphans Shack, I most certainly would not have been surprised, and I would bet *What Happened to Beatrice*, my prized triptych, that had you been there you would not have been surprised, either. Because you have probably guessed, as the Baudelaires guessed, why the man who was calling himself Coach Genghis was wearing a turban. A turban covers people's hair, which can alter their appearance quite a bit, and if the turban is arranged so that it hangs down rather low, as this one did, the folds of cloth can even cover the eyebrows—or in this case, eye*brow*—of the person wearing it. But it cannot cover someone's shiny, shiny eyes, or the greedy and sinister look that somebody might have in their eyes when the person looks down at three relatively helpless children.

What the man who called himself Coach Genghis had said about all orphans having perfect legs for running was utter nonsense, of course, but as the Baudelaires looked up at their new gym teacher, they wished that it weren't nonsense. As the man who called himself Coach Genghis looked back at them with his shiny, shiny eyes, the Baudelaire orphans wished more than anything that their legs could carry them far, far away from the man who was really Count Olaf.

CHAPTER Five

The expression "following suit" is a curious one, because it has nothing to do with walking behind a matching set of clothing. If you follow suit, it means you do the same thing somebody else has just done. If all of your friends decided to jump off a bridge into the icy waters of an ocean or river, for instance, and you jumped in right after them, you would be following suit. You can see why following suit can be a dangerous thing to do, because you could end up drowning simply because somebody else thought of it first.

This is why, when Violet stood up from the hay and said, "How do you do, Coach Genghis?" Klaus and Sunny were reluctant to follow suit. It was inconceivable to the younger Baudelaires that their sister had not recognized Count Olaf, and that she hadn't leaped to her feet and informed Vice Principal Nero what was going on. For a moment, Klaus and Sunny even considered that Violet had been hypnotized, as Klaus had been back when the Baudelaire orphans were living in Paltryville. But Violet's eyes did not look any wider than they did normally, nor did she say "How do you do, Coach Genghis?" in the dazed tone of voice Klaus had used when he had been under hypnosis.

But although they were puzzled, the younger Baudelaires trusted their sister absolutely. She had managed to avoid marrying Count Olaf when it had seemed like it would be inevitable, a word which here means "a lifetime of horror and woe." She had made a lockpick when they'd needed one in a hurry, and had used her inventing skills to help them escape from some very hungry leeches. So even though they could not think what the reason was, Klaus and Sunny knew that Violet must have had a good reason to greet Count Olaf politely rather than reveal him instantly, and so, after a pause, they followed suit.

"How do you do, Coach Genghis?" Klaus said.

"Gefidio!" Sunny shrieked.

"It's a pleasure to meet you," Coach Genghis said, and smirked. The Baudelaires could tell he thought he had fooled them completely and was very pleased with himself.

"What do you think, Coach Genghis?" Vice Principal Nero asked. "Do any of these orphans have the legs you're looking for?"

Coach Genghis scratched his turban and looked down at the children as if they were an all-you-can-eat salad bar instead of five orphans. "Oh yes," he said in the wheezy voice the

Baudelaires still heard in their nightmares. With his bony hands, he pointed first at Violet, then at Klaus, and lastly at Sunny. "These three children here are just what I'm looking for, all right. I have no use for these twins, however."

"Neither do I," Nero said, not bothering to point out that the Quagmires were triplets. He then looked at his watch. "Well, it's time for my concert. Follow me to the auditorium, all of you, unless you are in the mood to buy me a bag of candy."

The Baudelaire orphans hoped never to buy their vice principal a gift of any sort, let alone a bag of candy, which the children loved and hadn't eaten in a very long time, so they followed Nero out of the Orphans Shack and across the lawn to the auditorium. The Quagmires followed suit, staring up at the gravestone buildings, which looked even spookier in the moonlight.

"This evening," Nero said, "I will be playing a violin sonata I wrote myself. It only lasts about a half hour, but I will play it twelve times in a row."

"Oh, good," Coach Genghis said. "If I may say so, Vice Principal Nero, I am an enormous fan of your music. Your concerts were one of the main reasons I wanted to work here at Prufrock Prep."

"Well, it's good to hear that," Nero said. "It's difficult to find people who appreciate me as the genius I am."

"I know the feeling," Coach Genghis said. "I'm the finest gym teacher the world has ever seen, and yet there hasn't even been one parade in my honor."

"Shocking," Nero said, shaking his head.

The Baudelaires and the Quagmires, who were walking behind the adults, looked at one another in disgust at the braggy conversation they were overhearing, but they didn't dare speak to one another until they arrived at the auditorium, taking seats as far away as possible from Carmelita Spats and her loathsome friends.

There is one, and only one, advantage to

somebody who cannot play the violin insisting on doing so anyway, and the advantage is that they often play so loudly that they cannot hear if the audience is having a conversation. It is extremely rude, of course, for an audience to talk during a concert performance, but when the performance is a wretched one, and lasts six hours, such rudeness can be forgiven. So it was that evening, for after introducing himself with a brief, braggy speech, Vice Principal Nero stood on the stage of the auditorium and began playing his sonata for the first time.

When you listen to a piece of classical music, it is often amusing to try and guess what inspired the composer to write those particular notes. Sometimes a composer will be inspired by nature and will write a symphony imitating the sounds of birds and trees. Other times a composer will be inspired by the city and will write a concerto imitating the sounds of traffic and sidewalks. In the case of this sonata, Nero had apparently been inspired by somebody beating up a cat, because the music was loud and screechy and made it quite easy to talk during the performance. As Nero sawed away at his violin, the students of Prufrock Prep began to talk amongst themselves. The Baudelaires even noticed Mr. Remora and Mrs. Bass, who were supposed to be figuring out which students owed Nero bags of candy, giggling and sharing a banana in the back row. Only Coach Genghis, who was sitting in the center of the very front row, seemed to be paying any attention to the music.

"Our new gym teacher looks creepy," Isadora said.

"That's for sure," Duncan agreed. "It's that sneaky look in his eye."

"That sneaky look," Violet said, taking a sneaky look herself to make sure Coach Genghis wasn't listening in, "is because he's not really Coach Genghis. He's not really any coach. He's Count Olaf in disguise."

"I *knew* you recognized him!" Klaus said.

"Count Olaf?" Duncan said. "How awful! How did he follow you here?"

"Stewak," Sunny said glumly.

"My sister means something like 'He follows us everywhere,'" Violet explained, "and she's right. But it doesn't matter how he found us. The point is that he's here and that he undoubtedly has a scheme to snatch our fortune."

"But why did you pretend not to recognize him?" Klaus asked.

"Yes," Isadora said. "If you told Vice Principal Nero that he was really Count Olaf, then Nero could throw the cakesniffer out of here, if you'll pardon my language."

Violet shook her head to indicate that she disagreed with Isadora and that she didn't mind about "cakesniffer." "Olaf's too clever for that," she said. "I knew that if I tried to tell Nero that he wasn't really a gym teacher, he would manage to wiggle out of it, just as he did with Aunt Josephine and Uncle Monty and everybody else."

"That's good thinking," Klaus admitted.

"Plus, if Olaf thinks that he's fooled us, it might give us some more time to figure out exactly what he's up to."

"Lirt!" Sunny pointed out.

"My sister means that we can see if any of his assistants are around," Violet translated. "That's a good point, Sunny. I hadn't thought of that."

"Count Olaf has assistants?" Isadora asked. "That's not fair. He's bad enough without people helping him."

"His assistants are as bad as he is," Klaus said. "There are two powder-faced women who forced us to be in his play. There's a hook-handed man who helped Olaf murder our Uncle Monty."

"And the bald man who bossed us around at the lumbermill, don't forget him," Violet added.

"Aeginu!" Sunny said, which meant something like "And the assistant that looks like neither a man nor a woman."

"What does 'aeginu' mean?" Duncan asked, taking out his notebook. "I'm going to write down all these details about Olaf and his troupe."

"Why?" Violet asked.

"Why?" Isadora repeated. "Because we're going to help you, that's why! You don't think we'd just sit here while you tried to escape from Olaf's clutches, would you?"

"But Count Olaf is very dangerous," Klaus said. "If you try and help us, you'll be risking your lives."

"Never mind about that," Duncan said, although I am sorry to tell you that the Quagmire triplets should have minded about that. They should have minded very much. Duncan and Isadora were very brave and caring to try and help the Baudelaire orphans, but bravery often demands a price. By "price" I do not mean something along the lines of five dollars. I mean a much, much bigger price, a price so dreadful that I cannot speak of it now but must return to the scene I am writing at this moment.

"Never mind about that," Duncan said. "What we need is a plan. Now, we need to prove to Nero that Coach Genghis is really Count Olaf. How can we do that?"

"Nero has that computer," Violet said thoughtfully. "He showed us a little picture of Olaf on the screen, remember?"

"Yes," Klaus said, shaking his head. "He told us that the advanced computer system would keep Olaf away. So much for computers."

Sunny nodded her head in agreement, and Violet picked her up and put her on her lap. Nero had reached a particularly shrieky section of his sonata, and the children had to lean forward to one another in order to continue their conversation. "If we go and see Nero first thing tomorrow morning," Violet said, "we can talk to him alone, without Olaf butting in. We'll ask him to use the computer. Nero might not believe us, but the computer should be able to convince him to at least investigate Coach Genghis."

"Maybe Nero will make him take off the turban," Isadora said, "revealing Olaf's only eyebrow."

"Or take off those expensive-looking running shoes," Klaus said, "revealing Olaf's tattoo."

"But if you talk to Nero," Duncan said, "then Coach Genghis will know that you're suspicious."

"That's why we'll have to be extra careful," Violet said. "We want Nero to find out about Olaf, without Olaf finding out about us."

"And in the meantime," Duncan said, "Isadora and I will do some investigating ourselves. Perhaps we can spot one of these assistants you've described."

"That would be very useful," Violet said, "if you're sure about wanting to help us."

"Say no more about it," Duncan said and patted Violet's hand. And they said no more about it. They didn't say another word about Count Olaf for the rest of Nero's sonata, or while he performed it the second time, or the third time, or the fourth time, or the fifth time, or even the sixth time, by which time it was very, very late at night. The Baudelaire orphans and the Quagmire triplets merely sat in a companionable comfort, a phrase which here means many things, all of them happy even though it is quite difficult to be happy while hearing a terrible sonata performed over and over by a man who cannot play the violin, while attending an atrocious boarding school with an evil man sitting nearby undoubtedly planning something dreadful. But happy moments came rarely and unexpectedly in the Baudelaires' lives, and the three siblings had learned to accept them. Duncan kept his hand on Violet's and talked to her about terrible concerts he had attended back when the Quagmire parents were alive, and she was happy to hear his stories. Isadora began working on a poem about libraries and showed Klaus what she had written in her notebook, and Klaus was happy to offer suggestions. And Sunny snuggled down in Violet's lap and chewed on the armrest of her seat, happy to bite something that was so sturdy.

I'm sure you would know, even if I didn't tell you, that things were about to get much worse for the Baudelaires, but I will end this chapter with this moment of companionable comfort rather than skip ahead to the unpleasant events of the next morning, or the terrible trials of the days that followed, or the horrific crime that marked the end of the Baudelaires' time at Prufrock Prep. These things happened, of course, and there is no use pretending they didn't. But for now let us ignore the terrible sonata, the dreadul teachers, the nasty, teasing students, and the even more wretched things that will be happening soon enough. Let us enjoy this brief moment of comfort, as the Baudelaires enjoyed it in the company of the Quagmire triplets and, in Sunny's case, an armrest. Let us enjoy, at the end of this chapter, the last happy moment any of these children would have for a long, long time.

CHAPTER
Six

Prufrock Preparatory School is now closed. It has been closed for many years, ever since Mrs. Bass was arrested for bank robbery, and if you were to visit it now, you would find it an empty and silent place. If you walked on the lawn, you would not see any children running around, as there were the day the Baudelaires arrived. If you walked by the building containing the classrooms, you would not hear the droning voice of Mr. Remora telling a story, and if you walked by the building containing the auditorium, you would not hear the scrapings and shriekings of Vice Principal Nero playing the violin. If you went and stood beneath the arch, looking up at the black letters spelling out the name of the school and its austere—a word which here means "stern and severe"—motto, you would hear nothing but the *swish* of the breeze through the brown and patchy grass.

In short, if you went and visited Prufrock Preparatory School today, the academy would look more or less as it did when the Baudelaires woke up early the next morning and walked to the administrative building to talk to Nero about Coach Genghis. The three children were so anxious to talk to him that they got up especially early, and as they walked across the lawn it felt as if everyone else at Prufrock Prep had slipped away in the middle of the night, leaving the orphans alone amongst the tombstone-shaped buildings. It was an eerie feeling, which is why Violet and Sunny were surprised when

Klaus broke the silence by laughing suddenly.

"What are you snickering at?" Violet asked.

"I just realized something," Klaus said. "We're going to the administrative building without an appointment. We'll have to eat our meals without silverware."

"There's nothing funny about that!" Violet said. "What if they serve oatmeal for breakfast? We'll have to scoop it up with our hands."

"Oot," Sunny said, which meant "Trust me, it's not that difficult," and at that the Baudelaire sisters joined their brother in laughter. It was not funny, of course, that Nero enforced such terrible punishments, but the idea of eating oatmeal with their hands gave all three siblings the giggles.

"Or fried eggs!" Violet said. "What if they serve runny fried eggs?"

"Or pancakes, covered in syrup!" Klaus said.

"Soup!" Sunny shrieked, and they all broke out in laughter again.

"Remember the picnic?" Violet said. "We were going to Rutabaga River for a picnic, and

Father was so excited about the meal he made that he forgot to pack silverware!"

"Of course I remember," Klaus said. "We had to eat all that sweet-and-sour shrimp with our hands."

"Sticky!" Sunny said, holding her hands up.

"It sure was," Violet agreed. "Afterward, we went to wash our hands in the river, and we found a perfect place to try the fishing rod I made."

"And I picked blackberries with Mother," Klaus said.

"Eroos," Sunny said, which meant something like "And I bit rocks."

The children stopped laughing now as they remembered that afternoon, which hadn't been so very long ago but felt like it had happened in the distant, distant past. After the fire, the children had known their parents were dead, of course, but it had felt like they had merely gone away somewhere and would be back before long. Now, remembering the way the sunlight had shone on the water of Rutabaga River and the laughter of their parents as they'd made a mess of themselves eating the sweet-and-sour shrimp, the picnic seemed so far away that they knew their parents were never coming back.

"Maybe we'll go back there," Violet said quietly. "Maybe someday we can visit the river again, and catch fish and pick blackberries."

"Maybe we can," Klaus said, but the Baudelaires all knew that even if someday they went back to Rutabaga River—which they never did, by the way—that it would not be the same. "Maybe we can, but in the meantime we've got to talk to Nero. Come on, here's the administrative building."

The Baudelaires sighed and walked into the building, surrendering the use of Prufrock Prep's silverware. They climbed the stairs to the ninth floor and knocked on Nero's door, surprised that they could not hear him practicing the violin. "Come in if you must," Nero said, and the orphans walked in. Nero had his back to the door, looking at his reflection in the window as he tied a rubber band around one of his pigtails. When he was finished, he held both hands up in the air. "Ladies and gentlemen, Vice Principal Nero!" he announced, and the children began applauding obediently. Nero whirled around.

"I only expected to hear one person clapping," he said sternly. "Violet and Klaus, you're not allowed up here. You know that."

"I beg your pardon, sir," Violet said, "but all three of us have something very important we need to discuss with you."

"All three of us have something very important we need to discuss with you," Nero replied in his usual nasty way. "It must be important for you to sacrifice your silverware privileges. Well, well, out with it. I have a lot of rehearsing to do for my next concert, so don't waste my time."

"This won't take long," Klaus promised. He paused before continuing, which is a good thing to do if you're choosing your words very, very carefully. "We are concerned," he continued, choosing his words very, very carefully, "that Count Olaf may have somehow managed to get to Prufrock Prep."

"Nonsense," Nero said. "Now go away and let me practice the violin."

"But it might not be nonsense," Violet said. "Olaf is a master of disguise. He could be right under our very noses and we wouldn't know it."

"The only thing under *my* nose," Nero said, "is my mouth, which is telling you to leave."

"Count Olaf could be Mr. Remora," Klaus said. "Or Mrs. Bass."

"Mr. Remora and Mrs. Bass have taught at this school for more than forty-seven years," Nero said dismissively. "I would know if one of them were in disguise."

"What about the people who work at the cafeteria?" Violet asked. "They're always wearing those metal masks."

"Those are for safety, not for disguises," Nero said. "You brats have some very silly ideas. Next you'll be saying that Count Olaf has disguised himself as your boyfriend, what's-his-name, the triplet."

Violet blushed. "Duncan Quagmire is not my boyfriend," she said, "and he's not Count Olaf, either."

But Nero was too busy making idiotic jokes to listen. "Who knows?" he asked, and then laughed again. "Hee hee hee. Maybe he's disguised himself as Carmelita Spats."

"Or me!" came a voice from the doorway. The Baudelaires whirled around and saw Coach Genghis standing there with a red rose in his hand and a fierce look in his eye.

"Or you!" Nero said. "Hee hee hee. Imagine this Olaf fellow pretending to be the finest gym teacher in the country."

Klaus looked at Coach Genghis and thought of all the trouble he had caused, whether he was pretending to be Uncle Monty's assistant Stefano, or Captain Sham, or Shirley, or any of the other phony names he had used. Klaus wanted desperately to say "You *are* Count Olaf!" but he knew that if the Baudelaires pretended that Coach Genghis was fooling them, they had a better chance of revealing his plan, whatever it was. So he bit his tongue, a phrase which here means that he simply kept quiet. He did not actually bite his tongue, but opened his mouth and laughed. "That would be funny!" he lied. "Imagine if you were really Count Olaf! Wouldn't that be funny, Coach Genghis? That would mean that your turban would really be a disguise!"

"My turban?" Coach Genghis said. His fierce look melted away as he realized—incorrectly, of course—that Klaus was joking. "A disguise? Ho ho ho!"

"Hee hee hee!" Nero laughed.

Violet and Sunny both saw at once what Klaus was doing, and they followed suit. "Oh yes, Genghis," Violet cried, as if she were joking, "take your turban off and show us the one eyebrow you are hiding! Ha ha ha!"

"You three children are really quite funny!" Nero cried. "You're like three professional comedians!"

"Volasocks!" Sunny shrieked, showing all four teeth in a fake smile.

"Oh yes," Klaus said. "Sunny is right! If you were really Olaf in disguise, then your running shoes would be covering your tattoo!"

"Hee hee hee!" Nero said. "You children are like three clowns!"

"Ho ho ho!" Count Olaf said.

"Ha ha ha!" Violet said, who was beginning to feel queasy from faking all this laughter. Looking up at Genghis, and smiling so hard that her teeth ached, she stood on tiptoe and tried to reach his turban. "I'm going to rip this off," she said, as if she were still joking, "and show off your one eyebrow!"

"Hee hee hee!" Nero said, shaking his pigtails in laughter. "You're like three trained monkeys!"

Klaus crouched down to the ground and

grabbed one of Genghis's feet. "And I'm going to rip your shoes off," he said, as if *he* were still joking, "and show off your tattoo!"

"Hee hee hee!" Nero said. "You're like three—"

The Baudelaires didn't get to hear what they were three of, because Coach Genghis stuck out both of his arms, catching Klaus with one hand and Violet with the other. "Ho ho ho!" he said, and then abruptly stopped laughing. "Of course," he said in a tone of voice that was suddenly serious, "I can't take off my running shoes, because I've been exercising and my feet smell, and I can't take off my turban for religious reasons."

"Hee hee—" Nero stopped giggling and became very serious himself. "Oh, Coach Genghis," he said, "we wouldn't ask you to violate your religious beliefs, and I certainly don't want your feet stinking up my office."

Violet struggled to reach the turban and Klaus struggled to remove one of the evil coach's shoes, but Genghis held them both tight.

"Drat!" Sunny shrieked.

"Joke time is over!" Nero announced. "Thank you for brightening up my morning, children. Good-bye, and enjoy your breakfast without silverware! Now, Coach Genghis, what can I do for you?"

"Well, Nero," Genghis said, "I just wanted to give you this rose—a small gift of congratulations for the wonderful concert you gave us last night!"

"Oh, thank you," Nero said, taking the rose out of Genghis's hand and giving it a good smell. "I *was* wonderful, wasn't I?"

"You were *perfection*!" Genghis said. "The first time you played your sonata, I was deeply moved. The second time, I had tears in my eyes. The third time, I was sobbing. The fourth time, I had an uncontrollable emotional attack. The fifth time—"

The Baudelaires did not hear about the fifth time because Nero's door swung shut behind them. They looked at one another in dismay. The Baudelaires had come very close to revealing Coach Genghis's disguise, but close was not enough. They trudged silently out of the administrative building and over to the cafeteria. Evidently, Nero had already called the metal-masked cafeteria workers, because when Violet and Klaus reached the end of the line, the workers refused to hand them any silverware. Prufrock Prep was not serving oatmeal for breakfast, but Violet and Klaus knew that eating scrambled eggs with their hands was not going to be very pleasant.

"Oh, don't worry about that," Isadora said when the children slid glumly into seats beside the Quagmires. "Here, Klaus and I will take turns with my silverware, and you can share with Duncan, Violet. Tell us how everything went in Nero's office."

"Not very well," Violet admitted. "Coach Genghis got there right after we did, and we didn't want him to see that we knew who he really was."

Isadora pulled her notebook out of her pocket and read out loud to her friends.

*"It would be a stroke of luck
 if Coach Genghis were hit by a truck,"*

she read. "That's my latest poem. I know it's not that helpful, but I thought you might like to hear it anyway."

"I did like hearing it," Klaus said. "And it certainly *would* be a stroke of luck if that happened. But I wouldn't bet on it."

"Well, we'll think of another plan," Duncan said, handing Violet his fork.

"I hope so," Violet said. "Count Olaf doesn't usually wait very long to put his evil schemes into action."

"Kosbal!" Sunny shrieked.

"Does Sunny mean 'I have a plan'?" Isadora asked. "I'm trying to get the hang of her way of talking."

"I think she means something more like

'Here comes Carmelita Spats,'" Klaus said, pointing across the cafeteria. Sure enough, Carmelita Spats was walking toward their table with a big, smug smile on her face.

"Hello, you cakesniffers," she said. "I have a message for you from Coach Genghis. I get to be his Special Messenger because I'm the cutest, prettiest, nicest girl in the whole school."

"Oh, stop bragging, Carmelita," Duncan said.

"You're just jealous," Carmelita replied, "because Coach Genghis likes me best instead of you."

"I couldn't care less about Coach Genghis," Duncan said. "Just deliver your message and leave us alone."

"The message is this," Carmelita said. "The three Baudelaire orphans are to report to the front lawn tonight, immediately after dinner."

"After dinner?" Violet said. "But after dinner we're supposed to go to Nero's violin recital."

"That's the message," Carmelita insisted.

"He said that if you don't show up you'll be in big trouble, so if I were you, Violet—"

"You *aren't* Violet, thank goodness," Duncan interrupted. It is not very polite to interrupt a person, of course, but sometimes if the person is very unpleasant you can hardly stop yourself. "Thank you for your message. Good-bye."

"It is traditional," Carmelita said, "to give a Special Messenger a tip after she has delivered a message."

"If you don't leave us alone," Isadora said, "you're going to get a headful of scrambled eggs as a tip."

"You're just a jealous cakesniffer," Carmelita sneered, but she left the Baudelaires and Quagmires alone.

"Don't worry," Duncan said when he was sure Carmelita couldn't hear him. "It's still morning. We have all day to figure out what to do. Here, have another spoonful of eggs, Violet."

"No, thank you," Violet said. "I don't have

much of an appetite." And it was true. None of the Baudelaires had an appetite. Scrambled eggs had never been the siblings' favorite dish, particularly Sunny, who much preferred food she could really sink her teeth into, but their lack of appetite had nothing to do with the eggs. It had to do with Coach Genghis, of course, and the message that he had sent to them. It had to do with the thought of meeting him on the lawn, after dinner, all alone. Duncan was right that it was still morning, and that they had all day to figure out what to do. But it did not feel like morning. Violet, Klaus, and Sunny sat in the cafeteria, not taking another bite of their break- fast, and it felt like the sun had already set. It felt like night had already fallen, and that Coach Genghis was already waiting for them. It was only morning, and the Baudelaire orphans al- ready felt like they were in his clutches.

CHAPTER

Seven

The Baudelaire orphans' schoolday was particularly austere, a word which here means that Mr. Remora's stories were particularly boring, Mrs. Bass's obsession with the metric system was particularly irritating, and Nero's administrative demands were particularly difficult, but Violet, Klaus, and Sunny did not really notice. Violet sat at her schooldesk, and anybody who did not know Violet would have thought that she was paying close attention, because her hair was tied up in a ribbon to keep it out of her eyes. But Violet's thoughts were far, far away from the dull tales Mr. Remora was telling. She had tied her hair up, of course, to help focus her keen inventing brain on the problem that was facing the Baudelaires, and she didn't want to waste an ounce of her attention on the rambling, banana-eating man in the front of the room.

Mrs. Bass had brought in a box of pencils for her class and was having them figure out if one of them was any longer or shorter than the rest. And if Mrs. Bass weren't so busy pacing around the room shouting "Measure!" she might have looked at Klaus and thought that perhaps he shared her obsession with measurement, because his eyes were sharply focused as if he were concentrating. But Klaus was spending the morning on autopilot, a word which here means "measuring pencils without really thinking about them." As he placed pencil after pencil next to his ruler, he was thinking of books he had read that might be helpful for their situation.

And if Vice Principal Nero had stopped practicing his violin and looked in on his infant secretary, he would have guessed that Sunny was working very hard, mailing letters he had dictated to various candy companies complaining about their candy quality. But even though Sunny was typing, stapling, and stamping as quickly as she could, her mind was not on secretarial supplies but on the appointment she and her siblings had with Coach Genghis that evening, and what they could do about it.

The Quagmires were curiously absent from lunch, so the Baudelaires were really forced to eat with their hands this time, but as they picked up handfuls of spaghetti and tried to eat them as neatly as possible the three children were thinking so hard that they barely spoke. They knew, almost without discussing the matter, that none of them had been able to guess Coach Genghis's plan, and that they hadn't figured out a way to avoid their appointment with him on the lawn, an appointment that drew closer and closer with every handful of lunch. The Baudelaires passed the afternoon in more or less the same way, ignoring Mr. Remora's stories, Mrs. Bass's pencils, and the diminishing supply of staples, and even during gym period—one of Carmelita's bratty friends informed them that Genghis would start teaching the next day, but in the meantime they were to run around as usual—the three children raced around the lawn in utter silence, devoting all of their brainpower to thinking about their situation.

The Baudelaires had been so very quiet, and thinking so very hard, that when the Quagmires sat down across from them at dinnertime and said in unison, "We've solved your problem," it was more of a startle than a relief.

"Goodness," Violet said. "You startled me."

"I thought you'd be relieved," Duncan said. "Didn't you hear us? We said we've solved your problem."

"We're startled *and* relieved," Klaus said. "What do you mean, you've solved our problem? My sisters and I have been thinking about it all day, and we've gotten nowhere. We don't know what Coach Genghis is up to, although we're sure he's up to something. And we don't know how we can avoid meeting him after dinner, although we're sure that he'll do something terrible if we do."

"At first I thought he might simply be planning to kidnap us," Violet said, "but he wouldn't have to be in disguise to do that."

"And at first I thought we should call Mr. Poe after all," Klaus said, "and tell him what's going on. But if Count Olaf can fool an advanced computer, he'll surely be able to fool an average banker."

"Toricia!" Sunny said in agreement.

"Duncan and I have been thinking about it all day, too," Isadora said. "I filled up five and a half pages of my notebook writing down possible ideas, and Duncan filled up three."

"I write smaller," Duncan explained, handing his fork to Violet so she could take her turn at the meat loaf they were having for dinner.

"Right before lunch, we compared notes," Isadora continued, "and the two of us had the same idea. So we sneaked away and put our plan into action."

"That's why we weren't at lunch," Duncan explained. "You'll notice that there are puddles of beverages on our tray instead of glasses."

"Well, you can share *our* glasses," Klaus said, handing his to Isadora, "just like you're letting us share your silverware. But what is your plan? What did you put into action?"

Duncan and Isadora looked at one another, smiled, and leaned in close to the Baudelaires so they could be sure no one would overhear.

"We propped open the back door of the auditorium," Duncan said. He and Isadora smiled triumphantly and leaned back in their chairs. The Baudelaires did not feel triumphant. They felt confused. They did not want to insult their friends, who had broken the rules and sacrificed their drinking glasses just to help them, but they were unable to see how propping open the back door of the auditorium was a solution to the trouble in which they found themselves.

"I'm sorry," Violet said after a pause. "I don't understand how propping open the back door of the auditorium solves our problem."

"Don't you see?" Isadora asked. "We're going to sit in the back of the auditorium tonight, and as soon as Nero begins his concert, we will tiptoe out and sneak over to the front lawn. That way we can keep an eye on you and Coach Genghis. If anything fishy happens, we will run back to the concert and alert Vice Principal Nero."

"It's the perfect plan, don't you think?" Duncan asked. "I'm rather proud of my sister and me, if I do say so myself."

The Baudelaire children looked at one another doubtfully. They didn't want to disappoint their friends or criticize the plan that the Quagmire triplets had cooked up, particularly since the Baudelaires hadn't cooked up any plan themselves. But Count Olaf was so evil and so clever that the three siblings couldn't help but think that propping a door open and sneaking out to spy on him was not much of a defense against his treachery.

"We appreciate you trying to solve our problem," Klaus said gently, "but Count Olaf is an extremely treacherous person. He always has something up his sleeve. I wouldn't want you to get into any danger on our behalf."

"Don't talk nonsense," Isadora said firmly, taking a sip from Violet's glass. "You're the ones in danger, and it's up to us to help you. And we're not frightened of Olaf. I'm confident this plan is a good one."

The Baudelaires looked at one another again. It was very brave of the Quagmire triplets not to be frightened of Olaf and to be so confident about their plan. But the three siblings could not help but wonder if the Quagmires should be so brave. Olaf was such a wretched man that it seemed wise to be frightened of him, and he had defeated so many of the Baudelaires' plans that it seemed a little foolish to be so confident about this one. But the children were so appreciative of their friends' efforts that they said nothing more about the matter. In the years to come, the Baudelaire orphans would regret this, this time when they said nothing more about the matter, but in the meantime they merely finished their dinner with the Quagmires, passing silverware and drinking glasses back and forth and trying to talk about other things. They discussed other projects they might do to improve the Orphans Shack, and what other matters they might research in the library, and what they could do about Sunny's problem with the staples, which were running out quite rapidly, and before they knew it dinner was over. The Quagmires hurried off to the violin recital, promising to sneak out as quickly as they could, and the Baudelaires walked out of the cafeteria and over to the front lawn.

The last few rays of the sunset made the children cast long, long shadows as they walked, as if the Baudelaires had been stretched across the brown grass by some horrible mechanical device. The children looked down at their shadows, which looked as flimsy as sheets of paper, and wished with every step that they could do something else—*anything* else—other than meet Coach Genghis alone on the front lawn. They wished they could just keep walking, under the arch, past the front lawn, and out into the world, but where could they go? The three orphans were all alone in the world. Their parents were dead. Their banker was too busy to take good care of them. And their only friends were two more orphans, who the Baudelaires sincerely hoped had snuck out of the recital by now and were spying on them as they approached the solitary figure of Coach Genghis, waiting for them impatiently on the edge of the lawn. The waning light of the sunset—the word "waning" here means "dim, and making everything look extra-creepy"—made the shadow of the coach's turban look like a huge, deep hole.

"You're late," Genghis said in his scratchy voice. As the siblings reached him, they could see that he had both hands behind his back as if he were hiding something. "Your instructions were to be here right after dinner, and you're late."

"We're very sorry," Violet said, craning her neck to try and catch a glimpse of what was behind his back. "It took us a little longer to eat our dinner without silverware."

"If you were smart," Genghis said, "you would have borrowed the silverware of one of your friends."

"We never thought of that," Klaus said. When one is forced to tell atrocious lies, one often feels a guilty flutter in one's stomach, and Klaus felt such a flutter now. "You certainly are an intelligent man," he continued.

"Not only am I intelligent," Genghis agreed, "but I'm also very smart. Now, let's get right to work. Even stupid children like yourselves should remember what I said about orphans having excellent bone structure for running.

That's why you are about to do Special Orphan Running Exercises, or S.O.R.E. for short."

"Ooladu!" Sunny shrieked.

"My sister means that sounds exciting," Violet said, although "Ooladu!" actually meant "I wish you'd tell us what you're *really* up to, Genghis."

"I'm glad you're so enthusiastic," Genghis said. "In certain cases, enthusiasm can make up for a lack of brainpower." He took his hands from behind his back, and the children saw that he was holding a large metal can and a long, prickly brush. The can was open, and an eerie white glow was shining out of the top. "Now, before we begin S.O.R.E., we'll need a track. This is luminous paint, which means it glows in the dark."

"How interesting," Klaus said, although he'd known what the word "luminous" means for two and a half years.

"Well, if you find it so interesting," Genghis said, his eyes looking as luminous as the paint, "you can be in charge of the brush. *Here.*"

He thrust the long, prickly brush into Klaus's hands. "And you little girls can hold the paint can. I want you to paint a big circle on the grass so you can see where you are running when you start your laps. Go on, what are you waiting for?"

The Baudelaires looked at one another. What they were waiting for, of course, was Genghis revealing what he was really up to with the paint, the brush, and the ridiculous Special Orphan Running Exercises. But in the meantime, they figured they'd better do as Genghis said. Painting a big, luminous circle on the lawn didn't seem to be particularly dangerous, so Violet picked up the paint can, and Klaus dipped the brush into the paint and began making a big circle. For the moment, Sunny was something of a fifth wheel, a phrase which means "not in a position to do anything particularly helpful," but she crawled alongside her siblings, offering moral support.

"Bigger!" Genghis called out in the dark. "Wider!" The Baudelaires followed his instructions and made the circle bigger and wider, walking farther away from Genghis and leaving a glowing trail of paint. They looked out into the gloom of the evening, wondering where the Quagmire triplets were hiding, or if indeed they had managed to sneak out of the recital at all. But the sun was down now, and the only thing the orphans could see was the bright circle of light they were painting on the lawn and the dim figure of Genghis, his white turban looking like a floating skull in the night. "Bigger! Wider! All right, all right, that's big and wide enough! Finish the circle where I am standing! Hurry up!"

"What do you think we're *really* doing?" Violet whispered to her brother.

"I don't know," Klaus said. "I've only read three or four books on paint. I know that paint can sometimes be poisonous or cause birth defects. But Genghis isn't making us eat the circle, and you're not pregnant, of course, so I can't imagine."

Sunny wanted to add "Gargaba!" which meant "Maybe the luminous paint is serving as some sort of glowing signal," but the Baudelaires had come full circle and were too close to Genghis to do any more talking.

"I suppose that will do, orphans," Genghis said, snatching the brush and the can of paint out of their hands. "Now, take your marks, and when I blow my whistle, begin running around the circle you've made until I tell you to stop."

"What?" Violet said. As I'm sure you know, there are two types of "What?" in the world. The first type simply means "Excuse me, I didn't hear you. Could you please repeat yourself?" The second type is a little trickier. It means something more along the lines of "Excuse me, I did hear you, but I can't believe that's really what you meant," and this second type is obviously the type Violet was using at this moment. She was standing right next to Genghis, so she'd obviously heard what had come out of the smelly mouth of this miserable man. But she couldn't believe that Genghis was simply going to make them run laps. He was such a sneaky and revolting person that the eldest Baudelaire simply could not accept that his scheme was only as evil as the average gym class.

"What?" Genghis repeated in a mocking way. He had obviously taken a page out of Nero's book, a phrase which here means "learned how to repeat things in a mocking way, in order to make fun of children." "I know you heard me, little orphan girl. You're standing right next to me. Now take your marks, all of you, and begin running as soon as I blow my whistle."

"But Sunny is a baby," Klaus protested. "She can't really run, at least not professionally."

"Then she may crawl as fast as she can," Genghis replied. "Now—on your marks, get set, *go*!"

Genghis blew his whistle and the Baudelaire orphans began to run, pacing themselves so they could run together even though they had different-sized legs. They finished one lap, and then another, and then another and another and then five more and then another and then seven more and then another and then three more and then two more and then another and then another and then six more and then they lost track. Coach Genghis kept blowing his whistle and occasionally shouted tedious and unhelpful things like "Keep running!" or "Another lap!" The children looked down at the luminous circle so they could stay in a circle, and the children looked over at Genghis as he grew fainter and then clearer as they finished a lap, and the children looked out into the darkness to see if they could catch a glimpse of the Quagmires.

The Baudelaires also looked at one another from time to time, but they didn't speak, not even when they were far enough away from Genghis that he could not overhear. One reason they did not speak was to conserve energy, because although the Baudelaires were in reasonably good shape, they had not run so many laps in their lives, and before too long they were breathing too hard to really discuss anything. But the other reason they did not speak was that Violet had already spoken for them when she had asked the second type of "What?" Coach Genghis kept blowing his whistle, and the children kept running around and around the track, and echoing in each of their minds was this second, trickier type of question. The three siblings had heard Coach Genghis, but they couldn't believe that S.O.R.E. was the extent of his evil plan. The Baudelaire orphans kept running around the glowing circle until the first rays of sunrise began to reflect on the jewel in Genghis's turban, and all they could think was *What? What? What?*

CHAPTER Eight

"What?" Isadora asked.

"I said, 'Finally, as the sun rose, Coach Genghis had us stop running laps and let us go to bed,'" Klaus said.

"My sister didn't mean that she didn't hear you," Duncan explained. "She meant that she heard you, but she didn't believe that's really what you meant. And to tell you the truth, I can scarcely believe it myself, even though I saw it with my own eyes."

"I can't believe it either," Violet said, wincing as she took a bite of the salad that the masked people had served for lunch. It was the next afternoon, and all three Baudelaire orphans were doing a great deal of wincing, a word which here means "frowning in pain, alarm, or distress." When Coach Genghis had called last night's activities S.O.R.E., he had merely used the name as an acronym for Special Orphan Running Exercises, but the three children thought that the name S.O.R.E. was even more appropriate than that. After a full night of S.O.R.E., they'd been sore all day. Their legs were sore from all their running. When they'd finally entered the Orphans Shack to go to sleep, they had been too tired to put on their noisy shoes, so their toes were sore from the claws of the tiny territorial crabs. And their heads were sore, not only from headaches, which often occur when one doesn't get enough sleep, but also from trying to figure out what Coach Genghis was up to in making them run all those laps. The Baudelaire legs were sore, the Baudelaire toes were sore, the Baudelaire heads were sore, and soon the muscles on the

Smart, yes. Charming, yes. Able to survive austere situations, yes. But the children were not lucky, and so wouldn't use the phrase "if we're lucky" any more than they would use the phrase "if we're stalks of celery," because neither phrase was appropriate. If the Baudelaire orphans had been stalks of celery, they would not have been small children in great distress, and if they had been lucky, Carmelita Spats would not have approached their table at this particular moment and delivered another unfortunate message.

"Hello, you cakesniffers," she said, "although judging from the baby brat you're more like saladsniffers. I have another message for you from Coach Genghis. I get to be his Special Messenger because I'm the cutest, prettiest, nicest little girl in the whole school."

"If you were really the nicest person in the whole school," Isadora said, "you wouldn't make fun of a sleeping infant. But never mind, what is the message?"

"It's actually the same one as last time," Carmelita said, "but I'll repeat it in case you're too stupid to remember. The three Baudelaire orphans are to report to the front lawn tonight, immediately after dinner."

"What?" Klaus asked.

"Are you *deaf* as well as cakesniffy?" Carmelita asked. "I said—"

"Yes, yes, Klaus heard you," Isadora said quickly. "He didn't mean that kind of 'What?' We have received the message, Carmelita. Now please go away."

"That's two tips you owe me," Carmelita said, but she flounced off.

"I can't believe it," Violet said. "Not more laps! My legs are almost too sore to walk, let alone run."

"Carmelita didn't say anything about more laps," Duncan pointed out. "Maybe Coach Genghis is putting his real plan into action tonight. In any case, we'll sneak out of the recital again and keep an eye on you."

sides of the Baudelaire mouths would be sore from wincing all day long.

It was lunchtime, and the three children were trying to discuss the previous evening with the Quagmire triplets, who weren't very sore and not nearly as tired. One reason was that they had been hiding behind the archway, spying on Genghis and the Baudelaires, instead of running around and around the luminous circle. The other reason was that the Quagmires had done their spying in shifts. After the Baudelaires had run the first few laps and there was no sign of them stopping, the two triplets had decided to alternate between Duncan sleeping and Isadora spying, and Duncan spying and Isadora sleeping. The two siblings promised each other that they would wake up the sleeping one if the spying one noticed anything unusual.

"I had the last shift," Duncan explained, "so my sister didn't see the end of S.O.R.E. But it doesn't matter. All that happened was that Coach Genghis had you stop running laps and let you go to bed. I thought that he might insist on getting your fortune before you could stop running."

"And I thought that the luminous circle would serve as a landing strip," Isadora said, "for a helicopter, piloted by one of his assistants, to swoop down and take you away. The only thing I couldn't figure out was why you had to run all those laps before the helicopter showed up."

"But the helicopter didn't show up," Klaus said, taking a sip of water and wincing. "Nothing showed up."

"Maybe the pilot got lost," Isadora said.

"Or maybe Coach Genghis became as tired as you did, and forgot to ask for your fortune," Duncan said.

Violet shook her sore head. "He would never get too tired to get our fortune," she said. "He's up to something, that much is for sure, but I just can't figure out what it is."

"Of course you can't figure it out," Duncan said. "You're exhausted. I'm glad Isadora and

I thought of spying in shifts. We're going to use all our spare time to investigate. We'll go through all of our notes, and do some more research in the library. There must be something that can help us figure it out."

"I'll do research, too," Klaus said, yawning. "I'm quite good at it."

"I know you are," Isadora said, smiling. "But not today, Klaus. We'll work on uncovering Genghis's plan, and you three can catch up on your sleep. You're too tired to do much good in a library or anywhere else."

Violet and Klaus looked at each other's tired faces, and then down at their baby sister, and they saw that the Quagmire triplets were right. Violet had been so tired that she had taken only a few notes on Mr. Remora's painfully dull stories. Klaus had been so tired that he had incorrectly measured nearly all of Mrs. Bass's objects. And although Sunny had not reported what she had done that morning in Nero's office, she couldn't have been a very good administrative assistant, because she had fallen asleep right there in the cafeteria, her little head on her salad, as if it were a soft pillow instead of leaves of lettuce, slices of tomato, gobs of creamy honey-mustard dressing, and crispy croutons, which are small toasted pieces of bread that give a salad some added crunch. Violet gently lifted her sister's head out of the salad and shook a few croutons out of her hair. Sunny winced, made a faint, miserable noise, and went back to sleep in Violet's lap. "Perhaps you're right, Isadora," Violet said. "We'll stumble through the afternoon somehow and get a good night's sleep tonight. If we're lucky, Vice Principal Nero will play something quiet at tonight's concert and we can sleep through that as well."

You can see, with that last sentence, just how tired Violet really was, because "if we're lucky" is not a phrase that she, or either of her siblings, used very often. The reason, of course, is quite clear: the Baudelaire orphans were not lucky.

"In shifts," Isadora added, nodding in agreement. "And I bet we'll have a clear picture of his plan by then. We have the rest of the day to do research." Isadora paused, and flipped open her black notebook to the right page. She read,

"Don't worry Baudelaires, don't feel disgrace—
The Quagmire triplets are on the case."

"Thank you," Klaus said, giving Isadora a tired smile of appreciation. "My sisters and I are thankful for all your help. And we're going to put our minds to the problem, even though we're too exhausted to do research. If we're lucky, all of us working together can defeat Coach Genghis."

There was that phrase again, "if we're lucky," coming out of the mouth of a Baudelaire, and once again it felt about as appropriate as "if we're stalks of celery." The only difference was that the Baudelaire orphans did not wish to be stalks of celery. While it is true that if they were stalks of celery they would not be orphans because celery is a plant and so cannot really be said to have parents, Violet, Klaus, and Sunny did not wish to be the stringy, low-calorie vegetable. Unfortunate things can happen to celery as easily as they can happen to children. Celery can be sliced into small pieces and dipped into clam dip at fancy parties. It can be coated in peanut butter and served as a snack. It can merely sit in a field and rot away, if the nearby celery farmers are lazy or on vacation. All these terrible things can happen to celery, and the orphans knew it, so if you were to ask the Baudelaires if they wanted to be stalks of celery they would say of course not. But they wanted to be lucky. The Baudelaires did not necessarily want to be extremely lucky, like someone who finds a treasure map or someone who wins a lifetime supply of ice cream in a contest, or like the man—and not, alas, me—who was lucky enough to marry my beloved Beatrice, and live with her in happiness over the

course of her short life. But the Baudelaires
wanted to be lucky enough. They wanted to
be lucky enough to figure out how to escape
Coach Genghis's clutches, and it seemed that
being lucky would be their only chance. Violet
was too tired to invent anything, and Klaus was
too tired to read anything, and Sunny, still
asleep in Violet's lap, was too tired to bite anything or anybody, and it seemed that even with
the diligence of the Quagmire triplets—the
word "diligence" here means "ability to take
good notes in dark green and pitch-black notebooks"—they needed to be lucky if they
wanted to stay alive. The Baudelaires huddled
together as if the cafeteria were extremely cold,
wincing in soreness and worry. It seemed to the
Baudelaire orphans that they wanted to be
lucky more than they had in their entire lives.

CHAPTER Nine

Occasionally, events in one's life become clearer through the prism of experience, a phrase which simply means that things tend to become clearer as time goes on. For instance, when a person is just born, they usually have no idea what curtains are and spend a great deal of their first months wondering why on earth Mommy and Daddy have hung large pieces of cloth over each window in the nursery. But as the person grows older, the idea of curtains becomes clearer through the prism of experience. The person will learn the word "curtains" and notice that they are actually quite handy for keeping a room dark when it is time to sleep, and for decorating an otherwise boring window area. Eventually, they will entirely accept the idea of curtains, and may even purchase some curtains of their own, or venetian blinds, and it is all due to the prism of experience.

Coach Genghis's S.O.R.E. program, however, was one event that didn't seem to get any clearer at all through the Baudelaire orphans' prism of experience. If anything, it grew even harder and harder to understand, because Violet, Klaus, and Sunny became so utterly exhausted as the days—and, more particularly, the nights— wore on. After the children received their second message from Carmelita Spats, they spent the rest of the afternoon wondering what Coach Genghis would make them do that evening. The Quagmire triplets wondered along with them, so everyone was surprised—the Baudelaires, who met Genghis out on the front lawn after dinner again, and the Quagmires, who tiptoed out of the recital and spied on them, in shifts,

from behind the archway again—when Genghis
began blowing his whistle and ordered the
Baudelaire orphans to begin running. The Baudelaires and Quagmires thought that surely
Genghis would do something far more sinister
than more laps.

But while a second evening of running laps
might have lacked in sinisterity, Violet, Klaus,
and Sunny were too exhausted to notice. They
could scarcely hear the shrieks of Genghis's
whistle and his cries of "Keep running!" and
"Another lap!" over the sound of their own desperate panting for breath. They grew so sweaty
that the orphans thought they would give up the
entire Baudelaire fortune for a good long
shower. And their legs grew so sore that the children forgot, even with their prism of experience,
what it felt like to have legs that didn't ache
from thigh to toe.

Lap after lap the Baudelaires ran, hardly taking their eyes off the circle of luminous paint
that still glowed brightly on the darkening lawn,

and staring at this circle was somehow the worst part of all. As the evening turned to night, the luminous circle was all the Baudelaires could really see, and it imprinted itself into their eyes so they could see it even when they were staring desperately into the darkness. If you've ever had a flash photograph taken, and the blob of the flash has stayed in your view for a few moments afterward, then you are familiar with what was happening to the Baudelaires, except the glowing circle stayed in their minds for so long that it became symbolic. The word "symbolic" here means that the glowing circle felt like it stood for more than merely a track, and what it stood for was zero. The luminous zero glowed in the Baudelaire minds, and it was symbolic of what they knew of their situation. They knew zero about what Genghis was up to. They knew zero about why they were running endless laps. And they had zero energy to think about it.

Finally, the sun began to rise, and Coach

Genghis dismissed his orphan track team. The Baudelaires stumbled blearily to the Orphans Shack, too tired to even see if Duncan and Isadora were sneaking back to their dormitory after their last shift of spying. Once again, the three siblings were too tired to put on their noisy shoes, so their toes were doubly sore when they awoke, just two hours later, to begin another groggy day. But—and I shudder to tell you this—this was not the last groggy day for the Baudelaire orphans. The dreadful Carmelita Spats delivered them the usual message at lunch, after they spent the morning dozing through classes and secretarial duties, and the Baudelaires put their heads on the cafeteria table in despair at the idea of another night of running. The Quagmires tried to comfort them, promising to double their research efforts, but Violet, Klaus, and Sunny were too tired for conversation, even with their closest friends. Luckily, their closest friends understood completely and didn't find the Baudelaires' silence rude or discouraging.

It seems impossible to believe that the three Baudelaires managed to survive another evening of S.O.R.E., but in times of extreme stress one can often find energy hidden in even the most exhausted areas of the body. I discovered this myself when I was woken up in the middle of the night and chased sixteen miles by an angry mob armed with torches, swords, and vicious dogs, and the Baudelaire orphans discovered it as they ran laps, not only for that night but also for six nights following. This made a grand total of nine S.O.R.E. sessions, although "grand" would seem to be the wrong word for endless evenings of desperate panting, sweaty bodies, and achy legs. For nine nights, the Baudelaire brains were plagued with the symbolic, luminous zero glowing in their minds like a giant donut of despair.

As the Baudelaire orphans suffered, their schoolwork suffered with them. As I'm sure you know, a good night's sleep helps you perform well in school, and so if you are a student you should always get a good night's sleep unless you have come to the good part of your book, and then you should stay up all night and let your schoolwork fall by the wayside, a phrase which means "flunk." In the days that followed, the Baudelaires were much more exhausted than somebody who had stayed up all night reading, and their schoolwork did more than fall by the wayside. It fell *off* the wayside, a phrase which here has different meanings for each child. For Violet, it meant that she was so drowsy that she did not write down a single word of Mr. Remora's stories. For Klaus, it meant that he was so weary that he didn't measure a single one of Mrs. Bass's objects. And for Sunny, it meant that she was so exhausted that she didn't do anything Vice Principal Nero assigned her to do. The Baudelaire orphans believed that doing well in school was extremely important, even if the school happened to be run by a tyrannical idiot, but they were simply too fatigued from their nightly laps to do their assigned work. Before long, the circle of luminous paint was not the only zero the Baudelaires saw. Violet saw a zero at the top of her paper when she was unable to recall any of Mr. Remora's stories for a test. Klaus saw a zero in Mrs. Bass's gradebook when he was called on to report the exact length of a tube sock he was supposed to be measuring and was discovered to be taking a nap instead. And Sunny saw a zero when she checked the staple drawer and saw that there were zero staples inside.

"This is getting ridiculous," Isadora said when Sunny updated her siblings and friends at the start of another weary lunch. "Look at you, Sunny. It was inappropriate to hire you as an administrative assistant in the first place, and it's simply absurd to have you crawl laps by night and make your own staples by day."

"Don't call my sister absurd or ridiculous!" Klaus cried.

"I'm not calling *her* ridiculous!" Isadora said.

"I'm calling the *situation* ridiculous!"

"Ridiculous means you want to laugh at it," said Klaus, who was never too tired to define words, "and I don't want you laughing at us."

"I'm not laughing at you," Isadora said. "I'm trying to help."

Klaus snatched his drinking glass from Isadora's side of the table. "Well, laughing at us doesn't help at all, you cakesniffer."

Isadora snatched her silverware from Klaus's hands. "Calling me names doesn't help either, Klaus."

"Mumdum!" Sunny shrieked.

"Oh, stop it, both of you," Duncan said. "Isadora, can't you see that Klaus is just tired? And Klaus, can't you see that Isadora is just frustrated?"

Klaus took his glasses off and returned his drinking glass to Isadora. "I'm too tired to see anything," he said. "I'm sorry, Isadora. Being tired makes me crabby. In a few days I'll turn as nasty as Carmelita Spats."

Isadora handed her silverware back to Klaus and patted him on the hand in forgiveness. "You'll never be as nasty as Carmelita Spats," she said.

"Carmelita Spats?" Violet said, lifting her head from her tray. She had dozed through Isadora and Klaus's argument but woken up at the sound of the Special Messenger's name. "She's not coming here again to tell us to do laps, is she?"

"I'm afraid she is," Duncan said ruefully, a word which here means "while pointing at a rude, violent, and filthy little girl."

"Hello, cakesniffers," Carmelita Spats said. "Today I have two messages for you, so I should really get two tips instead of one."

"Oh, Carmelita," Klaus said. "You haven't gotten a tip for the last nine days, and I see no reason to break that tradition."

"That's because you're a stupid orphan," Carmelita Spats said promptly. "In any case, message number one is the usual: meet Coach

Genghis on the front lawn right after dinner."

Violet gave an exhausted groan. "And what's the second message?" she asked.

"The second message is that you must report to Vice Principal Nero's office right away."

"Vice Principal Nero's office?" Klaus asked. "Why?"

"I'm sorry," Carmelita Spats said with a nasty smile to indicate that she wasn't sorry one bit. "I don't answer questions from nontipping orphan cakesniffers."

Some children at the neighboring table laughed when they heard that and began banging their silverware on the table. "Cakesniffing orphans in the Orphans Shack! Cakesniffing orphans in the Orphans Shack!" they chanted as Carmelita Spats giggled and skipped off to finish her lunch. "Cakesniffing orphans in the Orphans Shack! Cakesniffing orphans in the Orphans Shack!" they chanted while the Baudelaires sighed and stood up on their aching legs. "We'd better go to Nero's," Violet said. "We'll see you later, Duncan and Isadora."

"Nonsense," Duncan said. "We'll walk you. Carmelita Spats has made me lose my appetite, so we'll skip lunch and take you to the administrative building. We won't go inside—otherwise there'll be no silverware between the five of us—but we'll wait outside and you can tell us what's going on."

"I wonder what Nero wants," Klaus said, yawning.

"Maybe he's discovered that Genghis is really Olaf, all by himself," Isadora said, and the Baudelaires smiled back. They didn't dare hope that this was the reason for their summons to Nero's office, but they appreciated their friends' hopefulness. The five children handed their scarcely eaten lunches to the cafeteria workers, who blinked at them silently from behind their metal masks, and walked to the administrative building. The Quagmire triplets wished the Baudelaires luck, and Violet, Klaus, and Sunny trudged up the steps to Nero's office.

"Thank you for taking the time out of your busy orphan schedule to see me," Vice Principal Nero said, yanking open his door before they could knock. "Hurry up and come inside. Every minute I spend talking to you is a minute I could spend practicing the violin, and when you're a musical genius like me, every minute counts."

The three children walked into the tiny office and began clapping their tired hands together as Nero raised both his arms in the air. "There are two things I wanted to talk to you about," he said when the applause was over. "Do you know what they are?"

"No, sir," Violet replied.

"*No, sir,*" Nero mimicked, although he looked disappointed that the children hadn't given him a longer answer to make fun of. "Well, the first one is that the three of you have missed nine of my violin concerts, and each of you owes me a bag of candy for each one. Nine bags of candy times three equals twenty-nine.

In addition, Carmelita Spats has told me that she has delivered ten messages to you, if you include the two she delivered today, and that you've never given her a tip. That's a disgrace. Now, I think a nice tip is a pair of earrings with precious stones, so you owe her ten pairs of earrings. What do you have to say about that?"

The Baudelaire orphans looked at one another with their sleepy, sleepy eyes. They had nothing to say about that. They had plenty to *think* about that—that they'd only missed Nero's concerts because Coach Genghis had forced them to, that nine bags of candy times three equals twenty-seven, not twenty-nine, and that tips are always optional and usually consist of money instead of earrings—but Violet, Klaus, and Sunny were too tired to say anything about it at all. This was another disappointment to Vice Principal Nero, who stood there scratching his pigtails and waiting for one of the children to say something that he could repeat in his nasty, mocking voice. But after a moment of silence, the vice principal went on to the second thing. "The second thing," he said, going on, "is that you three have become the worst students Prufrock Preparatory School has ever seen. Violet, Mr. Remora tells me that you have flunked a test. Klaus, Mrs. Bass reports that you can scarcely tell one end of a metric ruler from another. And Sunny, I've noticed that you haven't made a single staple! Mr. Poe told me you were intelligent and hardworking children, but you're just a bunch of cakesniffers!"

At this, the Baudelaires could keep quiet no longer. "We're flunking school because we're exhausted!" Violet cried.

"And we're exhausted because we're running laps every night!" Klaus cried.

"Galuka!" Sunny shrieked, which meant "So yell at Coach Genghis, not at us!"

Vice Principal Nero gave the children a big smile, delighted that he was able to answer them in his favorite way. *"We're flunking school because we're exhausted!"* he squealed. *"And we're*

*exhausted because we're running laps every night!
Galuka!* I've had enough of your nonsense!
Prufrock Preparatory School has promised you
an excellent education, and an excellent education you will get—or, in Sunny's case, an excellent job as an administrative assistant! Now,
I've instructed Mr. Remora and Mrs. Bass to
give comprehensive exams tomorrow—large
tests on absolutely everything you've learned so
far. Violet, you'd better remember every detail
of Mr. Remora's stories, and Klaus, you'd better
remember the length, width, and depths of Mrs.
Bass's objects, or I will expel you from school.
Also, I've found a bunch of papers that need to
be stapled tomorrow. Sunny, you will staple all
of them, with homemade staples, or I will expel
you from your job. First thing tomorrow morning we will have the test and the stapling, and
if you don't get As and make enough staples,
you'll leave Prufrock Preparatory School. Luckily for you, Coach Genghis has offered to homeschool you. That means he'd be your coach,

your teacher, and your guardian, all in one. It's a very generous offer, and if I were you I'd give *him* a tip, too, although I don't think earrings are appropriate in this case."

"We're not going to give Count Olaf a tip!" Violet blurted out.

Klaus looked at his older sister in horror. "Violet means Coach Genghis," Klaus said quickly to Nero.

"I *do not*!" Violet cried. "Klaus, our situation is too desperate to pretend not to recognize him any longer!"

"Hifijoo!" Sunny agreed.

"I guess you're right," Klaus said. "What have we got to lose?"

"*What have we got to lose?*" Nero mocked. "What are you talking about?"

"We're talking about Coach Genghis," Violet said. "He's not really named Genghis. He's not even a real coach. He's Count Olaf in disguise."

"Nonsense!" Nero said.

Klaus wanted to say *"Nonsense!"* right back at Nero, in Nero's own repulsive way, but he bit his exhausted tongue. "It's true," he said. "He's put a turban over his eyebrow and expensive running shoes over his tattoo, but he's still Count Olaf."

"He has a turban for religious reasons," Nero said, "and running shoes because he's a coach. Look here." He strode over to the computer and pressed a button. The screen began to glow in its usual seasick way, and once again showed a picture of Count Olaf. "You see? Coach Genghis looks nothing like Count Olaf, and my advanced computer system proves it."

"Ushilo!" Sunny cried, which meant "That doesn't prove anything!"

"Ushilo!" Nero mocked. "Who am I going to believe, an advanced computer system or two children flunking school and a little baby too dumb to make her own staples? Now, stop wasting my time! I will personally oversee tomorrow's comprehensive exams, which will be

given in the Orphans Shack! And you'd better do excellent work, or it's a free ride from Coach Genghis! Sayonara, Baudelaires!"

"Sayonara" is the Japanese word for good-bye, and I'm sure that each and every one of the millions of people who live in Japan would be ashamed to hear their language used by such a revolting person. But the Baudelaire orphans had no time to think such international thoughts. They were too busy giving the Quagmire triplets the latest news.

"This is awful!" Duncan cried as the five children trudged across the lawn so they could talk things over in peace. "There's no way you can get an A on those exams, particularly if you have to run laps tonight!"

"This is dreadful!" Isadora cried. "There's no way you can make all those staples, either! You'll be homeschooled before you know it!"

"Coach Genghis won't homeschool us," Violet said, looking out at the front lawn, where the luminous zero was waiting for them. "He'll do something much, much worse. Don't you see? That's why he's made us run all those laps! He *knew* we'd be exhausted. He *knew* we'd flunk our classes, or fail to perform our secretarial duties. He *knew* we'd be expelled from Prufrock Prep, and then he could get his hands on us."

Klaus groaned. "We've been waiting for his plan to be made clear, and now it is. But it might be too late."

"It's not too late," Violet insisted. "The comprehensive exams aren't until tomorrow morning. We must be able to figure out a plan by then."

"Plan!" Sunny agreed.

"It'll have to be a complicated plan," Duncan said. "We have to get Violet ready for Mr. Remora's test, and Klaus ready for Mrs. Bass's test."

"And we have to make staples," Isadora said. "And the Baudelaires still have to run laps."

"And we have to stay awake," Klaus said.

The children looked at one another, and then out at the front lawn. The afternoon sun was shining brightly, but the five youngsters knew that soon it would set behind the tombstone-shaped buildings, and that it would be time for S.O.R.E. They didn't have much time. Violet tied her hair up in a ribbon to keep it out of her eyes. Klaus polished his glasses and set them on his nose. Sunny scraped her teeth together, to make sure they were sharp enough for any task ahead. And the two triplets took their notebooks out of their sweater pockets. Coach Genghis's evil plan had become clear through the prism of the Baudelaire and Quagmire experiences, and now they had to use their experience to make a plan of their own.

CHAPTER
Ten

The three Baudelaire orphans and the two Quagmire triplets sat in the Orphans Shack, which had
never looked less unpleasant than it did now. All
five children were wearing the noisy shoes Violet
had invented, so the territorial crabs were
nowhere to be seen. The salt had dried up the
dripping tan fungus into a hard beige crust that
was not particularly attractive but at least did not
plop! drops of fungus juice on the
youngsters. Because the
arrival of Coach Genghis
had focused their energies
on defeating his treachery,

the five orphans hadn't done anything about the green walls with the pink hearts on them, but otherwise the Orphans Shack had become quite a bit less mountainous and quite a bit more molehilly since the Baudelaires' arrival. It still had a long way to go to be attractive and comfortable living quarters, but for thinking of a plan, it would do in a pinch.

And the Baudelaire children were certainly in a pinch. If Violet, Klaus, and Sunny spent one more exhausting night running laps, they would flunk their comprehensive exams and secretarial assignment, and then Coach Genghis would whisk them away from Prufrock Prep, and as they thought of this they could almost feel Genghis's bony fingers pinching the life right out of them. The Quagmire triplets were so worried about their friends that they felt pinched as well, even though they were not directly in danger—or so they thought, anyway.

"I can't believe we didn't figure out Coach Genghis's plan earlier," Isadora said mournfully, paging through her notebook. "Duncan and I did all this research, and we still didn't figure it out."

"Don't feel badly," Klaus said. "My sisters and I have had many encounters with Olaf, and it's always difficult to figure out his scheme."

"We were trying to find out the history of Count Olaf," Duncan said. "The Prufrock Preparatory library has a pretty good collection of old newspapers, and we thought if we could find out some of his other schemes, we might figure out this one."

"That's a good idea," Klaus said thoughtfully. "I've never tried that."

"We figured that Olaf must have been an evil man even before he met you," Duncan continued, "so we looked up things in old newspapers. But it was difficult to find too many articles, because as you know he always uses a different name. But we found a person matching his description in the *Bangkok Gazette*, who was arrested for strangling a bishop but escaped from prison in just ten minutes."

"That sounds like him, all right," Klaus said.

"And then in the *Verona Daily News*," Duncan said, "there was a man who had thrown a rich widow off of a cliff. He had a tattoo of an eye on his ankle, but he had eluded authorities. And then we found a newspaper from your hometown that said—"

"I don't mean to interrupt," Isadora said, "but we'd better stop thinking about the past and start thinking about the present. Lunchtime is more than half over, and we desperately need a plan."

"You're not napping, are you?" Klaus asked Violet, who had been silent for a very long time.

"Of course I'm not napping," Violet replied. "I'm concentrating. I think I can invent something to make all those staples Sunny needs. But I can't figure out how I can invent the device and study for the test at the same time. Since S.O.R.E. began, I haven't taken good notes in Mr. Remora's class, so I won't be able to remember his stories."

"Well, you don't have to worry about that," Duncan said, holding up his dark green notebook. "I've written down every one of Mr. Remora's stories. Every boring detail is recorded here in my notebook."

"And I've written down how long, wide, and deep all of Mrs. Bass's objects are," Isadora said, holding up her own notebook. "You can study from my notebook, Klaus, and Violet can study from Duncan's."

"Thank you," Klaus said, "but you're forgetting something. We're supposed to be running laps this evening. We don't have time to read anybody's notebook."

"Tarcour," Sunny said, which meant "You're right, of course. S.O.R.E. always lasts until dawn, and the tests are first thing in the morning."

"If only we had one of the world's great inventors to help us," Violet said. "I wonder what Nikola Tesla would do."

"Or one of the world's great journalists," Duncan said. "I wonder what Dorothy Parker would do in this situation."

"And I wonder what Hammurabi, the ancient Babylonian, would do to help us," Klaus said. "He was one of the world's greatest researchers."

"Or the great poet Lord Byron," Isadora said.

"Shark," Sunny said, rubbing her teeth thoughtfully.

"Who knows what any of those people or fish would do in our shoes?" Violet said. "It's impossible to know."

Duncan snapped his fingers, not to signal a waiter or because he was listening to catchy music but because he had an idea. "In our shoes!" he said. "That's it!"

"What's it?" Klaus asked. "How will our noisy shoes help?"

"No, no," Duncan said. "Not the noisy shoes. I'm thinking about Coach Genghis's expensive running shoes that he said he couldn't take off because his feet were smelly."

"And I bet they *are* smelly," Isadora said.

"I've noticed he doesn't bathe much."

"But that's not why he wears them," Violet said. "He wears them for a disguise."

"Exactly!" Duncan said. "When you said 'in your shoes,' it gave me an idea. I know you just meant 'in our shoes' as an expression meaning 'in our situation.' But what if someone else were actually in your shoes—what if we disguised ourselves as you? Then we could run laps, and you could study for the comprehensive exams."

"Disguise yourselves as us?" Klaus said. "You two look exactly like each other, but you don't look anything like us."

"So what?" Duncan said. "It'll be dark tonight. When we've watched you from the archway, all we could see were two shadowy figures running—and one crawling."

"That's true," Isadora said. "If I took the ribbon from your hair, Violet, and Duncan took Klaus's glasses, we'd look enough like you that I bet Coach Genghis couldn't tell."

"And we could switch shoes, so your running on the grass would sound exactly the same," Duncan said.

"But what about Sunny?" Violet asked. "There's no way two people could disguise themselves as three people."

The Quagmire triplets' faces fell. "If only Quigley were here," Duncan said. "I just know he'd be willing to dress up as a baby if it meant helping you."

"What about a bag of flour?" Isadora asked. "Sunny's only about as big as a bag of flour—nothing personal, Sunny."

"Denada," Sunny said, shrugging.

"We could snitch a bag from the cafeteria," Isadora said, "and drag it alongside us as we ran. From a distance, it would probably look enough like Sunny to avoid suspicion."

"Being in each other's shoes seems like an extremely risky plan," Violet said. "If it fails, not only are we in trouble but you are as well, and who knows what Coach Genghis will do to you?"

This, as it turns out, was a question that would haunt the Baudelaires for quite some time, but the Quagmires gave it barely a thought. "Don't worry about that," Duncan said. "The important thing is to keep you out of his clutches. It may be a risky plan, but being in each other's shoes is the only thing we've been able to think of."

"And we don't have any time to waste thinking of anything else," Isadora added. "We'd better hurry if we want to snitch the bag of flour and not be late for class."

"And we'll need a string, or something, so we can drag it along and make it look like Sunny crawling," Duncan said.

"And I'll need to snitch some things, too," Violet said, "for my staple-making invention."

"Nidop," Sunny said, which meant something along the lines of "Then let's get moving."

The five children walked out of the Orphans Shack, taking off their noisy shoes and putting on their regular shoes so they wouldn't make a lot of noise as they walked nervously across the lawn to the cafeteria. They were nervous because they were not supposed to be sneaking into the cafeteria, or snitching things, and they were nervous because their plan was indeed a risky one. It is not a pleasant feeling, nervousness, and I would not wish for small children to be any more nervous than the Baudelaires and the Quagmires were as they walked toward the cafeteria in their regular shoes. But I must say that the children weren't nervous enough. They didn't need to be more nervous about sneaking into the cafeteria, even though it was against the rules, or snitching things, even though they didn't get caught. But they should have been more nervous about their plan, and about what would happen that evening when the sun set on the brown lawn and the luminous circle began to glow. They should have been nervous, now, in their regular shoes, about what would happen when they were in each other's.

If you've ever dressed up for Halloween or attended a masquerade, you know that there is a certain thrill to wearing a disguise—a thrill that is half excitement and half danger. I once attended one of the famed masked balls hosted by the duchess of Winnipeg, and it was one of the most exciting and dangerous evenings of my life. I was disguised as a bullfighter and slipped into the party while being pursued by the palace guards, who were disguised as scorpions. The moment I entered the Grand Ballroom, I felt as if Lemony Snicket had disappeared. I was wearing clothes I had never worn before—a scarlet cape made of silk and a vest embroidered with gold thread and a skinny black mask—and it made me feel as if I were a different person. And because I felt like a different person, I dared to approach a woman I had been forbidden to approach for the rest of my life. She was alone on the veranda—the word "veranda" is a fancy term for a porch made of polished gray marble—and costumed as a dragonfly, with a glittering green mask and enormous silvery wings. As my pursuers scurried around the party, trying to guess which guest was me, I slipped out to the veranda and gave her the message I'd been trying to give her for fifteen long and lonely years. "Beatrice," I cried, just as the scorpions spotted me, "Count Olaf is

I cannot go on. It makes me weep to think of that evening, and of the dark and desperate times that followed, and in the meantime I'm sure you are curious what happened to the

Baudelaire orphans and the Quagmire triplets, after dinner that evening at Prufrock Prep.

"This is sort of exciting," Duncan said, putting Klaus's glasses on his face. "I know that we're doing this for serious reasons, but I'm excited anyway."

Isadora recited, tying Violet's ribbon in her hair,

> *"It may not be particularly wise,*
> *but it's a thrill to be disguised."*

"That's not a perfect poem, but it will have to do under the circumstances. How do we look?"

The Baudelaire orphans took a step back and regarded the Quagmires carefully. It was just after dinner, and the children were standing outside the Orphans Shack, hurriedly putting their risky plan into action. They had managed to sneak into the cafeteria and steal a Sunny-sized bag of flour from the kitchen while the metal-masked cafeteria workers' backs were turned. Violet had also snitched a fork, a few teaspoons of creamed spinach, and a small potato, all of which she needed for her invention. Now they had just a few moments before the Baudelaires—or, in this case, the Quagmires in disguise—had to show up for S.O.R.E. Duncan and Isadora handed over their notebooks so the Baudelaires could study for their comprehensive exams, and switched shoes so the Quagmires' laps would sound exactly like the Baudelaires'. Now, with only seconds to spare, the Baudelaires looked over the Quagmires' disguise and realized instantly just how risky this plan was.

Isadora and Duncan Quagmire simply did not look very much like Violet and Klaus Baudelaire. Duncan's eyes were of a different color from Klaus's, and Isadora had different hair from Violet's, even if it was tied up in a similar way. Being triplets, the Quagmires were the exact same height, but Violet was taller than Klaus because she was older, and there was no time to make small stilts for Isadora to mimic this height difference. But it wasn't really these small physical details that made the disguise so unconvincing. It was the simple fact that the Baudelaires and the Quagmires were different people, and a hair ribbon, a pair of glasses, and some shoes couldn't turn them into one another any more than a woman disguised as a dragonfly can actually take wing and escape the disaster awaiting her.

"I know we don't look much like you," Duncan admitted after the Baudelaires had been quiet for some time. "But remember, it's quite dark on the front lawn. The only light is coming from the luminous circle. We'll make sure to keep our heads down when we're running, so our faces won't give us away. We won't speak a word to Coach Genghis, so our voices won't give us away. And we have your hair ribbon, glasses, and shoes, so our accessories won't give us away, either."

"We don't have to go through with this plan," Violet said quietly. "We appreciate your help, but we don't have to try and fool Genghis. My siblings and I could just run away right now, tonight. We've gotten to be pretty good runners, so we'd have a good head start on Coach Genghis."

"We could call Mr. Poe from a pay phone somewhere," Klaus said.

"Zubu," Sunny said, which meant "Or attend a different school, under different names."

"Those plans don't have a chance of working," Isadora said. "From what you've told us about Mr. Poe, he's never very helpful. And Count Olaf seems to find you wherever you go, so a different school wouldn't help, either."

"This is our only chance," Duncan agreed. "If you pass the exams without arousing Genghis's suspicion, you will be out of danger, and then we can focus our efforts on exposing the coach for who he really is."

"I suppose you're right," Violet said. "I just don't like the idea of your putting your lives in such danger, just to help us."

"What are friends for?" Isadora said. "We're not going to attend some silly recital while you run laps to your doom. You three were the first people at Prufrock Prep who weren't mean to us just for being orphans. None of us have any family, so we've got to stick together."

"At least let us go with you to the front lawn," Klaus said. "We'll spy on you from the archway, and make sure you're fooling Coach Genghis."

Duncan shook his head. "You don't have time to spy on us," he said. "You have to make staples out of those metal rods and study for two comprehensive exams."

"Oh!" Isadora said suddenly. "How will we drag this bag of flour along the track? We need a string or something."

"We could just kick it around the circle," Duncan said.

"No, no, no," Klaus said. "If Coach Genghis thinks you're kicking your baby sister, he'll know something is up."

"I know!" Violet said. She leaned forward

and put her hand on Duncan's chest, running her fingers along his thick wool sweater until she found what she was looking for—a loose thread. Carefully, she pulled, unraveling the sweater slightly until she had a good long piece of yarn. Then she snapped it off and tied one end around the bag of flour. The other end she handed to Duncan. "This should do it," she said. "Sorry about your sweater."

"I'm sure you can invent a sewing machine," he said, "when we're all out of danger. Well, we'd better go, Isadora. Coach Genghis will be waiting. Good luck with studying."

"Good luck with running laps," Klaus said.

The Baudelaires took a long look at their friends. They were reminded of the last time they saw their parents, waving good-bye to them as they left for the beach. They had not known, of course, that it would be the last moment they would spend with their mother and father, and again and again, each of the Baudelaires had gone back to that day in their lives, wishing that they had said something more than a casual good-bye. Violet, Klaus, and Sunny looked at the two triplets and hoped that this was not such a time, a time when people they cared for would disappear from their lives forever. But what if it were?

"If we never see—" Violet stopped, swallowed, and began again. "If something goes wrong—"

Duncan took Violet's hands and looked right at her. Violet saw, behind Klaus's glasses, the serious look in Duncan's wide eyes. "Nothing will go wrong," he said firmly, though of course he was wrong at that very moment. "Nothing will go wrong at all. We'll see you in the morning, Baudelaires."

Isadora nodded solemnly and followed her brother and the bag of flour away from the Orphans Shack. The Baudelaire orphans watched them walk toward the front lawn until the triplets were merely two specks, dragging another speck along with them.

"You know," Klaus said, as they watched them, "from a distance, in the dim light, they look quite a bit like us."

"Abax," Sunny agreed.

"I hope so," Violet murmured. "I hope so. But in the meantime, we'd better stop thinking about them and get started on our half of the plan. Let's put our noisy shoes on and go into the shack."

"I can't imagine how you're going to make staples," Klaus said, "with only a fork, a few teaspoons of creamed spinach, and a small potato. That sounds more like the ingredients for a side dish than for a staple-making device. I hope your inventing skills haven't been dulled by a lack of sleep."

"I don't think they have," Violet said. "It's amazing how much energy you can have once you have a plan. Besides, my plan doesn't only involve the things I snitched. It involves one of the Orphan Shack crabs and our noisy shoes. Now, when we all have our shoes on, please follow my instructions."

The two younger Baudelaires were quite puzzled at this, but they had learned long ago that when it came to inventions, Violet could be trusted absolutely. In the recent past, she had invented a grappling hook, a lockpick, and a signaling device, and now, come hell or high water—an expression which here means "using a fork, a few teaspoons of creamed spinach, a small potato, a live crab, and noisy shoes"—she was going to invent a staple-making device.

The three siblings put on their shoes and, following Violet's instructions, entered the shack. As usual, the tiny crabs were lounging around, taking advantage of their time alone in the shack when they wouldn't be frightened by loud noises. On most occasions, the Baudelaires would stomp wildly on the floor when they entered the shack, and the crabs would scurry underneath the bales of hay and into other hiding places in the room. This time, however, Violet instructed her siblings to step on the floor in carefully arranged patterns, so as to herd one of the grumpiest and biggest-clawed crabs into a corner of the shack. While the other crabs scattered, this crab was trapped in a corner, afraid of the noisy shoes but with nowhere to hide from them.

"Good work!" Violet cried. "Keep him in the corner, Sunny, while I ready the potato."

"What is the potato for?" Klaus asked.

"As we know," Violet explained as Sunny tapped her little feet this way and that to keep the crab in the corner, "these crabs love to get their claws on our toes. I specifically snitched a potato that was toe-shaped. You see how it's curved in a sort of oval way, and the little bumpy part here looks like a toenail?"

"You're right," Klaus said. "The resemblance is remarkable. But what does it have to do with staples?"

"Well, the metal rods that Nero gave us are very long, and need to be cut cleanly into small, staple-sized pieces. While Sunny keeps the crab in the corner, I'm going to wave the potato at him. He—or she, come to think of it, I don't know how to tell a boy crab from a girl crab—"

"It's a boy," Klaus said. "Trust me."

"Well, he'll think it's a toe," Violet continued, "and snap at it with his claws. At that instant, I'll yank the potato away and put a rod in its place. If I do it carefully enough, the crab should do a perfect job of slicing it up."

"And then what?" Klaus asked.

"First things first," Violet replied firmly. "O.K. Sunny, keep tapping those noisy shoes. I'm ready with the potato and rod number one."

"What can I do?" Klaus asked.

"You can start studying for the comprehensive exam, of course," Violet said. "I couldn't possibly read all of Duncan's notes in just one night. While Sunny and I make the staples, you need to read Duncan's and Isadora's notebooks, memorize the measurements from Mrs. Bass's class, and teach me all of Mr. Remora's stories."

"Roger," Klaus said. As you probably know, the middle Baudelaire was not referring to anybody named Roger. He was saying a man's name to indicate that he understood what Violet had said and would act accordingly, and over the course of the next two hours, that's exactly what he did. While Sunny used her noisy shoes to keep the crab in the corner and Violet used the potato as a toe and the crab's claws as clean cutters, Klaus used the Quagmire notebooks to study for the comprehensive exams, and everything worked the way it should. Sunny tapped her shoes so noisily that the crab remained trapped. Violet was so quick with the potato and metal rods that soon they were snipped into staple-sized pieces. And Klaus—although he had to squint because Duncan was using his glasses—read Isadora's measuring notes so carefully that before long he had memorized the length, width, and depth of just about everything.

"Violet, ask me the measurements of the navy blue scarf," Klaus said, turning the notebook over so he couldn't peek.

Violet yanked the potato away just in time, and the crab snipped off another bit of the metal rods. "What are the measurements of the navy blue scarf?" she asked.

"Two decimeters long," Klaus recited, "nine centimeters wide, and four millimeters thick. It's boring, but it's correct. Sunny, ask me the measurements of the bar of deodorant soap."

The crab saw an opportunity to leave the corner, but Sunny was too quick for it. "Soap?" Sunny quizzed Klaus, tapping her tiny noisy shoes until the crab retreated.

"Eight centimeters by eight centimeters by eight centimeters," Klaus said promptly. "That one's easy. You're doing great, you two. I bet that crab's going to be almost as tired as we are."

"No," Violet said, "he's done. Let him go, Sunny. We have all the staple-sized pieces we need. I'm glad that part of the staple-making process is over. It's very nerve-wracking to tease a crab."

"What's next?" Klaus said, as the crab scurried away from the most frightening moments of his life.

"Next you teach me Mr. Remora's stories," Violet said, "while Sunny and I bend these little bits of metal into the proper shape."

"Shablo," Sunny said, which meant something like "How are we going to do that?"

"Watch," Violet said, and Sunny watched. While Klaus closed Isadora's black notebook and began paging through Duncan's dark green one, Violet took the glob of creamed spinach and mixed it with a few pieces of stray hay and dust until it was a sticky, gluey mess. Then she placed this mess on the spiky end of the fork, and stuck it to one of the bales of hay so the handle end of the fork hung over the side. She blew on the creamed-spinach–stray-hay-and-dust mixture until it hardened. "I always thought that Prufrock Prep's creamed spinach was awfully sticky," Violet explained, "and then I realized it could be used as glue. And now, we have a perfect method of making those tiny strips into staples. See, if I lay a strip across the handle of the fork, a tiny part of the strip hangs off each of the sides. Those are the parts that will go inside the paper when it's a staple. If I take off my noisy shoes"—and here Violet paused to take off her noisy shoes—"and use the metal ends to tap on the strips, they'll bend around the handle of the fork and turn into staples. See?"

"Gyba!" Sunny shrieked. She meant "You're a genius! But what can I do to help?"

"You can keep your noisy shoes on your feet," Violet replied, "and keep the crabs away from us. And Klaus, you start summarizing stories."

"Roger," Sunny said.

"Roger," Klaus said, and once again, neither of them were referring to Roger. They meant, once again, that they understood what Violet had said, and would act accordingly, and all three Baudelaires acted accordingly for the rest of the night. Violet tapped away at the metal strips, and Klaus read out loud from Duncan's notebook, and Sunny stomped her noisy shoes. Soon, the Baudelaires had a pile of homemade staples on the floor, the details of Mr. Remora's stories in their brains, and not a single crab bothering them in the shack, and even with the threat of Coach Genghis hovering over them, the evening actually began to feel rather cozy. It reminded the Baudelaires of evenings they had spent when their parents were alive, in one of the living rooms in the Baudelaire mansion. Violet would often be tinkering away at some invention, while Klaus would often be reading and sharing the information he was learning, and Sunny would often be making loud noises. Of course, Violet was never tinkering frantically at an invention that would save their lives, Klaus was never reading something so boring, and Sunny was never making loud noises to scare crabs, but nevertheless as the night wore on, the Baudelaires felt almost at home in the Orphans Shack. And when the sky began to lighten with the first rays of dawn, the Baudelaires began to feel a certain thrill that was quite different from the thrill of being in disguise. It was a thrill that I have never felt in my life, and it was a thrill that the Baudelaires did not feel very often. But as the morning sun began to shine, the Baude-laire orphans felt the thrill of thinking your plan might work after all, and that perhaps they would eventually be as safe and happy as the evenings they remembered.

Assumptions are dangerous things to make, and like all dangerous things to make—bombs, for instance, or strawberry shortcake—if you make even the tiniest mistake you can find yourself in terrible trouble. Making assumptions simply means believing things are a certain way with little or no evidence that shows you are correct, and you can see at once how this can lead to terrible trouble. For instance, one morning you might wake up and make the assumption that your bed was in the same place that it always was, even though you would have no real evidence that this was so. But when you got out of your bed, you might discover that it had floated out to sea, and now you would be in terrible trouble all because of the incorrect assumption that you'd made. You can see that it is better not to make too many assumptions, particularly in the morning.

The morning of the comprehensive exams, however, the Baudelaire orphans were so tired, not only from staying up all night studying and making staples but also from nine consecutive nights of running laps, that they made plenty of assumptions, and every last one of them turned out to be incorrect.

"Well, that's the last staple," Violet said, stretching her tired muscles. "I think we can safely assume that Sunny won't lose her job."

"And you seem to know every detail of Mr. Remora's stories as well as I know all of Mrs. Bass's measurements," Klaus said, rubbing his tired eyes, "so I think we can safely assume that we won't be expelled."

"Nilikoh," Sunny said, yawning her tired

mouth. She meant something like "And we haven't seen either of the Quagmire triplets, so I think we can safely assume that their part of the plan went well."

"That's true," Klaus said. "I assume if they'd been caught we would have heard by now."

"I'd make the same assumption," Violet said.

"I'd make the same assumption," came a nasty, mimicking voice, and the children were startled to see Vice Principal Nero standing behind them holding a huge stack of papers. In addition to the assumptions they had made out loud, the Baudelaires had made the assumption that they were alone, and they were surprised to find not only Vice Principal Nero but also Mr. Remora and Mrs. Bass waiting in the doorway of the Orphans Shack. "I hope you've been studying all evening," Nero said, "because I told your teachers to make these exams extra-challenging, and the pieces of paper that the baby has to staple are very thick. Well, let's

get started. Mr. Remora and Mrs. Bass will take turns asking you questions until one of you gets an answer wrong, and then you flunk. Sunny will sit in the back and staple these papers into booklets of five papers each, and if your home-made staples don't work perfectly, then *you* flunk. Well, a musical genius like myself doesn't have all day to oversee exams. I've missed too much practice time as it is. Let's begin!"

Nero threw the papers into a big heap on one of the bales of hay, and the stapler right after it. Sunny crawled over as quickly as she could and began inserting the staples into the stapler, and Klaus stood up, still clutching the Quagmire notebooks. Violet put her noisy shoes back on her feet, and Mr. Remora swallowed a bite of banana and asked his first question.

"In my story about the donkey," he said, "how many miles did the donkey run?"

"Six," Violet said promptly.

"*Six*," Nero mimicked. "That can't be correct, can it, Mr. Remora?"

"Um, yes, actually," Mr. Remora said, taking another bite of banana.

"How wide," Mrs. Bass said to Klaus, "was the book with the yellow cover?"

"Nineteen centimeters," Klaus said immediately.

"Nineteen centimeters," Nero mocked. "That's wrong, isn't it, Mrs. Bass?"

"No," Mrs. Bass admitted. "That's the right answer."

"Well, try another question, Mr. Remora," Nero said.

"In my story about the mushroom," Mr. Remora asked Violet, "what was the name of the chef?"

"Maurice," Violet answered.

"Maurice," Nero mimicked.

"Correct," Mr. Remora said.

"How long was chicken breast number seven?" Mrs. Bass asked.

"Fourteen centimeters and five millimeters," Klaus said.

"Fourteen centimeters and five millimeters," Nero mimicked.

"That's right," Mrs. Bass said. "You're actually both very good students, even if you've been sleeping through class lately."

"Stop all this chitchat and flunk them," Nero said. "I've never gotten to expel any students, and I'm really looking forward to it."

"In my story about the dump truck," Mr. Remora said, as Sunny began to staple the pile of thick papers into booklets, "what color were the rocks that it carried?"

"Gray and brown."

"Gray and brown."

"Correct."

"How deep was my mother's casserole dish?"

"Six centimeters."

"Six centimeters."

"Correct."

"In my story about the weasel, what was its favorite color?"

The comprehensive exams went on and on, and if I were to repeat all of the tiresome and pointless questions that Mr. Remora and Mrs. Bass asked, you might become so bored that you might go to sleep right here, using this book as a pillow instead of as an entertaining and instructive tale to benefit young minds. Indeed, the exams were so boring that the Baudelaire orphans might normally have dozed through the test themselves. But they dared not doze. One wrong answer or unstapled piece of paper, and Nero would expel them from Prufrock Preparatory School and send them into the waiting clutches of Coach Genghis, so the three children worked as hard as they could. Violet tried to remember each detail Klaus had taught her, Klaus tried to remember every measurement he had taught himself, and Sunny stapled like mad, a phrase which here means "quickly and accurately." Finally, Mr. Remora stopped in the middle of his eighth banana and turned to Vice Principal Nero.

"Nero," he said, "there's no use continuing these exams. Violet is a very fine student, and has obviously studied very hard."

Mrs. Bass nodded her head in agreement. "In all my years of teaching, I've never encountered a more metric-wise boy than Klaus, here. And it looks like Sunny is a fine secretary as well. Look at these booklets! They're gorgeous."

"Pilso!" Sunny shrieked.

"My sister means 'Thank you very much,'" Violet said, although Sunny really meant something more like "My stapling hand is sore." "Does this mean we get to stay at Prufrock Prep?"

"Oh, let them stay, Nero," Mr. Remora said. "Why don't you expel that Carmelita Spats? She never studies, and she's an awful person besides."

"Oh yes," Mrs. Bass said. "Let's give *her* an extra-challenging examination."

"I can't flunk Carmelita Spats," Nero said impatiently. "She's Coach Genghis's Special Messenger."

"Who?" Mr. Remora asked.

"You know," Mrs. Bass explained, "Coach Genghis, the new gym teacher."

"Oh yes," Mr. Remora said. "I've heard about him, but never met him. What is he like?"

"He's the finest gym teacher the world has ever seen," Vice Principal Nero said, shaking his four pigtails in amazement. "But you don't have to take my word for it. You can see for yourself. Here he comes now."

Nero pointed one of his hairy hands out of the Orphans Shack, and the Baudelaire orphans saw with horror that the vice principal was speaking the truth. Whistling an irritating tune to himself, Coach Genghis was walking straight toward them, and the children could see at once how incorrect one of their assumptions had been. It was not the assumption that Sunny would not lose her job, although that assumption, too, would turn out to be incorrect. And it was not the assumption that Violet and Klaus would not be expelled, although that, too, was a wrong one. It was the assumption about the Quagmire triplets and their part of the plan going well. As Coach Genghis walked closer and closer, the Baudelaires saw that he was holding Violet's hair ribbon in one of his scraggly hands and Klaus's glasses in the other, and with every step of his expensive running shoes, the coach raised a small white cloud, which the children realized must be flour from the snitched sack. But more than the ribbon, or the glasses, or the small clouds of flour was the look in Genghis's eyes. As Coach Genghis reached the Orphans Shack, his eyes were shining bright with triumph, as if he had finally won a game that he had been playing for a long, long time, and the Baudelaire orphans realized that the assumption about the Quagmire triplets had been very, very wrong indeed.

"*Where* are they?" Violet cried as Coach Genghis stepped into the shack. "What have you done with them?" Normally, of course, one should begin conversations with something more along the lines of "Hello, how are you," but the eldest Baudelaire was far too distressed to do so.

Genghis's eyes were shining as brightly as could be, but his voice was calm and pleasant. "Here they are," he said, holding up the ribbon and glasses. "I thought you might be worried about them, so I brought them over first thing in the morning."

"We don't mean *these* them!" Klaus said, taking the items from Genghis's scraggly hands. "We mean *them* them!"

"I'm afraid I don't understand all those thems," Coach Genghis said, shrugging at the adults. "The orphans ran laps last night as part of my S.O.R.E. program, but they had to dash off in the morning to take their exams. In their hurry, Violet dropped her ribbon and Klaus dropped his glasses. But the baby—"

"You know very well that's not what happened," Violet interrupted. "Where are the Quagmire triplets? What have you done with our friends?"

"*What have you done with our friends?*" Vice Principal Nero said in his mocking tone. "Stop talking nonsense, orphans."

"I'm afraid it's not nonsense," Genghis said, shaking his turbaned head and continuing his story. "As I was saying before the little girl interrupted me, the baby didn't dash off with the other orphans. She just sat there like a sack of flour. So I walked over to her and gave her a kick to get her moving."

"Excellent idea!" Nero said. "What a wonderful story this is! And then what happened?"

"Well, at first it seemed like I'd kicked a big hole in the baby," Genghis said, his eyes shining, "which seemed lucky, because Sunny was a terrible athlete and it would have been a blessing to put her out of her misery."

Nero clapped his hands. "I know just what you mean, Genghis," he said. "She's a terrible secretary as well."

"But she did all that stapling," Mr. Remora protested.

"Shut up and let the coach finish his story," Nero said.

"But when I looked down," Genghis continued, "I saw that I hadn't kicked a hole in a baby. I'd kicked a hole in a bag of flour! I'd been tricked!"

"That's terrible!" Nero cried.

"So I ran after Violet and Klaus," Genghis

continued, "and I found that they weren't Violet and Klaus after all, but those two other orphans— the twins."

"They're not twins!" Violet cried. "They're triplets!"

"*They're triplets!*" Nero mocked. "Don't be an idiot. Triplets are when four babies are born at the same time, and there are only two Quagmires."

"And these two Quagmires were pretending to be the Baudelaires, in order to give the Baudelaires extra time to study."

"Extra time to study?" Nero said, grinning in delight. "Hee hee hee! Why, that's cheating!"

"That's not cheating!" Mrs. Bass said.

"Skipping gym class to study is cheating," Nero insisted.

"No, it's just good time management," Mr. Remora argued. "There's nothing wrong with athletics, but they shouldn't get in the way of your schoolwork."

"Look, I'm the vice principal," the vice

principal said. "I say the Baudelaires were cheating, and therefore—hooray!—I can expel them. You two are merely teachers, so if you disagree with me, I can expel you, too."

Mr. Remora looked at Mrs. Bass, and they both shrugged. "You're the boss, Nero," Mr. Remora said finally, taking another banana out of his pocket. "If you say they're expelled, they're expelled."

"Well, I say they're expelled," Nero said. "And Sunny loses her job, too."

"Rantaw!" Sunny shrieked, which meant something along the lines of "I never wanted to work as a secretary, anyway!"

"We don't care about being expelled," Violet said. "We want to know what happened to our friends."

"Well, the Quagmires had to be punished for their part in the cheating," Coach Genghis said, "so I brought them over to the cafeteria and put those two workers in charge of them. They'll be whisking eggs all day long."

"Very sensible," Nero agreed.

"That's all they're doing?" Klaus said suspiciously. "Whisking eggs?"

"That's what I said," Genghis said and leaned so close to the Baudelaires that all they could see were his shiny eyes and the crooked curve of his wicked mouth. "Those two Quagmires will whisk and whisk until they are simply whisked away."

"You're a liar," Violet said.

"Insulting your coach," Nero said, shaking his pigtailed head. "Now you're doubly expelled."

"What's this?" said a voice from the doorway. "Doubly expelled?"

The voice stopped to have a long, wet cough, so the Baudelaires knew without looking that it was Mr. Poe. He was standing at the Orphans Shack holding a large paper sack and looking busy and confused. "What are all of you doing here?" he said. "This doesn't look like a proper place to have a conversation. It's just an old shack."

"What are *you* doing here?" Nero asked. "We don't allow strangers to wander around Prufrock Preparatory School."

"Poe's the name," Mr. Poe said, shaking Nero's hand. "You must be Nero. We've talked on the phone. I received your telegram about the twenty-eight bags of candy and the ten pairs of earrings with precious stones. My associates at Mulctuary Money Management thought I'd better deliver them in person, so here I am. But what's this about expelled?"

"These orphans you foisted on me," Nero said, using a nasty word for "gave," "have proven to be terrible cheaters, and I'm forced to expel them."

"Cheaters?" Mr. Poe said, frowning at the three siblings. "Violet, Klaus, Sunny, I'm very disappointed in you. You promised me that you'd be excellent students."

"Well, actually, only Violet and Klaus were students," Nero said. "Sunny was an administrative assistant, but she was terrible at it as well."

Mr. Poe's eyes widened in surprise as he paused to cough into his white handkerchief. "An administrative assistant?" he repeated. "Why, Sunny's only a baby. She should be in preschool, not an office environment."

"Well, it doesn't matter now," Nero said. "They're all expelled. Give me that candy."

Klaus looked down at his hands, which were still clutching the Quagmire notebooks. He was afraid that the notebooks might be the only sign of the Quagmires he would ever see again. "We don't have any time to argue about candy!" he cried. "Count Olaf has done something terrible to our friends!"

"Count Olaf?" Mr. Poe said, handing Nero the paper sack. "Don't tell me he's found you here!"

"No, of course not," Nero said. "My advanced computer system has kept him away, of course. But the children have this bizarre notion that Coach Genghis is actually Olaf in disguise."

"Count Olaf," Genghis said slowly. "Yes,

I've heard of him. He's supposed to be the best actor in the whole world. I'm the best gym teacher in the whole world, so we couldn't possibly be the same person."

Mr. Poe looked Coach Genghis up and down, then shook his hand. "A pleasure to meet you," he said, and then turned to the Baudelaires. "Children, I'm surprised at you. Even without an advanced computer system, you should be able to tell that this man isn't Count Olaf. Olaf has only one eyebrow, and this man is wearing a turban. And Olaf has a tattoo of an eye on his ankle, and this man is wearing expensive running shoes. They are quite handsome, by the way."

"Oh, thank you," Coach Genghis said. "Unfortunately, thanks to these children, they have flour all over them, but I'm sure it'll wash off."

"If he removes his turban and his shoes," Violet said impatiently, "you will be able to see that he's Olaf."

"We've been through this before," Nero said. "He can't take off his running shoes because he's been exercising and his feet smell."

"And I can't take off my turban for religious reasons," Genghis added.

"You're not wearing a turban for religious reasons!" Klaus said in disgust, and Sunny shrieked something in agreement. "You're wearing it as a disguise! Please, Mr. Poe, make him take it off!"

"Now, Klaus," Mr. Poe said sternly. "You have to learn to be accepting of other cultures. I'm sorry, Coach Genghis. The children aren't usually prejudiced."

"That's quite all right," Genghis said. "I'm used to religious persecution."

"However," Mr. Poe continued, after a brief coughing spell, "I would ask you to remove your running shoes, if only to set the Baudelaires' minds at ease. I think we can all stand a little smelliness if it's in the cause of criminal justice."

"Smelly feet," Mrs. Bass said, wrinkling her nose. "Ew, gross."

"I'm afraid I cannot take off my running

shoes," Coach Genghis said, taking a step toward the door. "I need them."

"Need them?" Nero asked. "For what?"

Coach Genghis took a long, long look at the three Baudelaires and smiled a terrible, toothy grin. "For running, of course," he said, and ran out the door.

The orphans were startled for a moment, not only because he had started running so suddenly but also because it seemed like he had given up so easily. After his long, elaborate plan—disguising himself as a gym teacher, forcing the Baudelaires to run laps, getting them expelled—he was suddenly racing across the lawn without even glancing back at the children he'd been chasing for such a long time. The Baudelaires stepped out of the Orphans Shack, and Coach Genghis turned back to sneer at them.

"Don't think I've given up on *you*, orphans!" he called to them. "But in the meantime, I have two little prisoners with a very nice fortune of their own!"

He began to run again, but not before pointing a bony finger across the lawn. The Baudelaires gasped. At the far end of Prufrock Prep,
they saw a long, black car with dark smoke
billowing out of its exhaust pipes. But the children were not gasping at air pollution. The two
cafeteria workers were walking toward the car,
but they had taken off their metal masks at last,
and the three youngsters could see that they
were the two powder-faced women who were
comrades of Count Olaf's. But this was not what
the children were gasping at either, although it
was a surprising and distressing turn of events.
What they were gasping at was what each of
the women was dragging toward the car. Each
powder-faced woman was dragging one of the
Quagmire triplets, who were struggling desperately to get away.

"Put them in the back seat!" Genghis
called. "I'll drive! Hurry!"

"What in the world is Coach Genghis doing
with those children?" Mr. Poe asked, frowning.

The Baudelaires did not even turn to Mr.
Poe to try and explain. After all their S.O.R.E.
training sessions, Violet, Klaus, and Sunny
found that their leg muscles could respond
instantly if they wanted to run. And the Baudelaire orphans had never wanted to run more than
they did now.

"After them!" Violet cried, and the children
went after them. Violet ran, her hair flying
wildly behind her. Klaus ran, not even bothering to drop the Quagmire notebooks. And
Sunny crawled as fast as her legs and hands
could carry her. Mr. Poe gave a startled cough
and began running after them, and Nero, Mr.
Remora, and Mrs. Bass began running after
Mr. Poe. If you had been hiding behind the
archway, spying on what was going on, you
would have seen what looked like a strange race
on the front lawn, with Coach Genghis running
in front, the Baudelaire orphans right behind,
and assorted adults huffing and puffing behind
the children. But if you continued watching,

you would have seen an exciting development in the race, a phrase which here means that the Baudelaires were gaining on Genghis. The coach had much longer legs than the Baudelaires, of course, but he had spent the last ten nights standing around blowing a whistle. The children had spent those nights running hundreds of laps around the luminous circle, and so their tiny, strong legs—and, in Sunny's case, arms—were overcoming Genghis's height advantage.

I hate to pause at such a suspenseful part of the story, but I feel I must intrude and give you one last warning as we reach the end of this miserable tale. You were probably thinking, as you read that the children were catching up to their enemy, that perhaps this was the time in the lives of the Baudelaire orphans when this terrible villain would finally be caught, and that perhaps the children would find some kind guardians and that Violet, Klaus, and Sunny would spend the rest of their lives in relative happiness, possibly creating the printing business that they had discussed with the Quagmires. And you are free to believe that this is how the story turns out, if you want. The last few events in this chapter of the Baudelaire orphans' lives are incredibly unfortunate, and quite terrifying, and so if you would prefer to ignore them entirely you should put this book down now and think of a gentle ending to this horrible story. I have made a solemn promise to write the Baudelaire history exactly as it occurred, but you have made no such promise— at least as far as I know—and you do not need to endure the wretched ending of this story, and this is your very last chance to save yourself from the woeful knowledge of what happened next.

Violet was the first to reach Coach Genghis, and she stretched her arm out as far as she could, grabbing part of his turban. Turbans, you probably know, consist of just one piece of cloth, wrapped very tightly and in a complicated way around someone's head. But Genghis had cheated, not knowing the proper way to tie a turban, because he was wearing it as a disguise and not for religious reasons. He had merely wrapped it around his head the way you might wrap a towel around yourself when getting out of the shower, so when Violet grabbed the turban, it unraveled immediately. She had been hoping that grabbing his turban would stop the coach from running, but all it did was leave her with a long piece of cloth in her hands. Coach Genghis kept running, his one eyebrow glistened with sweat over his shiny eyes.

"Look!" Mr. Poe said, who was far behind the Baudelaires but close enough to see. "Genghis has only one eyebrow, like Count Olaf!"

Sunny was the next Baudelaire to reach Genghis, and because she was crawling on the ground, she was in a perfect position to attack his shoes. Using all four of her sharp teeth, she bit one pair of his shoelaces, and then the other.

The knots came undone immediately, leaving tiny, bitten pieces of shoelace on the brown lawn. Sunny had been hoping that untying his shoes would make the coach trip, but Genghis merely stepped out of his shoes and kept running. Like many disgusting people, Coach Genghis was not wearing socks, so with each step his eye tattoo glistening with sweat on his left ankle.

"Look!" Mr. Poe said, who was still too far to help but close enough to see. "Genghis has an eye tattoo, like Count Olaf! In fact, I think he *is* Count Olaf!"

"Of course he is!" Violet cried, holding up the unraveled turban.

"Merd!" Sunny shrieked, holding up a tiny piece of shoelace. She meant something like "That's what we've been trying to tell you."

Klaus, however, did not say anything. He was putting all of his energy toward running, but he was not running toward the man we can finally call by his true name, Count Olaf. Klaus was running toward the car. The powder-faced women were just shoving the Quagmires into the back seat, and he knew this might be his only chance to rescue them.

"Klaus! Klaus!" Isadora cried as he reached the car. Klaus dropped the notebooks to the ground and grabbed his friend's hand. "Help us!"

"Hang on!" Klaus cried and began to drag Isadora back out of the car. Without a word, one of the powder-faced women leaned forward and bit Klaus's hand, forcing him to let go of the triplet. The other powder-faced woman leaned across Isadora's lap and began pulling the car door closed.

"No!" Klaus cried and grabbed the door handle. Back and forth, Klaus and Olaf's associate tugged on the door, forcing it halfway open and halfway shut.

"Klaus!" Duncan cried, from behind Isadora. "Listen to me, Klaus! If anything goes wrong—"

"Nothing will go wrong," Klaus promised, pulling on the car door as hard as he could.

"You'll be out of here in a second!"

"If anything goes wrong," Duncan said again, "there's something you should know. When we were researching the history of Count Olaf, we found out something dreadful!"

"We can talk about this later," Klaus said, struggling with the door.

"Look in the notebooks!" Isadora cried. "The—" The first powder-faced woman put her hand over Isadora's mouth so she couldn't speak. Isadora turned her head roughly and slipped from the woman's grasp. "The—" The powdery hand covered her mouth again.

"Hang on!" Klaus called desperately. "Hang on!"

"Look in the notebooks! V.F.D." Duncan screamed, but the other woman's powdery hand covered his mouth before he could continue.

"What?" Klaus said.

Duncan shook his head vigorously and freed himself from the woman's hand for just one moment. "V.F.D." he managed to scream again, and that was the last Klaus heard. Count Olaf, who had been running slower without his shoes, had reached the car, and with a deafening roar, he grabbed Klaus's hand and pried it loose from the car door. As the door slammed shut, Olaf kicked Klaus in the stomach, sending him falling to the ground and landing with a rough *thump!* near the Quagmire notebooks he had dropped. The villain towered over Klaus and gave him a sickening smile, then leaned down, picked up the notebooks, and tucked them under his arm.

"No!" Klaus screamed, but Count Olaf merely smiled, stepped into the front seat, and began driving away just as Violet and Sunny reached their brother.

Clutching his stomach, Klaus stood up and tried to follow his sisters, who were trying to chase the long, black car. But Olaf was driving over the speed limit and it was simply impossible, and after a few yards the Baudelaires had to stop. The Quagmire triplets climbed over the powder-faced women and began to pound on the rear window of the car. Violet, Klaus, and Sunny could not hear what the Quagmires were screaming through the glass; they only saw their desperate and terrified faces. But then the powdery hands of Olaf's assistants grabbed them and pulled them back from the window. The faces of the Quagmire triplets faded to nothing, and the Baudelaires saw nothing more as the car pulled away.

"We have to go after them!" Violet screamed, her face streaked with tears. She turned around to face Nero and Mr. Poe, who were pausing for breath on the edge of the lawn. "We have to go after them!"

"We'll call the police," Mr. Poe gasped, wiping his sweaty forehead with his handkerchief. "They have an advanced computer system, too. They'll catch him. Where's the nearest phone, Nero?"

"You can't use my phone, Poe!" Nero said. "You brought three terrible cheaters here, and now, thanks to you, my greatest gym teacher is gone and took two students with him! The Baudelaires are triple-expelled!"

"Now see here, Nero," Poe said. "Be reasonable."

The Baudelaires sunk to the brown lawn, weeping with frustration and exhaustion. They paid no attention to the argument between Vice Principal Nero and Mr. Poe, because they knew, from the prism of their experience, that by the time the adults had decided on a course of action, Count Olaf would be long gone. This time, Olaf had not merely escaped but escaped with friends of theirs, and the Baudelaires wept as they thought they might never see the triplets again. They were wrong about this, but they had no way of knowing they were wrong, and just imagining what Count Olaf might do to their dear friends made them only weep harder. Violet wept, thinking of how kind the Quagmires had been to her and her siblings upon the Baudelaires' arrival at this dreadful academy. Klaus wept, thinking of how the Quagmires had risked their lives to help him and his sisters escape from Olaf's clutches. And Sunny wept, thinking of the research the Quagmires had done, and the information they hadn't had time to share with her and her siblings.

The Baudelaire orphans hung on to one another, and wept and wept while the adults argued endlessly behind them. Finally—as, I'm sorry to say, Count Olaf forced the Quagmires into puppy costumes so he could sneak them onto the airplane without anyone noticing—the Baudelaires cried themselves out and just sat on the lawn together in weary silence. They looked up at the smooth gray stone of the tombstone buildings and at the arch with "PRUFROCK PREPARATORY SCHOOL" in enormous black letters and the motto "Memento Mori" printed beneath. They looked out at the edge of the lawn, where Olaf had snatched the Quagmire notebooks. And they took long, long looks at one another. The Baudelaires remembered, as I'm sure you remembered, that in times of extreme stress one can find energy hidden in even the most exhausted areas of the body, and Violet, Klaus, and Sunny felt that energy surge through them now.

"What did Duncan shout to you?" Violet asked. "What did he shout to you from the car, about what was in the notebooks?"

"V.F.D." Klaus said, "but I don't know what it means."

"Ceju," Sunny said, which meant "We have to find out."

The older Baudelaires looked at their sister and nodded. Sunny was right. The children had to find out the secret of V.F.D. and the dreadful thing the Quagmires had discovered. Perhaps it could help them rescue the two triplets. Perhaps it could bring Count Olaf to justice. And perhaps it could somehow make clear the mysterious and deadly way that their lives had become so unfortunate.

A morning breeze blew through the campus

of Prufrock Preparatory School, rustling the brown lawn and knocking against the stone arch with the motto printed on it. "Memento Mori"—"Remember you will die." The Baudelaire orphans looked up at the motto and vowed that before they died, they would solve this dark and complicated mystery that cast a shadow over their lives.

LEMONY SNICKET first received his education from

public schools and private tutors, and then vice versa. He has been hailed as a brilliant scholar, discredited as a brilliant fraud, and mistaken for a much taller man on several occasions. Mr. Snicket's researching skills are currently and devoutly concentrated on the plight of the Baudelaire orphans, published serially by Egmont Books.

Email to lemony.snicket@ecb.egmont.com

BRETT HELQUIST was born in Ganado, Arizona, grew up in Orem, Utah, and now lives in New York City. He earned a bachelor's degree in fine arts from Brigham Young University and has been illustrating ever since. His art has appeared in many publications, including *Cricket* magazine and *The New York Times*.

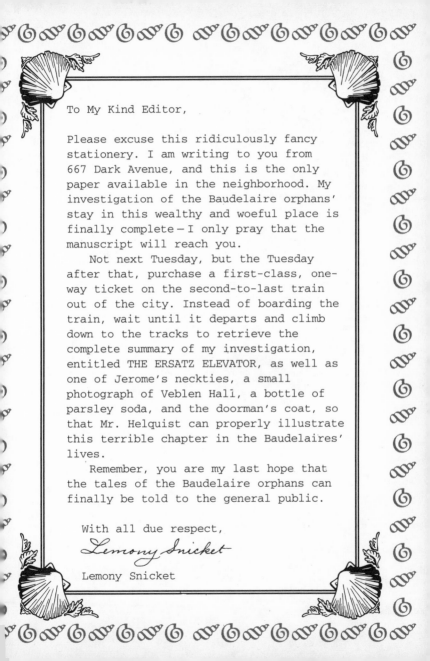

To My Kind Editor,

Please excuse this ridiculously fancy
stationery. I am writing to you from
667 Dark Avenue, and this is the only
paper available in the neighborhood. My
investigation of the Baudelaire orphans'
stay in this wealthy and woeful place is
finally complete — I only pray that the
manuscript will reach you.

Not next Tuesday, but the Tuesday
after that, purchase a first-class, one-
way ticket on the second-to-last train
out of the city. Instead of boarding the
train, wait until it departs and climb
down to the tracks to retrieve the
complete summary of my investigation,
entitled THE ERSATZ ELEVATOR, as well as
one of Jerome's neckties, a small
photograph of Veblen Hall, a bottle of
parsley soda, and the doorman's coat, so
that Mr. Helquist can properly illustrate
this terrible chapter in the Baudelaires'
lives.

Remember, you are my last hope that
the tales of the Baudelaire orphans can
finally be told to the general public.

With all due respect,

Lemony Snicket

Lemony Snicket